LOCKDOWN

FOR

LOCKWOOD

SAVAGE LAW: BOOK 3

LOCKDOWN FOR LOCKWOOD

SAVAGE LAW: BOOK 3

KIRBY JONAS

Cover design by Birgitta Bright

Howling Wolf Publishing
Pocatello, Idaho

Howling Wolf Publishing
1611 City Creek Road
Pocatello ID 83204

For more information about Kirby's books, check out:

www.kirbyjonas.com
Facebook, at KirbyJonasauthor

Or email Kirby at: **kirby@kirbyjonas.com**

Manufactured in the United States of America—*One nation, under God*

Publication date for this edition: November 2018
Jonas, Kirby, 1965—
Savage Law 3: Lockdown for Lockwood / by Kirby Jonas.

ISBN: 978-1-891423-31-4
Library of Congress Control Number: 2018909431

To learn more about this book or any other Kirby Jonas book, email Kirby at kirby@kirbyjonas.com

To Warren Webber—a.k.a. Jim Lockwood—
You’ve been a real character to work with, amigo

CHAPTER ONE

♦ *1972* ♦

Monday, December 18

Betty Lockwood was happily married. Bern Hargis, on the other hand, was simply married. Happiness was something Bern Hargis had long forgotten. And enough alcohol often made him forget that pesky "married" part as well.

For Bern Hargis, sometimes half a bottle of Olympia beer amounted to enough.

Two wind-worn, knotty juniper fence posts had been glued to an old, crusted saddle seat to form Hargis's hips and legs, topped by a torso that seemed to be crafted out of a frazzled board from some old barn. His head was a burl of lodgepole—twisted in more ways than one. Throw on a pair of run-down Justin boots, some 501 jeans with a belt that had four extra holes carved in it, wrapped half again around his waist, and was the one and only reason those jeans didn't fall down around his scrawny ankles, and a blue and gray plaid shirt with pearl snaps, and you had a good picture of Bern Hargis, who boasted shoulders like a snake. Ears the size of ear muffs, along with a shock of ratted orange-yellow hair, prevented a greasy black ball cap from sliding down to his neck and completed Hargis's stylish looks. Two missing teeth, like vacant windows beneath his thatch of mustache, rounded out an appearance that would live on in feverish nightmares.

Betty Lockwood liked to spend time with her quilting group, every Wednesday from two to four. As she sat there visiting with them and hand-sewing painstaking stitches into their current masterpiece, a Christmas tree on a red and white-checkered background, she had no idea that her husband was lying belly-down on a sheet of thin ice and trying to drag Sheriff Coal Savage to safety from a near-fatal dive into the icy waters of the Salmon River. But ignorance was bliss, and Betty and her four friends sipped their tea and hot cider and chatted aimlessly while Jim Reeves, Bing Crosby, Nat King Cole, and Johnny Mathis crooned Christmas songs on the big phonograph, one right after another, and Jinx, the wily black cat half the size of a beagle that came out of hiding for only one stranger—Betty Lockwood—purred and massaged himself against her legs.

When Betty finished, she decided to drive over to Rexall Drug in the baby blue sixty-three Chrysler New Yorker she loved so much. She had a tickle in the back of her throat that was leading to a cough, and nothing was going to stop it until she had some good cough drops—which, truth be told, she liked to suck on because she loved the taste. It was either that or horehound candy, and Jim would likely eat all of that. But Jim didn't like the taste of her cough drops.

Betty Lockwood was a handsome woman in spite of sixty-one years of age, with lustrous silver hair kept styled to the bottom of her neck. Her eyes resembled drops of melting dark chocolate, but when she looked at someone it was not her eyes, but that person who melted. She had a soft way about her and an elegant charm that could tame a rabid badger, and other than her silvery hair, the only obvious signs of age visible while she wore today's smartly cut lavender skirt and matching jacket were a few grooves in her neck, the wrinkles to the sides of her mouth, and crows' feet beside her eyes, formed there because she loved to laugh, and Jim Lockwood was just the man to make her do so. Unless Jim was not in a humorous mood, which led to the one other sign of age on Betty's face, generally beneath the hair on her forehead—wrinkles of worry.

Betty was leaving the drugstore with a brown paper sack containing her cough drops when Bern Hargis ran into her—literally. It happened to be one of those rampant days when a can of Oly made him forget he was married.

"Well, pardon me, Miz Lockwood," said Hargis, dipping the brim of his cap with a gnarled and nicotine-stained thumb and forefinger. "I surely didn't mean to run you over. My, my. Ma'am, you shore look beautiful today."

"Thank you, Mr. Hargis." Her words sounded polite, but her voice cool. She didn't waste breath reminding him she was a Missus, not a *Miz.*

Hargis caught her upper arm as she turned to go. In spite of his overall scrawny appearance, Bern Hargis owned a milk cow operation and for years had milked twenty cows by hand both morning and evening. The vise-grip of his fingers proved it.

"Excuse me, Mr. Hargis, but you're hurting my arm."

"Oh, I'm sorry again. Seems I cain't do nothin' right today, don't it? Say—I'll buy you a drink if you wanna come over to the Lantern with me. You know, to make up for hurtin' you."

"No, thank you. I had better be getting home. To start dinner for when my *husband* gets home. That should be shortly."

Bern Hargis chuckled. "Oh, shoot. Tha's right. I always forget yore still harnessed t' that old coot. Well, all right then. Maybe another time."

As she turned to go, he slapped her on the bottom, then let out a chuckle. Fuming, Betty kept walking, determined not to give him the satisfaction of turning to look back.

Betty was not going to say one word to Jim about this latest encounter. After the decades they had been together, she knew his temper too well.

But such plans are sometimes changed by fate.

Harvey Cupper, who owned Lemhi Valley Realty, had seen the entire encounter as well. And Cupper didn't mind passing the story along to his old friend Jim. Seeing Jim get red-faced and sputtery was always worth a laugh or two.

Cupper could not have known his mouth this fateful time would be planting the little bean soon to launch into a stalk of epic proportions the likes of which had not been seen for years in Lemhi County.

* * *

The monotonous *beep, beep, beep* coming from the monitor that hung along with IVs from a smooth, slender silver pole, and the pale blue dot that rose and fell in rhythmic cadence represented the heart of Deputy Todd Mitchell.

Coal Savage, recovered from his traumatic dip in the frigid waters of the Salmon River, stood over his deputy later that same day and watched him cling to life. Todd wore a clear non-rebreather mask over his face, which now was clean-shaven thanks to some nurse—maybe Annie Price. Two intravenous lines from ever-shrinking bags of lactated ringers dripped TKO—to keep open—into veins in either arm. Other than the slow rise and fall of his chest, there was nothing to give Coal hope that his deputy was going to emerge from this tragedy as anything but a vegetable.

Coal had spent time in an exam room himself upon returning to Salmon from his unfortunate but voluntary bout with hypothermia. He had chosen to ride in with Connie and the children, leaving Jim Lockwood with EMT Maura PlentyWounds at the scene of Bud and Linda Mileys' untimely demise. He didn't feel right about leaving Maura there. After all, they had gone there together, sharing in a common terror—the idea that they might lose the two girls they both adored, Cynthia Batterton and Sissy Miley. That very terror had bonded them together like little else could, and they had both watched as the red Buick Riviera driven by Bud Miley vaulted over the embankment and down into the icy and treacherous river. As far as either of them had known, Cynthia and Sissy had gone with it.

Then Maura had been forced to watch in horror while Coal attempted a rescue of the two girls, who ended up not even being in the car, and then nearly succumbed to the River of No Return himself.

Finally, he had left her standing on the sidelines near her ugly, rusted International Travelette as the big tow truck attempted to drag the car out of the river's deadly grasp. She had insisted that he go with his family, that he return to town to be looked over and rehabilitated. But even though it was her choice, it did not seem right leaving that woman behind. It had felt like Coal was deserting a partner. But it was a great comfort to know that rock-solid Jim Lockwood was there to watch out for her.

That river and this winter environment were nothing new to Coal. He had suffered mild hypothermia before. And so after all of the necessary dexterity tests and pulse and blood pressure checks, and the irritating questions trying to determine his mental status (Do you know what day of the week it is? What month is it? Who is the president? How many fingers am I holding up? Did you wear your clean underwear today like your mama always told you to?), he was released without being coerced into taking off more than his shirt—which incidentally prevented them from getting the answer to that last question which existed only in the corroded vault of Coal's twisted sense of humor.

By then, Annie, who was standing back with a spunky smile on her face and watching the proceedings as Doctor Leo Bent poked and prodded at Coal's bare torso, had let him know Ronnie Davis and Jay Castillo had brought Todd Mitchell in on the ambulance, unconscious and suffering a devastating head injury. This was actually good news to Coal, who had left the Batterton house thinking Todd dead. But according to all the doctor had to say, it sounded like Todd's chances of recovering were somewhere between that of a snowball in hell and a tort lawyer or lifetime politician making it to heaven. Of course those were Coal's own thoughts—but they seemed to line up with the doctor's blunt prognosis.

Coal stood with his hat hanging along his leg by the fingers of one hand, watching that blue dot go up, down, up, and back down, with that steady, rhythmic beep. He prayed it would just keep on beeping—against all odds.

Coal sighed. He couldn't help but wonder why Todd had been at the Mileys' in the first place. The way things looked, he might never know. The doctor had said his deputy would be lucky to pull through the night.

When Coal walked back into the hall and looked up and down it, there was no one in sight. He pulled in a deep breath. Because he had not done it himself, he assumed that no one had called Jan Mitchell yet to tell her about Todd. Once again, that kind of dirty job would fall to him.

Hearing footsteps, he turned to see Annie Price coming out of an exam room. She froze and looked at him. "You going to be okay?"

"Me? Sure. Why wouldn't I be?"

Annie smiled and walked close. She reached out and squeezed his hand. "Hey. Tough guy. I don't claim to know anything that goes on between you and your deputy. But I can see as plain as day that you care for him."

One side of Coal's mouth came up. "Yeah? That's funny. I guess I do. And I never thought I'd say that."

The sideways turn of her head and the squint of her eyes told him she was curious to know more about this cryptic comment. To her credit, she didn't ask. "So . . . you going to be okay?"

"The answer's still yes." Coal looked down at her for a moment before raising his hat and wiggling it down over his tousled, river-dirtied hair. "If you ever get a free day or two, maybe I'll tell you about all the misery I saw in Korea and Nam." He jerked a thumb over his shoulder at Todd's door. "This is just par for the course."

"Okay, Clint Eastwood. Right. I get it. But a hundred deaths of people you care about won't ever make the next one easier. They might even make it worse."

Coal just gazed at her. Inside, he knew she was right. But nothing would drag an admission out of him. He was supposed to be sheriff here, besides being an ex-Marine. If he let his emotions flood out into the open every time someone asked if he would be okay, he might as well go take up baking cakes, sewing frilly dresses, or flipping burgers at Wally's or the Salmon River Coffee Shop, and quit law enforcement altogether.

For a long time, Annie tried to match Coal's gaze, her lips pursed. Finally, she looked down at his third button, her thoughts frozen on her face. In time, she raised her eyes to his again and gave a little shrug and a sigh.

"Are you going to ask about me?"

"Umm . . . What about you?"

"Do you want to know if I'm going to be okay?"

Baffled, he let out a chuckle. "Uh, I guess I'll bite, but . . . Why wouldn't you be okay?"

"Oh, you're a typical man," she said, and taking a step forward she leaned against him and closed her arms around his middle. She took a lung-filling breath. "I had to listen to the radio traffic, Coal. To the dispatcher trying to find your Deputy Peterson. He finally answered, and she told him you were in a chase. In a private vehicle. Headed downriver."

His heart had begun to pound annoyingly as he heard her out. When she didn't speak again for a while, he said, "And?"

"And then she came on again and told him someone had called in on the phone, and that a car had gone in the river. And they said you had jumped in too."

"Well. Pretty accurate, I'd say." He wasn't sure what she was fishing for.

"Stop talking for just a second," she said, and she squeezed him so hard he almost couldn't breathe. "I was afraid we lost you, Coal," she finally said, easing off on the pressure of her arms. "I was afraid *I* had lost you."

CHAPTER TWO

As soon as the doctor was done checking him over, Coal had telephoned Ken Parks to talk him into going over to the Battertons' and fixing his flat tire. After calling him again to make sure it was done, he thanked him and then walked from the hospital over to Hope Street. He needed the walking time to think.

It seemed to Coal that somehow Annie Price had gotten overly attached to him. Part of him didn't mind. She was one of the most beautiful women he knew, and a real sweetheart, to boot. But his guts told him she wanted more from him than he was ready to give—or even *could* give. In spite of everything, he wasn't over Laura. Or perhaps it was only the traumatic way of losing her that still had his emotions twisted all around.

Either way, he wasn't ready for Annie's devotion. The truth was, it scared him. It was pretty plain there was nothing left of whatever imaginary magic he thought had started to spark between him and Maura, so that was no longer an issue, but . . . Was he fooling himself? He sighed. In spite of everything he kept saying in his head, his heart still had a big, empty hole in it that only Maura PlentyWounds seemed able to fill. And that was his biggest dilemma of all.

He reached the LTD and got in, sitting there for a few minutes with his head against the seat back and watching the quiet house. So much had changed since he had left this valley all those years ago. So many good friends were gone. He should have been used to that kind of loss, but somehow it never got easier. He just became more able to hide the pain.

Pushing those thoughts away, he started the Ford and drove up on the Bar to Todd Mitchell's house on Lincoln Street. The shoddy green house seemed either to be leaning against the bare-branched, destitute-looking elm tree in front, or the tree was leaning against it—maybe both. They seemed to be in need of as much support as Coal was right now.

Looking at the beat-down white station wagon in front, the pock-marked dirt yard, and thinking of the squalor inside, the slovenly, half-starved Jan Mitchell and her dirty-faced boys, made Coal cringe. He realized these people knew no different. They were poor and starving, and it was likely Jan had grown up that way. He had an inkling Todd had too. He had worried about them before—so much so that in the end he had dismissed a pretty serious charge against Todd so he could keep his job and continue to feed his family. But now things were different. What had happened to Todd now was nothing Coal could help. Only Doctor Bent, God, and time might save Todd Mitchell. And in the meantime, what became of his desperate wife and those little boys? Coal wanted to help, but he could only do so much. He couldn't save everyone. And right now it seemed like the whole world—or at least the part of it that he was responsible for—needed saving.

Again, like that time not so long ago when Todd was in jail, Coal stood here, smelling right through the poorly insulated door the old grease and stale cigarette smoke, the filth of cats, and the smell of some kind of food, this time unrecognizable.

Putting aside the thought of his nauseated stomach, Coal rapped on the door, three slow times.

Hurried footsteps sounded inside, and the door cracked open. It was Jan Mitchell, standing there in a bright pink dress that belied the dull and hopeless circumstances of her life with an underpaid Lemhi County deputy. Her low-heeled red shoes, against the clashing pink of the dress, hurt Coal's eyes.

She studied Coal's face. Hopeful light in her eyes fought back glowering clouds of old suspicion. "Can I help you?"

A look of expectation on her face had vanished like a hint of smoke. No greeting. No smile, not even a little one. Just a cold reserve on a face framed by languid grayish blond hair. Zero spark now flickered in her pale gray-blue eyes.

"Ma'am—Mrs. Mitchell—I need to come in."

She stared at him, trying to look strong—looking instead almost angry. Then confusion came over her face, and in the end the leap of sudden, inevitable fear.

"Why? What is it? Did Todd do something again? He's not here, you know."

"Just—" Coal stopped. Taking a deep breath, he sighed and insisted his way inside, pulling off his hat. The sound of a television and a glance into the adjacent living room showed two of the three filthy Mitchell boys huddled up on the couch, leaning forward to watch whatever was on TV. Only one, the six-year-old, had turned his intent gaze to Coal.

A scrawny gray cat slunk around a corner, saw Coal, and hot-footed it into the front room to dive behind the couch. Coal looked back at Jan Mitchell. Her eyes pleaded up at him.

"I know you're afraid Todd did something bad, ma'am, but he didn't."

Relief flickered like distant lightning through the woman's eyes. But her stare did not relent. Instead, it might have become a little more intense. This woman whose station in life, and whatever hard past she had lived, made her look more often at the floor than into someone's eyes, refused to look away this time.

Holding the shield of his hat between him and the woman, Coal told her all he knew about Todd, which was very little. For some reason, Todd, while on leave, had gone with a shotgun to where the Mileys were living. No one knew what he was planning—why he would have gone in so armed. But whatever the case, it wasn't enough. One of the Mileys had hit him on the back of the head with some blunt object, and Todd was now in a coma.

Staring, and too shocked to cry, Jan stood still. Coal shuffled his feet and looked over at the boys. The six-year-old was making his way to his mother, watching Coal with almost as much wariness as the gray cat. When he got close, Jan's slender claw of a hand reached out and jerked him to her, crushing him against her dress. "Hey, Bub, it'll be okay."

The boy looked up at her, then back at Coal. The look in his eyes accused Coal of being responsible for the bad news he had brought into the home.

Jan Mitchell looked back up at Coal, and a sudden rush of moisture filled her eyes. A long sigh came out of her mouth. "I know why Todd went to their house."

* * *

As Coal waited for Jan to feed her boys, Bub, Toby and little Jerry, some slapdash Spanish rice she had been fixing in a skillet, he mulled over everything the woman had revealed to him about her husband, and a big lump stayed in his throat. His deputy, desperate to prove himself to a man he thought was going to fire him anyway, had been doing his own detective work behind Coal's back. He had had the film of Bud Miley developed, sent the clearest photograph to the Missoula police, and then when it was proved that Miley was wanted for robbery, he had gone to their house all alone to apprehend them. In spite of the fact that the arrest had gone south and Mitchell was now in a coma, Coal could not put aside the knowledge of how badly Todd must have wanted his acceptance—and his forgiveness. That knowledge shook Coal to the core.

When their dinner was finished, he took them all out and loaded them into the Ford, thankful for vinyl seats, because the unwashed clothes that hung off this family would have soiled nice cloth ones. He drove down to the hospital and led them to Todd's room, where the doctor readily allowed them entry, with Annie there to supervise. Looking at the *blip* of the little blue light on the heart monitor, and the still face of his deputy, made Coal's heart start to pound dully as well.

Coal walked into the hallway. He wasn't even thinking about where he was going, so he nearly ran into a man who was coming out of another exam room. The man threw up both hands, trying to stop a runaway freight train.

"Whoa! Sorry, buddy." The man quickly gathered his wits and smiled, looking up from Coal's gold badge. "Sheriff, huh? You must have something big on your mind, trying to run *me* over. I'm not exactly the invisible man."

Coal tried to smile back. "Sorry about that. Yeah, too much on my mind." He started to turn away.

"Hey, before you go, let me introduce myself." The man stuck out his hand. "Ray Christian—from Reno, Nevada."

Coal turned back and looked the man up and down. He was well-built, with wide shoulders and a definite vee to his torso, set off by narrow hips. He stood a few inches shorter than Coal, perhaps an even six feet, and a solid one hundred eighty pounds. His well-groomed hair was very dark, parted neatly down one side, and his handsome, expressive face an olive-toned brown that hinted at some Hispanic or other Latin blood. A smear of almost blue color where a very thick beard would have been drew a sharp line just below round, hard cheekbones, and his eyes, complimenting his skin and hair, were a deep chocolate brown. A twinkle in them begged Coal instantly to like the man.

An obvious visitor to Salmon, Christian wore the clothing of someone who lived in a different place, clothing Coal usually saw only in catalogs, if he was particularly bored. He was dressed in a white shirt with crisscrossed red lines and red jeans with white oxfords. A fat red tie decorated with two rows of white dots plunged down the middle of his wide- and sharp-collared shirt.

"Hi, Ray. Coal Savage." He tried to hide a little smirk and forget the audacious look of the clothing. "Well, again, I'm sorry for not watching where I was going."

"No matter." Christian tossed the gaffe aside like used Kleenex. "I'm sure I'll live."

Coal laughed and looked at the man's left hand, which was bandaged. "Barely though, huh?"

Christian returned the laugh, with a shrug for punctuation. "Yeah, jeez. Flesh wound. I had a flat just out of town and about cut my finger off with my Handyman. I don't even know why I bothered coming in here. Should have just glued it back on with Super Glue. Cheaper and just as effective."

Coal grinned. "Better watch those jacks. They tend to bite."

"They do that!"

"So . . . you always wear a tie to change tires?"

With a laugh, Ray grabbed the bottom of his tie and gave it a downward yank. "Old habit, I guess. Speaking of which, I guess you and I have something in common—that badge. I used to be a detective myself—down in Reno. Man, am I glad to be out of there!"

This perked Coal's interest. "You don't say. I guess that explains the tie. Well, I'm doubly glad to meet you. Always good to run into someone else who packs a gun."

"*Packed,*" reminded Christian. "Like I said, I'm done with that."

"Right. Are you staying here in town?"

Ray sighed loudly. "Well, that's another thing I meant to ask about. I need a hotel, at least for the night—probably longer."

"Oh? You planning to hang out in our lovely village?" asked Coal with a tiny bit of fond sarcasm.

"Well, I wasn't exactly. But I took the Caddy in to get an oil change, and I asked the man to give it the once-over under the hood. He ends up telling me my power steering pump is about on its last legs—which I suspected already."

"Who'd you take that thing to?"

"Some big guy. Kevin? Not as big as you," added Christian, looking Coal up and down.

Coal chuckled. "Kevin, huh? Where's his shop?"

"About the middle of town. On that side." He pointed.

"Sounds more like Ken."

Christian's face lit up. "Ken! Yeah, that's it. Ken's Auto."

"Well, looks like you're in bad luck."

"Why's that?" asked Christian, cocking his head. "The guy's a crook?"

"No, not at all. I was just hoping to get you a second opinion."

"And you can't?"

"No need to. If Ken told you your pump's taking a dive on you, then it's taking a dive. Ken's as honest and as good as any mechanic in the valley."

Christian's face fell a little. "Oh. I was hoping you had some better news."

"Well, I might."

"Yeah?"

"How about we drive you over to a good hotel I know about—a new place on the way out of town—and then I'll drop you off at my friend Jay's for a good burger. Actually, I would ask you to come join me and my family for dinner, but it probably wouldn't be the best night for it."

Ray Christian glanced beyond Coal, at the closed door of the room he had just come from—Todd Mitchell's room.

"None of my business, but… Things aren't good, huh? Family of yours?"

Coal looked at him questioningly, then whipped his eyes toward Todd's door. "Oh! No. Well, a friend. My deputy, actually. Yeah, it's not so good."

"Man. Sorry to hear that. I lost a partner once in a fight over a prostitute. She was drugged up, and we were hooking her up when her old man—the pimp—he just waltzed right out of the hotel room and stabbed Pete, right in the kidney, all the way into his stomach."

Coal winced.

"Oh, jeez. Sorry, Sheriff! You don't need to hear that crap."

"No, no. I'm sorry about your partner. That can't be an easy memory."

"No. No, it's not. But that's the life of a man that wears a badge, right?" Christian shrugged.

"Yeah, I guess. A badge or a soldier's uniform." Coal wasn't sure why he even brought that up. It embarrassed him on the instant, being so open with a man he had just met. But he could tell Ray Christian was good people. It was easy to open up.

"You in the war?"

"Both of them. I did Korea as a Marine, then Nam as a soldier."

"Damn! I should buy you a drink."

"I don't do much of that, but thanks."

"Well anyway, *Semper fi!* I was a Marine myself. A year at El Toro, then a year at a base in Pleiku, in Gia Lai Province."

Coal grinned. "Nice, Ray. *Semper fi.*"

"So no drinking. Well, that's smart. But hey, do you think . . . ?" Ray looked toward the exit.

"Oh, yeah, the ride? You bet."

They both shrugged coats on, then went out and got in Coal's car, and he drove Christian to the Stagecoach Inn. An attractive and friendly woman with dark-framed glasses and a short-bobbed, full head of hair stood behind the desk, her nametag boasting not only the name Julie, but the title "Manager." Her blue eyes sparkled.

Julie was nice enough to give Ray a good price on a room on the river, since he was stuck in town against his will, and then Coal dropped him off at the Coffee Shop, stepping inside for just long enough to introduce Christian to his old friend, Jay Castillo. "Treat him right, buddy. He's an ex-cop, *and* a Marine."

Feeling a little bit better after the friendly companionship of Christian, but still worried about Todd, Coal said goodbye to his new friend, then drove back down the street to Steele Memorial and went inside. He had almost reached the door to Todd's room when Annie came out, shutting the door behind her. She looked up at him. "They're still in there. Looks like it might be a while. Hey—I'd like to sit with you, but I have another patient. You sure you're going to be okay?"

"Sure I am." Coal forced a smile and turned away.

With an aching feeling inside, he walked down to the waiting room and pulled his hat off, pinching the bridge of his nose between thumb and forefinger, squinching his eyes up tight. He heard the outer door open and felt a gust of cold air, and instinctively he looked up, dropping his free hand down near the butt of his gun.

Maura PlentyWounds stood there in front of the slowly closing door. A close-mouthed smile came over her face, and she walked to him with her boot heels clicking on the shiny, white linoleum floor. She sat down in the ugly mustard-yellow plastic chair next to his and knuckled the side of his leg. "Hey, Mr. Hero. Want to come out to my truck and get a proper kiss?"

Confused, he stared at her, and some thought of her own made Maura's cheeks pinken. Suddenly bolder, she grabbed his knee and shook it playfully. "Come on, buddy. I'm playing around with you. You act like you're still not with it."

"Huh." He let out a sigh and jerked his thumb down the hall. "Yeah, I just brought Todd Mitchell's wife and boys in and left them down there in the room with him."

“Wait. So… Todd’s alive?”

“Yeah, somewhat.”

“Wow. I was really afraid to ask.”

“With good reason,” Coal put in.

Maura frowned, looking down the hall, then back at Coal. “Will he get better?”

“He has a pretty bad skull fracture, and he’s in a coma. The doctor’s worried he won’t last out the night. Who can say for sure? I guess there’s a lot of swelling. I think Bent knows he’s got to drill to relieve the pressure, but he’s scared to do it. I’m no doctor, but if he doesn’t get going pretty soon I’m afraid whatever the damage is they won’t be able to fix.”

As if finally making a decision, Maura lifted her hand to his trapezius and gave it a squeeze. “He’ll pull it together, Coal. I’ve seen him on victims from some pretty bad wrecks. And for all we know, he might already have a helicopter en route from I.F. They’re a lot better equipped to handle something like this in Salt Lake City.” After a long pause, her hand still resting on his shoulder, she asked, “How about you? Are you going to be okay?”

“Everyone seems to be wondering that. I’m getting pretty worn out, Maura. Mom’s got the girls both back at the house. Knowing her, they’re making cookies about now. I should be with them. Instead, I’m here. When it’s time for Todd’s family to go home, I’ll have to take them, so I can’t even leave.”

“Your Deputy Peterson should be back in town soon, right? Can’t he do it?”

“There’s no way I can put that off on him. I’ve got to stay here in case . . .”

“Come on, Coal. Don’t think that way. It’ll be okay. So how about that kiss?”

Trying to seem playful, he said, “A little forward, aren’t you?”

She dropped her hand and gave his shoulder a hard shove with her fist. “Funny. Come on, knucklehead. Outside.” In the back of his mind, he started thinking maybe this wasn’t a joke after all. Was she really taking him outside to kiss him? In spite of himself, his heart started to pound with the thought.

She got up and held her hand down to him, then dropped it and darted her eyes away before he could even think about taking it. After a second he stood up too. Taking a last look down the hall to make sure Todd's family was still in the room with him, he followed her out the door into the deep and cold afternoon. Maura's rust-spotted, cream-colored International was parked in front in all its glory, and there inside, with an instant, huge grin plastered all over his face, was Burro—Coal still couldn't bear to call the dog any name the Mileys had chosen.

"Hey!" He went over, and Maura opened the door. Burro started wiggling all over, his tail making circles. Coal grabbed both sides of his face and gave him a playful scrub, and the dog barked right in his face, rattling his teeth. "Yeah, I can see a big kiss in my future, all right," he said, looking at the fat pink tongue. "But I think I'd better wait to get behind closed doors."

"May be," agreed Maura. When he looked at her, she winked.

Coal gave an amused grunt. It was easier to change the subject. "So how did things end up down at the river?"

"How *could* they end up? They finally got the car out, once they brought in a second truck and worked in tandem, and the Mileys were still inside. Of course. To be safe, they had me look at them, and as hard as they hit that water, it was like a brick wall. They probably didn't even live long enough to drown. What amazes me is this guy getting out without a bump."

Coal looked over at Burro. "The Lord really does work in mysterious ways."

"And he seems to love animals," said Maura with the shrug of one shoulder and a happy smile.

CHAPTER THREE

It was with a heavy heart and in total silence that Coal later drove Jan Mitchell and the boys back up on the Bar to their house. He dropped them off, then stood there at the open door of the LTD watching them trudge to the house in the half-dark and go inside. Jan Mitchell looked back at the very last, and her eyes were shining. She tried to smile, then disappeared inside.

Maura had wanted to ride with them up the hill, but since she had Burro and still needed to take care of him Coal wouldn't let her, and he had said goodbye to her at the hospital.

Still thinking about Annie, and Maura, the Mileys, and Todd Mitchell—and all the terrible things that had happened since his return to this valley—Coal drove on out the seven miles to Savage Lane. When he turned into it, he pulled to a stop on the frozen gravel and dirt, looking up at the looming Beaverhead Mountains. Somewhere, sometime, there had to be peace for Coal Savage. But he was beginning to wonder if it would be in this lifetime.

When he reached the ranch and pulled in, the first rig he saw was Maura's ugly Travelette. He paused at the opening of the drive, then finally went in and parked in his usual place, glancing over at the old dark blue Chevy pickup, now parked out near the barn. Sight of it made him think of the horrendous trip with Katie all the way home from Virginia, and at last a bright spot came into his mind. Katie… If nothing else good had happened since his return to this valley, bizarre circumstances had given him back his daughter. For that he could be thankful.

Snow had started to filter down, and big flakes settled on the windshield and turned to water as Coal watched the warm orange glow through the front room curtains, feeling the hot air from the floor vent push against the legs of his Dickies. He had to go inside a house full of traumatized women now, a place that was more frightening than any battleground in Korea, perhaps even worse than the Long Binh jail. But it was time. At least the dogs would be there to save him.

Opening the heavy steel door of the Ford allowed a brash rush of December air inside that almost burned with cold as much as the overactive heater did with heat. Coal got out and took a deep breath, then started for the front door of the house.

A peek inside the window showed him the television was off. That only happened on special nights. He eased the screen door open, then did the same with the wood one, and his stealth was effective, for Dobe and Shadow slumbered on near the Franklin stove. Neither of them even flicked an ear.

It was Connie who saw him first. She stood in the kitchen, facing the door, while the three girls sat on stools with their backs to him and the twins played checkers at the dining room table. His mother's eyes softened as they spied him over the heads of her girls. In spite of the presence of her pickup outside, Maura was nowhere in sight, and neither was Virgil.

Connie lowered her chin and said something quietly to the girls, and all three of them whirled in unison. It was Cynthia, however, who made the first move. After a look at her friend, Katie, as if for approval, she walked to Coal as fast as she could and threw her arms around him. Katie came second, hesitating as she drew near and watching Cynthia, who Coal realized now was crying.

Coal lifted his left arm from around K.T.'s little girl and held it out to Katie. A huge smile burst over her face, and she came in close, throwing her arms around both of them in what became a communal hug. Sissy, whose shyness was not going to disappear overnight, watched them, Cynthia's orange-brown Teddy Bear with its vacant, beady white eyes held tightly to her body and a thumb in her mouth—a habit Coal had never observed in her before, but one which was understandable, considering all she had just been through.

This family still had a long way to go, and the girls surely had a few more sessions due in Idaho Falls with Doctor Pearson, but at least for tonight they were home together.

After the children had returned to their work as cookie-making apprentices, Coal went around and hugged Connie from behind, kissing her cheek. She patted his hand. "I love you, Son."

He squeezed her more tightly, wishing those words would come more easily for him. "Hey, I don't suppose you'd like to tell me where the driver of that ugly white truck outside is, would you?"

Connie laughed. "Well, believe it or not, she's down the hall."

"Oh. The bathroom again, huh? Or is she asleep in your bed again?"

"First guess, yes. But it's not what you think. She's down there with Virg, so you should be safe to take a peek."

Coal gave her an odd look, then dropped his arms from around her and passed down the hall, feeling the warmth of the wood heat fold around him, smelling the pungent scent of smoking pine, an aroma that meant home.

He could hear giggling inside the bathroom now, and then the splashing of water. Knocking lightly, he eased the door open. Maura, crouched down beside the bathtub, was up to her elbows in suds, Virgil beside her. Maura looked up at him with her hair hanging in her face and a quarter-sized dollop of bubbles on the tip of her nose. Incredible beauty, undeniable. Some things never changed.

And there, the guest of honor, sat Burro, up to his midriff in sudsy water, and wearing a silly-looking hat made of bubbles, somewhat like a crown.

The look on the dog's face could have been described as nothing different than sheer embarrassment, and when Coal's eyes met his, the dog averted his eyes, most likely wishing himself back in the icy river.

"Doesn't Burro look kingly?" asked Maura, reaching out to put her hands under the dogs cheeks and raise them up, crunching his face all together in a sorry imitation of a grin.

"That's not exactly the word I was thinking of," replied Coal. "Mortified, maybe."

"Okay, but he sure is clean—and warm."

"Sure, until he gets out. That's when the cold sets in."

"That's what the Franklin heater's for."

Coal chuckled. "Smart move, coming over here to wash him so you wouldn't mess up your own bathroom."

She jerked her eyes up at his face, as if to see if he was joking. Then she sniffed and looked back down at the dog, picking up a plastic cup that she filled with water and let run down the back of his neck.

"Yep, that's the only reason I came over."

Coal wanted to say something more. He wanted to tell her how glad he was that she was there. Instead, he said, "I guess they're making cookies out there. Like that's any surprise."

"Yep." Maura's only response.

"So . . . I guess when you're done here . . ." Uncomfortably, Coal started to shut the door, then on a sudden thought searched the room with his eyes. "You got towels and everything?"

"Yes. Grandma Connie is always well-prepared."

Coal nodded, even though no one was looking at him. He went out to sink his exhausted body onto the black and white cowhide couch. Soon, Katie left the cookie-making and came to sit beside him, putting her head on his chest. There was no television playing. No music. Only the crackle of the fire, the scent of and softly glowing lights on a Douglas fir Connie had collected from up off Stormy Peak Road and decorated with the children in his absence—another important event his job had made him miss—and a house full of warmth and love.

* * *

Coal sat on the couch after the cookies were done and ate half of one, leaning back to divide his attention between the orange sparkle of dying embers and the glow of green, red, blue, orange, and yellow lights within the shiny red and green garland and the deep forest boughs of the fragrant fir. Cynthia had come to sit at the opposite side from Katie, so he was surrounded by two beautiful young girls. And there sat Maura in the La-Z-Boy, with Sissy on her lap.

After an initial welcoming ceremony, capped by the requisite butt-sniffing, the home guard had accepted Burro into their embrace, and all three dogs lazed about near the stove, although Coal predicted that in time all but short-haired Dobe would find a more temperate environment.

Connie had made the command decision to leave the television off, and instead she had put a couple of long-playing Bill Cosby records on the phonograph in the big old dark wood console. The one playing was named *Wonderfulness,* and the family was engrossed in Cosby's story of a chicken heart marauding through Manhattan and eating up the Jersey Turnpike. Connie sure knew how to set a mood.

The phone rang, and everyone froze. By the second ring, all eyes had turned to Coal.

Connie finally got up to lift the player arm off the record and pause the story, then headed for the phone. Maura looked over at Coal. "So I guess we forgot the part about taking the phone off the hook."

"I think we were planning that for tomorrow."

"I wish it could be forever."

"Yeah, me too."

Connie's surprised voice sounded from across the room. "Oh, hi, Kathy! Why, yes, he is here—for a change. Are you okay?" She glanced over at the clock on the wall. "Good, good. Sure you can talk to him. Hang on just a minute, okay?"

Coal untangled himself from girl arms and went to the phone, picking it up as he turned back to the faces in the room. "Hello?"

Hi, Coal. Just the two words. Then silence.

"Hi . . . Kathy, you okay?" A feeling of apprehension clutched him down deep.

Oh, yeah. Sure. I guess. I just . . .

"All right. What's wrong? Talk to me." Coal wrinkled up his face, looking over at Connie and shrugging in response to the look of concern on her face.

I think we're just missing a man in the house. Coal, I don't want to keep bothering you all the time. I know you're busy with your own family, and the job. But the girls and I were talking, and . . . We'd sure like to see you sometime.

The furrow in Coal's brow deepened, as did his frown. She obviously knew nothing about the day's events, and he decided not to tell her, at least not right now. He took a deep breath. "Hey, I'm sorry I haven't checked on you girls. Things have been real hectic here. When's a good time for me to come over?"

Any time, honestly. Any time at all. Just call and make sure we're here. She laughed, a sound that was more sad than joyous. *Like we're always out having a party or something.*

"All right. Maybe I can make it tomorrow." He instantly regretted saying that when Maura shot spears of correction into his eyes. Tomorrow was Sissy's birthday!

That would be nice, Coal. Maybe we can do something fun together.

"Sure. Sounds good. Have a good night, Kathy. And give those girls a big hug for me, okay?"

I sure will. See you soon then. Good night.

Coal hung up the phone, and his glance swung to his mother, past the gun barrels Maura referred to as eyes. He shrugged and shook his head.

Connie was still standing up, and she said, "Coal, would you let me have a word with you real quick?"

He frowned but nodded, following her down the hall to her room, where she shut the door behind them. Great. Another session behind the infamous closed door. That was Coal's thought, one he was prudent enough not to voice.

"I hope it doesn't make you mad for me to say this, but I'm thinking you've got a great big problem, Son." She gave him a direct gaze as she folded her arms.

"I know, I know—I told Kathy I might be able to come over tomorrow, and it's Sissy's birthday."

"Ha! Yes, it is. I'm proud of you for remembering. But that's not the problem I'm talking about. Coal, it seems that when a man like you comes into this valley it really stirs people up."

"Yeah, it has sure done that. Who are you talking about now, Maura?"

"No. Maura is stirred up, all right. And Annie Price. And who knows who-all else that I'm not even aware of. But I'm not talking about them, Coal. I'm talking about Kathy MacAtee."

"Huh?" Coal was a little slow on the uptake—sort of like a rag soaking up molasses by osmosis.

"Kathy, Coal. You remember her. Kathy?"

It was the look in his mother's eyes that finally made his senses clear. "Judas priest, Mom, cool it."

"Hey! Don't get a smart mouth with me."

"Sorry. But if you're hinting at what I'm thinking you are, please don't. Nothing could be further from the truth."

"Who's hinting? Kathy MacAtee is setting her cap for you, Son."

"Mom! Stop it already. Look at me! Jeez. You act like I'm some Adonis or something. Come on—this is just me, Coal Savage! A busted-down Marine with a low-paying job and no future. No money. No looks. Not really even all that smart. I'm not even all that ambitious about my future, to be quite honest. To hear you talk you'd think the whole world was waiting to swoon at my feet. Besides, Larry is hardly cold in his grave, and this is *Kathy* we're talking about here, for hell's sake—my best friend's wife!"

"Busted down! And no looks? Oh, brother. Okay, go ahead and act dumb, Coal. You can listen to me or you can ignore me. Either way, you're gonna have a rude awakening, and real soon, if you don't start deciding what you're going to tell Kathy MacAtee. She's a good friend and a real sweet lady, Coal. I know you think the world of her, and I do too. And yes, right now she's still hurting over Larry, and she probably will be for a long time. But speaking as a woman? To her, you are the closest thing to her man there is, because you were his best friend, and she knows that she's going to need a man in every single way somebody can be needed. You are in dangerous water, bud. If you think that river today was deadly, you just wait and see what's on its way."

"Mom, you're making me tired," Coal said with a sigh. "You're my mother, and you've always been the smartest person I know. But you're killing me here. First off, like you said, Kathy is just a great friend, and second, she is never going to let go of Larry MacAtee. It's not the way you think. She just wants me around because she's lonely and needs a friend. She would go the rest of her life as a widow before she would try to replace Larry."

"That's the way *you* think, Son, because you're a man. But I'm not talking about you and how you think. I'm talking about a lonely, heart-broken, devastated woman who is all alone with three daughters to raise, a ranch to run all by herself, and who could never see being disloyal to the man she has lost—unless it was with the one man who shared everything with him.

"Now personally, and quite honestly, I think the two of you would be great together. I'll say that flat-out. It might feel awkward at first, but you would work it out. So do whatever you want, even though I also think Maura would be one heck of a catch. But the main thing is, you had better start opening your eyes, or you are going to land yourself in more trouble than you have any idea what to do with."

CHAPTER FOUR

On the way back down the hall, Coal veered off into the bathroom on the inevitable errand and Connie kept on toward the main part of the house.

Finishing up, Coal zipped his jeans, and while washing his hands he looked in the mirror. He saw a tough-looking, dark-haired man with a round, upraised scar in the middle of his left cheek, a mustache that he had allowed to grow too big and bristly, and a face with big cheekbones and narrow, deep-set, steel-blue eyes. He saw rows of wrinkles now entrenched on his forehead, but surprisingly few anywhere else, and those few he had to look close to find. He saw a big, square jaw, a neck that was a good two inches in circumference larger than any shirt that was manufactured to fit his midriff, broad shoulders, and deep chest. In short, what he saw was something that he supposed in a man's world might be admired.

But in a woman's world? A world of Robert Redfords, Paul Newmans, and Ricky Nelsons? Coal Savage was not that kind of man. Maybe in the old world that his mother had grown up in women sought after men that looked rugged and strong. But that was the whole problem: His mother was living in the past. Coal had nothing, either in looks, charm, smarts, or in worldly means, to offer any woman. If Connie believed women were looking at him in any kind of romantic way, it was only because she was a mother, a mother who was almost unjustifiably proud of her son.

With a sigh, he dried off his hands and stepped back out of the bathroom. To his surprise, Maura was standing beside the front door when he came into the living room. All three dogs had gathered around her, along with little Sissy, who was holding onto one leg.

"You leaving?"

"Maybe."

"Ohh . . . kay." Was she fishing for something? Did she want to stay? Was she leaving an opening for him to beg her? Why did women have to be so cryptic?

"You have to work tomorrow, I guess."

Maura shrugged and gave a little shake of her head. The shrug of her shoulders extended into the expression on her face. "Actually, no."

Coal waited. He would have had better luck waiting for a train to pull up in the yard.

"So . . . then why are you leaving?"

"To feed the animals."

And yet still she stood there, with one hand squeezing Sissy to her leg, and her green down-filled coat dangling in the other hand.

Coal glanced over at Connie. She was watching him and didn't look away. She raised her eyebrows, turning her head a little to one side, and the expression on her face he could only have described as expectant—or hopeful. He returned his eyes to Maura, shoving his hands in his pockets and giving a shrug of his own.

"Maybe you could come back and spend the evening with us."

Maura quickly looked down, seeming to force out a smile while looking at Sissy. After a few moments, she blinked her eyes forcefully and looked back up at him, again trying to smile. "Yeah, okay. Well, I'd better hustle then."

She started putting on her coat. At the sound of Connie clearing her throat, Coal looked over. She gave him the meaningful "wake up, dummy!" face and jerked her head toward Maura.

And truly, in matters such as this, Coal *was* a dummy, but certain expressions could not be ignored, and this one came across as plain as a shotgun blast.

"I don't suppose you'd want any company, would you?"

Maura's eyes bounced to him. "Umm . . . Yeah, sure. I wouldn't mind. You mean you?"

Coal couldn't help chuckling. "Well, no, I was going to send the skunk that lives under our barn."

"Ha ha." Maura made a wry face. "If you want to come, you'd better get your coat. It's snowing." She crouched down before he could speak and took Sissy's tiny shoulders in her hands, looking into her eyes. "Hey, sweetie, I'm going to go feed the dogs and horses, but you know what? I'll be right back, before you know it. Okay? Can you do me a favor and let Grandma Connie hold you until then?"

A moment of concern crossed Sissy's face, but then she looked over the top of the couch at Connie, who was getting up to face her.

"We'll have fun, Sis," said Connie. "We can snuggle up and watch the TV. How about that?"

Sissy gave Connie a nod, and when she turned back to Maura, they shared a hug. By then, Connie had made it over to them, and she reached down her hand to her little angel. Sissy took it and smiled up at her. She even shot Coal a tentative smile.

At the last second, Connie gave Coal a look, and this time it came with a wink that let him know she was happy with him. In spite of the silliness of this whole thing, knowing he had made his mother happy gave him a warm feeling inside.

"Don't make any more cookies," said Coal as he walked to the coat rack and pulled down his leather coat.

Connie looked over. "Why not?"

"I'm going to get fat."

"Since when do you make the choices around here?"

Coal just grinned and shook his head. "Okay, have it your way. Then oatmeal chocolate chip."

He turned with Maura, and they squeezed out the door, leaving three devastated dogs behind.

Maura headed for the Travelette. "Hey, woman, that brings back bad memories," Coal spoke after her. When she turned, he jerked his head toward the LTD. "Can we go in mine?"

"Woman?" she said challengingly.

"Well, you're not a man, are you?"

She sniffed, trying to pretend she was offended. "So what's wrong with Ebenezer?"

"That name doesn't suit you."

After taking a moment for his corny joke to reach her, she laughed. "Real funny. Okay, so what's wrong with *my truck?"*

"The name, for one thing! Come on—Ebenezer? Jeez, we're not going to fight about it, are we?"

She shook her head and gave him a bewildered face. "Who's fighting?"

"Just get in the car, okay?"

"Okay, fine. Your heater works better anyway."

"Yes, and heaven knows it's going to be cold enough."

Maura had started toward the Ford, but now she turned back toward him. "What's that supposed to mean?"

"What?"

"It's going to be cold enough. Are you talking about me?"

Dismayed, Coal stared at her. Then he just started laughing. "You've got to be kidding me. A man can't say anything without some woman twisting it around." He walked over to the passenger door and opened it. Maura looked down at the opening for a moment. Finally, she looked back up at him with a blank face.

"What, am I driving?"

He gave her a wry smile and then a gentle shove. "Just get in, smart aleck."

When they pulled into her yard, Chewy and Dart, Maura's blue heelers, came out barking their normal greeting, and Homer, Sarah, Hilly, and Brusher all came to lean over the fence.

Coal glanced at the dark windows of the cold-looking trailer house. "So… I've been meaning to ask you something." He reached down to pet Chewy and Dart and try to keep them from jumping up and getting mud all over his pants.

"Okay."

"Your boys have been gone a while."

Maura's face went a little dark. "Yeah."

Coal stood frozen. He had the sudden feeling he had just hacked into an ice-covered pond he wasn't sure he could swim.

Maura turned and walked stiffly toward the corral and the horses, where she had thrown down two bales of hay earlier. She snatched an Old Timer from her pocket and popped out a blade, hacking savagely into the two strands of sisal twine on one bale before starting to hurl out three fat flakes for each horse. Coal eased over beside her, looking down at the second hay bale he knew she would need. He thought for a moment about cutting the twine himself, but instinctively left it to her. He sensed she needed to cut something up, and better the twine than his fingers.

Maura slashed into the second bale and launched out three last flakes for Brusher, the gentle chestnut that always had to wait for the other three horses to claim their feeding spot.

Taking a deep breath of the hay-scented air, which was icing over quickly as the day burned out to dusk and turned the mountains a dull blue, she turned back toward the house. Silent, Coal followed. He watched as she fed the ravenous dogs on the front porch and brought them clean water from the house.

Then, when all was done and they were standing and listening to the dogs munch their food, Coal drew from the last ounce of courage he was going to be able to summon that day.

"How are things going with the boys, anyway? I haven't heard much about them lately."

Maura locked her arms tight across her chest and looked out toward the horses—away from Coal. After a few moments: "Fine, I guess."

Coal froze and debated with sanity about whether to speak. *Fine?* What kind of an answer was that from a woman who loved her children? "Just fine?"

She nodded. She still wouldn't look at him.

Coal reached up and scratched under the back of his hat, pursing his lips and rubbing them together. Just something to do while he decided if he was going to start a little range war by feeding off his range or if Maura might actually need to talk. Maybe it was the lawman in him that just wouldn't let him mind his own stinking business.

"Hey, lady. You know you don't have to keep everything in all the time."

This managed to wring a chuckle out of her. "Like you, you mean?" She actually looked over at him, then realized the faux-pas in this and shot her eyes away.

He nodded, although she wasn't looking. "Uhh, yeah—like that." Silence. If a clock had been ticking, the thunder of it would have given him a concussion. "You having troubles?"

"My ex-husband could get shot today and I wouldn't bat an eye."

Well. That said something.

After a moment, Coal said, "Ohh . . . kay. Man trouble then. That's better than boy trouble—right?"

Maura turned fully to face him. "Coal, what am I going to do if he takes my boys? Nyle True Bear is a bastard."

She fought to hold back tears, a sudden rush that seemed to catch her off-guard. Coal stared at her. He was pretty sure he hadn't ever even heard this name, Nyle True Bear.

"Hey! Hey . . . Maura, it's not that bad, is it? What are you talking about, take your boys?"

A deep, chattering breath. She steeled herself. "Nyle's trying to take my boys away—again. He says I'm not a fit mother."

"Not a fit mother! My butt! You're a great mom even with kids that aren't yours."

"Tell that to the judge."

"They can't just take your boys on the word of your ex."

"Like I said, tell it to the judge. Nyle has all the money in the world, Coal. He hired a doctor to sign an affidavit swearing I'm mentally incompetent, and that doctor is bought and paid for. I have nothing to fight him with."

Coal was only stunned for a moment. "We'll see about that." His protective back was instantly up. Nobody, judge or otherwise, messed with his friends that way. And he had always been on the side of the down-trodden. "Where's all this happening?"

"He moved out of Terreton to Idaho Falls, and he has a big law firm hired there. And I think he might be friends with the judge that has the case, too."

"Well, that's the first thing we're going to address then. But let's not think about it tonight, okay? You told Sissy we'd be right back, and we can't let her see you sad."

Maura sniffled. "Yeah. I always have to be the strong one."

"That's what grown-ups do." Coal felt sheepish saying that. He had been broken up himself enough lately over Laura and Katie Leigh, and losing many of his oldest friends, to fill two lifetimes.

Maura looked up at him. Their eyes locked. For just a moment, he thought she was going to step up and try to kiss him. For just a moment, he was pretty sure he wanted her to.

At last, she stepped close but only put her arms around him, very softly, like the wings of a bird encircling its young.

She spoke to his coat. "Can I tell you a secret?"

"I guess so. If you're not breaking a promise."

"Well, I didn't really promise."

"Okay. What?"

"Your mom asked me to see if you would take me with you if you go see Kathy MacAtee tomorrow."

A feeling of indignant anger rushed through Coal after her words registered on him. In a bit, he took a deep breath, patting her back. Okay. It was okay. His meddling mother thought she was watching out for his best interests—doing him a favor. And it was obvious she really liked Maura. Maybe his mother had a bit more of the matchmaker in her than Coal had ever guessed.

He managed to chuckle. "All right. Good old moms, huh?"

"I guess. So, she didn't say why, but I think I know."

"Why?" Coal was afraid to hear the woman's thoughts, but too polite not to ask, because he knew Maura wanted him to.

"She thinks Kathy is going to take you away from . . . her."

Coal smiled to himself. From *her?* Not from Connie, he thought. From Maura! But what his mom didn't realize, and Coal did, was that any spark between them had already died.

Because it was easier to talk to this woman when she couldn't see his face, and because it hadn't gotten completely dark yet, Coal held onto her for a moment longer, keeping her from being able to look up at him. "So are you asking if you can go?"

"No. I'm going to tell her I remembered I had something else to do. That woman and those girls need a man over there—at least for a while. I would be the worst kind of intruder." She pushed away and looked up at him. "Is that okay? I know your mom means well, but I just think it would be terrible to interfere."

"It's okay. I don't think it would be *terrible* of you to go, but I think you're right not to." He wanted to promise her that nothing was ever going to happen between him and Kathy. But then he couldn't think of a reason why he should.

CHAPTER FIVE

Tuesday, December 19

Jim Lockwood went down to Wally's Café every few mornings, mostly to tease Beulah, to shoot the breeze and smoke a cigarette with Wally Richardson—as well as to argue whether Camels were really all Wally thought they were or if Marlboros were the only cigarette worth the thirty-two to thirty-three cents a pack they charged for them. It was also a good chance to sip down a few cups of coffee that wasn't Betty's. Not because he didn't like his wife's coffee, because he would always contend that it was the best in town, but because sometimes a man just had to wash the same old taste off his palate to keep it seeming fresh and alive.

So he sat on one of the stools at the counter in Wally's and told Beulah how beautiful her red hair was that morning and how if the noxious fumes from Camels ever choked Wally to death, and if Betty was no longer around, well then old Jim was just going to come calling, and he wasn't even going to give the gossips time to bet on how long it would take.

"Those Marlboros will kill you a decade before Camels take me down, you old bandit," said Wally with a laugh. "You ready for some more coffee?"

"Is it more of that Folger's?"

Wally looked at him askance and drew the steaming pot back toward himself. "What if it is?"

"Just making sure. If you were trying to poison me with Sanka or something I was fixin' to tear the place up."

Wally gave out a jolly laugh, almost sloshing the coffee. "Sanka!" he said with amused disgust. "Not a chance. Although I might say you could use a lot less caffeine in your life, bub. You get all riled up when you get a cup in you. I'd hate to see you if you ever got hold of any Black Beauties."

Jim matched Wally's laugh now and scrubbed at his horseshoe mustache with the web of his hand. "Nah, speed never was my style. I'm high enough all by myself. But wait a minute—how do you even know about Black Beauties?"

Grinning, Wally came close and leaned across the counter to top off Jim's cup. "You serious? You know I have teenagers in here all the time. And they love to talk about that stuff."

Chimes rang, and Jim twisted around to see the door click shut behind Harvey Cupper, owner of Lemhi Valley Realty.

"Mornin', ole Wally! Where's Red?" asked Harvey.

Wally laughed. "She's fixing some more coffee back in the kitchen. Jimmy's been drinkin' it like water." He waved his Camel around in front of him, sending smoke writhing in all directions.

Harvey, a thick-set man of medium height, whose crop of gray hair could barely be discerned among the pale blond that the girls had loved so much when he was young and single and it was still thick and wavy, looked over at Jim and shook his head as he took out a pack of Saratoga One-Twenties and shuffled one out, then slid a book of matches off the counter.

"Jeez, Jim, I hope you saved me at least a cup."

Jim grinned as Wally poured the last cup out of the pot into a porcelain mug and Harvey plopped down on the shiny red stool next to Jim's and took the mug.

Simultaneously as Harvey lit up the Saratoga, Wally and Jim said, "What the hell do you call *that?"*

Harvey frowned good-naturedly. "Wait till I finish my Saratoga!" he said, quoting the catch phrase from a currently well-known magazine ad and making the other two laugh with glee. "They're sure better'n what you're both choking on!"

"What do you know?" queried Jim as Wally went back to the kitchen.

"It's colder than a well digger's heel, I know that," said Harvey, embracing his coffee cup and putting it up by his nose so he could draw in a deep breath of its aroma. "You?"

"That's about all I know, too," replied Jim. Except it really wasn't all that cold. It hadn't even gotten below nineteen degrees that night. "Sellin' many homes?"

"Nah. Nobody wants to buy a home in the cold. Say! I was hoping I'd run into you sometime."

"Oh yeah? Well I'm not buyin'."

Harvey guffawed and waved Jim off. "Stuff it, you old turd. You're not gonna leave that broken down shack 'til they drag your wrinkly old carcass out of it. So, hey—you know old Bern Hargis?"

"Judas! Sure I do, to my regret. Who doesn't?" replied Jim, with a disgusted half-amused twist to his mouth.

"Ha!" Harvey opened his mouth like he was about to say something, then shut it abruptly. On a whim, he brought his cup to his lips and burned them good, made a face, then took a more careful sip to prove that he wasn't cowed by a little boiling coffee. Jim watched him patiently, but his eyes were wary. Every time he heard anything about Bern Hargis, it seemed like it was something he didn't like. Back when he was still sheriff, he had fed the scrawny beggar enough meals on the county's dime to keep a hobo alive for a year of Sundays.

Finally, Jim caved in. "So what about him?"

"Well, jeez, now that I brought it up, I'm a little unsure how to put this."

Jim's eyebrows lowered, and he squared himself on Harvey. "What's gnawing on you? Bern do something wrong? Again?"

"Well . . ." Harvey turned and met Jim's eyes. Suddenly, whatever he had started to say not only seemed unimportant, but it seemed painful. "Hey, I just remembered I was supposed to make a phone call first thing this morning, Jim." He started to stand up.

Jim lurched up too. "All right." As his old drinking buddy turned away, he grabbed his coat sleeve and eased him back around. "I pride myself on keepin' my hogs in their own pen when it comes to other folks' business, Harvey. You know that. But I'm guessin' there's somethin' in your craw about Bern Hargis. I'm even guessin' you came in here meanin' to tell me about it. What the hell's up?"

Harvey Cupper looked down at Jim's hand, which finally fell to his side. He returned his eyes to Jim's face. A worried look grew in his eyes, and all of his good humor fell away. "So yesterday I saw Bern come out and accost your missus on the sidewalk in front of the drugstore. Just being his usual charming self."

"Accost? What are you talkin' about?"

"Accost, yeah. That's the word I'm thinkin' of. He talked to her for a minute, and then… Well, he gave her a slap on the rear when she was walking away." Harvey's eyelids suddenly pinched up, like he was afraid Jim was going to punch him in the mouth.

Instead, Jim stood very quiet. When Jim Lockwood got that way, his eyes turning to steel, and his body tensing up, any man with two dimes' worth of sense either walked away, or started apologizing fast—for everything he might ever have done wrong. And some things he had never done at all. Just in case.

Harvey stared at Jim until he realized he wasn't going to get hit. Finally, he said, "Hey, it wasn't a big deal. Betty just kept on walkin' like it never happened, and Bern turned around and went back to his truck."

The corner of Jim's mouth twitched, and he turned just enough to set his trembling cup down on the countertop as Wally came back into the room.

Jim didn't say a word. He just walked out of Wally's.

* * *

Coal couldn't take Maura with him to the MacAtees'. She had flat-out turned down the whole idea, and she had given him reasons, all of them sound. He thought about taking Connie, but he was embarrassed enough already by her fantastic thoughts of how women were falling all over themselves to get to him. Fact was, he was worried about what she might say in front of Kathy and the girls. He felt bad admitting that, but not bad enough to invite her along. Did all aging mothers get meddling with their children like his did?

He did one thing he thought might appease her, and that was to invite Katie, Cynthia, and Sissy. A man in a room full of female emotions might be like a rabbit with a nose bleed swimming across a shark tank, but at least the move should set his mom's overactive imagination at ease.

There was a fifth member of this outing, perhaps the most important one: Burro.

Coal pulled into the MacAtees' driveway and took a calming breath, looking over at Katie Leigh. The other girls and Burro occupied the back seat.

"What do you think? We ready to go in?"

Katie shrugged. "I'm ready." Cynthia's agreement echoed hers, so Coal threw open the door and got out, opening the back door and watching Burro shoot out like a bullet. His immediate thought was how much nicer that name would have been for him: Bullet. Anything but Burro, or, worse yet, Rufus.

As the strange entourage made its way to the front of the house, the door swung open. Kathy MacAtee, with her dark hair already done and tasteful makeup applied, greeted them with a big smile on her face. In spite of himself, something stirred down in Coal's quiet heart.

"Wow! What do I owe all this company to?" Kathy asked.

"We thought you might like some new faces around," said Coal. He tried to act comfortable, but his own surprised reaction to Kathy's appearance, as well as his mother's warning words, kept rattling around in his head.

"And who's this?" Kathy asked, petting Burro as he came up and began exploring her pant legs.

"That's Burro. A friend and I rescued him off the road a while back and never could find an owner."

"Wow. He's a beautiful animal."

Yes, beautiful, thought Coal. "Yep. Full-blooded golden retriever, as far as I know."

"Can I let him inside?"

Coal shrugged. "Sure. He likes people a lot, and he's really well-behaved. Plus, he just had a good bath."

Kathy swung the door open the rest of the way, and the four of them and the dog trooped into the house with her. The girls were watching *The Dinah Shore Show,* with Rock Hudson as her guest. They were in the middle of a rendition of "The Twelve Days of Christmas." Just as those seven tired old swans began "a-swimming," Burro charged into the midst of them, waving his great big golden flag of a tail and grinning from ear to ear. Dinah and Rock were thrown violently aside in the following melee.

As Sissy huddled close to Cynthia, and Katie found herself a place on the couch, the three MacAtee girls loved on their new-found canine friend, and Coal watched them and smiled.

Kathy walked over and hooked her arm around his, squeezing it tight. He turned and gave her a hug, holding on maybe longer than he should. He guessed he needed her closeness as much as she must need his; each of them was the other's hold on Larry. At last, she let go of their embrace, but she continued holding onto his arm.

"So Burro's a new dog, huh? He doesn't seem to fit your tough-guy image of Rottweilers and Great Danes."

Coal laughed. "Well, in all honesty, I'm not interested in either of those."

"Okay, whatever. What is it then, Dobermans and shepherds?"

"As a matter of fact," he said with a smile.

"Hey!" Kathy turned to him, almost startling him. "I've been thinking of something I'd like to do with you. And it might be one of our last good chances before the roads get too bad."

"What's that?"

"Come with me." She turned to the girls, who were engrossed in the dog. Burro was in his element, soaking up all the attention. "Hey, girls? Girls!"

They all turned toward her voice. "Listen, Coal and I are going somewhere for a little bit. Will you be all right?"

"Sure!" came sixteen-year-old Milo's reply. "We have Burro!"

Coal smiled and with a little apprehension followed Kathy to the back door, where she picked up her quilted blue polyester coat, and he helped her slip it on. It made such a loud, whispering racket as she put it on that it made him think of a fellow he had gone hunting with a few years back who had insisted on wearing one a lot like it. That boy—Henry was his name—never got near any game animals, and he never seemed to figure out why.

With her coat on, and Coal having never removed his, Kathy opened the back door and led him out into the overcast day. Although it was brisk, the gloomy cloud cover seemed to be holding the little bit of heat down close to the earth, and it wasn't too much below freezing. Kathy reached out a hand, and Coal stared at it for a moment like someone had flung a tarantula at him. He had never felt that way before and would never have thought anything of the act but for Connie. It kind of made him mad, and with resolve he reached out and took her hand. It was very warm.

She led him to the garage and threw up the overhead door, then reached into her pocket and drew out a couple of keys on a ring. She held them out, jerking her head toward Larry's beautiful LeMans blue Camaro.

"Here you go, big guy. Take me for a spin."

Before he could even really think, a wave of goose bumps rolled over Coal's skin, and he beheld the car that had been his and Larry's dream machine. It was still perfectly dust-free, sparkling even in the low light. A dream if ever there was one. Kathy had told him the first time he saw the car that Larry came out and dusted it every day. He guessed she must be keeping that tradition alive now in Larry's honor.

Coal looked over at Kathy again. He tried to shake his head, but the movement was weak. "Kathy, I couldn't."

She frowned at him and shook the keys. "Yes, you can, honey. Coal, Larry's in there. He's been waiting for this moment for a long time. You wouldn't want to let him down, would you?"

Coal grinned through eyes gone misty. He was going to tell her she had a way with words, but he didn't. He couldn't speak.

Slowly, he walked to the passenger door and opened it, and Kathy bent down and slid onto the sleek blue seat. With just enough force to latch it, Coal shut her door, and on the icy blue steel his fingers lingered. His eyes roamed over the white vinyl top, along the hood with its fat stripes and gently raised scoop, then down the length of the doors and to the striped trunk and spoiler. Maybe Larry really was inside. Maybe he really would have liked knowing Coal was here, driving this wonderful machine, with Kathy beside him.

He went around to the driver's side, careful not to let his jeans rub the paint, and his fingers touched the door handle. Kathy was leaning over and smiling up at him through the glass, and he smiled back. As he opened the solid door, he seemed to hear Larry chuckling. *Come on, you big sissy,* Larry would have chided him. *Just drive the stinkin' car.*

Take 'er for a spin—if you're man enough.

CHAPTER SIX

Jim Lockwood was not a big, heavily-muscled man. At a passing glance, in fact, he might not have been anyone who would have drawn attention in a crowd. But to anyone, man or woman, who lived an active lifestyle, who spent any time in a gym or in a boxing ring, or even to a man of military or police background, a second glance at Jim, even at his age, was going to beg for still closer scrutiny.

There was something about Jim's craggy face, his vee-shaped torso, and his narrow waist, along with the stocky thighs that filled out his Levi's 501s, that would warn any man—unless that man was very drunk—that Jim Lockwood was not the kind of man you wanted to mess around with. There was something in Jim's narrow, blue-eyed gaze, something in the set of his mouth, surrounded by the gray horseshoe mustache, that screamed out to any sober, cautious man: *If it's mine, leave it alone. And if it's my woman, and you touch her, I will break you in two.*

Unfortunately, Bern Hargis was neither a very often sober, nor almost ever a very cautious man. And maybe he also thought that a man who had worn a sheriff's star would show more restraint with his fellow citizens. No one knew what Bern Hargis thought. Most people wondered if he thought at all.

When Jim swung his black nineteen seventy Thunderbird into the driveway, he sat there for a few seconds, trying to collect himself. He stared up at the front door of the house and thought of his sweetheart of all these many years. His princess. The woman he would fight and die for, at the drop of *anyone's* hat.

At last, feeling he had a grip on his anger, he got out and shut the door quietly. It stayed ajar, but he controlled his temper and didn't try it again. Instead, he walked up the concrete steps and went inside.

"Hi, honey! Where you at?"

"Back here, dear," came back the almost musical call. How Jim loved the sound of Betty's voice. Even after some forty years, it could send chills along his spine.

Jim took off his hat and hung it on its usual hook. He took another calming breath, then two more, and then he started toward the back part of the house.

Betty was in their bedroom folding a pair of his underwear when he first saw her, and teasingly she took both sides of them between thumb and forefinger and shook them back and forth at him. "Hi, big boy."

Jim tried—and failed—to grin. Betty stiffened. She dropped the briefs down to her waist. "What's wrong?"

"Honey, Harvey Cupper told me you ran into Bern Hargis."

"Oh, garbage," said Betty, waving Jim off with the underwear and glancing quickly away. "That busybody."

"Is he a busybody, honey? Did you or didn't you run into that filthy rat?"

"I suppose I did. It depends on what you call running into him. It was nothing, really."

"He said he saw him slap you on the butt."

There was a two-second pause, and then Betty held up the briefs, peering at them closer. Suddenly, she tossed them toward Jim, who caught them deftly out of the air. "I don't know why I'm still folding your drawers, do you? You're home as much as I am since you retired, and the way you rustle around in there trying to find things, nothing stays folded anyway."

Jim felt himself growing cold inside. "Woman, I want a straight answer."

Betty huffed, cocked her head to one side and put both fists on her hips. "So what if he did, Jim? Come on. I walked away, and that was all there was to it."

Jim's glance slanted over to where his shotgun leaned, in the same place it had for years, behind the door. He looked back at Betty. "You didn't like it, did you?"

Betty's eyes snapped up to meet her husband's. "What kind of a thing is that to say? Of course I didn't like it."

"Then it's battery. He can go to jail for battery."

"If I were to press charges. And if I wanted to waste time in court. Not to mention wasting taxpayers' money."

"There's comin' a time when Hargis is gonna go too far, Betty. A man can only take so much from somebody. At least if he intends to be considered a man."

"Honey." Her voice dropped like an oaken log into a metal drum. "Honey? Drop it, please? I don't want to hear anything more about it, and you are not going to say anything to Bern Hargis. All right? For me?"

Jim stared her down. Finally, he felt his heart softening. One side of his mouth twitched, and he reached up and scrubbed his mustache vigorously. He took a lung-filling breath. "Okay. For you. This time. But it's the last time, Betty. I swear it. He's used up all his rope."

* * *

When Coal turned the key in the Camaro's ignition, some three hundred and fifty horses roared to life beneath the hood and began to gallop. His heart raced with them.

With an almost-trembling hand, he reached down and flipped on the radio, and Neil Young had just started into "Heart of Gold." Coal closed his eyes and for a moment he listened. The song was fitting for his old buddy Larry, who most definitely had that heart of gold for which Neil Young had been searching.

Coal almost jerked when he felt Kathy's fingers settle like sun-warmed caterpillars on the back of his hand. He looked over at her.

"This was a dream for both of you, Coal," she said, searching his eyes. "So take it. Let's hit the road."

Coal could only nod, looking into the woman's deep, expressive brown eyes. Words had flown from him.

He shifted into reverse, then turned to look over his shoulder as he backed slowly out of the garage, almost expecting to see old Rowdy come flying up barking excitedly. He spun it around and puttered it to the front of the house. He was soaking it in, all of it. From the cold vinyl seat against his backside, to the icy feel of the leather-covered steering wheel, to the smooth, crisp clutch and gas pedal underneath his boots.

Up the driveway they went, and he paused once more at the highway. He looked at the pearl-handled Hubley Texan cap gun swinging from the rearview mirror, and as memories of boyhood escapades ran through his mind, he smiled to himself, then looked over again at Kathy and fell into her dark eyes, wondering why today they looked so different than they ever had before.

With a big breath, he put his foot down on the gas, eased off the clutch, and they roared out onto the highway, headed southeast. At that point, instinct took over, and before Coal knew what he was doing, he had gone through all the gears, and they were cruising at ninety-five miles an hour, floating like a leaf on the water. Coal didn't realize for a while that Kathy was gripping the sides of her seat. After a minute, she started giggling, as they flew past the first vehicle they came to going their direction, and then Coal had to start backing off because of all the curves in the road along the Lemhi River.

He glanced over at Kathy, who still had the giggles. "Sorry," he said finally. "I guess I got carried away."

"Jeez, Sheriff, I guess you did! I hope you don't plan on writing anybody any speeding tickets on this road!"

"Yeah, better not, I guess. At least not while I'm driving this."

Kathy sighed and sank back into her seat. Coal listened to her soft breathing and felt the magnificent, bold rumble all around them. She turned a little in her seat and put her hand on Coal's leg. "Larry would have loved this, wouldn't he?"

Coal nodded, his leg chilled in spite of the warmth in the fingers. "He sure would."

"Do you think he's here, Coal?"

He glanced over, then shot a look toward the back seat before returning his eyes to the winding road. He felt his skin rise in goose bumps. "You know, maybe he is. I could see him hanging around, just to make sure you girls are going to be okay. Not to mention his car." He chuckled at the thought. "What a car."

"Yeah. Do you think they have Camaros in heaven?"

Coal chuckled, feeling wistful. "Not a doubt in my mind. That's where they were created, and I wouldn't doubt it if God has one of his own—a gold hardtop Super Sport with a fat black nose band." Kathy smiled and squeezed his leg a little harder.

They were well on their way to the little settlement of Tendoy, and a crackling radio ad singing about the "Pepsi generation" and how "Pepsi's got a lot to give" had just ended when a song by the Bee Gees came on—their first number one hit in the United States, in fact: "How Can You Mend a Broken Heart".

The only sounds in the Camaro besides the song were the mighty rumble of the horses and the hum of the Michelins. Soon, Kathy began to sniffle, and Coal took his right hand off the wheel and squeezed her hand. He didn't dare look at her again so soon. The deepness of her eyes and the softness of her full lips had begun to disturb him in an impossible way, and driving while rattled was as bad as driving while intoxicated.

After another half a mile, they passed the little white Tendoy store, and he slowed down just beyond and pulled right onto Viola Lane, driving over the one-lane bridge that crossed the Lemhi and coming to a stop in the dead yellow grass that flanked the road of frozen gravel and mud. He couldn't bring himself to shut down the wonderfully humming engine, so he shifted into neutral and set the brake, and the Bee Gees kept on singing, mercilessly. Kathy seemed to think they were singing for her, and inside, Coal was beginning to wonder if they were singing to him as well. But unlike Kathy, he wasn't going to cry.

As she leaned toward him with the tears flowing down her face, Coal reached out and held her, and the tormenting words rang in his ears:

And how can you mend a broken heart?
How can you stop the rain from falling down?
How can you stop the sun from shining?
What makes the world go 'round?

And how can you mend this broken man?
How can a loser ever win?
Please help me mend my broken heart,
And let me live again.

Finally, the song faded to silence, and the deejay came on. Coal felt Kathy moving as she reached out with her right hand and shut off the purring engine and the prattling voice. Then she returned to her former place, leaning over from her bucket seat to burrow her left arm in behind the small of his back.

A hundred thoughts seemed to be racing through Coal's mind and heart at once. The foremost was, had Connie been right all along? Was Kathy developing some kind of feelings for him, the kind that could never be requited? Or was she just feeling natural sorrow and needing comfort from a friend, the way any woman would who had recently lost the only man she had ever loved?

And as for Coal, how *could* a loser ever win? And would he ever again truly live?

One thing kept coming into Coal's mind, and that was that if, on the off-chance Connie had been right, and Kathy made an attempt to try to kiss him, he had to keep that from happening, at all costs. It would change every single thing about their relationship, and neither of them would ever forgive themselves.

At last, Kathy sobbed herself into silence, and after holding onto him for what seemed like another fifteen minutes, and after his back had started to go numb, she let go and leaned back over into her seat, once again taking his hand.

With her red-rimmed eyes staring out across the grassy fields toward the snow-swept mountains, Kathy said, "Coal, do you ever find yourself wondering what the future holds for us?"

CHAPTER SEVEN

Coal had always hated questions like the one Kathy had just posed, questions which might have two completely different angles. Did she mean "us" as a unit, or "us" as separate individuals? Was there any graceful way to answer such a question? He found himself wishing they were someplace near his radio or a phone, because it seemed like more often than not lately he was saved from such potentially dangerous, or, at the very least, uncomfortable, questions by being dispatched on a call.

Put on your straight face, Coal, he told himself. *Start talking like a lawman, not as a human being.*

"Sure I do, Kathy. How could I not? We've both been through the mill, haven't we?"

"Yep. We have."

Kathy's eyes scanned the fields before them again. Black angus cattle meandered and grazed, scattered like old-fashioned "Nigger Babies"—the candy company's words, not Coal's—all over the landscape, with an occasional Hereford or red angus tossed in, like the obligatory cherry-flavored Nibs. Coal didn't usually think in terms of candy, but he had been feeling a sweet tooth come on for days now. Beyond the cattle, out more toward the hills, little boxes like Monopoly buildings dotted the grassy acres. Pastoral landscapes like this were Lemhi County's hallmark.

"Someday I hope we look back on these days and see God's will in all this," the woman said with a sigh. She squeezed his hand and then suddenly dropped hers away. Had she been testing his feelings for her with all this physical closeness? Had he mercifully failed? "I guess we should go back, huh?"

Coal knew some fortuitous opportunities came only once. "Yeah, I suppose." Without even a socially polite pause, he reached out and fired up the engine, then backed around and drove back out to the highway, this time driving much more like a respectable lawman as they headed toward Salmon.

Fifteen minutes later, they pulled into the MacAtee driveway. Swatches of blue sky had busted through the gray and white clouds now, and sunshine buttered the house and garage. As Coal pulled into the garage and shut down the engine, the cold shadows inside seemed like a shocking slap in comparison.

"We should get a nice cloth cover for this thing," Coal said as he opened the door for Kathy.

She stepped out and turned to survey the bold, crystal blue of the car, shiny even in the dim light. "Yeah, I guess. But I'd have to take it off every day anyway. Coming out to dust and polish it is how I keep Larry close."

Coal smiled down at her when she looked back up, putting her hands out and touching his sleeves in a way that seemed completely natural.

Coal didn't remember ever really thinking about Kathy as an attractive woman, mostly, he guessed, because she had always been his best friend's girl, long before he got to know her. But even with her page boy haircut, which was not his favorite, she was, he had to admit, an attractive woman. And today she had applied that little bit of makeup that somehow made her eyes as perfect as any he had ever seen. Furthermore, she had these incredibly white, straight teeth, and two striking dimples that all combined when that big, warm, wonderful smile broke over her face to melt a man's heart. Still, he had never thought about her looks, one way or another—beautiful or not. She was just Kathy, his best friend's sweetheart. He still couldn't find it in himself to contemplate her appearance much, and it made him wonder if down deep he really was a cold man, as Laura had accused him of being.

A truly caring friend might have given Kathy a hug right now. He could see a need for physical touching in her eyes that was borne out by her fingers on his sleeves. But a little warning bell was telling him not to, and he obeyed.

His eyes fell away from those brown ones that looked up at him with a sense of longing he hoped he was imagining only because of the seed planted by his mother. "We'd better get back in and see if we can catch those girls in mischief, huh? Poor Burro might need a rescue by now."

Giving a laugh that seemed forced, Kathy turned with him, and they headed for the house. On the way, she said, "Where in the world did you come up with a corny name like Burro, anyway?"

He told her how they had first discovered the retriever, all covered in burrs. When they got inside the house and took off their coats, they found the girls all gathered around the golden dog, with the television off and a Carpenters forty-five in the stereo playing the hit single, "For All We Know."

"Now there's a song for you," said Kathy, nudging Coal.

Coal had always liked Karen Carpenter's voice. But at the moment, he wasn't sure he liked having Kathy point out the song. Again, he might have been reading into things, but it seemed only one more in a long number of hints that perhaps his mother had been right about Kathy MacAtee. *And love may grow, for all we know.* The words, and Kathy's soft smile up at him, kicked Coal straight in the guts.

"So you don't think Burro is that great of a name, huh?" Coal asked. He wasn't good at much, but at changing the mood of the moment he was a master.

After a few seconds to catch up to the new track Coal was on, Kathy laughed. "Well, it doesn't sound very endearing."

"All right then. What name would you suggest?"

"Don't be silly! Coal, I'm not going to dictate the name you give to your dog."

"Then don't. He's not my dog. I brought him here to give to you."

"What?"

"With Rowdy gone, and this beautiful guy just popping up out of the blue and not able to find his owner, I wanted to see how you and the girls would take to him. It looks like he's already part of the family."

"Oh, no, Coal, we couldn't!"

Kathy's weak refusal of the gift was loudly overridden by the cries of her daughters. Sara and Jen jumped up and ran over to her, throwing their arms around her pleadingly. "Mom! Please! I want him!" It was almost like they had rehearsed their lines.

"Looks like you don't have a choice, Kathy. You're out-numbered."

Kathy looked at her daughters, and her momentary stubbornness gave way. "Oh, what am I going to do with a dog like that?"

"I'm not worried. The girls will think of something. Besides, you said yourself he's not my kind of dog."

"Yes, but… Oh, all right." The collapse of Kathy's resolve was swift and final when Sara and Jen threw their arms around her once more and squeezed her tight, then started doing a jumping dance of joy. The unrestrained delight warmed Coal's heart, even though when he looked at the shocked faces of Katie and Cynthia he had a tiny moment of regret.

Little Jen said suddenly and rambunctiously, "Let's name him Queen!"

"No, silly! Queen is a girl name," corrected Milo.

"Then King!" Sara threw in. "How about King?"

Coal's mind instantly u-turned back to the scene in his mother's bathroom with Virgil and Maura down on the floor bathing the dog and Maura saying he looked "kingly."

"King sounds nice," said Kathy, looking over at Coal for his approval.

He just shrugged. What could he say? It wasn't his dog, after all.

The Carpenters had stopped singing, and Mac Davis was performing, "Baby, Don't Get Hooked on Me," a much more suitable song for the moment, at least in Coal's mind. He wished he could point it out to Kathy, the same way she had The Carpenters. Instead, they stood watching the girls fall all over their newly adopted family member, formally dubbed "King," and it seemed like the woman stood a little farther away from him now. Just his imagination, or was she, too, listening to the words of the song?

In time, Mac Davis finished breaking some young girl's heart. Then a fresh forty-five dropped down the spindle, grinding against Mac Davis's hit in a jarring way Coal didn't think could possibly be good for it, the player arm came over and down, and after the brief sound of static as the needle bit into the outer grooves, Glen Campbell began singing "If You Could Read My Mind." It was a Gordon Lightfoot creation that was anything but romantic and happy, when one listened to the words. Sad, but hauntingly beautiful. On the instant, Coal was glad that Kathy couldn't read his mind, but it would have been so much easier for them all if she could—here and now.

* * *

Driving home, the car was silent. Coal already knew he was in trouble, but he hoped the storm clouds would roll over fast. He hadn't asked anyone's opinion about giving Burro away, but it had seemed only right. After all, he was the one responsible for the dog in the first place, and Burro hadn't been at the house long enough for anyone to get attached to him. Or maybe Coal just didn't know children very well.

At least he had gone to a great home, a home that had been missing its border collie, Rowdy, to say nothing of the man their family life had revolved around. And another plus was that an animal that might serve as an uncomfortable reminder of Annie Price, as well as Bud and Linda Miley, was well away from the Savage ranch. And it wasn't like the girls couldn't go visit the dog now and then if they really needed to.

But as it turned out, it was not the girls about whom Coal needed to worry.

When they arrived back at the house, the trio of female emotion trudged glumly inside, and Coal stood out by the LTD and suffered through his once-in-a-blue-moon longing to light up a Marlboro. But he hadn't lit one up since Nam, nor had he bought any since then, and he wasn't about to start now. A real man didn't need such a crutch. What he needed was a pound of venison steak and a plate of mashed potatoes.

After a few minutes, he followed the girls inside just in time to see Virgil coming downstairs. With an expectant gleam in his eye, he glanced at the two dogs fawning over his father, and then he searched the rest of the entryway and the living room. Finally, his glance settled on the girls, who sat together in silence on the couch, with some meaningless commercial about 1972 Plymouth Dusters playing on the television before them but affecting them about like one would expect of young females.

Virgil's glance came back and met his father's. To judge by the look on his face, he could almost hear the words before they came out of Virgil's mouth.

"Hey, Dad, where's Burro?"

* * *

The phone call from dispatch had come almost as a relief to Coal after word made the rounds about the vile, heartless evil he had done to his hapless clan in giving away their new dog. One would have thought he kicked someone's pet baby rabbit in the head, for the malice they all shunted his way.

With a promise that fell on the ears of a bunch of people who were currently indifferent to whether it was kept or not, the promise to return soon and not miss Sissy's birthday celebration, Coal drove off to the ranch of local millionaire Phil Harringer to field a complaint about some neighborhood squabble. Harringer was the thorn in the side who, thanks to Todd Mitchell's indiscretion, had been almost single-handedly responsible for K.T. Batterton's dismissal as sheriff.

When Coal drove the GMC pickup into Harringer's long gravel driveway, it was with a sick feeling in the pit of his stomach. He had no use for Phil Harringer, who had forced his friend out of a job he was doing so well, and he did not like to be reminded of how powerful Harringer's name was in this county. But looking at the two hundred yards of perfectly groomed gravel road and the huge manor Harringer called a fully bricked home, Coal had no choice but to be reminded. The house loomed tall and haughty among exquisitely lush pastures on the far side of the Lemhi River, on the southwest side of Highway 28. As unfortunate chance would have it, it also sat just off Barracks Lane, which on the north side of Highway 28 became Savage Lane, the location of Connie Savage's ranch. Yes, Coal had merely to drive down his lane and across the highway by a few hundred yards to run smack into one of the residents from Lemhi County that he despised the most.

The gaudy opulence of Harringer's house, fronted by several hundred square feet of concrete driveway and parking area and fully enclosed with an immaculate white board fence, sickened Coal, who knew so many people like the Todd Mitchell family, who seemed barely to have two dimes to rub together.

He pulled up on the pavement in front of the big red house, with its white trim and green, crisply shingled roof, and adjusted the .357 on his hip as he stepped out of the pickup.

Surrounding the fenced, manicured half acre of lawn—something Coal was sure Harringer did not take care of himself—stood many hundreds of yards of crossbuck fence, and in that lush acreage grazed fat Hereford cattle, looking somehow as clean and groomed as the estate itself.

The only blemish on the property was a long line of dead cottonwood trees that had been in place for possibly ten or fifteen years and had obviously been intended as a hedge between Harringer's road and the neighbor's property. Coal had driven past them on his way in, fifteen or twenty of them, and to all appearances they were only recently dead. Perhaps it was just normal winter dormancy, but most of the leaves still hung on them, brownish black in color. The leaves on a healthy tree should have turned a brilliant yellow at least by the end of October and fallen off naturally.

A brand-new Dodge pickup pulled around the corner of the house and screeched up alongside Coal's GMC on the pad wide enough for two more. Phil Harringer climbed out, adjusting a steel-gray cattleman's hat on his head.

Harringer was a broad man, with a once-muscular, wide jaw now beginning to slump into fat, creased with deep lines on either side of his mouth. His lips were wide and so tight as to almost seem like only a slit in his face. It was his pale green eyes, which were far too wide apart and stuck beneath a dark, overhung brow, that drew the most attention, however. They seemed to glow with anger in the shadow of his hat brim.

"About time you got out here."

Coal could have said several things, none of them proper for a fledgling county politician. But he was a warrior, not a vote chaser.

"I was about to say the same thing to you."

"What's that?"

"About time you got out here."

"Listen, mister, that tin badge doesn't give you any right to talk to the voting citizens of your county like a smug S.O.B. You want to take my complaint, or do you want to get off my property?"

Coal felt his eyes and face grow hard, disliking this man even more than he had planned to. *Speaking of smug S.O.B.'s,* he thought. "Are you offering that as a real choice? I didn't ask to come out here, Harringer. You called *me,* remember?"

Harringer turned red, and he tried to stare Coal down in a manner he was obviously accustomed to. "I'll admit I might be a little on edge, Sheriff. But I should tell you I have enough power in this county to have your job."

"Yeah, so I hear."

"What's that supposed to mean?"

"Listen, Mr. Harringer, I don't have time to stand around here exchanging pleasantries all day. I came out to take a report from you. If you want to fill me in, great. I'll write it up and turn it in. If not, I have a little girl's birthday party to be to."

"Why you cocky— All right." Harringer blew hard out his nostrils. "Did you see that line of dead trees along my driveway on your way in?"

Coal smirked. "Yeah, I saw them."

"All right, well sixteen years I've been growing those things, trying to keep the damn neighbor's hog and dairy stench from blowing all over my property."

"Okay. So?"

"Well, my neighbor killed them."

"Really. How'd he do that?"

"Hell if I know. I just know he did."

"Who's your neighbor?"

"His name's Bern Hargis."

"All right." Coal couldn't help the flicker of recognition in his eyes, and the curse word on his tongue. He had heard way too much from his mother about Bern Hargis. "So what makes you think Hargis killed your trees?"

"Did you see that little crap hole of a place he has over there on the other side of those trees?" Harringer jabbed a heavy finger in the general direction of his neighbor's house. Coal recalled a skinny two-story house on the other side of the line of cottonwoods that was a mere shack in comparison to Harringer's estate. In between all the swathes of trees, grassy fields overgrown with thistle and other weeds surrounded it, along with a scattering of black and white Holstein milk cows. It had seemed at a glance that the lines of barbed wire fence were in bad disrepair.

"I saw it."

"All right. Well, at the start of my property is where his road cuts off, but it goes back behind my property line—behind those dead trees."

"I'm following that much."

"Good. So some months back he comes to me, drunk as usual, and tells me he'd like permission to cut down a couple of my cottonwoods because they sit right in the middle of his view of the sunrise."

Coal raised his eyebrows. "You don't say."

"I *do* say. Some gall, huh? My trees, on *my* property, are blocking *his* sunrise. Since when does that become a property owner's problem, so he has to take down his own trees?"

"I don't think it is."

"Well, he apparently thought so. I flat-out told him no, and he said he had other ways of making things work out. I thought he was going to try to take it up with the county or something—maybe even the sheriff's department. I laughed in his face and told him to get lost."

"Then what?"

"Then what? What do you mean then what? You can see, can't you?"

"Yeah, I can see the trees look dead. But it is the middle of December, isn't it? Shouldn't they be dormant?"

"You don't know much about trees, do you? The leaves would have just turned yellow, like always, and then fallen off, if it was just autumn as usual. Instead, they turned black and brown and just *died.* Those trees aren't coming back, Sheriff. I can promise you that much."

"How did he kill them? Girdle them?"

"No, he didn't girdle them. I told you I don't know what he did. But that many established trees don't just up and die for no reason."

"I'll grant you that. So I guess I need to go talk to Hargis."

"I guess you do."

"I'll be coming back up here as soon as I have a word with him—Mr. Harringer. If you want to be civil while I'm here, then maybe we can pursue this further."

"Civil? Listen, you little peckerwood, you're on my property, and I'm paying your wages. I can buy you out of that badge any time I feel like it. So you think about this: I'll talk to you any way I please, and if you don't like it you can look for another job—in another county."

It wasn't fear that made Coal turn around and get in his truck without a reply. Not fear of Phil Harringer, at least.

It was just that he could see another Warrenton, Virginia, incident coming; he wanted like never before to punch a man in the face. And he was not so sure he could come up with another job he liked—particularly in this county.

With that incentive in mind, and his teeth nearly cracking under pressure, he drove back down Phil Harringer's endless road toward the Lemhi River.

CHAPTER EIGHT

After stopping and getting out at the line of dead cottonwoods to see if he could see anything peculiar about them, Coal drove another two hundred feet or so to where the road split off, turned left and rattled over a rusty cattle guard onto what Harringer had told him was Bern Hargis's property. He noted as he passed to the other side of the cottonwoods that there was what appeared to be a new road being made along them on Hargis's side, constructed in the most barbaric of fashions—simply by driving right along the edge of Harringer's barbed wire fence, over any vegetation and rocks in the path, and knocking it down until set-in tire tracks had begun to take shape. But the main road to the Hargis property veered off to the right and was coated meagerly in gravel, giving way to the mud beneath.

The Harringer and Hargis homes were about as different as white and black. Coal had seen that on his way by the first time, but it became glaringly more obvious the closer he got. Hargis's ramshackle, scrawny, board-sided home had been white at one time. Now it was more of a moth-eaten gray. It had been crying for a new coat of paint for a good number of years, and the ends of some of the siding were split beyond repair, in places where the corner boards had broken away. Like a friendless old dog, this house was beaten, crippled, and shamed. The shake shingles grew moss an inch thick in some places, and the yard consisted of dust, feral alfalfa, and thistles. Worst of all, the whole place stank of dairy cattle and pigs crowded into enclosures that were too small.

An old, filthy, gray mongrel lay ribby, scabby, and scarred to one side of the yard, obviously having long since worn himself ragged digging a hundred little future graves at haphazard locations around the house. He didn't even have enough residual energy to let out a bark, a howl, or a growl. He lifted his bony head, weighed the threat of this approaching stranger, then let his head flop again to the ground. Even the nearby gray tabby cat, which although obviously full-grown looked too small to be real, seemed the more threatening watch animal.

In the yard, near a cracked and spalling concrete pad that had been poured flat on the ground, squatted a late fifties Rambler sedan, once dark green with a white roof, now every bit as run-down and dilapidated as the house, with what appeared to be four green-dyed, faded rabbits' feet dangling from the rearview mirror. That brought a wry smile to Coal's face. Hargis had better hope those rabbits' feet brought him more luck than they had the rabbits.

The inner door of the house stood wide open, in spite of the cold. Before Coal could knock on the screen door, which had a jagged hole torn in the middle of it suspiciously about the size of someone's fist, a call came from an outbuilding that might once have had grandiose dreams of growing up to become a barn. The whole thing was tilted precariously to one side, as if trying to stand against a hurricane or getting set to flee the sure destruction of being a part of this property. From inside came the bawling of cattle.

The person hailing him approached. She was a large-boned woman wearing a floppy straw hat, and in one hand she held up an apron in curtsy fashion. A galvanized bucket hung from the other hand.

"Hello. Can I help you?"

"Sure, ma'am," said Coal, tipping the brim of his hat. "I guess I need to talk to Mr. Hargis, if he's around."

The woman stopped before him, standing some five-foot-eight, with dirty, straw-colored hair that looked unreasonably terrified of grooming implements, and lines creasing a face that didn't seem quite old enough to explain them all. Her thicker-than-feminine hand continued to hold up the front of the stained apron that contained a crop of brown eggs with manure and bits of straw stuck to them.

The woman's eyes flickered around the yard, darting only once toward the front door. "Well, Sheriff, he might be busy. I'm his wife Sherlene. Is there anything I can do?"

"No, ma'am, I really need to talk to your husband."

A younger dog, a blue heeler, came running in barking seemingly out of nowhere. Sherlene yelled at it in a stentorian voice Coal would not have expected to come out of her, even for all her size. She stomped a foot for emphasis. The dog stopped barking and made a wide circle around Coal, eying him as if it really needed to protect this place from him. To its credit, though, it never made another sound, and finally, it stopped next to Sherlene, leaning into her leg.

"Who is it, Sherl?" an immediately irritating voice yelled from inside the open door of the house.

Sherlene Hargis frowned, and a little shiver went over her frame. She wasn't dressed for the thirty-degree weather.

"Do you want to go inside?" he asked.

"Well, I guess we could, but . . ."

"Damnit, woman, who's out there?" came the man's voice again.

"I guess that would be the *Mister* Hargis," Coal said to Sherlene. To save her from replying, he called out, "It's Sheriff Savage, Mr. Hargis. I'm coming in to talk to you."

"Oh, Judas priest!" Coal heard the voice grumble as he opened the door and let Sherlene go in before him.

The room assaulted Coal's every sense and sensibility. Shades of gray defined it, like the outside, and shades of every rank odor with which a home should not be filled, from rancid grease to cigarette smoke to petrified dog manure and prehistoric urine in carpet. Rotting bodies might have filled the kitchen, for all Coal could guess. At a sniff, it made Todd Mitchell's house smell almost sanitized.

Soon, a rail-thin, unshaven man with overalls on over a tee shirt that had been white when Washington crossed the Delaware came into the room with bare, almost bluish purple feet shot with distended veins like grotesque blue night crawlers. The purple feet didn't surprise Coal, since it seemed nearly as cold inside the house as out.

"Thanks for tellin' me who it was, woman," the man growled. "What do you want, Sheriff? I'm in the middle of a show."

"You're Bern Hargis?" Coal asked, trying to be polite but already feeling pushed past the point of wanting to be. The man's attitude, true to local legend, stank even worse than his medieval dungeon of a house.

"Well, course I am. Who'd you expect?"

Coal gritted his teeth. There must have been something bad in the water along Barracks Lane. It spawned only people with a total lack of cordiality.

"I need to talk to you about Phil Harringer's trees, Mr. Hargis."

"What the hell? What *about* his trees?"

"Something killed them."

"Why ask me about it? Gol-dang, I'm tired of takin' the blame for everything in this valley. If a goat got knocked up they'd come sayin' it was me."

Coal didn't even take this blatant opportunity and invitation for derisive commentary—although later, deep in the night when he was alone, he might lie in bed and laugh himself silly over all the jabs he could have come back with.

"Nobody's being blamed, Hargis." Coal dropped the *mister*. This moth-eaten buffoon didn't deserve any such title. "I'm just here to ask some questions."

"Well, why're you takin' Harringer's part?"

"You're going to have to try listening to what I say, or this is going to end up being a pretty pointless conversation. I'm just asking you what you know about the trees."

"Hell, I knew when I saw them dead trees somebody'd be comin' down here to accuse me. I *knew* it! That's what happens when they's a poor man an' a rich one in a arga-ment."

"I have no idea what you're talking about, Hargis. How about grabbing a cigarette or something to calm your nerves?"

"My nerves are jus' fine. Why would you even say a thing like that? You come in here accusin' me of stuff, takin' Harringer's part against me, and then you start talkin' about my nerves. Why *wouldn't* my nerves be on edge?"

So *were* the scrawny idiot's nerves calm, or weren't they? The man couldn't even answer that himself. Coal had a hard time remembering very many times in his life when he had felt more immediately irritated by someone, even perhaps including Phil Harringer. It seemed like Hargis was either high on something, or flat-out crazy.

"Listen, Hargis, I told you I'm not accusing you of anything, and I'm not taking Harringer's part. I'm just doing an investigation, and you happen to be the one named as the only suspect."

"Dang it, I knew it! So you *are* accusing me!"

"All right." Coal's short fuse had just about burned out, and the sparks were near his dynamite. "You know what? Killing those trees is considered vandalism—" He had to raise his hands and throw them palm-out toward Hargis to keep from being interrupted again "—and because of how long it takes to grow a tree, they're pretty valuable, and I imagine this falls in the realm of a felony. Is that what you want, Hargis? A felony charge? Some prison time? You think that might shut you up?"

"I didn't kill the damn trees!"

Coal took a deep breath. "Well now maybe we're getting somewhere."

"What're you talkin' about? Am I under arrest or ain't I?"

"I don't even know where you got that idea."

"Well, if you're accusin' me of a felony, I'm assumin' bein' arrested is next on yer menu."

"That's why you need to stop making assumptions. Like I said, I'm doing an investigation. That's how these things get decided—or at least it's how I decide whether or not to cite or arrest someone. The sooner you settle down and cooperate, the quicker I can get out of here." *And I can't get out of here any too soon,* he thought.

Coal happened to glance over at Sherlene Hargis, who had divested herself of her bucket and dirty eggs and was leaning against the doorway into the kitchen. Her arms were folded, her face red, and she stared at the floor as if it were talking to her.

"Am I under arrest?"

"How much have you had to drink today?" asked Coal, exasperated.

"I haven't drank a thing."

"Well, if you're this big of an ass sober, I'd hate to talk to you when you're drinking."

"What the— Why you—"

"Shut up, Hargis!" Coal barked. His patience had gotten up and flown south. "I'm going to ask you a few questions, and if you'd like to cooperate, then great. If not, I'm done talking. I'm going to cite you on probable cause for felony destruction of property, and you can fight it out with Judge Sinclair and a local jury of your peers. From what I've seen between you, Harringer, and the judge, the three of you deserve each other."

Hargis swore. He looked over at his wife and growled, "Go get me a beer." Then he turned back to Coal. "Okay. *Okay!* So what do I have to do?"

"Thank you. That's the first sensible thing out of your mouth today. All right. Harringer says you had an argument about some of his trees. He said you told him they're blocking your view of the sunrise and you wanted him to take them down. Is that true?"

"Well, yeah, I guess so. Just some of 'em. But I—"

Coal threw his silencing hands up again. "It's my turn to talk. So then Harringer says his trees died."

"I reckon so."

"Did you kill them?"

"Hell no. I would have knocked 'em down with my chainsaw if I was gonna do it."

"So you didn't do anything to harm the trees? That's your story."

"Of course not."

"Have you ever had a run-in with Harringer before?"

"Only if I look at him."

"Be specific."

"All right, just mostly if our cows gets mixed up. He's got some high-falutin breed he says don't mix with mine. You know how them rich folks are."

High-falutin breed. Like Herefords. "Tell me about it."

"Well, our cows get in together, and I have a Holstein bull—a milkin' bull, you know."

Although Coal didn't want to know any more about the process of milking a bull, he kept this wry musing to himself.

Hargis continued. "Harringer doesn't want mixed blood cows—even though they're healthier and tougher."

"Well, in all fairness, his *are* beef cattle, and yours are dairy. I can't imagine *tougher* would do much for people wanting to eat the beef."

"Yeah, okay—whatever. Oh—and he gets mad about water, too."

"What about water?"

"Well, it's easier for cows to get down to the edge of the river on my place than it is on his because his bank is steeper and rockier, and he tried to get me to make arrangements so his animals could go down on the banks on my place and water at a certain time of day, and I was to keep my cows penned up out of the way until his was done. Imagine that. Who does he think he is? It's my damn stretch of river!"

The whole story had a big ring of truth to Coal, after having his own run-in with Harringer. "Nothing else?"

"Nothin'. So far."

"So this wasn't all that hard after all, was it?" asked Coal as Hargis turned and took the open beer his wife had been holding. He had no word of thanks for her, and the woman frowned, glanced over at Coal, then swung her eyes away. Coal felt immensely sorry for her. Her life here must be the next best thing to summer camp at the county dump.

"Well, it don't matter. Rich folks always get their way, in the end."

Coal thought back on losing his job with the FBI over punching the son of Justice Bryne. He thought of Harringer's complaints ousting K.T. Batterton from his job as sheriff. Hargis had an irrefutable point.

He drove back over to the Harringer place, and Harringer came out of his house in a gray wool sweater, nursing a porcelain mug of coffee. "So? What did that liar tell you?"

"He said he didn't do anything to the trees."

"Of course that's what he said. Did you cite him?"

"No, I didn't. It's your word against his. There's no evidence on either side, and I have no intention of wasting the county's time and money. Chances are those trees are going to come back in the spring anyway."

Harringer's face darkened as surely as if some invisible can of spray paint were coloring it. "Well, of course there's no evidence! Are you a fool? But when a man gets mad about some trees and wants them cut down, and then right after that they die, after sixteen years of doing fine, you would think that would be evidence enough."

Coal didn't know but that a jury just might find Hargis guilty on that one item of "evidence." However, in this case it would probably be hard to find twelve people who didn't hate either Harringer, Hargis, or both—considering what pleasant human beings they both were. So he didn't see any point in dragging the whole thing into court. And he still really wasn't sure those trees weren't going to sprout back to life in April anyway. After all, he was no arborist.

"It wouldn't hold up in court, Mr. Harringer."

The rancher snorted. "Well, it's pretty obvious to me, and it would be to my friends, too." Coal thought that a funny comment, as he doubted Harringer had a single one of those, and he ached to bring up this glaring fact but abstained because he didn't want to hurt Harringer's tender feelings.

"Sorry I can't help you. Anything else?"

"You make me laugh. *Anything else!* I should have known better than to call a little piss ant sheriff's department like this. I guess if you want something done, you have to do it yourself."

Coal looked Harringer square in the arrogant eyes. "Meaning?"

"Why don't you figure that out, Sheriff? Oh—one more thing."

"What's that?"

"You're going to find you've messed with the wrong man. I eat little nobodies like you for breakfast. I can buy your job in a heartbeat and leave you homeless."

"Yeah, you said that before. Are you threatening me?"

"Like they say, it's not a threat—it's a promise." Harringer stared Coal down, his eyes filled with ire, used to having his way and ready to tear up anything in sight now that he couldn't—not unlike one of his bulls during the mating season.

"Now get off my land and don't bother coming back here."

"Thank you. I honestly couldn't do that fast enough."

CHAPTER NINE

For the first part of his drive back home, Coal could think of little more than how fun it might be shoving sweaty, dirty socks down the throats of Phil Harringer and Bern Hargis. But after he got his temper under control, which he needed to do or risk running some innocent motorist off the road, his thoughts turned mostly to Todd Mitchell, his one-time barely tolerated deputy whom now he somehow missed. Funny how things could change when fate stepped in to make its play.

Thinking about that very same fate, Coal wondered if anything in particular had prompted him to think about Todd, and suddenly a gut-wrenching feeling came to him. When he got to Savage Lane, he slowed down, debating whether to turn, but then he gunned it and kept on going toward Salmon.

The closer he got to town, the harder it seemed to breathe, and the slower his pickup crept, until he was down from his original speed of seventy to now only fifty miles an hour.

He pulled into town and drove past the quiet businesses, finally turning onto Daisy and stopping in front of Steele Memorial. Taking a deep breath, he stepped out of the truck. Against all of the brick, rock, and concrete around him, the metallic sound of the slamming door rang in the narrowness of the streets. Coal heard distant voices conversing around the corner, on Main Street. They sounded relaxed, sort of the way he wished he could be and doubted he ever could, while he held down this job.

Looking at the hospital door for a moment, he composed himself, filled his lungs once more with a breath, and went around the hood of the truck to push inside the building. It was shockingly warm, even though fairly temperate outside as well, perhaps up to the high thirties.

Coal looked around, saw the receptionist back in an office making coffee, and went over to where he could see her better. His tentative query about Todd brought back a surprising answer: Dr. Bent had finally drilled a pressure-relieving drainage hole in Todd's skull, and he seemed to be improving, although still in a coma. They were now awaiting a team from the University of Utah hospital in Salt Lake City, who would transport Todd to their facility, where he could get much better treatment than Steele Memorial could offer.

Thanking the receptionist, Coal strode back to the room where he had last seen Todd, only slightly conscious of the receptionist's voice calling after him. When he got to the room and saw that it was empty, he turned to see the receptionist quick-stepping after him down the hall.

"He's in room twenty, sir," she said. "Sorry, I guess you didn't hear me."

"No, I had other things on my mind. Thank you, miss."

"You might as well call me Mandy," said the dark-haired, brown-eyed young woman, whose build was stocky but not unpleasant. "It seems like we see each other often enough."

"And we'll probably continue to," agreed Coal. "All right, Mandy. You call me Coal. Titles are for old people—or important ones."

Mandy laughed and held out her hand. Her grip was warm and pleasant.

When Mandy directed him toward Room 20, Coal followed her instructions and walked down the hall, surprised to see Annie Price exiting the room with dirty linen.

"Hi!" she exclaimed, her face brightening.

"Hi yourself. Do you ever take a day off?"

Annie threw her head to one side in an exaggerated manner. "Well look who's talking!"

"Oh, yeah. Right." He laughed. Then he motioned toward the room she had just left, where a white block of tile stenciled with a fat black ***20*** was glued on the wall just outside the doorframe. "How is he?"

"Still in a coma, I'm afraid. But his breathing is better, and his heartrate too."

"That's promising."

"Yes, very. Did you hear Doctor Bent is sending him on a plane to the U of U?"

"I did."

"Oh. Okay, well, we called his wife, but she can't come say goodbye unless she can find someone to watch her boys—and drive her down."

Coal sighed. He wished he could help. He wished somehow enforcers of the law like Todd could be deemed important enough by society to actually pay them what they were worth so their families would be taken care of when something like this happened.

"Maybe I should go get her."

"Or maybe you should spend some time with your own family. Right?" Annie's eyes got soft, and she tilted her head slightly to one side, searching his face. "Coal, you can't do everything for everyone. Believe me. I used to try."

Coal understood. At his age, he knew better. He had always tried too, and generally it was of no use. In fact, many times the people he tried to help either thought he was figuring out a way to take advantage of them, or they went the opposite way and tried to take advantage of *him*. Either way, helping people beyond something like stopping to give someone a ride or fix a flat tire usually ended up going bad.

"You think you're pretty smart, don't you?"

Annie laughed. "Well, I should. I've been around long enough!"

Coal gave another laugh. "Yeah, you're ancient."

"Older than you, I bet!"

"I must look young for my age."

"Yeah? Well, just how old are you?"

"That's not very lady-like, is it?

"Wait. Now you're assuming I'm a lady? I thought I taught you better."

"Funny. But to answer your question, I'm forty-two. And in July I'll be forty-three."

"Oh, wow! You *are* an old man!" Annie giggled, poking him in the stomach, which he instinctively hardened—a habit from his fighting days.

"Told you."

"Forty-eight."

"Huh?"

"I'm forty-eight. I'm nearly half a century old—and my birthday is coming before yours."

Coal stared at Annie, not knowing whether to laugh, simply smile, or tell her what a terrible liar she was. But in Annie's eyes Coal could see it: She wasn't lying.

"Huh," he said, scrambling in his mind to find better words. "I don't believe you, you know."

"Oh! Cops are so suspicious. Well, I guess for my ego that's a good thing. But if you want to come to my house I can show you my bona fide birth certificate. It says Annie Debra Barthlome, May fifth, Nineteen twenty-four. Honest!" She held up her right hand to mimic a Boy Scout. "Come over tonight. I'll show you my birth certificate, and then… Maybe we can go to the movies. If you've been trying to avoid me because you don't like disaster movies, you might be happy to know we missed *The Poseidon Adventure.* But Robert Redford is there now in *Jeremiah Johnson,* or *The Life and Times of Judge Roy Bean* is also playing. You like Paul Newman, don't you?"

"Sure, I guess so. Either one of those guys is great, and I'd actually love to go. Unfortunately, tonight is out."

Annie's face fell, but she recovered quickly. "Oh, I see how it is! Now that you know how old I am you don't want anything to do with me. Yep, I'm just a cradle robber."

Coal's laugh matched hers. "No, I don't think that at all. And your age doesn't bother me in the slightest." He wasn't sure if that was true, but the story was good. "But remember when you said I should spend time with my own family? Well, it's Sissy's birthday today, and I promised I'd be there to celebrate."

"Oh! Nice. Yes, you'd better do that. I'm sorry, I didn't know."

"Well, of course not. How could you?"

"Don't worry—we'll try to get to one of those movies before they end. Right?" she asked hopefully.

"Sure, I guess. But they still only show films at the Roxy for three days in a row, don't they?"

Annie's face fell, but she gave him a weak smile. "Oh. Well, yeah, but… So we can't make it tomorrow either? That would be the last day."

Coal offered her an encouraging smile in return. "We'll try. I really would like to see one of those."

Her smile got happier. And then: "So hey—how is Burro?"

Coal hesitated, unsure how she would take his news. "I gave him away today—to Larry MacAtee's family."

"Wow! I would have bet money you'd keep him."

"He's a great dog, Annie, but not really my type, and I already have two. I'm going to hold out for something special, and a pup. They die too soon as it is."

"That's true. So… what *is* your type, Coal? If I'm not being too bold asking."

There it was! Warning bells. Coal chided himself inside, but he sensed that Annie was not really asking about dog breeds. "A wolf, maybe. Half wolf, half shepherd or malamute. I'm hearing good things about them."

"Oh. So not a fox?"

Coal grinned, now certain she was playing with him. "No, don't get me wrong. I love a nice fox. But in the four-legged variety it's definitely a wolf cross I'm looking for."

Annie giggled again. "Okay, then. Just checking. Well, I have some more cleaning up to do, so I'll leave you with Mr. Mitchell, and then you'd better go home and be with your family."

A silly whim almost made Coal invite Annie over for the festivities, such as they would be, but then he remembered Maura was going to be there.

Unfortunately, Annie might have read his first thoughts in the expression that had come over his face, because the same silly whim came to her, and Coal froze when he heard her words. "Hey! I get off work at five today. I know, weird shift. Maybe I'll come over and bring little Sissy a surprise."

Coal's face felt stiff, and he had no idea how to respond, except like a rat with its tail caught in a drawer. "Uh, sure, if you'd like to. Maybe a little dress or shirt—or she seems to like stuffed animals." *Stuffed animals,* Coal thought. Like the stuffed deer-in-the-headlights he must be resembling about now.

"All right, then. I'll pick out something, then go home and shower and come over. It might be seven, but maybe sooner."

"Um, okay. That's probably fine."

With a big smile, Annie turned and walked down the hall, and Coal went into Todd's room, feeling like he needed medical attention himself now—for his sick stomach.

Todd's cardiac monitor was pacing along with a good, steady rhythm—seventy-two beats a minute. His breathing was strong. Bandages wreathed his head, but otherwise he appeared only to be asleep. Coal didn't really know what to do now. It wasn't like he could talk to his deputy and tell him he missed him. So he stayed for only a couple of minutes, then left the room. When he didn't see Annie, he said goodbye to Mandy the receptionist, went outside and saw old Jim's black T-bird parked in front of the Coffee Shop.

Crossing in the middle of the block, he went inside to be assaulted by the smells of fries, hamburger, onions, and the usual pall of cigarette smoke that made the Coffee Shop always seem a little warmer than it might actually have been. From his usual booth at the front of the restaurant, Jim had seen him coming, and he raised his hand and waved him over. Betty, in a prim powder blue blouse and darker blue skirt, sat across from him, with her back to the street, and she got up and gave him a strong hug—the best medicine she could have offered.

Jim reached up and shook his hand, his narrow blue eyes twinkling and an amused twist to his mouth beneath his gray mustache. "Have a seat, son. You're lookin' great."

"Thanks to you, buddy," Coal replied, sliding in next to Betty.

"Don't even mention it," said Jim, raising a cup of coffee to take a sip.

"Don't mention it?" Coal sat and stared into Jim's eyes for several seconds while he tried to form a reply. Finally, he reached over and almost unconsciously took Betty's hand and gave it a squeeze. He looked over at her. "You hear that, Betty? He pulls me literally out of the jaws of death and then he says 'don't mention it'." He returned his eyes to Jim, who was looking uncomfortably down to wipe up some ketchup with the fat end of a French fry. "It's pretty hard not to mention something like that. I owe you my life, Jim. You're probably going to be hearing me mention it for as long as you live."

A rush of mist came into Jim's eyes, and he waved off Coal's words. "Aw, come on. That's what friends are for. Really, cut it out."

Coal chuckled. Maybe Jim's embarrassment was for the best. He honestly couldn't think of any proper words to thank him for what he had done. Not only had he saved his life from the clutches of the River of No Return, but he had put his own life at grave risk doing it. All in a day's work, Jim would probably say. But it wasn't. Tough, courageous, selfless men like Jim Lockwood seldom came along in this life, and Coal was honored to call him his friend. He just wished he could tell him all these things out loud.

Betty leaned into Coal, pushing her shoulder against his and laying her head over on him. "I'm glad you're still with us, Coal. You're right—my Jim's a pretty neat guy. I think I might keep him."

They all laughed, and Jim raised a hand to scrub at his jaw, glancing around as if he really cared who else was in the room.

Tammy Hawley came over, her blond hair bouncing and with the usual great big smile lighting her face. Her deep brown eyes stood out wonderfully against the light color of her hair. "Hey, old man. I hear you decided to go swimming in the Salmon. Don't you know it's the wrong time of year?"

Coal laughed. "Yeah, that's what everybody keeps trying to tell me."

"Just kiddin' ya," Tammy said, returning his laugh. "I'm sure glad you're okay."

"Thanks. That's only because of Jim."

"Yeah, everyone keeps talking about him, too. He already told me he didn't do anything, though." She winked at Betty, then looked over at Jim, who was pretending to savage another fry. "Good thing you didn't mind your own business, Jim. Who knows what would have happened to Coal if you had."

Jim looked up and grinned sheepishly. "Man, I'm gonna have to go eat someplace else if I want any peace."

"Well, old buddy, don't let me bother you. I just came over to say thanks again." Coal stood up out of the booth.

"You're not ordering?" Tammy asked with a quizzical smile.

"Nope. Going home to my family this time for real. That little girl we took in has a birthday today, and I don't want to miss it."

"Good for you, Coal!" cut in Betty with a big nod. "Good for you. You give everyone a hug for us, okay? And be careful driving home."

Coal looked out the window at a day that was lightly overcast but had turned out very nice in comparison to some other days in the past few weeks. He looked back down at Betty and Jim. "I will. You two enjoy your meal. And Jim, thanks again. I mean it—I owe you my life, and I'll do whatever I have to to pay that debt."

When Coal turned, Tammy was right there, her pen in one hand and note pad in the other. "Speaking of hugs, Coal, I want one."

Coal laughed and gave her a hug, then left the café thinking how nice it was to have friends who had managed to stay out of the line of fire that had been so rampant since his return to the valley.

What he was about to find out was how awfully hard it could be to save one's friends from severe storms. And the coming storm was like no other Coal and Jim Lockwood had ever weathered.

CHAPTER TEN

Coal only reached the city limits before pulling over to stop at the curb. He knew he really needed to heed Annie's advice and head home. His family was waiting for him. But he couldn't go. Not yet. They were going to fly Todd Mitchell out to the University of Utah hospital any time, and his family hadn't been able to visit him and say goodbye. What if he never returned?

With a lump in his throat, he turned around and drove up on the bar to get the Mitchells. All he could think about was his own family if he had been in Todd's place.

After dropping the family off at Steele Memorial, he took a chance and called Jay Castillo at the Coffee Shop to see if he or someone he trusted could find time to go over after the medics picked Todd up, get his family, and take them back home. The arrangement was made with Jay's wife, Carrie, and with a good feeling in his heart, Coal went out and fired up the Ford again and headed back home.

Once Coal made it home, the entire family crowded into Connie's Chrysler to drive back into town and shop for Sissy's birthday. This time that family included Maura, who sat in the back with Sissy on one leg and Morgan on the other.

The only one who stayed home was Virgil, who had gone to his room and told them he was busy reading. He wouldn't say much to Coal, would only speak to others if spoken to, and then only briefly.

Coal instantly wrote it off as typical teenage behavior. He never stopped to consider the fact that Virgil wasn't a typical teenager.

For the first time that season, through the eyes of the children and Connie, Coal began to realize how beautiful his town looked, swathed in its rainbow of green wreaths and big red bows, with deep green evergreen trees inside almost every window, hung with shiny balls of every rich color, and draped in elegant, sparkly garland. At every turn bristled holly and mistletoe, and each store was infused with the intoxicating aromas representative of this magical time of year. Coal could not begin to name all of the different smells, but many came from stands of candles and from the trees themselves. Even latex and the different plastics from a thousand toys brought in to complete the season lent their own telltale scents that announced: *Christmas time is here.*

Coal could not remember the last time he had experienced this wonderful feeling of yuletide bliss. Even in the face of all the friends he had lost, and all of the dark moments he had passed through in recent times, the smiles on the faces of his children and other shoppers who passed filled his heart with peace and the spirit of the season. He saw and stopped to say hello to old friends and acquaintances from his past, and for the first time in two years it really felt like the time of loving happiness that this season was meant to be. Hearing the notes of Jim Reeves's version of "Silver Bells" piping out from one of the stores they passed capped it all off.

Out of all the places they saw that day, King's department store, on the north side of the street, was the most magical place for young people. Except for the plastic odor, Coal remembered some of the very same smells that surrounded him today from his own childhood, and for a while those bygone days came back to him through the excitement in the eyes of Sissy and the twins.

Coal wasn't really much of a shopper. Other than the Johnny West action figures his boys played with—and which he had already instructed Connie to buy them for Christmas—he had never had a very big hand in any of his children's birthday or Christmas shopping. Laura had taken care of all that.

And fortunately now Connie and Maura were here, for even if he had been inclined to pick something out, he had no idea what a little girl would like.

So he watched with disconnected interest as the girls did their shopping and the boys stood around dreaming over the wide array of Marx action figures in their colorful, neatly stacked boxes.

Later, after they had gone to Saveway Foodtown and bought boxed cake and frosting mixes, they went back home, and Coal forced himself to sit on the couch with the twins watching *The Andy Griffith Show* and then *Hogan's Heroes*. Actually, he wasn't really forcing himself, for although he had other things he needed to be doing, such as getting his workout in for the day or loading rounds for his weapons, these precious moments with his family seemed so few and far-between that he simply could not pass up this opportunity.

Connie came over after a while and asked about Virgil. "Did he ever come out of his room when we came home?"

"I haven't seen him," Coal replied distractedly—Colonel Klink was in the middle of one of his tantrums on the television.

"Maybe you should check on him."

Coal looked up and stared at his mother for a moment, trying to register what she had said. "Yeah, sure, Mom."

"But you're not going to, are you?"

"Probably not."

Connie grunted her disgust and went back to the kitchen. From the corner of his eye, Coal saw Maura hug his mother and then follow it up with a one-armed squeeze. Maura said something, and Connie found her laugh. For the time, it was nice to have another adult female in the house. But Coal dreaded the upcoming scene when Annie Price would be making herself a third.

He didn't have time to stew over it long, however, for suddenly his mother's voice rose in consternation. "Oh, darn it!"

"What, Connie?" asked Maura.

"I got so busy remembering the cake mix and frosting and everything else I forgot the candles. We can't have a birthday cake without candles to blow out."

Coal heard enough to read the writing on the wall. Before Connie could call out to him, but after she had turned her head to look his way, he said loudly, and with a little feigned annoyance thrown in, to make his reply sound realistic, "Yes, Mom, I'll head to the store."

Connie laughed. "Okay, now there's the good boy I know and love. Get the multi-colored ones."

Coal only nodded. The boys had jumped up, apparently having lost interest in *Hogan's Heroes* and their current attempt to escape prison camp, and were clamoring to go with him, so he told them to get their coats, and he grabbed his wallet, pulled on his coat, and clamped his hat on his head. "See you ladies later. I expect this house to smell pretty sinful by the time we get back."

Once in town, on a whim Coal pulled up in front of B and B rather than go back to Saveway, and as he and the boys got out Coal heard someone hail him from up the sidewalk. Turning, he saw Annie Price hurrying toward him. Just like they said, you start thinking of the devil and he's likely to appear. Or in this case, *she.* Annie had a huge smile on her face as she stopped where her pretty astro blue Buick LeSabre convertible was parked at the curb, opened her door and threw a paper bag into it, then hurried down the sidewalk to them, giving Coal a hug. She turned to look at Wyatt and Morgan, who had paused nearby, side by side.

Caught off-guard only for a moment, Coal said, "Annie, these are my two youngest. This is Wyatt, and that's Morgan."

"Hi, boys. You sure look handsome today." Annie's smile was big and genuine. Morgan grinned, but Wyatt looked up at his father, seeming unsure how to reply.

It had been too long since Coal was that age, so he didn't catch the concern in his little boy's face. "You following us around, Annie?"

"Very funny. I just got done at King's, and I need to buy some groceries too. I thought I'd just do it with you. No one wants to shop for groceries alone, do they?"

Coal laughed. *Did they?* “All right, come on.”

They stepped inside the warm store, which, although they carried different merchandise from King’s, still smelled of the holidays, foremost of cinnamon, oranges, peppermint, and pine.

Coal had only taken a couple of steps when he saw Betty Lockwood, her shoe heels clipping along the front of the store. She turned down the canned vegetable aisle without having seemed to notice him.

“I’m only here to grab some birthday candles,” he told Annie.

Annie tagged along with Coal, where he latched onto the first box of candles he saw that contained more than one color and turned around. Like any typical man, Coal was not one to stand around comparing prices.

“Now it’s my turn,” said Annie, grabbing his arm. “I just need to get some things on the vegetable aisle and some cans of soup.”

* * *

Jim and Betty Lockwood needed some food for their tiny Christmas Day feast, so they drove over to B and B Foods, on Main Street. The store, like the streets outside, was every bit as packed as it would be in the summer months when tourists came up to the quaint little town to see the River of No Return, made famous by the movie of the same name, and to brave its frothy rapids.

“We should just get a game hen,” said Betty as she ran her finger along her shopping list and checking things off mentally. She looked up at Jim. “I’m going to get some green beans and onions. Will you run and get a fat hen?”

Off Jim tromped dutifully, with nothing in his head but picking the biggest little bird he could possibly find.

Betty glanced over to see Coal Savage and the twins walk through the front door, but Coal wasn’t looking her way, and they had just visited, so in the interest of time she turned and walked straight down the front of the store to the canned food aisle, pushing her cart. She was thinking of her children and wishing they could be with them for Christmas this year. But all three of them had other plans with in-laws, so it was going to be a quiet Christmas. Perhaps she and Jim would go out and visit a few friends, but otherwise, they would watch the Christmas Day parade and all the Christmas programming and maybe pull out the old family photo albums. Betty liked doing that every so often because it made her tough old man get teary-eyed when he looked at his little babies, who were all grown up now and had families of their own. Those tears in his eyes always made Betty feel closer to him somehow.

She had put one can of green beans in the cart and was standing there trying to decide if she should take a second one as if that were the most important decision in the universe. Without warning, she felt arms close around her from behind, and she giggled. Jim's public displays of affection always made her laugh, especially because they were so infrequent.

"Oh, stop that! People are going to see us," she chided him, grabbing his hands.

At that moment, a man walked around the corner and stopped, only twenty feet away from her. He stared at her, confused, lowering a Cornish game hen to his side.

It was Jim.

After a moment of total consternation, Betty let out a laugh, realizing that Coal must have come up behind her. She had just started to turn and return his hug when a second man, along with a woman and two boys, turned the corner beside Jim, and he too stopped in surprise. Both men stared at Betty as the hands behind her fell away from her midriff.

The second man standing beside her husband at the end of the aisle was Coal.

And suddenly, the sour smell of stale beer and cigarettes assaulted Betty's nostrils. She turned to see him standing there smugly, in all his scrawny ugliness:

Bernard Hargis.

CHAPTER ELEVEN

As Betty's shocked eyes settled on rail-thin Bern Hargis, Jim dropped his game hen on the tile floor and charged. Hargis had started to laugh, but the look in Jim's face must have seemed deadly, for at the last second Hargis raised his hands to ward him off. Coal was still too stunned even to move.

Jim Lockwood's left hand flashed out and closed in a death grip over Hargis's throat. He power-drove two punches into his left eye, then came in with a knee into his groin.

Forgetting all about the boys and Annie, Coal ran in and grabbed Jim's trapezius muscle, trying to spin him around as he barked out his name. If his voice registered on Jim, he didn't show it. With his face burning red, he flung Hargis like a plastic doll against the shelves of canned goods, sending cans rocketing left and right like bowling pins. Just as he reached out with claw-shaped hands, trying to catch Hargis by both shoulders, Coal came in again, grabbing Jim around the middle and jerking him back.

"Jim! It's me, Coal! Cool it, Jim!"

Jim snarled like a rabid dog, throwing himself around and trying to break free from his friend's grasp as Hargis recovered from his pounding and his right hand dove down into his front pants pocket. He came out with a long pocket knife, whose blade he fumbled out of its channel just as his wife, Sherlene, was coming around the front end of the aisle to the sound of the ruckus. She must have known her husband well enough to know he would be at the heart of whatever was going on.

"Bern, stop!" Sherlene screamed. She had yet to see the knife.

In his wild ferocity, Jim managed to tear one arm out of Coal's grasp, and he grabbed a twelve-ounce can of tomatoes off the shelf and flung it like a pro baseball player at Hargis. The can caught him on the hand, making his arm snap backward. Hargis growled out a mouthful of curse words but managed to hold onto the knife.

Sherlene marched to him and laid a hand on his shoulder. "Bern, come on! Let's get out of here."

"Shut up!" Hargis growled, his face turning as red as Jim's. He whirled halfway around, the back of his hand catching Sherlene across the cheek and throwing her backward. She managed not to fall, but her hand came up to her face, and she stared at her husband in shock and pain.

As Jim reached for another tomato can, Coal grabbed the collar of his coat and flung him around, taking two steps forward so that he stood between Jim and his would-be victim.

Hargis slurred out a couple more curses at Jim and started forward with the knife held low. He seemed so intent on the ex-sheriff that Coal's presence didn't even register on his obviously beer-greased mind.

Tilting sideways, Coal delivered a devastating side kick to Hargis's pelvis under the palmed knife. It threw him backward like a sack full of rags. There were so many cans of food on the floor that Hargis's stumbling feet couldn't help but dance on a few, fairly ungracefully, and down he went on his back, landing hard on two or three of the cans. The knife flung out of his grasp and went scooting down the aisle, right between Sherlene's feet. In the back of Coal's mind he saw Sherlene Hargis retrieving the knife, and even as he watched for Hargis to get up he saw the woman snap the blade shut and pocket the knife. Coal had been trained intensively in making sure he knew the disposition of every possible weapon within an opponent's reach.

He had also been schooled in mortal combat, and in Coal's military training there was no notion of "fair play" or of allowing an enemy, once down, to regain his feet. All too often a man going to the ground was a gift granted only once.

Bern Hargis started to rise, and Coal lurched in and kicked him in the chest, then went forward and dropped a knee in the middle of that scrawny belly, driving all the air from his lungs.

By now, another man had come into the aisle, and he yelled out, "Sheriff! What do you want me to do?"

Coal looked up just in time to see Jim bearing down on him and Hargis. He wasn't sure by the look on his friend's face if it was even registering on him that Coal had the foe helpless on the ground. "Grab Jim!" Coal yelled at the man who had offered his hand.

The man jumped in and got hold of Jim just as he released a ferocious kick to Hargis's groin. "Hey, cut it out!" yelled the newcomer, holding the ex-lawman by the arms and jerking him backward. "He's down, man! He's down! Let it go!"

"Get off me!" Jim growled. "Let me loose."

"Calm down! Get a hold of yourself," the man ordered, obviously strong enough that Jim had no success getting away from him.

"Honey, stop!" Betty's voice cut in as she came close, getting in front of Jim so he could see her. She put both her hands on his chest, not pushing, but applying a steady pressure. "Sweetie, it's all done. Listen to me. You've got to stop now."

Jim turned to stare at her. He blinked a couple of times as if trying to figure out who she was. At last, his attempts seemed to bring recognition to his warrior's countenance, and his mouth twitched. His whole body sagged in resignation, and he sucked in a deep breath, turning deadly eyes back to Hargis as Coal was dragging the now very docile and disarranged milk farmer to his feet with the use of a none-too-gentle arm bar. Jim stood loose, for the man who had held him had backed off a couple of feet.

"I'll kill you the next time I see you, Hargis. You've pawed at my wife for the last time."

"Jim!" Coal barked. "Knock it off."

"Come on, honey." Betty stepped in close, taking his hand. "Hey. Hey. It's over now." She reached up and wiped at his brow. "It's all over. There was no harm done."

"I'll kill him, Betty," Jim averred, his jaw tight.

"That's enough, Jim," Coal ordered, his face hard. "You had your say. You won. I know how you feel, but you've got to back off."

Jim took another deep breath and raised a hand, waving it resignedly and dismissingly at Coal and turning to take Betty by the elbow. "Come on. Let's get out of here."

"What about our groceries?"

Jim looked around at the chaos throughout the aisle. "We'll come back tomorrow when the air in here is clearer. Or maybe we'll go to Saveway instead."

Betty turned embarrassed, apologetic eyes to Coal, then walked with Jim past Coal, Hargis, and Sherlene. Sherlene could only stare at the floor.

Betty pulled away from her husband as they walked, making him stop and turn to look at her. She put a hand on Sherlene Hargis's arm, which made the other woman shudder. "Are you all right, honey?"

Sherlene, still looking down, just nodded—too quickly. "Yes, fine. I'm fine."

Betty looked at the big red mark on the other woman's cheek, gave Jim a glance of concern, then another to Coal, and then she went docilely with Jim up the aisle, headed for the front door.

Coal, Sherlene, Coal's unexpected assistant, and a dozen onlookers were left in the cluttered war zone of an aisle with Bern Hargis. Coal put unnecessary force to Hargis's wrist, raising him up on his tiptoes and shoving his face against the now cluttered shelf. "That was battery, Hargis. Plain and simple. And I have to tell you you touched the wrong woman this time. I'm not going to arrest you right now because I don't have time for it. I've got things to do, and I'm off duty. But that doesn't mean this is over. I'll go over and talk to Betty and Jim Lockwood tomorrow, and if they want to press battery charges on you I'm going to let them. Is that clear enough?"

"You're breakin' my arm, man. Let me go!"

"I asked you if that's clear enough!" Coal bore down even more on Hargis's wrist.

"It's clear! It's clear!"

Coal immediately backed off, giving the other man a spiteful shove in the back that knocked him harder into the shelf and made two more cans topple to the floor.

When Hargis turned, trying to glare up at Coal through blood-shot eyes, Coal stood quartered to him, waiting—almost hoping for some move of aggression. At last, when it was obvious Hargis wasn't going to make any such move, he said, "I'd make a point of steering clear of Jim Lockwood for a few weeks."

He turned at last to thank the man who had stepped in at just the right time and was startled when he recognized him. It was the stranded traveler and ex-detective he had met at the hospital, Ray Christian.

"I'll be," said Coal. "Hi, Ray. You sure came along at the right time. Thanks for the help."

Christian grinned and reached out to shake Coal's outstretched hand. "I'm glad I did. I just thought I'd come in and buy a six pack and some pretzels. Thank heavens for my unquenchable appetite."

"No kidding," replied Coal. He stepped over by Sherlene Hargis. He already guessed her answer to the question he was about to ask. "Mrs. Hargis, do you want to press charges for battery?"

"No!" Sherlene shook her head almost violently, her eyes whipping toward Hargis, then falling away just shy of him. "No." The word was much quieter the second time.

"All right. I'll need that knife, though." He held out his hand.

The woman stared at him for a long moment, then blinked. She started to look over at Hargis, but at the last moment her glance fell away. Without a word, she reached into her pocket and withdrew the knife, placing it in Coal's open palm.

He turned and stared at Hargis. "I'll keep this until we find out the disposition of this case. If Jim wants to file charges for aggravated assault, I'll need to hang onto the knife for evidence, and you can expect me to come looking for you—soon. And the fact is, after what I saw I might just keep the knife anyway. I have enough to charge you whether they want to or not."

"What about him? He tried to choke me to death! And kicked me. And hit me with a can!"

"After battering his wife, you had a lot more coming to you than that, buddy. You'd better let it lie."

"Battering! I never hit his wife!"

"I'm not talking about hitting. In the state of Idaho, touching someone when they don't want you to is considered battery. And I guarantee you Betty Lockwood didn't want a hug from you."

"Ha! Well, no surprise," spat Hargis. "I never doubted you'd side with him over me."

"If it wouldn't have gotten him in a lot worse trouble, Hargis, I would have just walked out and let Jim have his way with you."

With that, he turned away in the direction he had come from. He teetered to a stop.

There, among the crowd that had gathered during the excitement, he saw Annie Price, her hands clutching the shoulders of his boys. They still stood at the end of the aisle, staring at Bern Hargis with morbid fascination. Of course, like all the other shoppers, the boys and Annie would have registered on Coal's unconscious brain as a non-threat even if he had noticed them during the altercation, so he had put them completely out of his consciousness. Forgotten in the heat of battle.

From out of the television screen into vivid life, this fight scene had erupted before the very eyes of Coal's innocent five-year-old boys. Coal would never have wished this scene upon them, or on Annie.

CHAPTER TWELVE

If a fly had burped in the LTD for the first several miles of the trip home, Coal would have heard it. The silence was excruciating. His boys sat huddled close together, staring straight out the windshield, but they were not sitting still. They were full of nervous energy, twisting their fingers back and forth, moving their little feet, and now and then filling their lungs to capacity before sighing the breath back out with every attempt to do it quietly. They seemed to feel like breathing out loud would break some kind of spell and perhaps re-create the recent explosion of violence in this very car.

While Coal drove and tried to put himself in those innocent little heads, he too was quiet. What words should he say to the boys, if any? Should he apologize? Should he assure them that the kind of violence they had just seen from their father would never be a threat to them? What was going through their minds?

Finally, the silence was too much for him. He glanced down at his two little shadows and braced himself.

"Are you boys all right?"

For a few seconds, the silence ran on. Wyatt looked up at Coal, his eyes big and full of questions. Suddenly, tears started running down his brother's cheeks, and Wyatt's reaction to it made the emotion well up inside Coal as well. Five-year-old Wyatt, wise and compassionate in his innocence, quickly put an arm around Morgan's shoulders and a hand around his upper arm and offered a reassuring squeeze. "It's okay," he told his brother in a quiet voice.

Coal clicked on his hazard lights and pulled over to the roadside near an iced-over pond on the north side of the road, where Angus cattle stood in the dappled sunlight beyond and stared at the sudden intruders.

Putting the car in park and leaving it running, Coal said, "Hey, guys. Come here."

With abandon, the boys flew up onto their father. Morgan was crying out loud now, and Wyatt had his strong little arm around him and around Coal's neck.

"It's all right now, boys. Everything's going to be fine. I'm sorry you had to see what happened at the store."

Morgan kept crying, and both boys squeezed tighter.

This was one of those moments for Coal, one of those moments that cried out for the three words he had always felt uncomfortable saying out loud. He took a deep breath, reaching deep inside himself. "I love you guys. You know that, right?"

Both boys nodded. Neither spoke.

He held onto them as a car or two flew past on the highway. He rummaged far back, into his ancient childhood memories and emotions. He was no psychologist by any stretch, but today he had to try to be—or at least an understanding father. And the only way was by picking his own five-year-old brain, if he could.

He remembered a time when some half-drunk man had fired his rifle at a deer that was trotting some seven or eight hundred yards away. His father had chosen that beautiful fall day to take his son out on his very first excursion into the world of deer hunting. Having his young son see that kind of misbehavior did not set well with big Prince Savage, and in his ire he nearly attacked the foolish so-called hunter. Coal had witnessed the tension in both of them, and although that instance had not ended in physical violence like the scene the boys had witnessed, it left its indelible mark on him as a little boy. It was the closest comparison Coal could find. What he remembered from the incident was the cold feeling in his guts—his first memory of true fear.

"Did that scare you boys pretty bad?"

Morgan nodded, his weeping beginning to turn now to sniffles. Wyatt said, "It scared *me*."

Coal had managed to hit the nail on the head. "I sure didn't want to scare you. I wish you didn't have to be there to see it."

"Is that man bad?" Wyatt asked, leaning back now to see into his father's eyes.

"At church they don't want us to say any man is really bad, but he sure was acting bad, wasn't he? I don't guess that man acts good very often."

"Was he going to cut that other man?"

It jolted Coal to realize his boys didn't know Jim Lockwood enough to call him by name, when to Coal the man was like a second father. That revelation made him feel almost worse than the entire rest of the incident.

"Yeah, he sure was. So I had to stop him. Understand?"

"Uh-huh." That time it was little Morgan's voice. It brought a surge of happiness to Coal's heart to hear it now.

"Say, don't you boys know who that other man was?"

Morgan had pulled away from Coal and was wiping his cheeks with the sleeve of his coat. They both looked at him and shook their heads.

"Well, I feel bad then," Coal went on. "That man is named Jim, and the woman who was with him is Betty. They are almost like a mom and dad to me. So they're kind of like a grandma and grandpa to you guys."

"But we already have a grandma," said Morgan, his eyes round and wondering.

"Sure you do," Coal replied. "But don't you remember your Grandma Sadie? She was your mom's mother."

"Oh yeah!" exclaimed Wyatt.

"So you have two grandmas, and you used to have two grandpas too—Grandpa Prince and Grandpa Ed. See?"

"Oh yeah. Did you hurt that bad man, Daddy?" asked Wyatt, ricocheting away from the mind-boggling double grandparent concept—although Coal had no doubt at all that his inquisitive little mind would return to visit it before the day was through.

"I guess I did kind of hurt him, Son. I had to so he wouldn't stab Jim with his knife. And maybe some of those other people."

"You said we can't hit anyone first. Right, Daddy?" asked Wyatt.

"Yes, I did tell you that."

"Then how come that old man hit the other man first?"

Coal chuckled. "Well, that old man—Jim—he was pretty mad. He shouldn't have done that. I'm not saying it was okay. But you know how I told you if someone is hurting your family you might have to stop them? Sometimes that might mean you have to hit them first."

The boys stared. The seeming double standard was going to take a while to break through their well-formed mental crust of not being the first to throw a punch. Finally, Wyatt said, "But he wasn't hurting anybody. He was hugging the grandma, right?"

This time Coal had to laugh out loud. He ruffled the boy's hair. "Well, Wyatt, that 'grandma,' Betty, she's Jim's wife, okay? That means he's supposed to take care of her."

"So other people can't hug her?"

Coal thought for a moment, scrunching up his face. "Well, some people can hug her—people she likes, like me, or Grand-ma—or you boys. But somebody just can't come up behind her and hug her without her thinking it's okay. If they do, then it's kind of Jim's job to make sure they let go."

"But he already let go before Jim hit him."

Coal nodded. "You're right, Wyatt. He did. Jim shouldn't have done what he did. But he was really mad."

A quizzical look came to the faces of both boys. "So it's okay to hit someone if you're mad?" Morgan finally asked.

Coal sighed. This was going to take some serious ironing out. "Boys, we'd better get back home with these candles. But let's talk about this some more later, okay? Just let me say that it's not really okay to hit someone if you're mad, but sometimes it's hard to think when you're mad."

"And when it's hard to think, you do bad things," Wyatt averred with a nod.

"When it's hard to think, you do bad things," Coal agreed. And he thought back to his first sight of Erin, standing in the Arlington Cemetery, so sad and alone—right when he and Laura were fighting so bad, and when it was so hard for Coal to think.

Once the first tension was out of the way, and the fears had been allayed, Coal found that the boys could not stop talking about the fight. Their way of dealing with what had been so scary was now to make a big story of it, keep reliving it, and above all else—talk all over what each other had to say. It seemed that once the fear was put to rest, their father had become some kind of hero, not unlike special agent James West, on *The Wild Wild West,* or Captain Kirk, on *Star Trek.*

Coal was relieved to pull into the driveway back home. The boys bailed out of the car and raced for the house, and this was one part of childhood no one needed to explain. Not unlike most adults, the boys were on a dead run to see who could get inside first and spread the news about the no-holds-barred battle at B and B Foods.

Coal took a deep breath, preparing himself for all the questions he was sure to be hit with on entering the house.

But as it turned out, there was hardly time to really talk it all out. The boys had no more than finished their side of the story, and Coal had started into his brief rendition of the real account, when the dogs started barking out their warning that someone else had pulled up outside.

Coal looked out the window to see Annie Price getting out of her Buick. He stared at her and wished he had had the common sense to warn the others of her promise to visit as he reached out with his senses and tried to feel if there were any bad vibes in the room around him—from either Maura or his mother.

Beyond the terrible barking of Dobe and Shadow, Coal couldn't have felt the vibes of Satan himself.

Feeling sheepish, he turned and deliberately looked right past Maura, who was frozen in place watching Annie approach the front door. "I forgot to tell you Annie said she was going to come over and bring Sissy something," he told Connie.

She frowned at him, but only a son who had been observing the nuances of a mother's facial expressions for forty-some years would have caught it.

"Oh, how nice." Connie smiled. In somewhat the same way wolves smile when they spy a prey animal.

Coal smiled back—in somewhat the way a dog that is caught next to a freshly chewed-up couch might smile, hoping the coming tirade and thrashing would be less than expected—and a little less than deserved.

Katie went dutifully and answered the door because Coal was imitating a clothed statue of David.

Annie stepped in with a beautifully wrapped package and met the next great ice age.

CHAPTER THIRTEEN

Coal greeted Annie with more reserve than he wanted to, because everyone was watching him. He wanted to give her a big kiss, just to spite them, but of course he refrained. Her entrance onto the scene was already changing the mood of Sissy's party, and that innocent little girl had done nothing to deserve that.

Maura stepped forward and shook Annie's hand, almost the most awkward move Coal could conceive, and then Connie stepped up to the plate.

"Hi, Annie. It's so nice of you to come. We were just going to start our celebration."

"Great!" Annie said, smiling as she looked around at the others. It was fairly warm outside for the end of December, now over forty degrees, but Coal judged as he watched her changing expression that she was sensing more cold on the indoors. She looked questioningly at Coal, but he just forced a smile.

"Come on, everybody. Let's go in the kitchen," he said.

"Where's Virgil?" asked Morgan.

Coal glanced around. Not seeing his oldest boy, he looked to Connie, who shrugged.

"I assume he's still in his room."

Coal frowned. "That must be some story he got caught up in."

"Didn't I suggest you check on him earlier?" Connie asked.

"Yes."

She cocked her head at him, narrowing her eyes. "Okay, and . . ."

"And . . . I told you I wasn't going to."

"Can you go get your son, Coal?" Connie said, giving him a level, no-nonsense look.

"I guess I will—now that you put it that way."

Coal turned, pushing the irritation down inside himself. How was it that a man could fight in the Marines, help quell one of the largest prison riots in history as an army M.P., arrest some of the biggest criminals in Washington, D. C., and solve the worst spree of killings in the history of Lemhi County, and yet his mother could still make him feel like a snot-nosed brat?

Everyone avoided looking at Coal as he walked away and climbed the stairs to Virgil's room. He tapped lightly, and nobody answered. Easing open the door, he stepped in to see Virgil on the bed with a Jim Kjelgaard novel open on his chest—*Snow Dog,* to be exact. He remembered Laura reading the same book to Virgil when he was very small, and he knew for a fact that his son had read it at least three or four times since—explaining the terribly faded cover and frazzled yellow pages.

Quietly, Coal stepped to his boy. He looked peaceful in his sleep, with his hair messed up and lying on his forehead. He wanted to cover him and just leave him there, enjoying his solitude, but Connie would not have stood for it. Besides, Virgil wouldn't be able to sleep tonight if he stayed sleeping now.

Sitting down on the edge of the bed, Coal picked up the book and reached over onto Virgil's nightstand for something to save his place. There on the night stand sat a pencil drawing of a beautiful golden retriever. It was the spitting image of Burro, and done in Virgil's obvious and very talented style. Next to it was an open notebook in which Virgil had been writing, a pen lying crosswise on its pages. It looked like quite an extensive amount of writing, and Coal peered at it closer, wondering casually if his son was taking up fiction writing himself.

Before he realized it was Virgil's private diary, the last lines registered on him: *Today Dad gave my dog away to some of his friends and didn't even tell me. I guess Katie was right. He doesn't even care about us.*

A sick feeling hit Coal in the guts, worse than the time he had gotten food poisoning early on in the Korean War from a bowl of *gejang*, in which spoiled crab meat had been used. He hurriedly shut the book, looking over at his son, who in his sleeping state seemed so free of care. Ironically, this sleeping boy had just given him far more information about himself than his waking incarnation would have in a month of coaxing.

Coal took the pen and put it into the Kjelgaard book before shutting it, then shook his boy's shoulder gently. Virgil's startled eyes came open, and he stared up at Coal for a few seconds, blinking to clear his vision.

"Hi, Son. We're going to have some cake and ice cream."

Virgil turned dull eyes away. "Okay."

"Do you want to come down? Grandma's going to insist."

"Sure, I guess." The boy's face remained emotionless. For just a second, Coal thought about telling him he had seen his journal. But would Virgil think he had been snooping? Was there any good way to tell someone you had read their most private thoughts, even if you hadn't meant to? In the end, he stood up to let Virgil get off the bed, and he made a quarter turn as Virgil walked zombie-like past him and went out of the room, moving quietly, like a streamer of smoke.

So he had done it again. As a father, he was failing. He thought back on the words in the journal: *Today Dad gave my dog away* . . . His dog? How had he gotten the idea that the dog was his?

Then he remembered once more the loving way Virgil had crouched beside the bathtub with Maura, giving Burro his big bath, and laughing at the bubbles on the dog's head. He remembered how proud he had seemed drying him off and brushing him, making his golden coat shine. The Savage family had a German shepherd and a Doberman pinscher. Coal never dreamed they would want anything more. Apparently, as usual, he had been wrong. More likely, his big boy just wanted a dog to call his own.

And now Burro was in the loving arms of a woman and three girls who had just been devastated by the loss of their husband and father, and then the death of Rowdy. There was no way he could go ask for that dog back. There was no fix for this Coal-ism.

*   *   *

The cake was delicious. He could think of no time when Connie's cakes weren't absolute prize winners, except for the one glaring incident when a burlap sack full of rattlesnakes the fifteen-year-old Coal had caught granted themselves freedom through a seemingly very small tear in the sack and escaped off the kitchen table into all the dark recesses of the house. And on that historic occasion, she had had fourteen perfectly valid, slithering excuses for the lapse of memory that ended with the charred remnants of that particular birthday cake, which had been meant for his brother Dan on his sweet sixteenth.

Coal still remembered the choking pall of dark gray smoke that had nearly ended the lives of his limb-less captives and put an end to his first—and last—attempt at going into business providing fresh venom to the hospital from which to make antivenin. The same event had also ended with his inability to sit on a hard surface without pain for the following week, once Prince Savage returned home from a horse ride to the smoke billowing out of every open orifice of his house. But as bad as the pain was, the smoke smell in the house had lasted much longer, and sometimes Coal fancied he could smell it to this day.

Connie came over beside Coal while Sissy was opening all of her presents and leaned up beside him. She didn't say a word, but Coal sensed that she was thinking about the same things he was, about how this little girl had suffered so much life-changing drama, all in so short a time. Would she be able to function from now on like a normal person?

Sissy seemed almost frightened, for a while, about all the attention that was centered on her. But once she had opened her first gift, a little blond Teddy bear not too different from Cynthia's "Buddy", she seemed almost to become lost in the celebration. She would look up, now and then, usually straight at Maura or at Connie, and both of them would give her the warmest of smiles. She didn't seem to understand the use of the words *thank you,* and that was all right. She said it in spades with her actions and her eyes, and the smile that sometimes flashed across her face, seemingly without her even knowing it. Surrounded by the love of her new family, little Sissy was going to be just fine.

She especially seemed to enjoy the huge white rabbit Annie had chosen for her, so at least in that, Annie's being here was a success.

Coal sat back and listened to Connie, Maura, and Annie chatting. Without seeming too obvious, he kept an eye on the three of them, and sometimes on Katie, trying to discern whether or not after the evening's festivities ended he was going to have to make a run for shelter. Not that men are famous for their powers of discernment, but from all signs it seemed the evening had come off without a hitch. In his own defense, Annie had sort of invited herself over anyway. But it was good to see the tension had melted away and to listen to the music of their voices.

The only moment when the room seemed to grow cold again was when Annie brought up the fight, and both Connie and Maura glanced over at Coal involuntarily. Apparently, he had forgotten to mention the fact that Annie was with him during the fight. It didn't take a genius to guess what conclusions his mother and Maura must be drawing from that teensy revelation.

After a while, he excused himself and took the dogs outside to offer them their daily sacrifice of dogfood. A ceiling of cloud had come glowering in to seal off all the stars in the sky, and it had cooled off fast. A light sifting of freezing rain had begun to fall. Coal walked out with his lined Wrangler jacket his only protection from the cold and threw hay to the horses, made sure they still had a full water trough, and then stood for a while inside the barn, listening to the water that dribbled off the roof of the loft onto the main roof, both of which were covered in sheets of rusted tin.

Christmas Day was just five days away, and he prayed for peace that day—or at least he would have prayed, but he was starting to wonder if there really was any use in it. He pondered the chances of finding a pup for Virgil before then and instantly decided against it. No human being alive was going to crowd Coal Savage into buying a dog he had no time to approve of and which might not make Virgil happy anyway. That was a gift no smart man gave lightly, no matter the wounds one was trying to heal.

He took a deep breath of the fragrances of the old barn. Here was a kind of heaven—one of many a person could find in Lemhi County. Molasses feed, fresh hay, and even the aged remnants of bales that had fallen apart. The wood gave up its own odor, especially now that the old pine boards were wet with the soaking rain, and leather and horse sweat completed the sense of a horseman's heaven on earth.

As Coal stood out in the barn, a soft, beautiful light suddenly flooded the yard, and he looked over in surprise. It took him a moment to realize where the light was coming from. Connie had somehow managed without his help, during all of his escapades in and about town, to line the eaves of both the house and the garage with the huge, colorful light bulbs she loved so much, and she had just now plugged them in. The multitude of warm, softly glowing colors spilled their glow over the yard, and the feeling of Christmas was complete.

Unfortunately, that feeling was not to last.

* * *

When the little party ended, Coal and the others said good night to both Maura and Annie, and they left together, walking out side by side to their vehicles under the onslaught of slush now plopping down.

Coal waited at the big front window, watching to make sure Annie and Maura got into their vehicles and safely on their way. But to his surprise, they did not immediately go. Instead, they stood out in the slush talking, seeming oblivious as their hair got more and more wet and even began to stick to their foreheads.

Just when the curiosity in Coal from watching them and trying to make something of their impromptu conclave became almost unbearable, something strange happened, alarming him more than anything that had been said or done throughout the rest of the night: Maura thrust out a hand, which Annie took, and they shook briskly, then broke apart to go to their separate vehicles.

Neither of them seemed to sense that he had been watching them, and neither would guess that he stood there silent and thoughtful for a half hour after the Christmasy cherry glow of their taillights had faded into the night.

Finally, Coal put on his coat and stepped back outside, taking the dogs. While they ran out toward the road, sniffing everything they had smelled hundreds of times but seemed still to find every bit as interesting as before, he stood under the overhang of the garage roof and listened to the gentle drip of slush out of the sky.

He had just called the dogs back and turned to go in when he heard the gears of a vehicle grinding out in the dark, and he paused out of curiosity, seeing the rig coming up the road from the highway with just its left headlight glowing. It finally reached their property, and only thanks to the sparkle of Connie's Christmas lights could he make out any details of it in the dark. It sped on past, a beat-up, beat-down early fifties Ford pickup that appeared to be dark blue or green but with a mismatched driver's door, either white or yellow in color, or possibly just painted with light gray primer. It was rattling so badly as it went by he half-expected it to fall to pieces right there in the road.

Wednesday, December 20

At ten-thirty the next morning, Coal sat at his desk in the sheriff's office. He had come in early to use a brand-new coffee grinder to grind some beans he had purchased, and as he leafed through paperwork, he sipped at a cup of java as perfect as any he had ever tasted, black as his name and full of body.

The phone rang, and he picked it up, irritated at the gall of it, ringing in such a moment of peace and tranquility.

On the other end of the line he heard the voice of Wilma Frank, Judge Sinclair's secretary. *Good morning, Sheriff Savage. Judge Sinclair would like you to come up and see him as soon as possible.*

"What's it about?"

I'm not privy to that. She lowered her voice. *But just to warn you, he sounds very angry about something.*

Coal thought about asking her to just put the judge on the phone. But maybe by going up there and talking to him in person he could build something of a bridge between them, which so far he had had no luck with.

"All right, Wilma, thanks. I'll be right up."

Coal looked out at the parking lot before opening the door. It was promising to be even warmer than it had been the day before, and a blanket of dark gray clouds hung low to make sure any heat stayed down near the earth. A tiny bit of drizzle was still detectable in the air, but hardly enough to call it that. New, wet snow that had fallen in the night was now mostly gone, even in the shadows, but the gorgeous mountains ringing the valley were laced in white. It would be small comfort for snow lovers, for down here in the valley Coal was starting to wonder if this year's Christmas was going to have any white at all.

As he went up the concrete steps to the parking lot, he was surprised by a man standing nearby looking at the upper floor of the courthouse, holding a tan overcoat draped over one arm.

"All right," Coal said. "Now I know you're following me."

It was the helpful Reno, Nevada, detective—or *former* detective, Ray Christian. He wore an ugly polyester suit coat over a white dress shirt, a maroon sweater and black polyester pants, flared slightly at the leg, with black oxfords on his feet. He gave Coal a huge grin. "Hey! Yeah, you caught me. No denying that."

Coal walked to him and gave him a hearty handshake. Even in the cold, Christian's hand seemed extra warm. "Can I help you with something?"

"Yeah. Well, maybe."

"Name it. I sure do owe you."

"Owe me? What for?"

"For stepping in yesterday."

Christian grinned. "Jeez, Sheriff, you don't owe me a thing!"

"Okay, first off, it's Coal, not Sheriff. And second, we both know I owe you for saving my bacon in that fight, so cut that crap right now."

Christian gave a grin and one big, hearty nod. "All right. Fair enough. Well, as you know, I'm kind of stuck in that hotel until my Caddy's fixed, and it's going to get real old real fast watching soap operas all day. So I wandered over here hoping maybe you wouldn't mind if I just sort of hung out with you for a while. I promise not to be a bother."

"You serious?"

"Well, sure. You're the only person I've connected with in this town, plus I feel pretty safe hanging out with the big shots."

Coal laughed. "Well, I'm not sure how much of a big shot I am, but you're welcome. I don't know if you'd like to wait downstairs or come up with me, but I have to go meet with the judge for a few minutes."

"Ha! I've had enough of judges. I'll wait for you down there—if it's all right."

"You bet. Make yourself at home. Finish up the coffee if you want. It's freshly ground. I shouldn't drink any more anyway."

While Ray Christian went down into the office, Coal entered the courthouse and took the steps two at a time, topping out and smiling at Wilma.

She made a cautious face at him, and jabbed the point of a yellow number two pencil toward the judge's quarters. "Good luck."

Coal rolled his eyes as he went back and knocked on the door.

"Enter."

He walked in and took off his hat, holding it in one hand by the crown. "What would you like to see me about?"

The judge frowned at him. Maybe he was expecting some title to accompany Coal's question. But Coal was happily out of the military now. Nobody but the very deserving was going to get a title out of him.

"I have sworn out a warrant for the arrest of Bernard D. Hargis."

The name took Coal aback. For a moment, he just stared. "Who's that again?"

"Bern Hargis?"

Coal's mind caught up. "That was fast."

"Pardon?"

"Never mind. This is for the altercation at B and B last night?"

Now it was Judge Sinclair's turn to look puzzled. "Apparently I've not heard about that."

Coal was irritated on the instant. "What's this about then?"

"Mr. Hargis was to be in my courtroom at Oh-nine hundred hours. He did not show up, and he didn't call. He is to be brought in and placed in a cell until he can be arraigned."

"He's probably hung over in bed," said Coal. "He was pretty drunk around four o'clock yesterday."

"Fine. I suppose that is a reason, but it's no excuse."

"What's the warrant for?"

"I said—failure to appear."

Coal steeled himself and bit his tongue. "Sorry. I mean what was the original charge?"

"Disturbing the peace, of course. Oh, I forget—you are new to the position of sheriff here. Let me enlighten you on Mr. Hargis, in that case. He has been in this court no less than eight times in the last three years, almost always for the same type of behavior: disturbing the peace, public drunkenness, and things of that nature. One time for malicious injury to property, and another for battery on a police officer. So you might want to take some assistance with you."

"How did the battery go?"

"It wasn't much, granted. He was drunk, and he spit on the shirt of our last police chief. Then poked him in the chest."

"I guess that's enough," said Coal with an unintended grin. "All right, I'll go get him. It will be my pleasure."

"Say." The judge's voice stopped Coal turning around, and he turned to face him again. "It's almost Christmas. That means Mr. Hargis will have to spend the holidays in jail, because this is my last day before the holidays. Imagine the odds of that."

Coal cocked his head at the judge, trying to read behind the mask on his face. Finally, he realized there was a little smile on his lips—barely discernable. "Yeah," he agreed. "Imagine the odds."

The judge held up a hand, a signal for Coal to wait further, and he leaned down and opened a desk drawer. From inside it, he pulled a wooden box, which he placed on his desk. With one finger, he tipped the lid open, revealing a row of expensive cigars, and from the row he drew one out, then a second, after a brief moment of thought went across his face.

"Here, Sheriff." He held the two cigars out to Coal. "Merry Christmas."

CHAPTER FOURTEEN

As Coal hit the bottom of the steps, he looked through the glass in the door and saw Christian rummaging through papers on his desk. He shoved the door open, and a startled Christian dropped whatever he was holding and looked up.

"Crap! You scared me. Sorry, Coal—you caught me red-handed leafing through some of your files. Old habits."

Coal laughed. "I imagine they're hard to let go. So you really want to hang out and see what law enforcement officers do out here in the sticks?"

With a shrug, Christian replied, "Don't tell me you've got something already. I was afraid I might have to watch you read paperwork all day or capture stray cows."

"You'd be amazed," replied Coal. As they trooped outside, he began to tell his new shadow about all the recent adventures with which Lemhi County had welcomed their new sheriff home. Christian admitted reading about it even in the *Las Vegas Sun.*

"The *Sun?* I thought you said you were from Reno."

Christian hesitated, then laughed lightly. "Sure, but that doesn't mean I can't see a Vegas rag now and then."

The roads were going to be a little muddier than Coal wanted to chance with the LTD, considering the warmer weather and the drizzle coming down, so they took the GMC out to Hargis's place. He didn't bother calling anyone for backup. He had handled a thousand men three times as tough as Bern Hargis and a lot more unpredictable, and he had already seen enough of his new-found friend, Ray Christian, to know he would be handy in another mix-up with Bern Hargis, if it came to that.

As soft rain dampened the windshield and conversation died off for a minute, they listened to Bing Crosby singing about his "White Christmas", and Coal found himself pondering on Judge Sinclair's surprise gift back at the courthouse. He wasn't going to make use of the cigars, because even when he *was* smoking he had never liked the smell or taste of a cigar. But the thought that a man who came across as surly as the judge would want to give him a gift of any kind was, to say the least, startling. He still had a hard time finding anything to like about Sinclair, but he was brought up short in thinking that he already knew everything he needed to know about him.

He turned on a whim to Christian. "Say, you don't happen to smoke cigars, do you?"

"Sure do!" His hand darted toward a coat pocket. "Want one?"

"No, no!" said Coal with a laugh. "Thanks. No, the judge just gave me these, and I don't smoke them." As he finished, he produced the two cigars and held them out to his friend.

"Wow! Those look high quality. He must like you."

Coal made a half-contemplative frown. "Well, you sure would never have known it. Quality, huh?"

"Oh yeah. No doubt these cost him a bundle! Thanks," he said, stowing his new treasures in the inside pocket of the ugly brown suitcoat with whatever others he was keeping there.

Where Hargis's dirt road turned right off Barracks Lane, after crossing the little bridge over the Lemhi, Coal stopped. He had told Christian some of the story about his confrontation with Harringer over the dead cottonwoods, and now he pointed out Harringer's opulent house, farther along the road.

The difference in the two roads was marked. Harringer's was covered inches-deep in compacted road base; Hargis's had a few one-inch cobblestones here and there, along with some angular gravel, but most of it was dirt—which today meant mud. Again, he took note of the newer road—he thought of the term loosely—that took off of Hargis's lane and went straight along this side of the cottonwoods and barbwire fence, headed toward the base of the mountains. Idly, he noticed there seemed to be newer tracks there than those he had seen before.

Continuing along the lane, Coal pulled into the cluttered yard and got out, not happy about being back here again so soon. But at least this time he was here with a warrant for Hargis's arrest, so he guessed it was all worthwhile. The downside was now he had to have the little low-life in his jail, and he also had to feed him. This would be the prime example of bittersweet.

In the yard near the green Rambler, there was a mid-forties Chevrolet Stylemaster coupe that had not been there the day before. It had once been a high-class, stylish big boat of a car, but now, like the buildings and property, it was in the throes of death, as far as Coal could see, with a huge dent in the left rear quarter-panel and a rusted-out spot two feet long on the bottom of the driver's door. Its only windshield wiper was on the driver's side, and the tires were as bald as beach balls.

Coal looked around, smelling the sweet scent of wood smoke and noticing a broken curl of it huffing out of the chimney. Rain dripped in a steady rhythm off the rusty tin roof onto another piece of roofing that had apparently been placed at the left front corner of the house to shuttle moisture away. Judging from the rough channel still visible, the water was used to running along and probably making a swimming hole around the concrete pad at the front of the house.

In the near-distance, a cow bawled.

Sickly orange light soon flickered in the house, and Coal saw movement. At the same time he saw someone moving around out in the barn. While he was trying to decide which way to turn, with his right hand on the butt of the .357 and Christian stationed behind his right shoulder, the front door creaked open. Sherlene Hargis stood back a ways in the shadows provided by the top of the doorframe. The light behind her continued to flutter, made obviously by a live flame, not an incandescent bulb.

"Good morning, Mrs. Hargis."

"Mornin', Sheriff. How are you?"

"I'm good, ma'am. How about you?"

"I'm fine. Just fine." Deep, dirty shadow continued to envelope her.

"This is a friend of mine, Ray Christian."

The woman looked past Coal's shoulder and gave Christian a long, squinting look, then finally nodded.

"Is your watchdog around?" Coal asked, referring to the young blue heeler, since the older dog could be considered almost anything but a watchdog.

The woman paused, and her eyes skipped around. "No sir. I haven't seen him for a while."

With a feeling of semi-relief, Coal said, "Good. So I don't want to spoil your Christmas for you, Mrs. Hargis, but I came out to see your husband. Is that him out in the barn?"

Sherlene Hargis's face swiveled that way, and in the changing light he saw her right eye was swollen nearly shut, and that side of her face almost appeared to be one large bruise. The right side of her mouth was also swollen, and her lips were split.

"Ma'am, if you don't mind my remarking, it looks like you might have run into a door or something since I saw you at the store. Do you need to have a doctor look at that?"

"What's that?" A startled look leaped into her face, and she shook her head, trying too late to move back deeper into the shadows. "No, I'm just fine."

"Well, if that's Bernard out in the barn I'm going to need to see him. And I'll need you to come out there with me too."

"That's not Bern," she replied. "That's my son, I think."

"You think?"

"Well, he brought home a friend of his. Likely, they're both out there."

"And Bern's inside?"

"I'm not sure where Bern is, Sheriff. Haven't seen him since I woke up."

Coal sighed. Nothing was ever easy. "Well, I'm going to need to search the property, Sherlene. You don't suppose I might find him hiding around here somewhere, do you?"

She shook her head. "No sir, I don't suppose you will." Her eyes fell away right after she said it. He sighed again.

"All right. Hold on a minute then." He went back to the car and radioed for someone from the police department to pick up Jordan Peterson and drive out to assist him. There was a possibility that he might need a few more sets of handcuffs before this morning's work was done. Christian might be useful in a fight, but he surely wasn't carrying cuffs.

Going back to the house, where Sherlene still stood at the door, he said, "Ma'am, I would sure like to see your face closer. I've seen a lot of hurt people, and I might be able to help."

"No sir. Thank you kindly, Sheriff, but I really don't need no help. This is nothin'." What she meant, he figured, was that she was used to it.

"All right. I guess you'll have to be the judge of that. Can you call your son and his friend out here for me?"

"Sure. Boys! Y'all come over here, would you?"

Soon, two burly men sauntered out of the barn, one of them sporting a scraggly, unkempt reddish beard of several inches and a greenish John Deere ball cap that had been trampled by a flock of filthy sheep and nibbled by a herd of nervous goats. He wore denim overalls that covered a patched up red plaid shirt he had grown out of around the tender age of twelve.

The other one was younger—barely even a man, if he could be called one at all, and his shoulders were sloped and weak-looking, his belly huge and flabby beneath an ugly, grease-stained blue coat of quilted polyester. The coat hung open, and so did the younger man's fly, from which part of a faded yellow shirt tail protruded. Coal picked up a look on the heavy-set youth's face that said in huge neon lights, *Vacancy.* There was space for rent in this boy's head—a lot of empty space.

"Moby," said Sherlene, "you tuck in your shirt and zip your fly, honey. We have company, can't you see?"

Moby looked over sharply at Coal, his round eyes innocent but wary. Maybe even almost frightened.

"Sheriff," said Sherlene, "this is our boy, Moby."

"What was that? Moby?"

"Yes sir, Moby."

Coal would have hazarded a guess that the boy's middle name might be Dick, as if named after a famous white whale that was nearly maybe all of three times his ponderous size. But in all likelihood, the Hargises weren't familiar enough with literature to make any such connection. Besides, whenever this boy had been named, they couldn't have had any idea he would grow up to these proportions.

"Hello, Moby. I'm Sheriff Savage." The boy tried to look at him as he was fumbling to zip his fly, but his eyes seemed incapable of staying in one place. His hands suffered the same malady, as well as his feet, which Coal would have referred to not as dancing, but plodding in place.

"And this here is Leroy Yarwood, Sheriff. Leroy and Moby have been friends for a lot of years."

Coal prayed neither of them would want to shake hands. By a glance at both of their big paws, he wasn't sure what there was more of—dirt and grease, or skin. Come to think of it, there were probably several other things he didn't even want to contemplate.

Leroy Yarwood stared at Coal for a moment through pale blue eyes, then looked at Sherlene. "Is somepin' wrong, Ma?"

Sherlene laughed, a forced, nervous sound. "No, Leroy, everything's fine." She had come out farther into the light now, probably inadvertently, and it disturbed Coal to see her badly beaten face. On top of the facial injuries, she was holding her right hand in a queer-looking fashion, sort of curled up like a claw. It was the same hand she had used to pick up Hargis's pocketknife, and there had not seemed to be an issue with it.

"Ma'am is your hand all right?"

"Oh, sure. I just… I shut it in the door," she blurted.

"Shut it in the door? How in the world did you do that?"

"I'm clumsy. Clumsy as can be. Bern always told me that."

"Clumsy, huh?" Coal repeated after a moment's pause.

"Yessir. Sheriff, do you want some coffee?" she blurted.

"Not if your husband's in there, no, ma'am." In truth, he wouldn't have taken any coffee made in this house under any circumstances. He turned and looked at the other two. He wanted badly to have all of them in handcuffs, and soon, but beyond not having enough cuffs, there was another reason he didn't try. He had a gut feeling things were going to go down the toilet fast with this Leroy fellow once the cuffs came into view. He did not like the look of him.

"Bern's not in there," Leroy Yarwood cut in. "We haven't seen him t'day."

"No?"

"Me and Mobe came in this mornin' from the Falls," Leroy went on, seeming slightly more normal now that he was talking than Coal had taken him for. "Bern was already gone."

"What does he drive?"

"That car," said Moby, and pointed over by the barn. "Papa drives that car."

Coal glanced over at the side of the barn to see a dark blue Oldsmobile 98, probably 1950 or so. A car he hadn't seen the day before. Like everything else on this property, it had seen much preferable days of wine and roses.

"So he *is* here," said Coal.

"No, he ain't," said Sherlene. "When I got up, he was gone. The boys came in about a hour after I got outta bed. You ain't seen him, have you, boys?"

Leroy had already sworn they hadn't seen Hargis that day, but roly poly, plump and white Moby "Dick" Hargis turned his eyes from his mother to Coal. "I hain't, not today. I promise, I hain't." And there was no ability to lie in that boy's face. Coal truly believed him.

"Let's talk about you, Mrs. Hargis," Coal said, now stalling for time until his extra handcuffs arrived. "The truth. What exactly happened to your face? And your hand."

"Nothing."

"Really? You didn't look like that at the store. And in fact, I remember you grabbed your husband with that hand—right before he hit you. You picked up his knife with it, too."

Sherlene's face flushed. "He was drunk, Sheriff. I'm sorry about all that."

"Yeah, so am I. Can you just tell me where Bern is, ma'am? It will sure go a lot easier for him—and you folks too."

"I don't know, Sheriff. I wish I could tell you. He was really drunk last night. And yes, he hit me some. It ain't no big deal. But then he must have felt bad, so he left. He started walkin' over yonder way." She started to point toward the line of cottonwood trees but jerked her hand back down.

Coal began to take more notice of what she was saying. Something decidedly strange was afoot here. What if she really was telling the truth? "So you say that's his car? And it's all he drives?"

"That's his baby," replied Sherlene.

"Does he often leave like this when he gets drunk?"

"Yeah. And I'm not usually awake when he comes back."

"But he's usually back by morning?"

"Usually, yeah."

"And he went walking that way?"

"I'm not sure."

"You seemed pretty sure a minute ago."

"Well… I guess I just saw him go out the front, and I thought he'd walk over that way."

Coal furrowed his brow. "Does he often walk that way?"

"Yes. Or well, no, he usually drives." She caught herself and blushed. "I mean—not like he drives drunk or anything. Leastway not out on the highway."

"Why does he drive over there?"

"He's been clearin' off a new road there."

"What's that for?"

"Not sure. He told us we ain't allowed to go there, to follow him, to see what he does. He told us he just wants to be left alone."

"So that's what you did? All of you?"

She stared at him. To reply must have seemed futile.

"Yeah, never mind. I guess with a temper like his it would be a good idea to do what he told you."

"He never beats us, though. I promise."

Coal chuckled, shaking his head. It hadn't been one minute before that she had told him, *He hit me some.* "Ma'am, I'm not going to worry about that right now. I just need to see your husband."

A few minutes later, a city police car turned into the long driveway, slipping and sliding all the way to the yard. Bob Wilson and Jordan Peterson got out, cursing the greasy road.

"Hello, Bob. Jordan. I need to have you help me search this place. Ma'am, I'm going to ask you one more time: You don't know where your husband is, right?"

"Hey, she told you she ain't seen him!" cut in Leroy Yarwood. His face had gone red. He turned his eyes to look suspiciously at Jordan Peterson. Suddenly, for no apparent reason, he winced and swatted at his left side, then just as quickly dropped his hand away. Defiant eyes stared through Coal.

When Leroy's hand moved, Coal had seen Ray Christian grab for his waist and go into a partial crouch, and he looked back at him, seeing something flash behind his belt buckle before his coat flipped down.

He looked back at Leroy Yarwood. "Whoa, Mr. Yarwood. Simmer down, okay? I'm just doing my job."

Leroy continued for another five or ten seconds to stare, and the tension in the air ran high. At last, he cringed again, and a grimace crossed his face. He flashed a look over at Sherlene that Coal could only describe as a plea.

The fact was this whole thing certainly wasn't worth any kind of a fight. Coal had been running a big bluff. Nothing more. A misdemeanor arrest warrant didn't give him the right to search this house or any of the other property without permission, and both he and Bob Wilson knew it. Bob had probably told Jordan on the way there as well, so none of them was under any illusion about how things were going to go. He had simply wanted an officer from town in case Hargis showed up and things went south. The simple truth was unless one of these people gave Hargis up, or if they consented voluntarily to a search of the property, Coal and the others were just going to have to wait until next time Hargis came to town to make the arrest.

"Ma'am?" Coal directed his gaze at Sherlene Hargis. "Do you mind if we search the house and all the outbuildings?"

After a long pause, she replied, "I'd really rather you didn't."

Coal sighed. "Okay, then I guess we won't. I believe you're telling me the truth anyway. I don't think Bern is here. But I do need to see him. As soon as he comes home, will you tell him to call me?"

"Sure, Sheriff," said Sherlene. "Soon's we see him."

Coal turned back to the pickup just as he heard traffic coming over his newly installed radio. Neither he nor the others were able to make anything of it.

He reached the pickup and climbed partway in, taking the mic and calling dispatch. “Did you have traffic for me?”

Scratchy words: *Sheriff, we’ve just received a report from your home phone. Something about finding a body.*

Coal pulled the mic away for a second and glared at it, then put it back to his mouth. “Wait—Flo? Ten-nine! I thought you said a body.”

Yes, a body. Sheriff, you need to call your house.

Coal’s heart wanted to beat right out of his chest. He clicked the mic again. “Is my family all right?”

Yes, I think so. But they hung up on me, said Flo.

“Who called?” Coal could feel a touch of panic rising in his voice.

Please just call home. It was your mother.

Coal stepped out of the truck and stared at Bob Wilson. “Bob, I might need you.”

“What did you make of that?” asked Bob, staring Coal down.

“No idea. I’m just afraid it’s all starting over again.”

CHAPTER FIFTEEN

Coal felt almost nauseous stepping into the Hargis home, but this call could not wait. He had to walk carefully because the only light source was the candle he had perceived earlier, and strangely, Sherlene didn't offer to turn any on. She just pointed him to the phone.

Coal dialed Connie's number. The phone sounded like it was jerked off the hook halfway through the second ring.

Coal?

"Yeah, Ma, it's me. Is everyone all right?"

Hi, honey! Yes, we're fine. It's not us. But you've got to get home right away! Shaw Hardy is here—you remember him, from back down Lemhi Road? He's here and he says he found a body up Wimpey Creek when he was hunting.

"Who is it, Mom?"

We don't know that, Son. Just hurry up home. Shaw says he'll wait right here with us.

"Okay, hang tight. I'll be there as fast as I can." Coal dropped the phone back on the receiver. He wanted to ask if he could wash his hands, but he couldn't imagine the faucet handles being any cleaner than the phone, and with the stench that filled this disgruntled, dark old house, he wanted to dash for safety.

He went back outside, into the daylight and fresh air, where Christian, Bob, and Jordan waited for him. His explanation was as brief as the one he had received, and then he got in the truck with Christian, fired it up and wheeled it around in a tight circle to gun it and speed back out the way they had come, throwing mud and gravel up behind.

They were about to pull across the highway when Coal, still looking straight forward, said, "Hey, Ray, I need to say something to you."

"Okay." He sensed the man looking at him, but he didn't look over as he waited for a logging truck and a pickup to pass.

"Since around the first World War, we've had a law in Idaho against concealed firearms carry."

"Oh, yeah?"

"Yeah. I mean, a sheriff could still issue someone a permit, at his discretion, but..."

Ray sighed. "Okay. So I guess you saw."

"I saw."

"Sorry. I guess I should have asked. Old habits. All those years I packed this thing. Pretty hard to just let go, you know?"

Coal could understand. A handgun became a part of you. And in Coal's estimation there were far too few sheepdogs standing between the innocent sheep of the world and the wolves that would love to tear them apart. But a law was still a law.

"I know."

"So... I'll put it away when we get back. Good enough?"

Coal thought for a moment. "Ray, I guess you and I are in sort of a brotherhood, really. How much stronger does it get than law enforcement *and* Marines, right? I don't feel bad letting you have it. When we get back, just give me your driver's license, and we'll write up the form for the permit. It's a snap."

"No, it's okay. I'll just put it away."

Coal looked over at him. "It's no problem. It'll just take a minute. I'm sure you'd feel naked without it."

"Hey! Man, really, it's okay. I'll just lose the gun."

Coal returned his eyes for a moment to his friend. He raised his fingers up off the steering wheel, sort of a casual salute to a shrug. "Okay, that's fine too. Just trying to be helpful."

There was a feeling of tension in the cab that took a moment to melt away. They sat there waiting for a line of traffic to pass that must have been caught behind the logging truck for some distance. Finally, Christian reached out and flipped the radio on. Ray Price was at the tail end of "For the Good Times," and then Merle Haggard came on singing "The Fighting Side of Me." Ray Christian let out a laugh, and he relaxed back against the seat as Coal was finally able to gun it and speed across the highway onto Savage Lane. It was as if a big sigh went out of the pickup.

"Hey, man—sounds like me! The 'fightin' side of me'. Sorry about that back there. I don't want to be a bother, and to be perfectly honest, I don't trust the government much. The less they have on me the better."

Coal looked over at him again and grinned. "No problem, Ray. I can understand that."

Christian started singing along with Merle just as Coal turned off and pulled up in the yard.

A mud-splattered blue late sixties Ford was parked in front, and as they stopped next to it the front door of the house vomited out what seemed to be a dozen worried faces, with Connie and Shaw Hardy in front.

Hardy, although up in his early seventies, was a fit and good-looking rancher old Prince Savage had at one time traded breeding stock back and forth with, in the days when the Savage Ranch was actually a working cattle operation. Hardy loved to hunt, and Coal figured he'd be at it until the day he died.

Wearing a gray cowboy hat and a quilted, tan vest and green plaid shirt, with a gun buckled around his waist, Hardy strode straight to Coal and thrust out his hand.

"Howdy, Coal. Sorry to be bringin' bad news to you again after all the garbage you've been through since ya got back."

"Part of the job, Shaw. So tell me what you found."

"Well, it's a body. A man, I'm almost sure. He's face-down, and I didn't turn him over because I didn't want to mess up anything."

A feeling of relief washed through Coal. "Thank you. That's huge, and I can't tell you how much I appreciate it. All right." He turned to make sure Bob and Jordan had pulled in behind them. When the two lawmen came up, Coal explained the situation and said, "Hey, Bob, do you care to go up there? It's still a ways up in there from here—four miles or so, right, Shaw?"

Hardy nodded. "Impressive, Coal, for a feller who hasn't been around much lately."

Coal gave a half-grin. "My old stomping grounds." He turned back to Bob, and they agreed that he should return to his own bailiwick. Jordan would ride back up with Hardy in his Ford, and Ray Christian was more than happy to continue riding with Coal.

"Not trying to make light of anything," Ray told Coal as they left the yard, "but I sure didn't expect to end up in the middle of an adventure when I came to ride around with you."

Coal didn't look over at him. He just pursed his lips. After a minute or two of the only sound being that of the pickup bouncing over the terribly muddy road, he said, "I'm about tired of adventures, myself."

To that, Ray Christian had no reply.

Coal had brought with him only one thing from the house, and that was his personal camera. Everything else—notebooks, measuring tapes, writing implements, and tags and bags he would need to collect evidence at the scene of the dead body—he had started keeping in a backpack behind the seat of the pickup.

Shaw Hardy had been instructed to stop well shy of the body, so he pulled up out on the main road. Coal parked and got out, then walked up to Hardy's window. When the older man rolled it down, he said, "I don't suppose you two would mind if Ray and I get in the back of your pickup for the rest of the ride in, would you? I'd like to have as few tire tracks in there as possible, and your rig was already in there."

Hardy agreed, and Coal and Ray climbed into the back of his pickup. Coal looked at Ray and cleared his throat. "You said it was homicide you were in, right, Ray?"

"Yeah. Years of it."

"Hey, I don't want to take advantage of you, but . . . You know, other than one week-long class two years ago, I really haven't been trained in murder investigations, although I have followed along on a few that someone else was working. Would you mind if I kind of relied on you to help me through this? I've been forced into doing a lot of it lately, but I'm anything but comfortable." It pained him to admit this, since he was supposed to be the big cheese lawman in charge of the whole county.

"Of course, man! I'd be honored to help out," replied Ray. "Thanks for asking."

Hardy drove down to within a hundred feet of the body, then pulled over and opened his window. Coal leaned over, and the old rancher said, "Is this good enough? This is where I stopped before."

"It's perfect," replied Coal.

They all got out, and after a careful walk of seventy feet, trying to stay single file, in Hardy's tracks as much as possible, they saw the body, face-down in Wimpey Creek, below.

Ray started giving Coal careful instructions. He took a page of notes and two or three rolls of film, recording the body from all angles, as well as footprints and the one set of new tire tracks, which went in and then back out. They also made measurements of the footprints, and the stride that went with each, and measured the tire tracks from inside to inside and outside to outside.

During this so-called "general impression," then scrutiny of the terrain and everything that might be pertinent, Coal had had plenty of chances to study the characteristics of the body itself: lean, to a degree that few people Coal knew could match; the right height; the right kind of clothing; boots he well remembered.

Had this dead body been that of anyone other than Bern Hargis, Coal would have been speechless, but he never mentioned his thoughts to the others throughout the process of gathering evidence.

When at last they moved in close and turned the corpse over in the icy waters of the trickling creek, Coal was speechless anyway, but it wasn't out of surprise. It was simply that nothing needed to be said.

But inside, all Coal could think of was Phil Harringer, Hargis's hateful, and much-hated neighbor, the man who made claims like, *If you want something done, you just have to do it yourself.*

Well, it appeared he had done it. He had taken care of his problem with Bern Hargis, and he owed nothing to Coal for it. Now it was going to be up to Coal to figure out how he had done it—and, perhaps more importantly, to live through his own investigation. It would seem that Harringer was willing to kill, or at least powerful enough to have it done—not a man to take lightly.

Coal and Jordan were able to take Hargis by the shoulders of his coat and by his ankles and get him up out of Wimpey Creek and into the back of Hardy's Ford without much struggle. Even with his clothes soaked, he didn't weigh over one hundred fifty pounds, a barbell weight Coal could curl, and one he was fairly certain Jordan wouldn't balk at either.

Coal turned to see Shaw Hardy standing there with him and Jordan, but Ray Christian still squatted with his feet on a couple of big round rocks that humped up out of the creek. Reaching down, he stirred around in the water with his hand as if he was unwilling to cease his search for evidence.

All of a sudden, he reached down and fished something out of the water and looked up quickly, as if about to say something. He gave a blank stare when he saw Coal already watching him. "Hey! This must be his, huh?"

Coal peered closer, but all he saw was something that looked silver and shiny. Christian was twenty-five feet away down the slope from where the truck was parked, and Coal's eyes weren't what they used to be. "What is it?"

"A broken watch," said Christian with a shrug. He held it up higher, as if by some magic that would make it more visible to Coal.

Finally, he stood up and leaped from rock to rock, coming up out of the creek bottom and stopping a few feet away, breathing heavy and making frost burst out of his mouth in quickly dissipating clouds. He held out his hand, palm up, and the watch lay across it like a dead fish. The band had separated right at the body of the watch on one side, leaving the buckle still fastened.

The watch was very recognizable, but not as Hargis's. Coal had seen it many times before. It had a large ivory elk tooth inlaid into the band on either side of the watch. Those teeth came from a royal bull elk taken up Wood Tick Creek, off of Panther Creek, back in 1947, when Coal was still a junior in high school. He remembered that hunt almost as if it were yesterday—his father's last hunting season before tragedy took him away forever. The hunter had been so proud. The elk mount still hung on the wall of a log home Coal knew well, its antlers perfectly dusted and polished, the tan, red, and dark brown hairs of its cape kept painstakingly groomed and vacuumed.

The owner of this watch was not Phil Harringer. It was Coal's friend, Jim Lockwood.

CHAPTER SIXTEEN

The look on Coal's face must have been much like the evening when he discovered that the signature in his high school yearbook of the supposedly long-dead war hero, Hague Freeman, matched the writing on the hit list he had found in Roger Miley's pocket.

Ray Christian had been watching Coal, seeming to expect some kind of reaction. Jordan and Hardy looked up expectantly from the watch as well. Their faces froze when they saw Coal.

"What's up, boss?" Jordan was the first one to break the silence. He suddenly looked back down at the watch, a startled look in his eyes, then snapped his glance to Coal's face again. "Hey, isn't that—" The big deputy stopped mid-sentence, and his eyes swept the other two men's faces before coming back to Coal. He had clamped his lips shut.

Shaw Hardy was the last man to have his face overcome with recognition. His head jerked up, and he stared at Coal. The odd man out was Ray Christian. He looked back and forth at the others for a few seconds longer, his hand remaining open out in front of him. At last, he closed his fist, and it dropped to his side. "What?"

Coal's mind was racing. He looked at Jordan and Hardy, both of whom he knew had recognized the watch. Anyone who had been around Salmon very long would have known it, although most weren't as intimate with Jim as Coal was. And although Jordan probably had not known a thing about Jim Lockwood one month ago, he had spent a lot of time with him since then, so the appearance of this remarkable watch was something he couldn't miss.

Coal looked back at Christian. A part of him wanted to say why he and the others had gone so quiet. That part of him needed to break the silence, to scream out that what the three of them were looking at could not possibly be real. And he knew curiosity must be killing this stranger to the valley, and it was no fun being the only one in the dark—like the only one who didn't understand a hilarious joke in a room full of people. But he could dredge up no words to address this discovery.

He raised dull eyes to Ray Christian. "Can you think of any more measurements we might need? Or photos?"

As if shaken from a trance, Christian blinked and looked around. "Uhh… No, I can't. We were pretty thorough."

"Yeah. Okay. Good."

Just words. Pointless sound, spoken to hide the shock.

Coal stared at his new cohort a moment longer, then said, "All right, well, you're the one with all the years of experience at this. So you think all my bases are covered?" Not for a second did he stop to think how repetitive he sounded.

Christian nodded. Coal could tell he knew there was something grave about this situation, something beyond the mere murder of a man. His expression was that of someone trying mentally to work through the sudden change in the atmosphere. "Yeah, Coal, like I said, you've gone over it all pretty well. Maybe you can take some more photos—some good directional ones—of the tire tracks on the way out, maybe see which direction they came in from. And later on, we should come back and try to get some plaster casts. The only thing you might want to get now is a few soil samples from where the tire tracks are. Otherwise . . . I think you got it, buddy."

"All right. Thanks. Gotta get the body down to the coroner," Coal said. "Right away."

Jordan and Hardy nodded automatically, bobbing head dogs on the dash of a car on a washboard road.

"And of course you'll want to go back to Hargis's, right?"

It was Ray Christian who had spoken, and Coal looked over at him. Stared. A raccoon in a spotlight. He had to get his mind clear! Everything right now seemed like a fog. Of course they had to go back to Hargis's—to the job Coal hated perhaps worse than any other.

"Oh yeah. Right. We'll go there first."

Everyone was silent for five or ten seconds, thinking of nothing, thinking of everything. Dreading the rest of this day.

"You got one of those evidence bags?" asked Christian at last.

"Uh, yeah. Sorry." Coal looked down at the watch cupped carefully in Christian's hand and hurriedly looked away, like it was something forbidden, or as if it would burn his eyes if he looked at it too long. He pulled a baggie from his pants pocket and handed it to Christian, who slipped the watch into it and rolled it up safe. After a baffled look at Jordan and Hardy, he handed the package to Coal.

Coal took it wordlessly in his left hand and reached across to let it slide into the right chest pocket of his coat. His eyes were fixed on Hargis's body, lying in the truck bed. After a moment, he realized his hand was still at his pocket, as if sewn there. He dropped it away, and without looking at anyone else, he said, "Better get moving."

"You still need me, Coal?" Hardy asked.

Coal stared through the rancher for a moment before the words registered. "Umm… No, Shaw, you should be good for now. But you probably should take down some notes when you get home, everything you can remember about this morning. And then I'll need you to come down to the courthouse and fill out a report in the next day or two. Call me first."

"What about me, Coal?"

He looked at Jordan. "Uhh . . . Oh. Yeah, I *will* need you. Why don't you ride down with me and Ray? Your butt's skinny enough to fit in with us."

Jordan tried to smile. Coal looked away, down at the creek bed, where the water gurgled among the rocks and thin ice, reflecting the dull gray of the sky, turning non-descript round stones into wonderful treasures of deep, rich color.

Coal was pretty sure Shaw Hardy said something by way of farewell. He was next to positive that he got in his Ford and fired it up. He would have bet money the rancher was backing up and then driving away. But for a time, nothing registered on Coal but a long, persistent ringing in his ears.

Then his senses became clear again—ultra-clear, in fact. He heard black-capped chickadees in the brush along the creek, and he heard the rustling, singing water. A passing raven, high against the gray canopy of sky, gargled out its throaty cry, the call of wilderness. He smelled the wet earth. He felt the cool breath of air wanting to play winter as it chilled his cheeks and neck. No word could describe the beating of Coal's heart.

Taking samples of soil out of the suspect vehicle's tire tracks in four different places as they walked, and more photographs, they climbed up out of the west fork of Wimpey Creek.

When they got close to the pickup, they saw Hardy's Ford sitting just past it, and he was on the tailgate smoking a cigarette. Before Coal could say anything, Hardy said, "I thought you might rather take the body with you than have me take it home."

Even though Coal and the others were embarrassed that not one of them had even thought about that problem when they let Hardy go, it gave them their first chance at laughter now, and in spite of the situation, it felt good.

They transferred the body over to Coal's pickup bed, then said goodbye once more to Shaw Hardy, followed him out onto Bohannon Creek Road and down to Lemhi, finally veering off of it left onto Savage Lane while Hardy remained on Lemhi. Most of the time, Coal could feel Christian studying him.

Just beyond the fork in the road nestled the house. Connie and the children would be inside, waiting for some kind of word. But there *were* no words—at least none that could make this better. What would he tell them? He offered a passing salute, three sharp taps of his horn. He hoped Connie would hear it. He had no heart to stop and talk to her. Later, she would understand.

Coal hit Twenty-Eight, paused to wait for a silver Chevelle to pass, and then revved it across the highway onto Barracks Lane. He had a sudden urge to slow the truck to a crawl. How would the Hargises take the news? How could anyone have even tolerated Bern Hargis, much less loved him? How could anyone possibly care that he was dead, beyond the simple fact that it would change how the dairy operation was run, maybe even if it stayed open at all?

Unnecessarily slow, the GMC crept along the muddy brown road, among the willows and other brown, gray, and red-branches that had surrendered their vestments of green to the insistent wiles of autumn and this strange pseudo-winter. They rattled over the one-lane Lemhi River bridge and soon drew within sight of Phil Harringer's palace and the muddy fork in the road that slanted off to the Hargis dairy. With a sigh, Coal turned onto Hargis's lane and drove up it into the apathetic, worn-out yard.

This time, the Hargises' old dog struggled up off the ground onto its haunches and gave one tired, begrudging bark, turning to look at the front door in hopes that its warning would be considered ample. It didn't bother to get all the way up. Maybe it couldn't. The younger dog, the blue heeler, once again made no appearance. Probably out prowling.

Looking out toward the work shed, Coal saw movement, and within the shadows he made out Leroy and Moby. Both stood with their hands hanging at their sides, watching his truck.

Sherlene came once more into the shadows at the front door, but she didn't emerge. Coal climbed out. He was about to tell Jordan and Christian to wait for him in the truck, but a lawman's caution told him he might need witnesses to the coming scene.

"Don't suppose you two would consider getting out and listening in on this—for moral support, if nothing else."

Both jumped out, and the two doors slammed as one. Beneath the overcast sky, the sound seemed somehow trapped in a tunnel, unnaturally loud. When Jordan and Ray came over to Coal, Christian put his hands on both of their arms and said, "Pay close attention to everything you see and hear. It might play a big part later."

Jordan looked over at Coal, and Coal's eyes went to Christian.

"Hey," said Christian, "I know there's something you're not telling me. I feel like you've already made up your mind about who killed this guy. But trust me when I say things aren't always what they might seem. Just remember, everybody is a suspect—until they're not."

Coal swallowed. After a moment, he just nodded his agreement. Inside, the suspect in this case seemed far too certain.

Coal started toward the front door, followed by his backup team. Sherlene Hargis seemed to make a decision, and she pushed the door open and stepped onto the concrete pad. "Hi, Sheriff. Somethin' else I can do for you?"

"Uh, yeah. Mrs. Hargis, can you call your son out here? May as well bring Leroy too."

"Why Moby? He wouldn't understand nothin' you had to say no-how."

Coal cocked his head, trying to digest that. Finally, he replied, "Just . . . Call them both, would you please?"

With a little frown, she turned and called to Leroy. "Can you come here? And bring Moby too." She turned back to Coal. She had a hard time meeting his gaze.

When Leroy and Moby were standing there with them, Coal cleared his throat. "I don't know exactly how to tell you this. It's not easy. But we just found your husband's body, ma'am. Up on the other side of the highway."

Sherlene's eyes flickered. It took five or ten seconds, but finally she said, "What do you mean, his body?"

"His body. I'm sorry, ma'am, but your husband is dead."

The same flicker in her eyes. She stood for several seconds, staring at him, her brow knitted. Finally: "Oh. How did it happen?"

"Not sure yet," he lied. By the blood stains in Hargis's clothing and the hole in the right front portion of his skull, it was obvious he had been murdered, but somehow it didn't seem the time to talk about it.

Sherlene Hargis turned to her son and Leroy. Leroy's gaze met hers, and held. Moby stared at the ground. "You hear what the sheriff said, Mobe? Yore daddy won't be comin' back no more."

The boy's eyes jerked up toward her, then dropped before their two gazes could make contact.

"Mobe! You hear me? Yore pop's dead."

Moby's glance shot up to his mother, then over to Coal and the others. His lip started quivering, but he didn't cry. He just returned his eyes to the ground, and like a wounded deer trying to hide in plain sight, he stared and appeared to wish the three strange men away.

Inside, Coal swore. He suddenly wished he had another vehicle, so he could leave Jordan here to guard this property. He had to keep reminding himself of what Ray Christian had said: *Everyone is a suspect until they aren't.* They were going to have to try and get a warrant and do a thorough search of the place, on the chance that this could be where the murder had occurred, and as if they didn't already know who the killer was. Wimpey Creek appeared to be nothing more than a dumping place.

"Is there anything I can do for you folks?" Coal asked. He didn't know what he could do, but he felt like he had to say something.

"No, not really," Sherlene replied.

"We'll try to find the murderer, and we'll let you know if we do. In the meantime, we'll take Mr. Hargis in to the coroner's office." He didn't tell her they would be back to search their property. He didn't tell her they would be considered suspects, even though the killer already seemed so obvious. Some cards had to be held close to the vest.

Sherlene stared at him. "Um . . . Okay." That was it. Simple and straightforward. And more awkward than if there had been weeping and wailing and gnashing of teeth.

* * *

They got to the morgue, which was coroner Kerry Updyke's mortuary. After carrying the body inside and talking to Updyke for a few minutes, Coal started to leave.

Once out of sight of the coroner, Ray Christian put a hand on Coal's shoulder to stop him from going outside. Coal turned and looked at him. "What's up?"

"Well, I didn't want to say anything back in there—you know, just for the sake of decorum—but you should probably go over that body a little more before we just leave him here. Take some more photographs. Do a little more digging. Once we walk away, you never know what might be changed before we see him again."

Still feeling a little numb, Coal glanced back toward the room where they had left the body. "Oh, sure. Yeah, you're right." He turned to Jordan. "Hey, will you run out and grab my camera and the backpack from behind the seat?"

"Sure thing, boss." Jordan turned and went outside.

"You might also want to call your prosecutor and see if he wants to get involved in this right off the bat. He might not be happy if you take off with something like this without notifying him first."

"Sounds good," Coal replied. He was too embarrassed to admit that the prosecutor hadn't been consulted one time during all of the murder investigations that had taken place in the county since his return home.

Coal tried to call the prosecutor, figuring that if he wanted to be involved it would be before they even searched Hargis's body. There was no answer. Apparently, he and the judged worked on the same calendar.

Having failed once again at getting the prosecutor involved, Coal and Ray went back into the room where Kerry Updyke was putting on latex gloves. He heard the door and turned to look at them. "Oh! Hi. Did you forget something, Sheriff?"

"Nothing big," said Coal casually. "Just wanted to take a few more photographs and look him—that is, the body—over a bit more before we take off."

"Oh, sure. Sure. Take your time," said Updyke. "Just let me know when you're done." He took the gloves back off, then glanced down at Coal's hands. "You'll probably want a few pairs of these, won't you?"

Coal's eyes fell to the still-soaking wet body, thinking how anyone who ever dealt with Bern Hargis, even when he was alive, should have desired a pair of good rubber gloves. "Sure, if you have more."

"Of course. I'll be right back."

Once Updyke was out of the room, Ray looked at Coal. "This is your show, Coal. I'm just here to support you. I want this to look like I'm just an observer."

"Why?"

"Well, you're the one who has to live here with these people. They'll be looking to you to know how to do these things. You know, buddy—sometimes it's all about smoke and mirrors, right?"

Coal nodded. "Yeah, I guess that's true." Again, he couldn't help but think about all the recent killings where he had followed almost none of these steps Ray seemed so bent on.

Updyke came back in with a box of extra-large gloves, then left again. After gloving up, Coal gave the body a long look. He took in a big, lung-filling breath as Jordan came back in with his camera. "Well, here goes."

Taking way more photographs than he could imagine they would ever need, Coal slowly began to disrobe the corpse. He unbuckled Hargis's belt and pulled a cased Buck knife off, unsnapping the case and pulling out the folding knife. Without even popping open the blade, he could see there was blood crusted on it.

"The man had no end of knives," Coal said.

Jordan nodded. "And this one's bloody. That's a little strange."

"I don't know," said Coal with a shrug. "He was a pretty big slob. I can see him not washing his knife after he used it."

They went through all of Hargis's pockets, photographed and tagged everything as they put it in bags. When Updyke returned, they took off the last of his clothing and put it in larger plastic garbage bags provided by the undertaker. With the nearly emaciated body lying nude on the table before them, Coal took more photos, pretty much of nothing, and of everything. Then he gave Ray a glance, which was met by an almost imperceptible nod.

Coal looked at Kerry Updyke. "I guess that's it for us, Mr. Updyke."

"Are you going to order an autopsy?" Ray cut in.

"Why?"

"All sorts of reasons. You never know what might turn up."

They discussed this for a few minutes, deciding that it was pretty obvious that the murderer had struck from the left side, leading to the assumption that he was likely left-handed. Other than that, it didn't seem like there was much an autopsy could tell them, and Coal wasn't interested in wasting taxpayer money on frivolity.

Finally, Ray shrugged. "Okay. Suit yourself. It's your county."

With all the formalities finally taken care of, Coal went out to the pickup again and laid his fingers on the door handle. He looked across the back of the truck at Jordan and Ray, both of them watching him for some kind of word.

"Jordan, I think I could use a little moral support."

"Huh? For what, boss?"

Coal stared at him. Did he actually have to say it? Until he said it, he was still able to pretend this was all a dream. Seconds passed. Word fought word inside his brain. Lightning flickered, thunder rumbled. In his head, and in his heart, was a storm.

"I have to let him know he's our number one suspect, and depending on what I find, make the arrest. And we can't wait for any more evidence to get old."

"Make the—" Jordan stopped. "Oh. Sure." He glanced sideways at Ray.

"So . . . you do have a suspect," said Ray. "I wondered. The owner of the watch, I assume."

Coal nodded.

"And what about me?"

"What about you?" Coal repeated.

"Yeah. What do I do?"

"Ray, I should probably take you back to your hotel."

Ray gazed at him for a long moment. It was the first long look they had shared for quite some time. "Hey, I know I'm a stranger in this valley, but I did what you're doing for quite a while. I'd like to be around to help if I can. Now I know you have a suspect in mind, and nobody's acting too happy about it, so I'm guessing he's some friend of yours—or someone important around here."

Coal felt himself nodding once more. An unplanned reply followed. "You may see things from here on that will make you a witness in court. Is that what you want? It's a long ways from where you live to sit in on a murder trial that's none of your affair. And if there's one thing I know it's that murder trials can go on for a hell of a long time."

"We'll talk more about that later, all right? For now, I kind of miss it, to tell you the truth."

"Miss it bad enough to move to Salmon for a while?"

"Well let's face it, buddy—I've already seen quite a bit. They'll probably have to subpoena me anyway. Why stop now?"

Coal nodded. "All right. Have it your way. You were right, Ray. This isn't just some nobody. It's going to get ugly. That watch belongs to the most beloved sheriff this valley's ever had—and he also happens to be a good friend of mine."

It was finally Ray's turn for shock to wash over his face, though he tried to hide it. He took a deep breath, glancing at Jordan. "Okay. I'm getting it now. But remember, just because his watch was there isn't proof of murder."

"No. But you saw the fight in B and B yesterday. That's the ex-sheriff I'm talking about. You heard as well as I did when Jim told the dead man he was going to kill him. Twice. In front of quite a few witnesses. Fifteen hours later, he's found dead. And likely died within just a few hours of the fight, I'm going to guess."

Ray stared at Coal. Coal stared at Ray. "I . . . didn't realize it was your friend from the fight. Okay," said Ray. "Son of a . . . Damn."

Coal nodded at Ray and agreed: "Yeah: damn."

CHAPTER SEVENTEEN

"All right. Well, hell or high water, as you cowboys up here say." Ray kept staring at Coal. "I'm already in it. I've been with you since you found out Hargis was missing, right? I never could leave a fellow cop hanging out alone—no offense, Deputy," he said to Jordan.

Jordan smiled. Speaking seemed pointless—even almost irreverent.

Coal drove up to the courthouse, where he got the keys to the LTD and handed the pickup keys to Jordan. "Follow us."

He and Ray got into the LTD, its ice-cold seats an insult to their warm backsides, and they drove down Courthouse Drive and out south of town to the Lockwood home. It was a fitting abode for one of the best-known men in the county. Made of expertly joined logs, antiqued brown with time, its two stories likely came to three thousand square feet, with a dormer in the front that overlooked a deep, solidly railed porch. All of the window and door trim was painted in jade green, the roof shingled in brown, and on the end of the house, where there was an expanse of still-green lawn, towered an imposing chimney of finely fitted river rock.

Betty Lockwood badgered Jim to keep the roadside premises in top shape, so the place looked like somewhere a respectable lawman might live. It was only in the back, where Jim worked on his vehicles and the firearms operations that couldn't be performed in his house, that someone would have said, *Only a man would keep a place like this.*

Coal pulled up in the gravel drive that edged the grass, and Jordan parked the truck behind the LTD.

Coal stared at the front door. It was painted a deep brown, and for the season it was decorated with a huge wreath of fir boughs, an overbearing red bow pinned in place top-center. At night, the multi-colored lights would smile from beneath the eaves as if Betty Lockwood and Connie Savage had hired the same decorator.

In five days, it would be Christmas Day. The judge had already said this was his last day at work until after the holidays. If they arrested Jim, unless the judge agreed to make a decision based on a phone call, Jim could stew throughout the holiday season in jail, and his beloved bride Betty might spend it alone. Yet in this murder, the evidence against Jim Lockwood—Phil Harringer's angry, idle comments aside—was like a mountain, or maybe a well-designed fort. It was pretty large, pretty obvious, and pretty hard to shoot holes through, and it was going to be difficult to knock over. Like it or not, Coal could not imagine any reason why Jim Lockwood's watch would have been at the murder scene unless Jim had done the murder.

God, please let Betty say Jim has been with her since that fight. Coal spoke the words only in his head.

Coal took a breath the size of his body, wiggled the .357 around on his belt, out of habit, took another breath, and started for the door. It was the only time in his life he could remember not wanting to lay eyes on Jim Lockwood.

Betty answered Coal's knock, with Jordan and Ray to either shoulder and behind him. "Why, Coal! Hi!" Her huge smile overcame her face, and she started forward to touch him. She stopped. Her smile flew. She searched his face, seeming to find something, even in the shadows of the overhanging roof, that frightened her. Her hand flopped to her side.

"Coal? Is something wrong?" Her eyes jumped to either side, picking up Ray and Jordan.

"Betty, can we come in? Is Jim here?"

"Yes, sure he is. Sure. Come in." She stepped aside as the three of them eased past her, nodding in greeting.

They all paused in the front room, shuffling their feet on the hickory floor Jim had had shipped in from Missouri and put down with Coal's help while he was on leave from the Army in sixty-three. The walnut cabinet to the left, displaying immaculate white and blue china, the

Charles Russells on the wall, and the bookcase full of Zane Grey, Ernest Haycox, Luke Short, Louis L'Amour, John Steinbeck, and Ernest Hemingway titles registered only dimly on Coal's senses. The aroma of fresh bread and roasting meat from the kitchen had no effect on him. The thing that slapped him in the face was the huge elk mount from forty-seven, the very same bull elk which had given up its ivory teeth as decorations on the watch that now stood as stark evidence against Jim in the murder of Bern Hargis.

Coal stood with his hat in his left hand and waited for Betty to close the doors and come to stand in front of them.

She patted at her hair, trying to smile. "You want me to get Jim?"

"Please."

She went from the room for all appearances as if she were after a fire extinguisher. Hat off and bald dome shining, Jim led the way back in just fifty seconds later, wiping a hand across his wide mouth and horseshoe mustache. He had sawdust on his jeans and a rasp in his left hand.

"Hi, Coal." He glanced at the others, nodding at Ray and speaking Jordan's name, before returning his eyes to Coal. "What's up?"

Coal clenched his teeth. He tried not to look at Betty. He wanted to pretend she wasn't in the room.

"Jim, I have to ask you something. Where is your watch?"

Jim glanced down at his wrist, looking confused. With a sudden spark in his eye, he looked back up, starting to speak. Then he looked into Coal's face again, followed the glance on over to the others, and the beginnings of a smile faded from his face. "I'm guessin' you know that better than I do, but you're not lookin' happy to present it to me. Hey, what's goin' on here?"

Coal looked over at Betty. "Excuse me, Betty." He put his hat back on his head and dug into his coat pocket. He soon produced the little package that was the baggie containing Jim's watch. He held it a ways out in front of him.

Jim tried to grin. "That must be a pretty important watch, seeing as it took three of you to deliver it back to me."

Coal couldn't return any semblance of a smile. "Aren't you even going to ask me how I got this?"

"No, I figured you'd tell *me.*"

"I will. But before I do, is there anything you need to say?"

"I'm not followin' you."

Coal searched the older man's eyes. He found no guile there. He expected to, and he didn't. He wasn't sure if that made him feel better, or worse. All he saw was confusion, bordering on irritation.

"This is your watch, right?"

"Oh, for hell's sake, Coal! You know the answer to that." Jim looked down at the package, then back up at Coal. "Come on, what's goin' on?"

"Jim, tell me flat-out if it's your watch or not."

Jim's face darkened, and the corners of his mouth turned down. The happy side of Jim Lockwood was fading fast. "Of course it's my damn watch."

"All right. It was found under the dead body of Bern Hargis, above my house on the west fork of Wimpey Creek."

Jim stared. Betty gasped. The room was a dead stalemate of people staring at each other and barely breathing.

Finally, Jim's eyes shot across the other two men before coming back to land on Coal. A full ten seconds had gone by. "You ain't joshin' me, are you? *Bern Hargis?* He's dead?"

"He's dead."

"Up *where?"*

"I think you heard."

Jim gaped. The shock was painted all over him. Then his eyes flattened out, and a look of flint came into them that Coal had seen before, but was always directed at someone else.

"Up Wimpey Creek. And I guess by the way you came in here you think you have your suspect."

The only move Coal could make was a slight twisting sideways of his hand that held the watch, almost like a shrug. He cocked his head at his old friend.

"I didn't do it, Coal."

The statement and the guiltless look in Jim's eyes brought the first tiny hint of relief to Coal since finding the watch, but his face didn't change. "Can you tell me why your watch was there?"

"I wish I could. I have no idea."

"Where were you last night, Jim? Where have you been since the fight at B and B?"

"Here. We came straight back home."

Coal looked at Betty. A warning told him to stop asking questions now, but it was already too late. The woman had heard Jim's story, and the damage had been done. The only chance now was to catch some nuance of change in her facial expression.

"Betty? Is that true?"

It was there. A flicker of her eyes. It first came out as a look of sickness, a faltering. She then glanced sidelong at her husband, and at last her glance came back to Coal. She froze. Any person whose story agreed with Jim Lockwood's would have found no cause to hesitate. Her reply would have been a resounding yes.

"Don't answer that, Betty. Not if you have to lie."

The woman stared at Coal. Shock began to change to fear, then fear mixed with anger. She reached out and grabbed Jim's left shoulder, trying to turn him toward her as she took a step closer. "Jim? Jim, talk to me!"

Jim clenched his teeth and pursed his lips. He grimaced, then raised his hand to rub at his mustache.

The room was still. A buzzer started going off in the kitchen, but Betty's only acknowledgment of it was a quick glance that way. She seemed to feel obligated to excuse the noise, and she hurriedly shook her head. "The roast," she mumbled.

Jim Lockwood's shoulders slumped. "I didn't kill Hargis, Coal. The last time I saw him was in the store."

"Where were you last night, Jim? And this time the truth would be good."

"I don't know."

"You don't know! What the hell does that mean?"

"It just means I don't know. I . . . Well, I guess you better get out the cuffs."

"Why?"

"Don't pretend there's anything hopeful about this situation, Coal. I was in your shoes not that long ago, remember? Apparently a man got murdered, right after I said in front of half a dozen people that I was gonna kill him, and you found my watch with his body. Pretty much sums it all up, right? And I have no alibi."

Jim turned around, looking thirty years older than he had the day before, and put his hands behind his back.

Coal hesitated. He knew all eyes were on him.

"I'm not going to cuff you, Jim."

"You damn sure will." Jim's face was turned away, but Coal could tell by the angle of it that he was avoiding looking at Betty.

"I damn sure won't."

Jim whirled back around. His steely blue eyes looked almost wild. "That's how cops get killed. Put them cuffs on me, damnit. I could kill you easy."

"Knock it off. I'm not cuffing you."

Jim stared up at Coal's face, his eyes defiant. Finally, he looked over at the other two. A couple of seconds passed before Ray took a step closer, his left side toward the old sheriff.

"I can handcuff him if you'd rather, Coal."

"Nobody's cuffing him!"

"So I'm not under arrest?"

Coal's eyes swiveled back around to meet Jim's. A thousand memories seemed to whirl in a maelstrom between them. Under arrest? How did he say those words to this man, one of the two men who had mentored him since childhood?

"I guess you are."

"Am what?"

"Under arrest," Coal said softly. "You're under arrest." And the heart inside him seemed to die.

CHAPTER EIGHTEEN

Things were done differently in Lemhi County. Things with which no big city law enforcement agency would have ever put up were just a way of doing business for men like Coal Savage. That was in part because life itself was different there. And in part because Coal was a different kind of man.

Asking Ray Christian if he would mind riding back up to the court-house in the pickup with Jordan, Coal put Jim in the back seat of the Ford—his single nod to Jim's demand that Coal "treat this like a real arrest"—and he let Betty ride up front in the seat beside him. All the way to the courthouse, Coal wanted to talk. He meant to try to say something to them about how they would "fix this," and how he knew Jim didn't murder Hargis. But the problem was each time he tried to come up with the words, he found instead a truth he didn't want to face, a truth he never dreamed he would *have* to face. He really couldn't tell Jim that he knew he was innocent. In fact, he really *didn't* know. Going by what Coal could glean from Jim's defense so far, *he* didn't know either.

They got to the jail, a jail through whose door Jim Lockwood had walked literally thousands of times in his life, and for the first time he rode into this parking lot as other than a free man.

Betty had managed to keep her emotions in check up to this point. Likely because she was still in shock, like Coal. But when Coal opened her door for her, and then they stood beside each other as he opened the back door for Jim to disembark, Coal sensed her beginning to cave in. He listened to the music of the creek that splashed along down in a gulch behind the jail as he tried not to look at Betty, and failed. When he did, her chin was trembling, her eyes moist. Yet still, she held it in.

Jim got out, and Coal shut the door. The ex-lawman turned to face his wife, and he stiffened his chin, causing the pockmarks to become etched there like old stab wounds from a sharp pencil. He reached out and took Betty's elbows. His jaw muscles worked for a few moments as their emotions passed between them.

"I promise you I didn't kill that man, Betty." It had taken all his strength to finally say it.

She searched his eyes, and then she began to cry. Like the tough woman she had always been, however, she stopped almost right away, before her nose could get runny.

"I believe you, honey. You know I do."

Jordan pulled the pickup in and parked a few spots away. Until Coal, Jim, and Betty started walking toward the jail, he and Ray didn't get out of the truck, but then Coal heard their doors shut, more quietly than normal, and he knew they were following.

On the old concrete steps that were starting to spall from the effects of weather and time, they went down to the jail, the place Jim was so familiar with from all the years when this had been his domain. Coal pushed open the ugly yellow metal door, and Jim walked in ahead of him. He glanced around the room as he walked, then stopped mid-room and turned to look at Coal, thrusting his fingers into the pockets of his 501 jeans. "There's weapons all over this place, Coal."

Coal raised his eyebrows a little. "As usual. And?"

"And I ain't got any handcuffs on. You don't let a prisoner walk loose in a room full of guns, and especially if you're dumb enough not to handcuff him."

Coal relaxed, cocking one hip. "Jim, if I thought you would go for a gun and try to shoot me, I'd hand my own to you."

Jim gave his friend a half smile. He ran a hand back over the shine of his bald head. "Now what?"

"Now I guess we Miranda, so I can start an official interview."

"Stuff that."

Coal chuckled. "I can't. I have to be able to swear in my reports and in any future proceeding that I followed the rules."

"You haven't followed any rules so far. I rode all the way up here unsecured behind you in the car. You haven't even searched me. Why start following any rules at this point?"

"I didn't do any of the rest because I'd rather be dead than live knowing somebody I looked up to my whole life tried to kill me."

Jim smiled. Then he nodded. Check mate. "Okay, let's repeat this together then: You have the right to remain silent…"

Coal just stood with a half smirk on his face and let his friend go through the entire Miranda rights warning. When he was finished, Coal said, "Yes. That. So do you wish to waive your rights to talk to an attorney?"

"Sure."

"In writing?"

"Sure."

Coal went to his desk and pulled out a blank legal pad and a pen. He slid them both to Jim, who looked down at them, then back up at Coal. "What am I supposed to do with that?"

"Sign it."

"Yeah. There's nothing on it."

"Sign it. I'll write something in later."

Jim managed to laugh. "So you just write a confession in there, and bam! It's over."

"If you don't trust me, don't sign it."

Jim rubbed his mustache, then reached down to pick up the pen and scrawled his sloppy former lawman signature to the bottom of the blank sheet on top of the pad. "Just don't write anything in there about me being a child molester or a queer."

"Funny. All right, Jim, do you want to be interviewed first, or Betty?"

By this time, the other two men had come into the room. For the moment, Coal ignored them.

"Can you talk to Betty? Then maybe Jordan can take her back home so at least one of us can have a peaceful day."

Coal frowned. He hated thinking of Jim spending a night in jail, and he intended to do everything in his power to make sure that didn't happen. "All right." He looked over at Jordan and Ray. "Hey, Jim, this gentleman is a former homicide detective from Reno. Ray Christian. Betty, this is Jordan Peterson, my top deputy at least until Todd Mitchell recovers."

Jordan gave a sheepish shrug. "*Only* deputy."

Betty forced a smile. "It's nice to meet you both." One of the most over-used phrases in the English language, particularly in a case like this.

"So Jim, I hope you don't mind sitting in the back while I talk to Betty. As you know, we don't have an actual interview room."

"I'm fine." He turned and walked into the cellblock, and Coal motioned for Jordan to go in with him. Then he turned to Betty. "Betty, do you want a cup of coffee or anything?"

"No. I've heard from Jim what's happened to the coffee down here."

Coal smiled at her obvious attempt to lighten the mood. He couldn't quite make himself laugh. "No, that's Todd and Jordan. If I make it you'll like it."

"No, no, sweetheart. I'm just playing with you. I'm fine, really."

"Then a Tootsie Roll or something? Some candy corns? Some gum—Juicy Fruit? Blackjack? Cloves?" He named the only three kinds of gum he knew to be in his desk drawer.

Betty smiled patiently. "No. Thank you, though."

"Okay. Listen, Betty." He gazed into her eyes, aching inside. "I'm really sorry you have to go through this. I wouldn't be doing this for anything if I had a choice."

"It's not your fault, Coal." She stepped closer. "Hey, we know you're just doing your job, okay? There've been a lot of times when Jim had to do things that went against the grain."

"Okay. I'm sure it's all just a technicality. Everything will work out fine." Her eyes filled with a sudden rush of tears, causing Coal to leap sideways for his desk and grab a box of Kleenex. "Hey, hey. What's wrong?"

"I'm not sure it's going to work out fine, Coal. That's the whole problem."

Coal stared at her. Now his heart really started to pound. "Okay. Okay, maybe you need to sit down, and let's start from the beginning."

She complied, sitting on the chair in front of his desk while Coal remained standing. He held onto the Kleenexes, hoping both of them wouldn't need them before this was all done.

"I'm going to record this, all right? I don't take notes so fast."

"That's fine."

From a bottom desk drawer, Coal pulled out a shiny silver cassette recorder, got a new tape out of the same drawer, opened it, and slid it in. He pushed down on *record* and *play,* then slid the machine over closer to Betty.

In a slow, clear voice, he spoke the date and time, along with the case type and who was involved. He then said, "First interview, Betty Lockwood, wife of suspect number one." He couldn't look at Betty as he spoke those words, but when he was finished, he looked into her eyes.

"We're just going to jump right in, okay? What happened after you and Jim left the store?"

"He drove straight home."

"Did you talk on the way?"

"Of course."

"What was Jim saying?"

"What do you think? That he was going to kill Bern Hargis."

"Not what I hoped to hear."

"Come on, Coal, you know my husband. He has a slow fuse, but when it has a reason to get lit, it takes a long time to burn down."

"Yeah. I do know your husband. So… How many more times did he say that after you left B and B? I had already heard it twice in the store."

"I can't tell. Four or five, at least. I kept begging him not to say that, but he was *so* worked up over everything that happened."

"He was just mad at Hargis, right? Not at me."

"No, no! Of course not. He knew you were just trying to keep him out of trouble."

"So what did he say when you asked him to quit saying he was going to kill Hargis?"

"He kept telling me nothing was ever going to change until somebody did something about him. That Mr. Hargis was getting worse and worse, and there couldn't possibly be a good end to it."

For several seconds, Coal was still. He cringed each time he thought of this conversation going onto permanent record on the cassette. It was sounding worse and worse for Jim. The sad truth was in the end it might be Betty's blunt honesty that hung him.

"Did he ever say anything specific about how he was going to kill Hargis?"

"Yes. I don't like to even talk about it, but… He said he'd like to get his .45 and shoot him between the eyes. What happened, Coal?" she asked suddenly. "How did he die?"

"Let's keep that quiet for now," Coal said. "But just know for now that he wasn't shot."

"Thank heavens!" She sighed with relief. "At least that's something, right?"

"It's something. But truthfully not much."

"But whatever happened, it couldn't have been an accident, could it?"

"No. It wasn't an accident."

"And what is all the proof against Jim?"

"The word of several witnesses how angry Jim was in the store—almost out of control—and how he threatened twice to kill Hargis. Then Jim's watch was under the body when it was found. And now… I hate to say it."

"You mean my testimony."

"Yeah. They'll ask you to tell the court what you told me, Betty. You know that, don't you?"

"Yes."

"How do you feel about it?"

"I don't think Jim would want me to lie. But I know he didn't kill that man."

"Then you know more than Jim does."

She was silent. She looked down at her hands, folded in her lap. Coal waited for a good twenty seconds. Finally, he said, "Betty, look at me. Tell me what Jim's going to say when I ask him about that. He already said he doesn't know. Why would he say something like that? What's he talking about?"

Betty gave out with a sobbing sigh after holding her breath for several seconds. "Coal, we've been hiding this for several years. Jim has a condition. No one knows but us, his doctor, and the kids. Well, and possibly two other doctors."

"You've got to trust me."

She nodded. "I know. I know. Okay, so when Jim gets really stressed, sometimes he blacks out. It's bad enough that if we were to drive to a city somewhere, once we got into the city he would make me drive."

"Wow. That sounds bad. Betty, why haven't you told anyone?"

"Oh, Coal! You know Jim. His pride. He doesn't want people feeling sorry for him."

"And this is a verifiable condition? His doctor can present testimony?"

"Yes, of course. He's been dealing with it for . . . Well, it actually went for the whole last year he was in office. People thought he left in the middle of his term to give K.T. a chance to prove himself so he would have a better chance in the election. That really wasn't it at all. Jim wouldn't have minded staying in the job longer. He just couldn't. He never knew when one of his episodes was going to happen."

"Is it like epilepsy?"

"Maybe. Sort of. It's a seizure disorder, caused by stress. That's all they know for sure. And it seems like the worse the stress is, the more of his memory it can knock out—sometimes hours of it. He just blacks out, and when he comes out of it, he doesn't remember one thing."

"So let me ask you this . . ." Coal was feeling sick, and was afraid to ask his question. He was afraid of the answer. "While he's in this blacked out state, what exactly do you mean? Is he actually passed out, unconscious?"

Betty shook her head. "No. That's the scariest part. He seems wide awake. You would probably recognize that he isn't quite there, but you wouldn't think he's having a medical issue. He went downstairs and loaded three boxes of ammunition like that one time, and when he came out of it he had to start all over again. He saw the can of powder still sitting there, unopened, and realized he hadn't put one grain of powder in any of the cases."

Coal found himself thinking back over the fight at B and B. "What about the fight at the store? He didn't even seem to know me."

"I think he was on the verge of going into one of his episodes then. But he wasn't yet, because he remembers the fight. And he remembers driving home."

"Then what could have set him off?"

"Coal, I don't..."

"What?"

She sighed, and at last she reached for a tissue and daintily blew her nose—at least as daintily as anyone can perform that chore. "I know he will hate having this known, but it's going to have to come out."

"I'm sorry."

She shrugged one shoulder. "It's okay. Life. You know? So we had a fight when we got home. I think I can count our real fights on one hand, Coal. Our entire life, even back to the War."

"Real fights? What do you mean?"

"Well, not like hitting each other or anything. Just really loud yelling, and me screaming back at him. I finally told him if he kept acting like that I was going to leave him. I can't stand it when he gets so furious, and his face turns all red, and it just looks like he's going to explode. I hope you know I would never really leave him. I was just so frustrated. He wouldn't stop! One more time of him saying how he was going to kill Bern Hargis, and I thought about calling you over there to try and talk to him."

"I sure understand that. And then what happened?"

"Well... When I told him that, he stuck his finger in my face and started shaking all over. He told me if I wanted him gone, then he would just go. He grabbed the keys to his pickup, and started going out. I tried to stop him, but by then it was way too late. When he went out and slammed the door, I followed him, but he was so mad when he got in the pickup and started backing out in the street I decided just to let him go. I knew he didn't have a gun with him, because his gun was still under the seat in the Thunderbird, and he usually doesn't keep any others in the vehicles."

"Where did he go?"

"I don't know."

"When did he get back?"

"It must have been midnight."

"What did he look like?"

"What did he look like?" she repeated quizzically.

"Yeah. What was his expression? What was his physical appearance? What did his clothes look like?"

"Honestly, I had gone to bed. By the time he came in and lay down by me, I was still so mad and upset I was pretending to be asleep. When I got up this morning, he was already up and drinking coffee, reading the news."

Coal watched her and listened intently. In fact, he couldn't take his eyes off her, and he could feel her anguish at that moment as if it were his own. Instead of merely listening, he had the urge to walk over and put his arms around her.

"Did he say anything to you?" he asked when she finished.

"He sure did. And I'll never forget his words, Coal. He looked up over those reading spectacles of his—which were stuck on the end of his nose and made him look like some grandfather out of a Norman Rockwell painting—and he said, 'Mornin', babe. I made you coffee and hash browns and bacon'."

"That's all?"

"No. When he saw how surprised I was, he said, 'And I want to apologize for last night, honey. I'm sorry I acted like that.' And those words, Coal, I will swear to on a stack of Bibles. He was talking to me like there wasn't one thing in the world wrong."

For a moment, Coal stood there nodding, feeling a surge of love for his old buddy, his friend, and the friend of his family since long before he was born. Then he sucked in a big breath.

"Betty, there's one more thing I need to know."

"Okay."

"Did you see his clothes? Especially whatever he had on his feet when he drove off? Was it the boots he has on now?"

She gazed at Coal, and he could tell she was nervous about saying anything. "Yes, I did. I saw them. And no, it wasn't the boots he's wearing. Coal, where did you say Bern Hargis was found?"

"I don't know if I did. Answer my question first, and then I'll tell you."

She swallowed and seemed to steel herself. "His boots were soaking wet. All the way through. And the soles were covered in mud so bad I had to put them out on the back porch so I can clean them later."

Coal had the sudden urge to leave. Simply to turn and walk out of the room, leave Betty sitting there, and go for a drive all alone. He had a task to do, to go down to the Lockwood home and confiscate Jim's boots, and to inspect his truck and its tires and take measurements. Maybe also take soil samples from the tires, if there was any to be had.

But the truth was, he no longer felt any need for all of that. It was only going to seal this case.

He had never wanted in a worse way to be proven wrong. Jim Lockwood might have a defense, thanks to whatever his seizure condition was, but it seemed like there could be very little doubt that Jim, aware or not, had killed Bern Hargis.

He had sworn he would, and Jim Lockwood seldom made idle threats.

CHAPTER NINETEEN

When Coal interviewed his friend, after Betty said goodbye and Jordan left the jail with her, the mood was somber. He knew that no matter what happened from here on, it was going to be a long, difficult road, both for Jim and Betty, and for anyone else who was close to them. He tried to stay positive and objective, but there was only so much a man could believe. And Betty's testimony, sadly, had pretty much proven her husband's guilt to Coal. As much as he hated to believe it.

He could still take hope in knowing that Jim wasn't really *lying* to him when he said he didn't kill Bern Hargis. After all, it seemed there was a good chance that he really believed he hadn't, and as long as he believed it then it wasn't a lie.

To help Coal remain on track, and so the distraction of his relationship with Jim would not affect the case, and particularly the interview, in any negative way, Ray Christian had asked to be involved in the process, telling them he would stay back out of the way and would only intercede if he saw any issues or thought of any pertinent questions that were missed. Both Coal and Jim were amenable to that, because for Jim, he didn't feel he had anything to hide, and for Coal, he felt the sudden, dire need for the moral support of a man who had been in the profession of homicide investigations as Ray had.

The first thing Coal made sure of was that they started out on an equal footing, with Jim knowing that Betty had informed him all about his medical condition. He didn't want his old friend to feel like he had any further reason to hide it.

Coal asked Jim numerous questions about what happened to him after he left the house. Without any professional knowledge of what might be the underlying cause of Jim's issues with memory lapse, he was trying in some hopeful, completely amateur way to jog his memory, to bring him back to the reality of whatever had taken place last night. But Jim, embarrassed, kept insisting he couldn't remember a thing. He never even admitted to knowing he had gone out to the pickup.

Finally, Coal was ready to give up. His heart had never been much heavier. "Jim, what's the first thing you have any clear memory of after your fight with Betty?"

"I only remember waking up with her. I knew I must have had one of my blackouts, and I thought I must have gone to bed right after we had our fight. I got up and made breakfast and read the newspaper for a while. I wanted to let her sleep as long as she would. I figured I owed her that."

"So you're telling me you finally retired because you were worried about doing your job, right, Jim?"

"Yeah."

"You know you probably shouldn't be driving anymore either, right?"

Jim stared at him for several seconds. It was as if that idea had never occurred to him. At last, a breath gusted out of his mouth. "Might as well take away my right to be a man, Coal. At that point, how can I even take care of my sweetie pie?"

A wave of sadness came over Coal. How was he going to take care of her anyway, if they locked him away in prison?

Ray witnessed the whole proceeding, and throughout it all he did not interrupt. His face remained thoughtful, his eyes watching Coal at times, but most of the time studying Jim.

Finally, Coal looked over at Ray. He was trying to seem calm. "What do you think, Ray? Did we miss anything?"

Framing his chin with a thumb and forefinger, Ray furrowed his brow, and he pursed his lips and began to shake his head, almost imperceptibly. Finally, the sideways shake became pronounced, and he dropped his hand. "No. No, I don't think so. That's pretty much all I would have asked too—at least for the time being."

Coal nodded thanks and looked back at Jim. For a moment, their eyes locked. "I'd never tell you how to do your job, Coal, but maybe you could consider letting Betty come up and have some kind of little Christmas dinner with me, huh? I sure would appreciate it."

Coal took a deep breath. He nodded, then looked over at Ray. At last, he sat up straighter on his chair, and then, making a final decision, he stood up.

"I'll go you one better. You're not some psychotic murderer, Jim. I've got things to do at Christmastime besides hang out at the jail, and so do Jordan and Victor. Come on. I've got to do some things down at your house anyway. So I'm taking you home. The judge is off until after Christmas, and apparently the prosecutor is too, because I couldn't get him on the phone. We're just going to have to wait and deal with your status after the first. You don't plan on leaving the country, do you?"

Jim managed to grin, although not the grin of a carefree retired man happily married to a beautiful wife. "Thanks, Coal. No, I plan on staying right here in town, and if I do decide to leave I'll probably invite you to come with me."

* * *

They returned to Jim's house, where Jordan was still sitting with Betty in the parlor, trying his best to comfort her. When they heard the front door, and Betty came to peek out and see who was there, she broke into tears, flying into Jim's arms.

He squeezed her to him and whispered into her silvery hair, "I'm sorry, babe. I'm so sorry."

Coal and the others left quietly, and they retrieved the measuring tape and camera from the pickup. Not wanting to perform this part of his job, Coal forced himself to go out to Jim's light blue pickup, a sixty-one Ford.

He cringed when he saw the pickup. A vehicle that Jim tended to keep clean and tidy was covered around the back fenders and the tailgate with mud and bits of grass and gravel. On close inspection, it appeared to be the same color as the soil as that up Wimpey Creek, and when he pulled out his own samples from the scene, they seemed a nearly identical match. It took only a glance to see that the tire pattern was close as well, although the tracks on the road had been hard to see, in places. But just before where the vehicle had turned off Wimpey Creek Road onto Bohannon, there had been a good, clear spot in the mud, and thinking back on those prints, they were a near-perfect match to these. The width between them was also the same. Everything seemed to match, even the mud on Jim's boots, which Coal confiscated to take back and tag for evidence.

He went back to the tires and studied the tread closer, then turned to look at Ray. "Do you remember the tracks? They didn't seem to have this much tread, did they?"

Ray gave a sad frown. "Not really, buddy, but you've got to remember all the mud they already had in 'em. Tread's not going to look quite as deep when it's full of mud."

Coal nodded. "Maybe not the middle, but the edges should."

"Now that might be something," said Ray, his face brightening. "Are you good enough at photography to trust the photos? Otherwise, maybe we can go back up there and take another look now that we've seen these tires. We really should try and go get some of those plaster casts I talked about anyway."

Again, Coal nodded. He had no desire to go back there, but he knew they had to. He took a calming breath. "What about the tread, though? The pattern?"

Ray looked sadly at Coal. "I hate to say it, but if I remember it right, it looks pretty much the same."

Coal didn't even want to go back in the house to say goodbye.

Jim Lockwood was going to need the best lawyer in the world, and every Christmas from this one forward was going to bring back a sour memory of a black spot in Coal Savage's life. Christmas might never be the same.

God, Coal found himself thinking, *we don't talk much, and I guess maybe You can see why. I don't know what I've done, but I guess it must be pretty bad, for me to land in the spot I've been in since I came back to the Lemhi. When I think things are as bad as they can get, they get worse.*

The truth was, he was starting to wonder if God really cared about people at all. Or if, like they supposedly had with Job, the devil and the Lord were playing some big, heartless gambling game with the life of Coal Savage.

CHAPTER TWENTY

When they got out to the vehicles again, after saying a quick—and, for Coal, hopeless—goodbye to Jim and Betty, Coal told Jordan he could call it a day and thanked him for all his help.

Jordan pulled away in the LTD, and Coal and Ray Christian stood in the gray day and looked at the gray street. Coal's whole existence seemed now to be shades of gray, or black.

"Christmas will be here in no time," commented Ray. "That was good of you to let him spend it with his wife."

"Yeah. I'm guessing it might be the last for a while."

"He's no spring chicken," Ray pointed out, glancing toward the house, then back at Coal. He sniffed. "You think he's up to spending time in the pen? That's done in a lot of tough men."

Coal felt glum. He was sure it showed. "No idea. But it's sure going to change his life forever."

"Do you think he really did it?"

Feeling confused at the question, Coal looked at Ray. "What do you mean? Don't you?"

Ray shrugged his shoulders under his brown suitcoat, which was turning dark under the day's moisture. "I don't know."

"You don't know?"

"Ah, yeah. I don't know. There's just something that doesn't feel right to me."

"Ray, I'm not an investigator. It sounds like you've done a lot more of this kind of thing than I ever dreamed of. But I'm having a hard time thinking of a more solid case."

"I know. Yeah, you're right." Ray shook his head, pinching up his lips. "I don't know, though. I'm not going just by evidence, you understand. I'm going by my guts."

Coal didn't really know why, but this gave him a strange sense of hope he hadn't felt even one minute earlier. Then his cynical side took a figurative ax and hacked that hope into kindling and threw it on a gasoline fire. "You've got more hope than I do then."

"Hey, brother, if we don't have hope in this life, what *do* we have? I'm just saying, I sure wouldn't give up on my friends without a fight. Sometimes they're all we've got in this life that's worth fighting for. You know?"

"You're something, Ray. Say, you want to go for a drive? Or maybe grab a bite to eat?"

"You up to it?"

The gloominess inside Coal matched the gray feel of the whole day. "Not particularly."

"Then why don't we go make those plaster casts and then go back to your place? Go see your family. You got any dogs?"

Coal looked up at him, puzzled. "Actually, yeah. A couple of them. Why do you ask that?"

"Go get a proper dog greeting then. Nothing like a doggie welcome to make a man feel like things aren't so dire after all."

Coal felt himself actually smile. It was a strange sensation.

"All right. Yeah. I'd like my family to meet you. You sure you don't have anything you'd rather be doing?"

Ray jerked his head severely backward, giving Coal a weird look. If his head hadn't been sewn on tightly, it would have gone rolling. "Yeah, man, like what? Go down to the river and watch the ducks?"

Coal laughed. "You wouldn't be the first. That's considered high entertainment around here—although usually you're watching them with a shotgun in your hands."

Grinning, Ray slapped Coal on the shoulder. "Come on, partner. And come to think of it, I *am* getting pretty hungry."

* * *

On the way out to Savage Lane, Coal had time, and the inclination, to mention Burro—now King—to Ray and to tell him the story of his big gaffe with Virgil. Ray listened quietly to the story, sort of the way Coal had guessed he might, hanging on every word, and seeming to care deeply about the outcome, and the people involved—even the ones he didn't know.

"Man, dads do some stupid things, don't they?" he said after Coal finished.

Coal looked over at him, then found himself laughing. "Yeah, I guess we do. You have any kids?"

"Yeah. Well, I did."

That reply shut Coal up for a moment. "Sorry. I hope I didn't bring up any bad memories."

"No, man, you couldn't know. And it's not like they're dead, so I shouldn't say *did.* I've still got 'em—in the world, anyway. My wife, God bless her pea-pickin' little heart, poisoned them against me as bad as she could, then got custody and headed out to her folks' place in Georgia. I haven't seen those kids in ten years."

Coal almost broke out in a laugh when he heard the phrase "pea-pickin' heart." He thought only his mother said that. But it didn't seem like the time for laughter. He thought of all his issues with his own children. All of them seemed suddenly very small.

"Sorry to hear that. I can't imagine life without my kids."

"Yeah? What about your wife? I see you're not wearing any ring."

"Never liked jewelry," Coal replied quietly. "But I still wear it sometimes."

"Oh, I get it."

Cursing himself inside, Coal sucked in a breath. "No, sorry, man. It's tough to talk about, but actually, my wife's dead. Her name was Laura. She was a beautiful woman—from right here in the valley."

"Yeah?"

"Yeah." Coal stared at the road. They were getting close to Savage Lane.

Coal could tell Ray was reading behind his thoughts and finding something more there. But his only reply was, "Huh."

Coal pulled the pickup off the road onto Savage Lane and stopped. He threw it in neutral and set the brake, turning to look at Ray. "Hey, I guess I should tell you, just in case . . . My wife, Laura . . . Well, she killed herself. Yeah. Hanged herself in our barn out in Virginia. Not long ago. I was working for the FBI. My life fell apart. My daughter blamed me. Maybe my boy Virgil too, but I never could tell that for sure. I've got twins, a couple of rambunctious five-year-old boys, and I think they're all right. But yeah. Not to be a downer, but I just thought it might be good to know, so you don't get into any uncomfortable spots with my family."

Ray sat there quietly nodding, studying Coal's face. He reminded Coal, at least at the moment, of Larry MacAtee.

"Hey, brother, that's a rough patch. I've never heard much harder than that. I appreciate you letting me know, all right? Man!" He paused and took a deep breath. "I sure wish I knew something to say."

Coal smiled and slapped the seat between them. "Nah, don't worry about that. You know, just talking about it helps sometimes."

"Sure. Sure. Then I'm glad you told me. Say, let's go meet this family of yours—and those dogs."

With a sigh, and a lighter heart, Coal drove the rest of the way up the road and parked in the yard. He saw that now only Connie's Chrysler and the dark blue sixty-four Chevy, old Betsy, which still bore its black and white Virginia plates, were parked in the drive. He didn't know if he felt more relief or sadness not to see Maura's pickup. He was starting to wonder if allowing her to take her horses and dogs back home would start to keep her away from the Savage place more and more often, since she wouldn't have that excuse for coming over.

Getting out, he and Ray kicked the dirt off their boots on the porch, and Coal stepped inside, fighting off the dogs as they scrambled to get the most attention the fastest. Ray pushed in behind him, closing the door to fight back the cold air. Coal found himself laughing at Dobe and Shadow. They seemed even more rambunctious than normal.

Ray watched for a while from in front of the door, then started laughing as well. "See, what did I tell you? Now we're even laughing. I always say a dog is the best medicine for a man."

The sound of his voice had drawn the attention of both dogs, and Dobe came over to greet this stranger that his master seemed to think was safe to have in the house. Ray rubbed the Doberman's sleek back and scratched behind his sharp upright ears. Shadow, on the other hand, sniffed at him, then shied away when he reached for her.

"That's weird!" said Coal. "She never does that."

"She senses evil, I guess!" replied Ray, laughing.

Connie and the children had started gathering around by now. Even Virgil was in the room, since they had all been snacking on a huge silver bowl of popcorn—something that drew his children much like monkeys.

Coal introduced everyone. He realized partway through that he had made the faux pas of forgetting to tell his new friend about Cynthia and Sissy, so when he shared their names he simply said they had recently joined the family, and left it at that. The way things were going so far, Ray was probably going to end up knowing about them too, and the circumstances that had brought them to be under this roof. But there was no place for that kind of talk in a light-hearted moment like this.

The entire Savage household seemed to take to Ray Christian immediately. He had an easy, friendly, and caring way about him that drew people to him in a matter of sentences—and in cases like Coal's even made people want to share some of the deeper secrets of their lives.

Once she found out about his stranded circumstances, Connie promptly invited Ray to stay with them for the remainder of the day, if he was so inclined, and supper as well. It was a supper Coal could already smell cooking—one of his mother's famous Dutch oven meals, he guessed. That was a treat he had tasted all too seldom in the last twenty years.

Everyone gathered in the living room while Connie began whipping up some of her trademark cookies—not that she had any particular cookie trademarked. It was cookies in general that were her stock in trade.

Coal quickly realized that his popularity, even with Dobe, had taken second place, at least while Ray Christian was here. The children found out that he was from Reno, that he had been a detective there, as well as a street patrolman before that, and all the questions began then in earnest. All of them, even Katie, were fans of *Adam 12* and *Mannix*—and although Mannix wasn't exactly the same type of detective Ray had been, to the children that fact was irrelevant.

Coal watched his friend, feeling a strange sense of pride in having brought him home, as he entertained the children with his vivid—but not too gory—stories of life as a big city policeman. It baffled Coal that Shadow never did warm up to Ray, and in fact it was just the opposite. She kept looking at him suspiciously and then would give him a wide berth and get back over close to Coal to be protected—or perhaps to protect *him*. The only other one who wasn't drawn to Ray, predictably, was little Sissy. In fact, the man's mere presence seemed to drive Sissy over the edge onto Coal's lap, and he took the welcome opportunity and held onto her tightly.

At that point, he hadn't dared say one word to Connie or anyone else about Jim Lockwood and the investigation, even though the murder was obviously on Connie's mind. The afternoon had become filled with cheer, and there was no point in ruining it with the news that, unless something else big broke, Jim Lockwood was heading for lockdown.

Eventually, Coal and Ray broke away, gathered a few supplies from town, and then went back up to Wimpey Creek to make plaster of Paris casts of the tire tracks. The footprints were barely good enough to make useful casts of. Photos and width and length measurements would probably serve their purposes just as well. Coal and Ray studied them for some time, but in the end decided there was no conclusive evidence as to whether the footprints had been obliterated purposely, or if the ground was simply too soggy to support readable prints.

When they had finished all they could do at the crime scene, Coal and Ray returned to the house, and the adults made a careful point of not bringing up any of the morning's activities. The children coaxed Ray for more tales of Reno, and it didn't take much to convince him to cave in.

A fire crackled in the Franklin Heater, which Virgil stoked now and then, between Ray's stories, with additional pine logs. While Coal sat and listened, sometimes with only half his attention, to Ray's voice, he half started to doze off. He had been thinking about Maura, wondering if she was just at work and if maybe she would come by later—or maybe even stay the night. As much as he hated to admit it, he kind of missed that. But he wasn't about to ask Connie about her. Some spirits simply weren't worth inviting in.

Ray had been entertaining everyone for more than an hour and a half, and he seemed to be just warming up, when the phone rang. Connie had finished her chore long since and satiated them all on chocolate chip and frosted sugar cookies and icy cold fresh milk. She jumped up and got the phone, and in a moment she turned and crooked a finger distractedly at Coal, while still talking into the receiver.

He got up and started to set Sissy back down on the chair, but for the first time she grabbed onto his neck and wouldn't let go. That sent a feeling of warmth all through him. It amazed him what a little child could do for one's soul, especially a little child who had for so long seemed unreachable. He guessed that in that way children were like dogs—a show of love from them could heal a broken heart.

Holding on tight to Sissy, as she held to him, he went to Connie, and as he got close she put her hand over the transmitter and gave him one of her big-eyed, knowing looks. "It's Kathy."

Coal took the phone, rolling his eyes to show how he felt about his mother's take on the whole Kathy situation.

"Hello?"

Hi there, big boy. You know something? I miss ya.

"Well, dang it—me too! What's new? How are you getting along with King?"

Oh, buddy! You created a monster, Mr. Savage. These girls don't ever go outside in the cold, but they won't even stay in the house for ten minutes now. They're always up and down the road with that dog. It's actually starting to make me feel a little like chopped liver.

Coal laughed. "Well, we can't have that!"

No way! So how about you taking me out?

Coal heard her. He just wasn't sure how to reply. He tried to buy himself a moment to think. "Wait—what's that again? The phone was scratchy." *You liar,* he chided himself.

I said how about taking me out? This time Kathy laughed lightly. It was the kind of laugh intended to cover a moment of awkwardness.

"Take you out? Really? You mean now?"

No, you silly man! Well, unless you want to! But I was thinking about maybe for breakfast. These girls will sleep till the Lemhi freezes over anyway, if I let them.

"That sounds nice, Kathy. What time?" And it did indeed sound nice, but Coal hated thinking about Connie's inevitable comments after the end of the phone call.

Early! In the dark.

"Wow, woman. You've lost your mind."

Kathy's laughter sounded particularly merry. Maybe she was feeling better. Or maybe she had been testing wine. Coal smiled at that thought.

I haven't lost my mind. I just know about how your days seem to go, and I want to get my time in early.

Coal didn't say anything about how this particular day had gone, but he thought: *Wow, Kathy. If you only knew.*

"So how is six o'clock? I bet the Coffee Shop would love to see your smiling face that early in the day. I doubt it's ever happened before!"

Oh, come on! I'm a rancher's wife . . . Momentary silence . . . *Well, I mean* was *a rancher's wife. I'm up earlier than you.* The mood of the call had sobered.

Coal's thoughts stalled. Only for a moment. "So . . . six then?"

Yes, six sounds good. Can you come get me on your fiery steed? She tried to bring back the merry mood, but ice had fallen down its neck.

"I sure can. See you then." He started to hang up, then thought better of it and said, "Hey!"

Yeah?

"You doing okay, Kathy?"

Just a little sniffle. *Yeah, I'm okay. Thank you for asking.*

Coal hung up, aching inside for Kathy, his best friend's wife. And then he happened to look over where the spotlight shone brightest in the living room: at Ray Christian.

CHAPTER TWENTY-ONE

As it ended up, Ray Christian not only stayed for supper with the Savages. He stayed the night as well. Julie, down at the Stagecoach Inn, was gracious enough to let him out of his rental agreement for the night because she knew Coal would recommend the Stagecoach to other travelers in the future. And Connie had the wonderful idea of calling Maura at McPherson's and having her go to the Inn to pick up Ray's luggage, since she was already in town.

Coal had his own thoughts about that whole development. First, it meant that for whatever reason his mother seemed to be keeping pretty close track of Maura's schedule. And second, if he wasn't mistaken, she also liked to jump at any opportunity to get Maura over to the house. As for Coal, he wasn't sure if either one of those thoughts bothered him—and the fact that he *wasn't* sure bothered him more than anything else.

As for Connie, she got the night off of going out in the cold to feed the horses when Ray offered to go out and do the job with Virgil, who really seemed to have taken a shine to him. Coal went out with them, just to tag along.

Maura arrived while they were out with the horses, and to Coal's private dismay, by the time they came back in she had already excused herself and gone home, she said to take care of her animals. Coal couldn't help but wonder if it didn't have more to do with her conversation with Annie after Sissy's birthday party, and the handshake they had shared out in the night. He also couldn't help but wonder why he should care, and with that thought he banished the whole subject from his mind.

When the children were gone to bed, Coal took Ray to a place that had been special to him during his childhood, and even in the times returning home when he had an hour or so to kill. That place was up in the hayloft, where they opened the front door, which hay was thrown through to stack for the winter, set up chairs, and shared a thermos of coffee while looking out over the little Savage Ranch.

They were sitting there drinking coffee, in one particularly long moment of thoughtful silence, when a thought struck Coal, instantly followed by a feeling of almost-guilt. He realized how much he had come to enjoy the company of Ray Christian, maybe because he reminded him so much of Larry. And then he wondered if perhaps he was replacing his best friend too soon—thus the guilt.

When their talk eventually came back around to Jim Lockwood, which even when they weren't speaking of it had filled Coal's chest to overflowing, Ray listened quietly to Coal. He just couldn't believe, even in spite of whatever disorder his old friend had, that he had murdered someone in cold blood. When Coal was done venting, he sipped quietly at his coffee, his heart at war with his head. It was in this moment that Ray Christian proved his full value as a friend.

"Coal, can I speak openly to you?"

He turned to look at him and shrugged, feeling a little bewildered. "Sure. I wouldn't have it any other way."

"It seems to me like you're throwing a pretty solid lifetime friend to the wolves way too easily."

"What?"

"I just don't know how you can be so sure Jim is guilty."

"I don't know how you're still not. Even after having all this time to think about it? I've never seen a much more ironclad case, even on TV."

Ray chuckled, looking at Coal with an expression almost of understanding, almost of disbelief. There was no other way Coal could have described it, even if his own thoughts made no sense at all.

"You mean you actually believe what you see on TV? Coal! Come on, buddy. Really? You haven't heard of ironclad cases that suddenly fell apart?"

"I guess maybe. I just can't think of one right off."

"Well, I sure have, and I'm still not convinced Jim did it."

There. It was out between them once more, like a stone dropped into a mud puddle. Coal Savage, willing to believe in the guilt of a man who was almost like a father to him, meet Ray Christian, stranger to the valley, knowing nothing about Jim Lockwood as a person, yet unwilling to relinquish the possibility of his innocence.

Coal felt more shame at that moment than he had over anything else in a long time.

Thursday, December 21

In the morning, Coal woke to the spitting of wet snow against his window. Connie was out with the horses already, so he got up and went out to help. Other than thanking him, she said nothing until finally they were back in the barn, which was lit in yellow and orange tones by a single kerosene lantern.

"I haven't wanted to pry into your job, Coal, but I sure have to admit I'm curious."

"About what, Mom?" Of course he knew. It was just his stubborn streak that made him force her to be specific.

"Oh, come on! I have to ask? Fine. The body yesterday—would it be anyone I know?"

Coal breathed in deeply of the icy air, watching the little flakes of snow-rain drip down out in the yard between the house and barn. "Yeah. It was."

She waited.

"It was someone *everybody* in Salmon would know: Bern Hargis."

Connie drew a sharp breath. "*What?* You can't be serious."

"I almost wish I wasn't."

She gave him a questioning look. After a moment, she followed it with: "I don't want to sound heartless, but… if it has to be someone we know, I can't imagine anyone whose death would be more of a relief than a cause for sorrow."

Coal stood like a stone. His heart had started to pound. He wished once more to be back in Washington, dealing with complete strangers. Connie sensed his feelings.

"Coal? Honey, what is it?"

"I don't want to say."

"What? Now you *can't* be silent. What's wrong?"

"There's a reason I wish it wasn't Hargis. Mom, it looks for all the world like…" He actually swore, and his mom didn't even correct him. "It looks like Jim might have done it."

If Coal could have had his hand wrapped around his mother's heart, he was pretty sure he would have felt it stop beating, just for a few seconds. He tried to meet her gaze, then finally pulled his eyes away and looked out again at the plummeting snow, shoving his hands deep in his coat pockets.

At last, he sensed when his mom was about to speak. "Coal, you must be mistaken. Jim? Jim Lockwood? I don't believe that for a second." Her voice was filled with shock.

"Believe it or not, Mom. Every piece of evidence points right at him, and there isn't one piece I can refute yet. When we didn't stop on the way back by here yesterday, that was why: We were going to the Hargises', then the coroner's, and then to Jim's house to place him under arrest."

It was Connie's turn to swear. She used it to full privilege. Another time, Coal might have had a fun time pretending to remind her how terrible that kind of language sounded. Right now, he felt no sense of humor at all.

* * *

Leaving a very somber, dark house, Coal drove the GMC out to Kathy MacAtee's, watching deer bob in and out of his headlights. He had badly wanted to invite Ray along with him, partly because he was starting to feel like he and Kathy needed a chaperone, and partly, he admitted with a feeling of guilt, because he wondered if Kathy wouldn't fall for Ray, relieving him of one of the most complicated situations he had ever felt himself get into. But Ray was sure to move on soon, so any connection between the two of them would end up for naught. And besides, she had basically asked Coal on a date. It would be in extremely poor taste to show up with a third wheel.

Kathy waited inside like a good girl until Coal parked the car and went up to the door. She wouldn't want to look too anxious.

But she had a huge smile for him when she threw open the door at his knock. She gave him a hug, making him feel, on the moment, like the most important person in her world. And because of the seed his mother had planted in his head, that was exactly what worried him. He could hear King back in the girl's bedroom, moving around excitedly. Kathy, however, obviously intended to keep Coal to herself.

As much as Coal would have liked to take the Camaro into town, they left it in the garage, because he didn't care to get it all muddy on the messy roads and then have to take the time to wash it later—although that was a job he would gladly have taken on during a warmer time of year.

As it turned out, Coal was pretty sure breakfast with him wasn't exactly what Kathy envisioned it would be. He was distracted, to say the least, and the hard part was he couldn't even tell her why. There was one part of him, down deep, that almost hoped she would find his aloofness and moroseness a serious turn-off and decide to move on. That was, of course, if his mother was right about Kathy being interested in him in the first place.

The thing for him to do, if he was half a man, would be just to come right out and ask Kathy what she expected from him. There was always a chance that even in the face of that kind of frankness she would continue to keep her cards hidden. But at least then the burden would be on her rather than him.

He guessed he just wasn't ready to hurt her, if hurt her he eventually must. After all, unless she came right out and told Coal she wanted him, he would be able to go along pretending she didn't. He had hurt other people, and it always hurt him too. Sometimes it was simply better to put off the pain.

Tammy Hawley was their server at the Coffee Shop, looking sprite and lovely in a short-sleeved brick-red blouse and white skirt, with a brief white apron over the top of it. She tried to make small talk with Coal and Kathy, but Coal's attention was elsewhere, and Kathy was beginning to act like getting up so early wasn't all she had dreamed it would be.

Eventually, Tammy got the hint, and the next time they saw her was when she brought the check.

Later, Coal dropped Kathy back off at her house, and he walked her to the door, simply because his mother and father had trained him that way. He wanted to get away from her fast, but when she invited him in, he caved. She looked lonely and hopeful, and Coal Savage was, at heart, a sap.

It was while they were inside the house, before he could make his escape, that the phone call came in. Kathy asked him to wait while she took it, and he stood impatiently at the door.

"Hello. Oh, hi!" She stood listening to whoever was on the other end of the line, and at first it was obvious that she intended to ask if she could call them back later. Then a shocked look came over her face, her hand went to her mouth, and a little gasp escaped her.

"Wait. Are you serious? How did you hear that?"

She looked over at Coal while trying to absorb whatever answer was coming across the receiver. At last, she jumped in and said, "Hey, Lonna, can I call you back in a bit? I actually have company. Okay. Talk to you soon—bye-bye."

She hung up the phone and instantly returned her eyes to Coal. He waited for her to speak. And *kept* waiting.

"What?"

"That was Lonna Deroe. Coal, I owe you an apology."

"Huh? What do you mean?"

"I didn't know."

"Didn't know what?"

"About Jim."

Silence. Cold and still. At last, he took a big breath.

"Wow. Small towns never change. Well, there wasn't any reason you should have known, Kathy. Or could have known. I was kind of trying to keep it quiet."

Kathy nodded and came close, putting out her hand to squeeze his. "I'm not even going to ask you any details, but . . . Are you going to be okay? This is terrible."

"I'll be okay. But yes, it is terrible. And…" He looked down at the phone. "Since it's obvious Lonna's going to call you back with all the seedy details, I guess I'd better stay and give you our side of the whole story first—so you aren't getting secondhand information that might not even be true."

So he told Kathy what he knew, as far as the fact that Bern Hargis was indeed dead and that there was, as rumor suggested, plenty of evidence linking Jim Lockwood to the crime. Jim was, however, not in jail, he admitted, and that was one thing he asked Kathy to keep to herself.

But the wheels of the rumor mill had already begun to turn, and some things cannot be kept under a lid.

* * *

Coal drove slowly away from Kathy's, thinking about Jim. Now that the word had gotten out, things would start happening, and fast. He didn't stop to question where the leak had come from. The truth was he didn't want to know. He didn't want to have anyone to blame it on. Shaw Hardy was a good guy, but he wasn't in law enforcement, and he could have told his wife or anyone else, not even thinking that it might be something that should be kept under wraps. It might have been Jordan, but Coal couldn't blame him either. Coal hadn't told him not to tell anyone, and he hadn't been in law enforcement long enough to give much thought to the possible repercussions of letting this kind of information out to the public too soon. He knew the leak wasn't with Ray Christian. He was the last one Coal would suspect in the first place, but he and Coal had been together the entire time. Anyway, the moth had erupted from its cocoon, and now it was going to grow and flourish—in all its multiple, and sometimes hideous forms.

Once Coal started thinking about it and about the implications of this full story hitting the news, he began feeling queasy. He raced the rest of the way home to find Ray out on the road walking Dobe. His friend informed him that Shadow wanted nothing to do with walking if he was the one going along with her. Coal grinned and shook his head. Who could figure out what made a dog tick? That would be on a par with figuring out some women! To be fair, he thought then—*all* people.

Parking the pickup, Coal went and caught up to Ray and Dobe and informed his new-found friend of the latest news. "Just curious—what would have happened in Reno when something like this broke a little early?"

"Well, for one thing, I don't know how people would take it that the number one suspect was walking loose. That could come back to bite you."

"You think so?"

"Well, yeah. For one thing, you didn't even call the judge and ask if it was okay to release him. And he didn't bond out or even sign an O. R. form."

"O. R. form?"

"Own recognizance."

"Oh. Yeah." Coal stared at Ray for a few seconds. "So I'm the sheriff, and I'm the one who made the arrest."

"Well, I know, but in Reno, and I think in most other places too, once someone's arrested, and especially for murder, you have to run it by the judge if you feel there's a good enough reason to let him go before his hearing."

Again, Coal stared. "Why didn't you say something before?"

"I don't know. I guess I just didn't want you to feel like I was stepping on your toes. Besides, I don't really know how you do things up here."

"Well, I guess I don't either. I've never had to deal with it before. Anyway, this is Jim Lockwood. He's a good friend, and . . ."

"Yeah, I understand. And it's Christmas, and you can't bear to see your buddy locked away. I really do understand that. I'm just not sure everyone else will."

"What you said about Jim earlier—are you interested in looking into this any further? I wouldn't blame you if you just want to get your Cadillac and fly. But the one person I would have relied on in this case happens to be the main suspect. Kind of hard to look to him for any kind of advice. I think I'm in over my head, Ray."

Ray chuckled, although not with a lot of humor. "I've spent a lot of the night lying awake thinking about this, my friend. I agree. You're in a real bad spot. I would never want to be where you are today. I'm not sure where to even start looking to try and exonerate your friend, but it seems like a shame if we don't at least try. So I was thinking, with your main deputy in the hospital, not even able to do anything, and your other deputy a pretty smart guy, but obviously pretty green . . . What would you think about making me a temporary deputy? I'd feel a lot better if I had some kind of authority, and I think your constituents would too."

Coal only had to think for a moment. It wasn't like he had been at his job for years, but from everything he knew, he was pretty sure he had the right to deputize anyone he wanted.

"I'd be happy to have you on board, Ray. But do you seriously plan on hanging around long enough to do anything?"

"What are you talking about, Boss? I already got involved in the investigation, and remember I'm probably going to be subpoenaed into court as a witness anyway. I might as well be official."

Coal almost wanted to give Ray a hug. Instead, he simply swore him in right there at the house to the position of deputy, Lemhi County, Idaho. He conveniently failed to mention the fact that he had never been sworn in himself. That was a strange oversight someone was going to have to deal with later—if anyone ever even realized it had been overlooked.

When the ceremony, such as it was, was over, with Connie and Sissy the only witnesses, Ray went to take a shower. It wasn't one minute later when Maura's ugly Travelette pulled into the yard and parked. Coal's heart started to beat a little harder, and he hated that. On a whim, he went out to meet her.

He stood on the porch with the fingers of both hands thrust down into the pockets of his blue Wranglers. Seeing his stance, Maura stopped and folded her arms, looking up at him in her Lucchese boots, flare-legged blue jeans, and down-filled dark green coat with its fur collar. In spite of the flared legs, the outfit looked good. But then anything on Maura looked good.

The look on her face was inscrutable, for a few seconds. Not mad, not sad, not happy. She simply seemed to be reading him.

Then, without warning, her mask seemed to break into lines of relief, she unfolded her arms and came to climb the steps, surprising him by throwing her arms around him. Into his ear, she whispered, "Oh, Coal, I'm so sorry. I heard about Jim." He guessed she didn't feel bad about Hargis. He had to fight the humorous side of himself not to say that.

"Thanks." What else could he say?

She held onto him for a long time before pulling away. He half expected her to take his hands. She didn't. Instead, she stowed her own away in her pockets. It always amazed him to see that pants so tight could still fit more flesh into them, even if her hands weren't all that big.

"What happens now?" she asked.

"What do you mean?"

"Well, I mean… Coal, it's almost Christmas. What about his family?"

He shrugged. "I let him out."

She stared at him. "Let him out? Can you do that?"

"I think that's what I'm about to find out. I have to go out to the judge's house and try to get a search warrant for the Hargis place, and while I'm there I'm going to tell him what I did. I guess I'll see what he says."

Maura pursed her lips, studying his eyes. Her own were clear and blue and full of compassion. It was a look she had been hiding from him for a while. "Can I go with you?"

He tried to process her request and figure out why she would want to go. Then in spite of being a man he suddenly understood one thing: She was offering herself up to support him, and if he said no, he would be slapping her in the face. And truth be told, her company would be more than welcome. Besides, it would give him a chance to introduce her to his new deputy.

"Sure. Yeah, if you want. I don't know that it'll be all that exciting."

She gave him a soft smile. "Maybe not. That's okay. I'm not up for any excitement today."

Coal took her inside, and Connie greeted her with her usual hug. She had to sit down after that, because Sissy came and climbed all over her, and she was too big to hold for very long. While Connie started making Maura a couple of pancakes, Coal said, "Hey, I've got a new deputy."

"Is that the guy I brought the luggage over for last night?"

"Yeah, him. I thought you would have stayed and met him." Coal tried to keep his tone non-accusatory.

"I had to feed the animals." She slid her gaze away from him and gave Sissy a tighter squeeze.

"You'll like him," said Coal. "Everybody likes him."

Maura just smiled in reply and gave a thoughtful nod. When her pancakes were done, she did her best to eat them around Sissy. The child didn't want to let go.

Connie took Maura's plate when it was empty, and Coal looked up to see Ray coming from the hallway with a towel in one hand, his hair still damp and ruffled.

He stopped there at the entry into the living room in his fancy, citified clothing, this time a dark brown dress shirt and tan, plaid pants, flared slightly at the leg, with dark brown oxfords, and a tan and dark brown knit sleeveless sweater, which seemed to be a thing with him. Coal thanked his lucky stars that he had been born and raised a country boy in Salmon, Idaho, and had been immune to any notions of trying to follow the styles of the day. For all his strut and flare, and even his devilish, dark-skinned handsomeness, Ray Christian looked pretty ridiculous in a town like Salmon. Still, Coal had to like the guy. And seeing him standing there with a holster inside the front of his waistband and a gold badge on the left side of his chest made the picture much easier to swallow.

Ray had started to raise the towel up to dry his hair, but when he saw Maura sitting there he lowered it slowly back down. Maura's eyes met Ray's just as Coal said with a smile, "Ray Christian, this is Maura, one of our local EMTs—the best one, in fact."

Throwing his towel over on the La-Z-Boy, Ray walked closer, grinning. He thrust out his hand. "Hi, Maura. Great to meet you."

Maura's hand left Sissy's midsection slowly. It was even slower going out to Ray. She took his hand, then dropped hers away only a little less quickly than if she had been burned. Her eyes flickered over to Coal before she looked back at Ray. She said only, "Hello."

Coal would agree with anyone who said he didn't know women. But he could sure read when someone disliked someone else, and the coolness in the air right now was palpable. He fought back a frown. Typical Maura, he guessed. She just didn't warm up to any man very quickly. Her reaction irritated him more than it should have. He had been trying to show both of them off, but she sure had not acted in any way that would have impressed his new friend. In fact, quite the opposite.

"You ready?" Coal turned back to Ray.

"Just about."

"Good. Maura's going to come into town with us."

Maura's face snapped around, and she stared at Coal. He stared back. The room was silent, at least until Dobe let out a big, snoring sigh from over by the Franklin Heater.

"You still want to go, right?"

Maura's eyes flickered toward Ray. "Uh… Yeah, sure." She spun back on her chair to face Connie. "Hey, thanks for the pancakes, Connie. Delicious like everything you make."

"Thank you, dear," said Connie, and with her usual sense of timing she came near and gave Maura a hug. That was one lady who knew when to dole out the hugs.

Coal, Maura, and Ray went out to the GMC, and Coal noticed that Ray held his door open and stood away from it, leaving an obvious opening for the woman. Instead, she hurried to the driver's side, and when Coal flung open the door, she pushed past him to climb in the middle of the seat. Ray looked a little confused, but he recovered and got in.

Coal sat down, almost having to shove Maura over with his hip to fit all the way in and shut the door. A piece of cellophane wouldn't have fit between their legs.

Backing the pickup around, Coal got onto Savage Lane and headed for the highway. The gravel crackled under their tires, and the motor hummed. Otherwise, and except for the winter, Coal thought he would hear crickets.

At the highway, he turned toward town, and Ray stopped pretending to study the countryside. "So you live nearby, Maura?"

A moment's silence. "Sure. A ways up."

Longer silence.

"They don't have full-time EMTs here, right?"

"No."

This time the silence broke Coal's eardrums.

"Maura works at McPherson's. It's a western store downtown." He had to offer something that sounded conversational. Every reply by Maura was delivered like a punch in the mouth.

"Oh, great. Yeah, I've seen the place." Ray spoke and then stopped talking. His glibness had run its course.

Coal didn't try to break the silence anymore. He was no miracle worker. He only knew Maura needed a spanking. She sure could make things more uncomfortable than sitting on a cactus.

For the rest of the trip into town, Coal thought about Judge Wiley Sinclair. That was one tough bird, and a hard shell to crack. How did he go about admitting that in his ignorance he had set Jim free? Maybe if he sounded humble enough it would garner him some lenience.

But speaking humbly to haughty people was not Coal Savage's most polished ability.

CHAPTER TWENTY-TWO

After a quick stop at the courthouse to look up the judge's number and make a phone call to get permission for a visit, Coal drove the five or six miles out to the judge's house, which sat at the far end of ten or fifteen acres of pastureland surrounded by perfectly kept white two-by-six fencing out on Highway 93, headed toward Montana. Two good-looking chestnuts that appeared to have some warmblood in them and a long, sleek gray that must spend all his nights in a barn stopped grazing on the few remaining hummocks of grass to watch Coal's truck as it passed.

Coal walked up newly swept concrete steps to a crisply white door with a half moon-shaped window at the top and knocked. The judge came to the door holding a folded newspaper in his left hand and wearing black-framed spectacles a ways down the bridge of his nose, a black tee shirt, and tan slacks with house slippers. He glanced from Coal to Ray. His eyes roved to Maura and lingered there longest. Finally, he looked back at Coal. "Good morning, Sheriff."

"Good morning. I think you might know Maura Plenty-Wounds, one of our local EMTs?" His fingers feathered the back of Maura's arm.

"Yes, of course." Sinclair's smile at Maura was larger than any he had ever offered Coal. "Good morning, Maura. Nice to see you."

She nodded and took his hand in quick greeting.

"This is Ray Christian," Coal then introduced his new deputy. "He was in homicide with the Reno P.D. He's agreed to help out with the investigation, so now he's a deputy."

Judge Sinclair looked Ray up and down, including a glance over his glasses at the badge pinned to his sweater, then finally held out a stiff hand, the newspaper dropping forgotten to the side of his leg. "Nice to make your acquaintance, Mr. Christian. It will be good to have some experience on this case." He turned back to Coal, not tumbling to how slighting his comment might have sounded. "So what can I do for you, Sheriff?"

"Well, sir, we really need to do a search of the Hargis property if at all possible, while any evidence out there is fresh. Maura's just riding along."

"That won't be any problem. I expected as much after hearing the news."

"Yes sir. And there's something else," Coal went on. He was irritated to realize how nervous he suddenly felt.

"All right. Let's hear it."

"Well, word seems to spread around this valley like wildfire, so I wouldn't be surprised if you've already heard this, but . . . Well, let me just lay it out there. My prime suspect is Jim Lockwood."

The judge nodded, raising the rolled paper and using it to slap the palm of his other hand. "Yes, so I hear. The *Recorder-Herald* beat you to it. I think you all better come inside."

Coal put his fingers on the small of Maura's back to invite her in before him. She jerked away and looked over at him, her eyes flickering to Ray, then back. Reaching down to give his fingers a squeeze, she mouthed the word *Sorry*. Hoping Ray hadn't caught the exchange between him and the woman, he followed her into the immaculate entryway of the two-story gabled house, stepping onto an exquisite floor of chocolate-colored tile, with massive honey-blond oak baseboards bordering it all around. The walls were a beautiful deep olive green, with an oak chair rail and crown molding of the same color.

Coal's glance briefly took in the beauty of the room, then returned to Judge Sinclair. The judge drilled him with his eyes.

"Please debrief me, Sheriff."

Coal ran over all the details of the case, speaking fast to get through without interruption.

The judge sighed, slapping the folded paper against his leg. Another sigh. "Well, I have to admit this certainly wasn't anything I expected right before Christmas."

"No sir. But there's something else I doubt the paper says."

"Yes?"

"Sir, I've known Jim Lockwood my whole life. His wife is here in town, and he loves her more than anything. I know he isn't a flight risk."

The judge gave him a questioning look. "And? I suppose you want to let him out on bail."

"Well, sir…" Coal shot a quick glance at Ray. "I actually already let him go home after booking."

The judge continued to stare Coal down until finally he drew a deep breath. "I see." Another deep breath, another sigh. He cleared his throat. "Well, Sheriff, by your tone I'm assuming that you now realize a phone call to me would have been in order. Once you've made a felony arrest for a crime of this magnitude, I would like to at least be in on any decision to let our most important suspect out."

"Yes sir. I apologize for that. I didn't want to bother you."

"Sheriff, that would have been no bother. In fact, bothering me should have been the least of your worries. This is a case I would have really liked to be informed about from the beginning, in fact. Seeing it in the paper was not my favorite way to wake up."

"For that I apologize. It won't happen again. But with the holidays, and you being off . . ."

The judge stared Coal down, his face stern, lips tight. Finally, he gave what for him was the equivalent of a smile, although nothing like the smile he had offered Maura. "I realize your situation, Sheriff. Hold on a moment—may I call you Coal?"

Coal looked at him blankly. "Uh . . . Yes sir. You bet." This was a request Coal wouldn't have expected from this seemingly self-important figure if he had been around him for years. And certainly not right now, considering the new tension he had introduced to the room.

"Thank you. Coal, as I said, I realize your situation. You have been friends with Jim Lockwood for years, and he has been somewhat of a mentor to you, if I understand correctly."

"That's true."

"Well, he has become a man I'm proud to call my friend as well, Coal. Does that surprise you?"

Coal shrugged. "I wouldn't have guessed either way."

"No, of course. Anyway, it's true. And I value my friendship with Jim Lockwood. I'm not going to reprimand you for your decision. In your shoes, I might have done the same thing. But please, in the future, just call. Have you at least been in touch with Mike Fica or Bryan Wheat?"

"Umm . . . I'm at a disadvantage now. I don't know them."

The judge raised an eyebrow. After a moment, he chuckled. "Well, I suppose you *have* been pretty preoccupied since your return to the valley. According to the papers."

"Yes sir."

"Well, I expect you to get to know Fica and Wheat—soon. And well. Fica is our county prosecutor, and Wheat is his deputy."

Inside, Coal cringed. The way Judge Sinclair said this, he knew it was considered important that he get acquainted with those two, and he made a mental note of it. "I'll do that, sir. Thank you."

The judge nodded. "Now. About that warrant."

"Yes," replied Coal, still a little shocked at the judge's reaction. Maybe this tough-acting, no-nonsense judge was actually a little human after all. "There is a little something more."

He went on to outline the situation that had existed between Phil Harringer and Bern Hargis, the obvious enmity between them, and the thinly veiled threats Harringer had made. He then asked if it would be possible to include the Harringer place in the search warrant.

Judge Sinclair's face changed, almost imperceptibly. He looked from Coal to Ray, then back. He ran the tip of his tongue around inside one cheek, then huffed out a breath. "I don't think so, Sheriff. Coal, I mean. Not at this time, anyway. Let's see what you can find at the Hargis place first, shall we? If you don't find what you need there, then give me another call."

Coal had to hide his surprise. It seemed to be a morning of surprises. He would have to ask Ray about this later, but to him it seemed perfectly reasonable to search the Harringer place also, under the circumstances. However, his relationship with the judge was just beginning to soften up. His guts told him this was not the time to muddy the waters by questioning his decision.

"Yes sir. Thank you for your help."

After the judge typed up a brief warrant, detailing the property to be searched and the items that would be seized if located—namely, a suspect vehicle, murder weapon, and anything that could reasonably be pointed to as evidence in this investigation—he handed it to Coal, and Coal thanked him again and went out to the truck, still disappointed at having no legal right to search Harringer's place. Hopefully, they would find any evidence they needed at the Hargis property. But Coal continued to fear that the suspect vehicle was the one they had already found—Jim Lockwood's pickup.

On the way back to town, Flo called Coal on the radio to pass on a message that Ken Parks was waiting for a call back, down at his shop. Coal looked at his watch after hanging up the mic, then looked at Maura.

"You still have some time?"

She only nodded. It wasn't the ideal answer, but if she didn't have time she should have come right out and told him.

"Let's just go down to Ken's then," Coal said. "Save time going back to the courthouse to call him."

"Great!" said Ray, looking like a little boy on Christmas morning. "Now you're going to see a *real* car!"

Coal looked at Maura and caught a frown on her face. It didn't fade when their eyes met. "Is that okay with you? We'll try to be quick."

"It's fine. But I only have a half hour."

Coal grimaced. "When we're done, can I drop you off, then come and get you when you're off? We're not going to have time to go get your truck and get you back in time."

The woman looked at first put out, but then some private thought made a little smile come to her face, and she shrugged, reaching over to squeeze his leg. "Sure."

They drove downtown to Ken's Automotive, and once again Coal noticed—and kind of liked—how close Maura was crowded up against him. The seat was wide enough that there was still enough room between her and Ray to set a can of soda, but Coal wasn't going to complain.

The big blue Cadillac was parked out in front of Ken's in such a way as to attract the attention of everyone who passed. Coal had to admit Ray was not exaggerating. This was indeed an incredible piece of machinery.

When Coal and Ray climbed out, Maura chose to slide out under the steering wheel rather than descend on Ray's side, where he was holding the door. Coal sensed Ray looking at him, probably wondering what was up with the woman, but he didn't have any explanations to offer, so he didn't make eye contact with his deputy. Maybe Ray could explain women to *him. He* sure wasn't going to try.

Ken Parks saw them park and came outside, wiping his hands on a rag. His door bells jingled as he shut the door, making Coal think of the Christmas in the Salmon air that he had been paying all too little attention to.

"Caddy's done," Ken said, looking at Ray.

Ray gave a huge grin. "Man, she looks beautiful."

Ken laughed. "I agree. Not anything I did, though. But at least she's running right. Turns like a dream now."

The automobile was a 1957 Eldorado Biarritz, a convertible in General Motors' Lake Placid blue iridescent, with an immaculate white top and four tires whose walls were almost completely white, as if all of the black had been frightened away. The car was long and sleek, the hallmark of any Cadillac, with two huge fins on the rear fenders that resembled the backs of breaching dolphins.

Coal made a slow circle of the car, gawking at it. Any man who admired great beauty in an automobile couldn't help it.

"You seem to be staring," remarked Ray with a grin.

"I can't deny that."

"Well, what do you think? Be honest."

"Surprised you didn't go for red or white."

"Could've had a red," Ray admitted. "But I don't really like to be showy."

Coal let out a hard laugh. "Yeah, I can tell! Well, I almost don't know what to say, Ray. Wow. I can't say that I've ever seen a prettier car. These were almost eight thousand dollars way back when they were built, weren't they?"

"More," said Ray proudly. "And I'll show you why." He pointed to a brass box located on the hump between the floor pans, in front of the front seats. "See that? It's a special sensor I ordered that detects rain or moisture in the air and automatically closes the top."

Coal had no words. He could only utter another laugh of unbelief. He looked over at Maura, but the dour look on her face soured him to saying anything.

Ray slapped the top of the hood. "A three sixty-five under here, three hundred twenty-five horsepower—which is a damn good thing, because this baby weighs in around forty-nine hundred pounds. Power windows, power search radio, power seats, air conditioning. I mean, buddy, G.M. put everything in this baby! You've gotta go for a ride with me."

"I would have been heart-broken if you never asked." He looked again at Maura.

"I have twenty minutes," she reminded him.

"We'll do it in less."

"I'll get in back," she said without looking at him.

Ken stood and watched them drive off, after Ray paid twelve dollars for the repairs, seven dollars for the water pump, and eighteen dollars for the brand-new whitewall tire—after all, he had had to have it shipped special all the way from Idaho Falls.

Ray only drove up and down Main a couple times, rather than out on the highway, which was all right with Coal—and certainly would be with Maura. As much as Coal enjoyed the Caddy, his priority was trying to find out all he could about Bern Hargis's murder as fast as he was able, and getting Maura to work before he had any other murders to deal with—foremost his own. A longer ride could wait. Now that word was out about the murder, including Jim Lockwood's possible involvement, there were all kinds of terrible scenarios running around in Coal's head as to what could happen in the next few days prior to Christmas.

They stopped in front of McPherson's, and Coal jumped out and let Maura slide out of the back. He had a strange urge to give her a kiss, but he refrained. He didn't need to. She gave him one instead, on the cheek. She followed it with a hug that warmed him down to his toes and left him wondering why the sudden change in her—and why the first kiss, here in front of the world?

She stepped away. "I hope you're going to be okay."

"Thanks, Maura." He had wanted to ask about her treatment of Ray. He sure wasn't going to now.

"I'll be off at six."

"And I'll be here."

"I've heard that before."

He grinned. "I'll be here. With bells on."

She reached out and squeezed his fingers, and he felt for a moment like maybe there was still a chance for them.

He watched her into the store because a red-blooded man couldn't not. Then he climbed into the Caddy, looking straight ahead and trying to hide the stupid look on his face.

"She's something," Ray said.

"Yeah. She sure is that."

There was more that lay between them about Maura PlentyWounds, but Ray had the couth not to bring it up right then, and Coal blissfully didn't care.

* * *

Ray drove back to Ken's, where they picked up the GMC, and then Ray followed Coal in the Cadillac back out to Savage Lane and left it parked there, for safe keeping, before they headed back to the Hargis dairy.

This time it was only the two of them, for even though Coal would have liked to see Jordan Peterson get some good experience in investigations, Jordan was nearly worn out from working as much as had been required of him lately, and Coal was going to need a well-rested man in the county tonight. The rowdy element of Salmon was not going to sleep, regardless of whatever dire trouble one of its most beloved citizens was in.

Driving back toward the highway, Ray looked at Coal. "I don't know much about your judge, Coal, but… What do you make of his reaction when you asked about the warrant involving Phil Harringer?"

A surge of adrenaline seemed to explode in Coal's stomach. He shook his head, throwing a glance at Ray. "I don't know. Did that seem strange to you too?"

"It did. But like I said, I don't know him."

"Well, Harringer seems to be pretty powerful in this valley, or at least he sure thinks so. And as you can see, he has more than his share of money. Maybe Sinclair's scared of him."

Ray gave a little conciliatory shrug, mostly with his eyebrows. "Huh. Yeah, I guess maybe. How well do you know the judge, if you don't mind me asking?"

"Not well."

"Okay. So… Well, I just can't help but think maybe Harringer had too much to do with getting him elected or something. You think? Maybe?"

Coal nodded thoughtfully as they drove over the Lemhi River and then turned into Hargis's lane. "Anything's possible. Not much we can do about it, though, even if that's true."

"No. I guess not. But I've just got a bad hunch about this Harringer fellow, and I haven't even met him."

This time Coal looked over and met Ray's eyes, letting the pickup track along in the muddy ruts. "So… What exactly are you saying?"

"Well, I guess it all depends on what we find here at Hargis's place, but… I sure don't think we should rule out Harringer. Not after what you've said."

"What is that, exactly?"

"Well, when Harringer made his threats, it sounds like he was pretty cold and calculated, where when Jim made his, he was in the heat of battle. In my experience, a man who makes threats when he's calm is more likely to go through with them than the man who makes them because he's ticked off."

Coal nodded. He agreed with Ray, but agreeing and getting the judge to change his mind, strictly on the tone of the comments Harringer had made during Coal's investigation, might be two widely separated things.

"I won't give up on pursuing what I can, Ray, but I have a hunch that's going to be an uphill battle."

By this time, they had pulled into the yard, and Coal stopped the pickup fifty feet out from the house, where the yard was wide open. "What do you think? Okay to park here?"

Ray looked around, studying the layout. At last, he nodded. "Sure, good as any place. We can start out taking photographs from right here, in fact."

After taking photographs around the yard, with no young heeler in sight, and his older compatriot sitting near the house and staring at them with only an occasional flap of his tail against the ground, Coal hollered out, and Sherlene Hargis soon appeared in the front doorway. She looked out toward them, saying nothing.

"Well, come on," Coal told Ray, and they walked closer. Coal stopped in front of the woman, holding up his piece of paper between thumb and forefinger, letting it flap in the tiny breeze.

"Ma'am, this is a search warrant."

"A what?"

"A search warrant. I'm sorry for any inconvenience, but we have to start our evidentiary search right here at your property."

Sherlene's gaze faltered, but she tried to maintain eye contact. "But he was found somewhere else. Why would you need to search here?"

Ray Christian cut in: "Ma'am, there is too much to explain, but if you would like you might want to contact an attorney. We really need to search your property, because this is the last place we know about where anyone saw your husband alive. But we'll be quick about it, all right?"

Sherlene had turned to stare at Ray. It was obvious she was torn now about who to give her attention to. She looked at Coal again. "Do you think I killed him?" He detected a slight quiver to her voice.

"No, ma'am. Well, at least . . . Ma'am, you just have to understand that until we get further into our investigation and have done a thorough search for evidence, *everyone* is going to be on our list of suspects. It doesn't mean we think you did it. But we have to go slowly to rule people out. It's just a technicality."

Sherlene stared at Coal and blinked rapidly until she couldn't hold his gaze, and her eyes fell away. Like a dog who knew it was about to taste the whip, she nodded. "Are you searching the inside of the house too?"

"Yes, ma'am." Ray just nodded affirmation.

"Well, there aren't any lights," she offered.

"What do you mean?"

"Bern was having a problem with the power company, and they said they were going to cut off our power. Yesterday morning, before you came, they shut everything off. Don't even have a stove to cook on now—just the wood stove."

Coal thought back to the darkness in the house when he went in to use the phone. Now it made sense. It was going to be impossible to do an effective search for evidence inside that place. It was dark as a bear's belly. With this knowledge, he thought of calling Judge Sinclair again. But then he remembered his friend Leif Sellers had been working at the power company the last time he was in town. He didn't know if Sellers owed him any favors, but maybe Sellers wouldn't remember either.

Fortunately, the phone was still operational inside the house, and although Coal cringed once again to have to touch it, he got permission from Sherlene Hargis to make a phone call, and after taking the phone book outside to look up the power company's number, he stumbled back through the dark house to the phone and called to ask for Leif. As luck would have it, he was on another job, but the secretary said she would have him come out and make contact with him at the Hargises' as soon as possible.

In the meantime, Coal and Ray started their search on the outside the house. Coal went to the right, while Ray went left. Coal stopped at the right rear corner of the house and stared at the ground. What appeared to be a large area of dried up blood stained the ground there. When Ray got around to him, he pointed at the spot.

Ray crouched down and dug in the hard dirt with the blade of his pocket knife. He looked up at Coal, and their eyes locked. Even in the cold ground, the blood had soaked in maybe a quarter inch, and it was every bit as big around as a couple of tortillas melded together.

"That's a good deal of blood," said Coal.

Ray stared at him for a moment longer. The look on his face seemed to be one of confusion. "Uh . . . Yeah, you're right. Quite a bit." He looked back down and swept the area with his gaze. "You don't happen to have one of those baggies, do you?"

Wordlessly, Coal pulled the backpack from the shoulder where he had slung it. He unzipped one pocket and pulled out a baggie, handing it down to Ray, who first stepped back and took a few photos with Coal's camera, which he had slung around his neck, and then dug up a portion of the dark earth and scooped it into the bag with the knife blade. He used a twist tie to close it, then stood up and handed it to Coal.

Having found this large area of obvious blood loss, they backtracked to the front of the house, and now, with something concrete in mind to look for, they were able to follow a trail of blood drops all the way back to the front door, most of them no bigger than the head of a six penny nail. There were even some faint splatters on the concrete pad. All of this, Ray took photos of.

Coal and Ray hardly spoke.

At that point, Coal scanned the yard and the barn and outbuildings. "That blood… That's a lot," Coal said again. Ray nodded. "Do you suppose he was killed right here? Head wounds bleed like there's no tomorrow."

Ray gave a shrug. "If he was… Well, we should know something when we go through the house. Whatever happened was inside the house, judging by the blood trail. But why would he leave the house and go around to the side and bleed out?"

"Why would anyone do anything?" Coal replied. "You're the detective."

Ray managed a laugh. It had a shaken sound to it. "Yeah, of course. Speaking of which, there's one more thing."

"What's that?"

"Well, you saw that hole in Hargis's head."

"Yeah."

"Okay, so I've seen a lot of people do a lot of strange, unbelievable things with a bullet in the heart or lungs or somewhere. But a hole in the head that big? I'm having a hard time picturing somebody walking out of the house and clear around to the back with a hole like that in his head."

Coal nodded. "Good point. That's why you're the detective."

With no better idea of how to proceed, Coal took Ray to watch Sherlene, Leroy, and Moby while he went out and nosed around in the barn and behind the house and all the other buildings, looking for vehicles. There was nothing of any consequence but the vehicles he and Ray had already seen. He had Sherlene open the trunk of Hargis's car, which was empty, of blood or any other evidence. When he did the same with Leroy's, as the trunk came all the way up and rocked to a stop, his heart seemed to jump. There, smeared just inside the trunk lid and splattered profusely inside, was obvious blood, and in one place, half-hidden underneath a toolbox, was a flaky, dried up pool.

Coal looked up at Leroy, and Leroy froze.

CHAPTER TWENTY-THREE

Reading Leroy's body language and his facial expression, Coal slowly raised his hand up until it encircled the butt of his .357. Leroy licked his lips. His left eyelid twitched.

"Something you want to tell me about, Leroy?"

"No sir."

"You know you aren't under arrest, right?"

Leroy swallowed. "Yeah, I guess so."

"All right. So I'm thinking this looks like blood in your trunk. In fact, I'm sure it is."

This time Leroy only stared. Sherlene and Moby, who stood behind either of his shoulders, stared too. But Moby was staring at his feet.

"Want to tell me why there's blood in the trunk of your car, Leroy?" Coal pressed.

"I don't know." Leroy's eyes widened, then narrowed again, and his gaze slid away.

"Well, I'm going to take a sample of this blood with me." Coal's hand tightened on the butt of the gun. Leroy stood seven feet away. Warding him off if he made a move was going to take a good kick to the solar plexus before Coal would have time to draw his gun. But the truth was, that kick would likely be enough. A good blow there was more effective at extinguishing the fight in a man than a blow to the privates.

"Do you understand what I'm saying, Leroy?"

"I guess so." The young man suddenly cringed and grabbed at his ribs. On the moment, his hand fell abruptly away.

"They'll test this blood, and it will show a blood type. The coroner did the same with Hargis's body, so pretty soon we'll know his type. Still nothing you want to tell me?"

Leroy shook his head. He looked over at Moby, who sensed the look and tried to meet it but couldn't. Coal looked at Sherlene, who was staring at the two young men. In spite of himself, a feeling of hope was starting to come over him. Could these two, or at least Leroy, by himself, be the killer? Could finding Jim Lockwood innocent be this easy?

"Does anyone have anything they'd like to say?" Coal asked, hand still on his gun butt.

Sherlene continued to stare at Leroy and Moby. "Boys?"

Moby's eyes flickered up toward her, then back down. His face seemed paler than before. Leroy looked at her and said, "It ain't nothin', ma'am. Probably just blood from some geese I shot last year."

Coal pierced Luther with his eyes. "Geese, huh? Last year? That's the story you want me to write down?"

Leroy nodded, seeming to gather courage. It was only distractedly that he made a strange face and pawed at his side again, wincing. "Yeah, that's it. Some geese."

Coal nodded. Stepping back, he pulled the backpack off his left shoulder with just the use of that hand, holding it out to Ray. "Ray, grab a sample of that blood, would you?"

While Ray was taking care of the blood sample, Coal studied the tires on the car, and he felt up under the fenders. There was mud on both, but it appeared to be the exact same mud as in the yard, and the amount under the fenders wasn't enough for this to have been the vehicle used to dump the body. This car wouldn't have been able to climb into and out of Wimpey Creek anyway. Coal shrugged off his faint disappointment. But none of that meant the blood wasn't Hargis's, anyway. This vehicle might simply have been used to transfer the body to another one, with four-wheel-drive.

There was no other evidence to be found, either around the outside the house or in the outbuildings. No murder weapon, no blood in any other vehicle.

Coal was trying to decide what to do next when he saw a power company truck coming up the road. He held up a hand for the truck to stop when it was near the GMC. A middle-aged man with a walrus mustache and huge sideburns got out and waved at Coal, then started walking his way.

As Leif Sellers got close, a big grin came to his face. "Hey, Coal! Welcome home, buddy!"

Coal smiled back and walked close enough to shake hands. "Hi, Leif. You're looking good. That's a great set of chops."

Sellers let out a laugh. "Yeah, you know, man—it's all the rage. Where are yours?"

Coal grinned. "Well, that's the one place I can't grow decent hair. Luckily, that saves me from looking like a dork."

Sellers laughed again, then let his eyes slide toward Sherlene and the two young men. The humor quickly left his face, and he lowered his voice. "Is her ass of a husband around?"

Coal shook his head. "You haven't heard? He's dead."

A shocked look came into Sellers's eyes, but it was quickly pushed away. "Oh! Hey, I heard there was a murder, but I never heard who it was. Dang!"

"Yep. Gone. Just like that. Listen, Leif, I'm going to need to have you get their power back on. We're trying to serve a search warrant inside the house, and I can't see a wooly mammoth in that place."

With one of his typical grins, Sellers came back with, "Maybe there's not one in there! But if you still need to look . . ."

Coal chuckled. "I do."

"All right, boss. Give me a few minutes."

Coal and Ray waited while Sellers monkeyed up the power pole and tied in. Within ten minutes, he hollered down. "Should be on now!"

He scaled back down the pole to where Coal stood as Ray stepped just inside the front door of the house and flipped the nearest light switch. Coal could see the room inside the front door get lighter, and even from twenty feet away he heard Ray swear.

"Coal? You'd better come over here."

"Wait!"

It was Sherlene Hargis whose agitated voice had stopped Coal from walking to the house. He turned and looked at her, casting a quick glance toward her son and his friend.

"Do you need to say something?"

"Yes. About the house."

He turned fully to her. "What about it?"

"It . . . It's . . . bloody."

"It's *bloody?"* He looked over at his friend Leif Sellers. Sellers shrugged. The look on his face was bewildered.

"Yes, bloody. My husband shot the dog."

Coal stared into her eyes for several seconds. That comment had blindsided him. "The *dog?"*

"Yes. Our heeler. He was... You know, my husband was mad at me, and . . . And so . . . So the dog didn't like it, and he growled at him and bit his leg. Bern started bleeding, and he went and got his gun. He shot the dog, and it ran outside."

"Outside where?" asked Coal.

"There." Leroy pointed toward the corner of the house where Coal had seen the blood.

"You're sure that was the dog?" Coal asked. He had started to believe nothing these people said, and to believe more and more everything Jim Lockwood had said. It was the muddy boots, truck, and tires, and of course the broken watch that Coal kept coming back to, in spite of everything else. Could Jim and all of these people possibly have been involved in this together?

"I need to see the house," Coal reaffirmed.

Sherlene looked beaten. "Okay."

Before Coal made it to the house, walking alongside a petrified looking Sherlene Hargis, he heard another vehicle pull onto the Hargises' lane and head his way. Under his breath, he said, "What is this, Grand Central Station?"

He turned around to see an ugly white Travelette slopping its way along the muddy ruts. "Oh, Judas. Now what?"

Sherlene looked over at Coal, then back at the truck. Maura, obviously taking her cue from the fact that both Coal and Leif Sellers had parked in the same area, pulled the Travelette up there and got out. Before Coal knew what was going on, two cannon balls shot out of the truck behind her and started running around the yard. The cannon balls were Dobe and Shadow, doing some exploring until suddenly they caught his scent and stopped to scan the property. The moment they saw him, they charged his way to give a proper greeting.

"Hold on a minute, Mrs. Hargis," said Coal without looking toward her. "I need to see what this is about." He yelled out to Ray to wait for him, then walked out to meet Maura halfway. The dogs, of course, had long since reached him and were sniffing at his hands and rubbing against him, showing their master what true love was all about. But with Maura walking toward him in her tight jeans, it was all Coal could do even to acknowledge them.

The look on the woman's face as she got close was one of gladness melted into a pot of caution. She searched his eyes, ostensibly waiting for him to break the silence between them.

"What's up? Come to join the circus?"

His words would have been an invitation to joviality, but he guessed she must have read the clearer message in his eyes, one of surprise that he was sure could only be seen faintly through a veneer of irritation. He had been told that he was terrible at hiding his feelings and that they showed on his face as clear as a hand-painted map.

"Well, Scott showed up down at the store because he read the schedule wrong. He lives fifteen miles out of town down the river, so instead of making him go all the way home I volunteered to let him have my shift and I'll just take his tomorrow instead."

"And the dogs…" He couldn't hide the question in his voice.

"Well, your mom had to come and get me to take me back and get Ebenezer, and she came with the dogs, so I just…" A look on her face that wanted to be one of happiness mixed with anticipation sluffed away, and her shoulders slumped a little. Her hands now hung tight at her sides. "I guess I shouldn't have come, right?"

Coal, you're an ass. He said the words only in his mind, but he guessed she might be thinking them too. "No! No, I'm glad you came. I just… No, I was just surprised, that's all."

A mask had covered her face. "Well, yeah, that was kind of the plan."

"It was a good one," he managed to reply.

"Things aren't going good, are they?" Maura asked suddenly, nodding toward the house.

He frowned. "This whole thing is a mess. I don't know how I'm ever going to sort it all out."

"Any hope yet for Jim?"

Coal shrugged. "Yeah, actually. At least I think so. But I still can't explain the watch and several other things. And then there's the fact that he told Hargis he was going to kill him, and he kept on telling Betty that all the way back to their house."

The dogs had charged away by now, and they were running around over by the dead cottonwood trees, both of their noses fast to the ground. Suddenly, Shadow stopped to pay particular attention to one place and began to dig.

"Shadow! No!" The barked command made Maura jerk, and he looked at her sheepishly. "Sorry." Before she could react, he turned back to Shadow and Dobe. "Shadow! Dobe! Come!"

Dobe bolted his way. Shadow, after one last intent sniff where she had started digging, followed her buddy back to the man whose every command she knew she must obey.

Coal put his hands on both of the dogs' heads and looked at Maura. "Hey, will you hold these guys for a second?" He turned and hollered toward the house for Ray, and then before his deputy could respond, he walked briskly toward where Shadow had stopped to dig.

His German shepherd loved to dig. Between digging and shedding, he didn't know what pursuit she excelled at most. Before they had started keeping her in the house in her older age, to decorate all their furniture with a fringe of fine tan hairs, she had dug some holes in the back yard they easily could have buried her in. But digging was only something she did out of boredom, and as she had just descended from Maura's truck into a new area to explore, she had hardly found time to be bored yet. That was the thing that had Coal intrigued.

When he reached the place, it was obvious. Blood. A lot of it. He swore. He began to pivot, scanning the area around him. What he was looking for was a blood trail, something that led either to this place or away from it.

But maybe there was no reason to look. By the amount of blood that had been shed right on this spot, perhaps whoever had left it had both been wounded and died—right here on this little piece of Hargis Dairy real estate.

CHAPTER TWENTY-FOUR

"Flo, I need you to do me a favor. Can you look up a gentleman by the name of Eric Hansen and give him a call? Tell him I need his help out here as soon as possible, and to bring his dogs."

Coal was sitting in the front seat of the pickup talking to his lead dispatcher over the radio while Ray Christian stood out by the blood, studying the ground around it.

A few minutes later, Coal heard the scratchy sound of his radio speaker opening up, following by Flo's voice. *Salmon dispatch to Sheriff Savage.*

"Go ahead," he said disconnectedly into the mic.

Is there any way you can give me a call? What Mr. Hansen said wasn't good.

Frustrated, Coal growled back, forgetting to temper the sound of his voice, "What did he say?"

He said to tell you he doesn't work for free anymore.

Coal snapped the button down on the mic. "Please tell him I don't expect him to. I just need him."

Yes sir, I actually told him that. He said . . . Sir, I don't suppose you could call me on the phone.

Lack of patience was quickly turning to anger for Coal. Why did people have to bother him with stupid things? "Flo! The phone here is . . . Hey, can you just tell me what he said?"

A long pause. Flo must be trying to compose herself, or maybe she was simply thinking of a gentle way to relay Hansen's message. *Sheriff, he just said it may be a cold day, but it isn't a cold day in . . . Well, you know.*

Coal jerked the mic away and stared at it. Then he hit the button again, prepared to yell into it. He managed to stop, looked out at Ray, then over at Maura and the dogs. At last, he started laughing. He punctuated the laughter with a couple of curse words.

"Thanks, Flo. Why don't I just call you?"

Immediate reply: *Why don't you call me, Sheriff?*

Coal had a gut feeling his dispatcher hung up her microphone with a laugh.

Stepping out of the cab, he slammed the door, and it rang against the house and outbuildings and lost itself in the dense trees masking off the river. He tramped along the wet ground to Maura and the dogs, and after looking down for a moment at the hopeful looking faces of Dobe and Shadow, with her flag of a tail thrashing and Dobe's stub wriggling, he laughed. He gave them both a brisk scrub of the head and ears, then swore out loud and looked up at the woman.

"And if you tell my mom I said that I won't ever let you ride me again. I mean *with* me!" he corrected, blushing.

"Freudian slip?" Maura questioned. He didn't have a word for the look in her eyes other than perhaps mischievous. Whatever it was, he kind of liked it. And he liked this feeling that maybe he and the woman were reclaiming some of their previous fun banter, in spite of the bad situation.

"Don't use your big city words on me," he teased.

"Oh, yeah! Because I grew up in such a big city."

He chuckled. "Come on. I've got to make a couple of phone calls. And I guess you might as well see the inside of the stink house." He yelled over to Ray to follow them, and together they filed over to the house.

Coal took several deep breaths of the cold, fresh outside air and prepared to gag away his appetite. Sherlene and her son, along with Leroy, were all standing beside the front door, having been ordered by Ray not to set foot inside the house. Even in his distracted state, Coal couldn't help but be disturbed by the look on Leroy's face, a look he couldn't quite define. But if he had to pick a word, it would be painful.

"I need to make some phone calls."

"Okay," replied Sherlene. "Sheriff?"

"What?"

"Never mind."

It was significant that she didn't ask him what they had found out by the line of cottonwoods. It seemed like any normally curious person would have.

Leaving Ray and the dogs with the Hargises and Leroy Yarwood, Coal flicked his fingers for Maura to follow him, and they started into the house. Immediately, Coal began to see the blood. The prints of several bloody fingers on a doorframe. More on the edge of a hutch. A brown smear left in the middle of the hall by a badly carried out swipe of a rag. In short, as he walked and looked around, it looked like some half blind person had attempted to clean up a slaughterhouse with a toothbrush—a half blind person, or someone working in a house with no electric lights.

He had third and fourth thoughts about the phone.

Taking a latex glove out of his hip pocket, he shoe-horned it onto his right hand; they didn't make gloves in his size, apparently. He went to the phone, trying to keep the high level of disgust from his face when he looked at Maura, whose whole countenance shone with distaste and a look like she had just walked into an overheated frat house five hours after a chili-eating contest. He had to fight back a grin.

He picked up the handset of the phone and lay it on the desk with his gloved hand, then dialed Flo with the same hand. Busy signal. Again, he swore, the same outhouse word. He didn't even apologize to Maura.

"Busy?"

"Yep."

She stood there for a few seconds, studying him. "You told me once that I shouldn't swear in front of you because you didn't swear in front of me."

He stared at her just for a moment before blurting out his canned answer: "The hell I did."

She giggled, but even so, he frowned and let out a big sigh. "You're right, Maura. I'm sorry. That's not how I was raised, and I won't let it happen again. Thanks."

She gave him a close-lipped smile and reached out to rub his arm. "It's all right. Just keeping you on the strait and narrow."

He tried the number again. It was busy again, and again he almost swore. He looked at Maura just in time and stopped with a word on the tip of his tongue. It tasted bad leaving it there, so he swallowed it, and that tasted worse.

She let out another giggle. "It hurts, doesn't it?"

"Not as bad as breathing through my nose in this house hurts."

She gave a grunt of hearty agreement.

Coal was about to go back out to the truck radio and yell at his dispatcher, and Maura knew it as he turned toward the door. She caught his arm and gave him a patient smile. "Come on, grumpy. Give her a minute. Maybe she's taking another call."

Again she was right, and so again he waited and sighed. Finally, taking a deep breath of air that shouldn't be breathed by mankind, he dialed the number once more. This time it rang.

It immediately came off the hook. *Salmon dispatch.*

"Flo. The number's been busy." It was the least accusatory thing he could think of to say.

Yes, Sheriff. I'm sorry. Another call came in. Uh . . .

Coal didn't like the tone of her voice. There was something she needed to say, and she wasn't saying it. "What is it, Flo? Who called?"

Sheriff, it was the attorney general's office. His secretary. She said it's urgent for you to call him back immediately.

"She didn't say what it's about?" The words had no sooner left Coal's lips than suddenly a bad feeling came over him. Maybe he didn't *want* to know what it was about.

No. Nothing. But she sure didn't sound very nice.

Coal drew in another deep breath, trying to calm himself, trying to block out all of the bad thoughts that were trying to crowd in. "Okay, I'll go back to the courthouse when I'm done here and call. But I need Eric Hansen's number first."

Okay, Sheriff, but just so you know, he's not happy.

Coal nearly laughed. "Yeah, so I gathered."

She gave him the number, and they disconnected with a short good-bye.

Coal dialed Eric Hansen's phone number. It rang seven times before picking up. *Yeah!*

"Hansen?" Coal queried.

Yeah, who's this? The sheriff?

"Yeah, Sheriff Savage."

Okay, well I already told your dispatcher the answer's no. I'm tired of bein' jerked around by the government. I don't work cheap, and I sure don't work free. You need to find yerself somebody else. There's other hounds around here.

"Hansen, hang on a minute, all right? I don't know what happened before. But I'll make it right."

Didn't you hear me? There's other hounds.

"Hansen, there sure are other hounds out there. Cougar hounds, bear hounds, and some coon hounds. But I need man hounds. And more important, I need the man behind the hounds. Hansen, it's you I really need. I don't like to beg, but the well-being of somebody I believe to be an innocent man is hanging in the balance here. I can't trust this to anyone but you."

Lengthy pause. *Who's the somebody?*

Something told Coal he should keep that under his hat. But he couldn't start out this relationship by dishonesty. He was going to have to lay everything on the line. "Jim Lockwood."

No reply from the other end of the line. Finally a sigh. *I figured. I heard the news. I'm not helping, Savage. Good luck.*

Coal had started to reply when he realized the line had gone dead. He held the phone away and stared at it for a moment. The words that were on his tongue would have offended a high seas sailor. He felt

Maura's will. He pursed his lips. He swallowed his words, like swallowing sulfuric acid. He lost his sense and took a deep breath through his nose, then almost gagged. The smell of stale cigarette smoke, grease, dog urine and feces mixed with filthy rugs and decades of cow and pig manure tracked in from outside was even more offensive than the words he had fought so hard to keep back.

He slammed the handset down on the base and turned away, gritting his teeth. Maura tried to put a gentling hand on his arm, but when he kept going she had to bear down with her grip, and she used her other hand as well. "Wait, Coal."

He turned slightly back. "For what?"

She managed to persuade him with her hands to turn fully and face her. "What's this man's name?"

"Eric Hansen?"

"Yeah. Him."

"Eric Hansen," he said, trying out a grim smile.

"Very funny. Can I call him back?"

"Ha! Good luck. He won't even pick it up."

"Can I try?"

Coal made the mistake of looking into her dusky blue eyes. They seemed to be mining into his soul. After he lost the battle of wills, he let out another sigh, then looked around for a moment on the cluttered desk until he found a pencil. He wrote on a used envelope the number he had kept in his head. He held it up to Maura. "Want me to leave, so you can talk dirty to him?"

She shoved his shoulder hard with her fist. "Stop it, ya creep." She fought to hold back a smile. "And you know I only talk dirty to you."

That time she made him chuckle. "I guess I'd forgotten."

She eyed him levelly, a cool, good-humored stare. Then, mumbling something about how *any* conversation held in this house was going to be disgusting and filthy, she turned and picked up the phone, dialing the number on the envelope. Coal wanted to leave, but something made him stay. He could hear, or at least thought he could hear, the phone ringing non-stop. Just when he was certain Maura would disconnect, it picked up, and he heard a man's voice yell into the receiver. Startled, Maura jerked the phone away from her ear. When the yelling subsided, and just when it was probably going to go dead, she spoke sharply into the mic.

"Hey! Please don't hang up."

There was a pregnant pause. Finally, the man's voice again, this time softer. *Who is this?* Coal could hear because she was still holding the phone away from her ear in case Hansen started yelling again.

"Someone who wants to be a friend. My name's Maura."

Whatever Hansen said this time was soft enough that it came to Coal only as mumbling.

"No, it's not a joke. Please, Mr. Hansen, can you at least meet with me for a few minutes? I'll pay you for whatever time you spend and for your mileage to where I am and back."

No sound from the other end that was audible to Coal. He was mad now. Mad that she would offer this aggrieved, volatile piece of work a dime, and that she would do it in such a soft and sweet voice—nothing like the voice he had first heard her use against him, the night of his encounter with the moose. He couldn't bear to see her crawl, so he walked out of the house.

Half a minute later, Maura stepped out to find him sulking several feet out into the yard, just about where air with oxygen in it started again.

He gave her a direct gaze for several seconds, which she held without blinking. She didn't speak. Apparently, she could see the words forming in his eyes, and she wanted to wait for him to stick his foot in his mouth.

"Got yourself a new boyfriend, huh?"

Even for Coal, it was an incredibly juvenile thing to say.

"What? Listen, Coal, I did that for you. Wow. I can't believe you just said that."

"Oh, come on. I was kidding."

She glared ice crystals at his eyes. It was a staring contest he was destined to lose. He took a step closer to her. "Hey. Sorry I'm a jerk. Thanks for calling Hansen for me. Is he coming?"

She took a deep breath, speaking as the air gusted out of her with a sound more of relief than anger. A lucky, timely apology had perhaps avoided another war. "Yeah, he said he'd come over. He said he could only give us a few minutes."

Coal grunted. "Well, I think it might take a lot longer than that."

It was half an hour later, and Coal, Maura, and Ray were sitting in the cab of the idling pickup, to stay warm, when a brown sixties Jeep Wagoneer pulled onto the road and stopped nearby. At a glance, one couldn't tell where the brown paint ended and the myriad splotches of rust began. The front bumper was bent several inches out on one side, and that headlight was shattered.

The Hargis clan was sitting in Leroy's car because Coal had refused to let them go back in the house until the search was complete. There was a thick blue cloud chugging from the tailpipe. When Eric Hansen descended from his Jeep, no one in the Hargis car followed suit. Coal, Maura, and Ray started out to meet him, and Maura managed to work her way into the lead.

She turned to Coal and glared him down. "Could you just wait here for a minute?"

Taken aback, Coal looked at her. He decided to let her have the show, for now. Without saying a word, he and Ray stopped. Ray thrust his hands deep in the pockets of his tan coat, while Coal folded his arms across his chest—his typical stance when he wasn't happy with something. He knew the message it sent people, but for some reason he seemed helpless to stop it. And maybe sometimes it made him feel happy not to look happy.

Maura and Eric Hansen stopped a few feet from each other. Hansen was a little younger than Coal had expected, younger than Coal by at least a few years. His hair was dark, and his beard bushy and long. In a word—overgrown. The beard wasn't becoming, but it wasn't hard to erase it with some imagination and see that Hansen's heavy-set face was handsome, his nose fine, his hazel green eyes expressive. He was dressed in a camouflage coat and black wool pants, with Danners on his feet and a long-barreled, fairly new Ruger Single Six revolver in a hunter holster extending down his right leg.

Maura and Hansen spoke for a few minutes too quietly for Coal to pick it up. A couple of times Hansen glanced past Maura at Coal. The first time, he looked away the moment he saw Coal watching him. The second, he held his gaze for a few seconds. Finally, Maura thrust out her hand for the first time, and the two of them shook. Maura turned and motioned Coal over.

When Coal stopped beside Maura, Hansen studied him with a cool, shrewd eye. He had a savvy look about him, the look of a man who could be hard but also might be a good ally.

"Coal, I guess you've already met Mr. Hansen over the phone," said Maura.

Coal nodded. He wanted to look friendly, but after Hansen's attitude on the phone he wasn't feeling it, and it was something he'd never been able to force. "Howdy, Mr. Hansen."

Hansen sighed. A half-amused look came into his eyes, but not to his mouth. "All right. First off, I'm not *Mister* anything. You were doing better on the phone earlier. You can call me Hansen or Eric, if you want. Or some people like to call me Trax—with an X. I'm not going to stand on ceremony."

Coal studied him a little longer. "I never had anything to do with anything that happened to you, Eric. Is that right, or am I forgetting something?"

Hansen shook his head. He bunched up his lips. "No, you're right. I was kind of short with you earlier. I just don't usually hit it off that well with people who wear badges."

Coal nodded. "Understood. If it's all right with you, I'd like to start all over." He stepped closer and put out his hand in a peace offering. "Coal Savage, if you don't remember. You can call me Coal."

Hansen almost smiled as he reached out and took Coal's hand. "So your dad's pretty much a legend around these parts," he said as his hand fell away from their grasp.

Coal allowed himself a little smile. "Some people tell me that. He's been gone a long time."

"Legends never die," Hansen quipped.

Coal chuckled. "No, I guess not." On an afterthought, he introduced Ray. Then Hansen asked about the case and what Coal needed.

Before replying, Coal looked over to see a much larger German shepherd than Shadow in the front seat of Hansen's Jeep, with a couple of hounds, a Walker and a blue tick, in the back. All were big, muscular animals, obviously males.

"Those are the boys. The shepherd is Luke. Don't ask why. The blue is Bogart, and the Walker is Clint."

Coal cocked his head and grinned. "Clint?"

His response got a chuckle back from Hansen. "Yeah, my family's all pretty big on the old *Cheyenne* T.V. show. It seemed like a big shame to get a Walker hound and waste the name."

This time Coal gave a laugh. In spite of a rough start, he had a feeling he and Eric Hansen were going to hit it off.

"So what do you need me to do, anyway?"

"Well, Eric, we've got a mess here. Or do you prefer Trax?"

Hansen smiled with one side of his mouth. "It was meant as a joke when it started, but I kind of like it. It says a lot more about me than Eric."

"Trax it is then," agreed Coal.

He went on to tell Hansen about the case in as much detail as he could, and he told what his own untrained dogs had discovered, the newest spot of blood. "That spot's been snowed on, though, and it looks like somebody might even have driven over it a few times. I just don't dare try to make anything of it myself, and you're the best known tracker in this county, so . . ."

Hansen actually smiled, although his lips never parted. "So the old sheriff got himself in a spot. He's sure got a temper. It would be hard to say it surprises me."

Coal's first gut response was anger, but he pushed it aside. After all, Hansen was right.

Hansen told the others to stay back, and leaving his dogs in the Jeep, he slipped off his Danners in favor of a pair of well-worn elk hide moccasins. He began to soft-foot around the area where the blood had been found.

After half an hour, he came back over, not inviting the others into the area he had been working.

"I can see a couple of things you might want to take notes of. One, there were at least two different people who tried to either hide the body or drag it off. The first one had on sneakers, and as far as I can tell he dragged the body for a few feet into the grass, then tried to break off some brush and cover it. Then somebody else with a pair of sharp-toed cowboy boots tried to drag the body off farther but ended up dropping it and running away. There were two or maybe even three other people over there, and every one of their tracks at some point blotted out at least one of the cowboy boot tracks—but the cowboy boot tracks blotted out some of the sneaker tracks. On the other hand, the cowboy boot tracks aren't on top of any of the others, just the sneakers. And later, the sneakers showed back up, but that time on top of the cowboy boots." Hansen stopped for a few seconds, apparently catching on to the lost look in Coal's face. "Confusing enough?"

"Uh . . . Yeah, something like that."

"Sorry. I'm going too fast. Okay, so basically some guy with sneakers was here first, dragged off the body from where it first fell, and tried to cover it up. Then the guy in the cowboy boots came and dragged the body for maybe another fifteen feet. Then I'm guessing maybe the others scared him off—including the guy in the sneakers, coming back for a second time."

Cowboy boots, thought Coal. Like what he wore himself—and so did Hargis's fun-loving neighbor, Phil Harringer. He tried to push away his feeling of elation about Jim Lockwood. Since there was more than one person involved, maybe they had just about proven him innocent, right on the spot. Only there was still nothing to explain Jim's watch, the muddy truck and boots.

"So they tried to drag the body . . ."

"That way," Hansen finished Coal's sentence, jerking a thumb toward the barbwire fence that separated Hargis's property from the line of cottonwoods and from Barracks Lane, which continued on past the Harringer place and then into the yellow grass and sagebrush foothills of the Lemhi Range.

"And which way did the guy in the cowboy boots run off?"

"Same way," said Hansen. "He jumped the fence and headed that way down Barracks Lane."

He pointed.

Right in the direction of the Harringer ranch.

CHAPTER TWENTY-FIVE

Throughout the rest of the search warrant service, Coal couldn't stop thinking about Harringer. They didn't have permission to do any searching on his property, but that fact sure didn't keep Coal from wanting to. However, to do this right he was going to have to wait. If he threw aside the Fourth Amendment, went over there now, and found something damning, the evidence would be ruled inadmissible in court anyway.

Even so, Coal had Trax Hansen follow the cowboy boot tracks up the road to make sure they kept on going toward Harringer's.

The curve was they didn't.

After a while the tracks went back into the brush and grass along Hargis's side of the road, and eventually they lost them. Even after Hansen got his hounds and Luke the German shepherd out of the Jeep, there had been too much moisture and the passage of time working on the tracks for them to follow them to a solid conclusion.

Before they left the area, however, Hansen pointed to one particularly clear track on the edge of the road, mostly in mud rather than gravel. "I'd take a photograph of this track, and put a note somewhere about this. This is his right boot, and you see that ugly nick out of the outer edge of the heel? Somethin' that simple has sealed up a whole murder case before."

They all went back to the house, where Hansen decided of his own accord to stay and help in the search. The house was something out of a bad horror movie. Apparently because the power had been off, although there had been an attempt to clean up all the spilled blood, assumedly either by flashlight or candlelight, it hadn't been effective. There was blood on the floor, on some of the furniture, and even some still in the sink and bathtub.

The only thing Sherlene Hargis kept claiming was that she had struck her husband in the nose, and he had done the same to her, and they both bled a lot. Then he had shot the dog, and he had bled all over the place as well before Sherlene had finally opened the door, and he limped outside and around the corner of the house. That part Coal guessed was true, since the heeler had never shown up again, and there was a large pool where he must have died.

"Can you show me where the dog's body is?" he asked.

Sherlene nodded. "He's buried, but I can show you where."

"Okay. But we might have to dig him up and re-bury him."

That time she frowned but didn't speak.

They took samples of blood in a dozen different locations, noting on each baggie where the blood had come from. They took photos and made sketches of the layout of the house and did anything that Ray could think of that might be useful later in the investigation. Then finally they had to face the inevitable: They still had found no murder weapon and no transport vehicle that matched the tire tracks at the scene, and Coal had to get back to town and make a phone call to Mark Hepner, the attorney general. What in the world could that be about?

Coal assumed that the blood in Leroy's trunk had something to do with the murder, but it was obviously not the transport vehicle that made the trip down into Wimpey Creek. And then there were the fleeing cowboy boot tracks. It was simply too bizarre to think that the Hargises could somehow be involved with Harringer in this whole case. Coal actually felt himself get sick when he realized that if anything the case was more muddled than when he began his search. But the one thing that seemed more hopeful was the thing Coal cared most about: This murder wasn't likely committed by one person, and to him that made the chances of Jim's being guilty seem pretty slim.

The last thing he needed to do was to go home and get his plaster of Paris and make some casts of all the tracks, since he hadn't thought to bring it with him. He needed to get himself more organized.

Saying goodbye to Hansen, he watched him get in the Wagoneer and drive off up the road. Oddly, both of his hounds stayed perfectly quiet as they rolled away. Coal had seen a lot of hounds in his day, and being quiet was not their strong suit.

He turned and looked at Sherlene Hargis, who stood alone because Leroy and Moby had gone out to the milking barn. "I'm going to have to come back, Mrs. Hargis. Try not to disturb things any more than you have to. And I assume the power company will be coming back out later to turn your power back off. Are you sure you can't pay that bill?"

"No, I can pay it," Sherlene admitted. "Bern was just being hard-headed. We have plenty of money."

Coal gave her an odd look. *Plenty of money?* One sure wouldn't have known that by the run-down look of the place. "You'd probably better pay it then. Pretty miserable eating cold food—and even more miserable freezing to death."

Coal drove the pickup away with one last glance toward the milking barn. It gave him a jolt to see Leroy Yarwood standing there staring after them. Moby stood at his side.

* * *

Coal couldn't put off returning the attorney general's call any longer, so he postponed making the casts of the tracks. Maura wanted to stay with Coal, so they convoyed back to the home place to drop off her truck and the dogs. Then on the way into town, Coal, looking straight ahead, said, "Anybody want to grab a bite to eat?"

He felt both Maura and Ray look over at him. It was Ray who finally spoke first. "I guess I am pretty hungry, now that you mention it."

Maura seemed not to think about it as she laid her hand on his leg. "Coal, what about calling the attorney general?"

He gritted his teeth, making his jaw muscles bulge. "What about it? I'll get to it."

They passed the feed store before Maura squeezed with her hand that was still on his leg. "It sounded kind of important, didn't it?"

"Or something," he replied after a moment. "The attorney general can wait."

They stopped at the Coffee Shop and sat down at the front booth. A glance down the deep room showed several people Coal knew, but he only waved their direction as he was sitting. He wasn't in the mood to socialize. In truth, he wasn't really in the mood to eat, either. He wouldn't admit it to anyone, but he was only stalling. His guts told him something bad was in the air. Calling the attorney general would prove it.

Tammy wasn't in today, so Jay Castillo's wife, Carrie, came and took their orders, after Coal got out of his seat and gave her a big hug and they chatted for a bit. Carrie, like her husband, was one of Coal's favorite Salmon people, always full of vigor and spirit, and always ready to jump into political discussions with all her energy. She was also fairly intuitive, and somehow she could tell that Coal wasn't his normal self, so she took the orders and left in a fraction of the time she and Coal would have talked had he been in his usual mood.

Finally, the meal was finished, and Coal checked his watch. It was two forty-five, under a heavily overcast sky. He pulled in a deep breath and picked up the napkin from his lap, throwing it down on the table. "Well, I guess it's time to find out what bur's under the attorney general's saddle."

He slid out of the booth, waiting there for Maura so he could help her put her coat on, and then, leaving a crisp ten dollar bill on the table to pay for their meals and the tip, he led the way outside, hollering goodbye to Carrie and Jay and throwing up a hand in farewell to the diners who flung goodbye greetings after him.

He parked the pickup in the lot of the courthouse. They all got out in a silence accentuated by the rustle of the creek in the gully and trudged inside, stomping their feet at the bottom of the steps out of habit.

The jail was cold. Coal cranked up the radiator and started to make coffee. He didn't get far before he felt Maura beside him, and her hand came out and closed over his as he was scooping coffee out of the can.

"Go make the call. I can do coffee."

He looked over at her, trying to appear calm, and glad she couldn't see how he felt inside. At last, he sighed, glancing over at the phone. Ray was sitting in the chair at his desk. He too was looking at the phone.

Coal took a big breath, walked over and shuffled through his Roll-a-Dex, finding the attorney general's number. He dialed it, and a woman in a nasally voice answered. "Hi, this is Sheriff Savage, over in Salmon. I got a message to call Mister Hepner?"

Oh, yes sir, said the woman through her nose. *I'll go get him. Hold on.*

He heard the phone *clunk* down on her desk. While Christmas kept creeping closer and closer, he waited for the A.G. to get his phone. Apparently, Coal wasn't that important after all. He thought about hanging up and forcing Hepner to call back. He hated self-important people who kept him waiting. He hated—

This is Mark Hepner. Am I speaking with Sheriff Savage?

Or someone who's claiming to be him, Coal wanted to say. "Yes, that's me."

Well, Mister Savage, I regret that I couldn't be there in person, but this needed to be dealt with immediately. The governor is out for the holidays, and I am going to be out myself immediately after this phone call. So I hope you understand why this must be done over the phone.

This must be done? What was he talking about?

"Yes sir," Coal replied. "But I'm not sure what we're doing."

Hepner cleared his throat loudly. Then again. *Well, Mister Savage, I understand from your local judge—Wiley Sinclair, correct? That there has been a miscommunication, and some other problems have arisen as well.*

"How's that?" Coal countered. "What kind of a miscommunication?"

Well first of all, in short, I understand that there was never a swearing-in ceremony when you took office. Is this the case?

That's what he was calling about? Judas priest. They didn't have anything more important to worry about? Coal frowned. Couldn't this have waited until after the holidays?

"Um… Yes, I guess that's true. I'm sorry. No one ever brought it up. Things were pretty hectic when I first got back to the valley. What do I need to do?"

Well . . . Let's hold on just a minute. As I said, some other problems have arisen, so perhaps the swearing-in ceremony would be a bit premature anyway.

Whatever vise was on Coal's heart seemed to tighten. "I'm not sure I understand."

Okay, well I have to be a little blunt here. Without getting into dates and other details, is it true that you willingly and knowingly let a prisoner out of a cell to go downtown and feed himself, and that this prisoner was then attacked by ruffians and in fact died of the wounds they gave him?

In his head, Coal swore. It was coming back to haunt him. He had feared this, but it had taken so long! There was nothing he could do. He couldn't deny it.

"Yes sir, that is what happened." He could explain that letting model prisoners out of their cells to take care of their own nutritional needs was not a new way of doing things in Lemhi County. But in this case, he didn't think it was going to matter. A man had died, and the State would be looking for a scapegoat.

And is it furthermore true that you released the prime suspect in a murder case without conferring with the proper authority, which again would be Judge Sinclair?

Coal was silent for a moment too long, and the man spoke again. *Mister Savage? Are you still on the line?*

"Yeah, I'm here. And yes, I released a prisoner. He lives nearby and isn't a flight risk. He's the former sheriff of Lemhi County." That was more explanation than he felt like giving. He didn't like the sound of this man's voice, and he was quickly finding that he didn't like the man himself.

So you freely admit that these two charges are true. Do you have anything to add?

"Not anything I expect would do me any good." Coal's voice had gone hard and cold. He knew it, Hepner would hear it, and somehow he could do nothing about it. Or maybe he just didn't want to.

All right, Mister Savage. Are you at your office?

"I am."

That's fine. I need to make a quick phone call or two. I would advise you not to leave this phone until you have heard back from me. Do you understand?

By this part of the conversation, Maura's obvious concern over Coal's state of mind had drawn her to put her ear close to his, and she heard this last advice.

Mister Savage. Do you understand?

Coal was thinking about Phil Harringer, who had cost K.T. Batterton his position as sheriff and who had vowed that he could have Coal's job as well. A betting man would have put all his money down on the guess that Harringer had been busy on the phone the past day or so. “Yes,” he replied, too brusquely. “I understand things a little too well.”

Pardon? What was that?

“Hurry if you’re calling back,” Coal said into the transmitter. “I have things to do.”

Then he hung up. And in his guts he knew that his job as sheriff of Lemhi County had come to an end, on the ruthless chopping block of rancher Phil Harringer.

CHAPTER TWENTY-SIX

“So now we have to wait here?”

Maura had heard that part of the conversation pretty plainly.

“Well, that’s what the A.G. says. I never said it.”

“Coal…” He looked down into the woman’s beautiful eyes. Even when he was frustrated and angry and wanting to punch someone in the mouth, her eyes still looked incredible. “Don’t do anything you’re going to regret.”

What Maura meant was that he shouldn’t leave until the attorney general called back. What he heard was that if he didn’t get a search warrant on Phil Harringer’s property *now* it was going to be too late.

He picked up the phone and dialed the judge’s number, which was still sitting on a pad on his desk. No answer. But no busy signal, either. Was the judge only outside? Or was he gone? Coal had to take a chance. He headed for the door.

“Where are we going?” said Maura, as she hurried after him. Even in his anger, he liked how she immediately included herself.

“Back to the judge’s.”

The three of them piled back into the GMC, and Coal sped north on Highway 93. When they were only a mile or so from the judge’s place, they caught up to a black Lincoln Mark IV that inconsiderately insisted on going the speed limit. Coal looked at his speedometer. Fifty-five. On the money. Damnit, he wished Maura wasn't in the vehicle with him. There were so many creative things he needed to say, and all of them were constructed around swear words. He calculated how long it would take to get around the Lincoln and if he would be recognized in that time as the sheriff. And then how would they know he wasn't going on an important call anyway? The fact was, they couldn't. And he was tired of waiting for slow drivers who had nothing important on their schedules. So he gunned it.

As he was coming alongside the Lincoln, and already up to seventy, Ray Christian said one of the words that had been burning a hole in the tip of Coal's tongue. "What?" He looked over distractedly at Ray as they flew past the Lincoln and back over into the right lane before the driver of a white Caprice coming from the other way shook his fist out the window at them.

"Oh, nothing."

"Then what's the cussing about? There's a lady here."

Ray nodded, and his eyes flickered over at Maura. "Sorry, Maura."

"So what are you swearing about?" asked Coal as he veered too fast off the highway and almost took out the judge's mailbox, then splashed through a big puddle of mud in the middle of the road and coated most of a section of the judge's formerly immaculate white fence.

"That was the judge you just passed." Ray said the words almost too quietly, holding onto the dash and staring straight out the windshield.

Coal drove for a moment in dead silence as in the rearview mirror he saw the Lincoln turn into the lane behind them, much more sedately than the pickup had done. He started going through the alphabet in his head, trying to think of a swear word that started with every letter. He did fairly well until he got to *i*.

The pickup had slowed down to the speed of a farm wagon by the time it reached the judge's house, and Coal eased it to a stop and set the brake. The judge's Lincoln rolled in slowly beside them. All of a sudden, it looked an awful lot like a hearse.

All four of them debarked at the same time.

The judge's face was red. He stared over the top of his car at them. Coal thought of all the flowery things he could have said in his own defense. The thought took about two seconds. There *was* no defense for driving like the demons of hell were after him, especially when, as the top lawdog in Lemhi County, he was rocketing past the one man who could throw his butt in a cell.

"Sorry about that display back there, Judge." Coal wondered if his voice sounded as meek as he suddenly felt. It wasn't a feeling he was used to or cherished.

Judge Sinclair drew in a deep breath. His gaze went to Maura and held for a moment. He blinked. Slowly, his eyes came back to Coal, who sensed that his own best self-defense was no defense at all, but the mere presence of a woman with whom the judge was apparently taken—as any red-blooded American would have been.

"May I ask to what I owe that display of . . . *driving ability,* Sheriff?" The *Coal* of earlier was significantly absent.

"Stupidity," Coal said. "I needed to see you fast."

"Well, apparently you didn't see me fast enough."

"No-o." Coal drew the single syllable out into two. "I need you to issue a warrant on the Harringer place," Coal said, surpassing all niceties. After all, he had already apologized, and they were running out of time.

"I thought we talked about that." The judge's eyes went again to Maura, as if he were trying to decide if his admiration of her was enough to keep him from exploding.

"We did, but we found evidence at the Hargises' that makes it look like Harringer is involved. Whoever did it ran from the scene and jumped the fence onto Harringer's road, then ran toward his house." He didn't bother mentioning the fact that he had then also run back onto the Hargis property.

The judge stared at Coal. In his face, Coal could see the wheels of his mind turning.

"You're sure of this?"

"I am. We had the best tracker in this valley helping us."

A gust of breath came out of the judge's mouth. A look of fatal determination came over his face, and the muscles of his jaw bunched. "All right. Then I guess that's that. Come inside."

They stepped once more into the judge's house, and he went to his typewriter, a shiny blue Underwood. As he was setting it up with a crisp new piece of paper, he spoke without looking at them. "Now remember, you are looking for a murder weapon and a vehicle, correct? And apparently whatever proof you need that the tracks you saw actually belonged to Mister Harringer—which I assume will include finding boots to match the tracks. The moment you find these things, the search is over. Understood? Or is there anything else?"

"No," said Coal. "Nothing else I can think of. Boots, a vehicle, and a weapon."

The judge started typing, but he only got five or six sentences before the phone rang. His honor looked over at it irritably. Coal looked at it frantically. Maura and Ray stared at Coal. By the looks of dread on their faces, they both knew what he was going to do.

Coal's heart was in his throat. "Do you want me to get that for you so you can keep typing?"

The judge, his fingers frozen on the keys of his typewriter, stared at him. "Yes, would you just take a message real quick? Thank you."

Coal walked over and grabbed the phone off the hook on the sixth ring. "Hello?"

Is this Judge Sinclair? said a voice that only half an hour earlier Coal had been blissfully unaware even existed.

"Hello?" he repeated.

Yes, hello. Hello, can you hear me? I'm looking for Judge Sinclair."

"Huh," Coal grunted, and the black handset rattled back down on the receiver. "Dead silence."

The judge looked over distractedly. "Well, sometimes I get strange calls like that. I often wonder if it's someone I sentenced, just harassing me." He looked back at his fingers for a moment to gather his thoughts, then went on typing. Coal stared at the phone. He looked at the plug going into the back of it. He had to unplug that. He reached his hand out slowly, feeling both Maura's and Ray's eyes glued to him.

The ring of the phone made Coal jerk and almost swear. He looked over at the judge, who suddenly shoved back his chair. "Oh, I'll just get it. Maybe they're dying to hear my voice. Hold on."

As Coal stood frozen, Judge Sinclair walked over and lifted the phone off the base, bringing it to his ear. For a moment, he held it there, seeming unsure whether or not even to answer.

Then he said, "Hello? Oh, yes, hello, Mister Hepner." A few moments passed. Then: "Well, that's strange. I had company, and I was busy, so I had him answer it. He said it was just silence."

Coal stared. What was he was going to say if the judge accused him of lying about the call? Fifteen seconds passed while the judge listened intently to the caller.

"Well, yes, as I said earlier, he did release Mister Lockwood, but he told me about it later, and I told him— Well, yes sir. Yes sir. I know, sir, but—"

A look of angry frustration came over the judge's face as he glanced over and met Coal's eyes.

"Yes sir . . . Yes sir . . . Yes, I think that is about how it happened … Yes sir, but that is a pretty well-known way of— What's that again? No, sir. No. Yes, perhaps a questionable practice. I suppose that's correct."

Coal was ready to grab the phone out of the judge's hand and tell Attorney General Mark Hepner exactly what he thought of his family lineage. He glanced over at the search warrant for Phil Harringer's property, still in the typewriter, half-typed. Something inside him fell. Sick to his stomach, he looked back at the judge, who continued talking into the phone.

"Well, yes sir, but it *is* almost Christmas, after all, and I seriously don't think there's any risk that he'll try to leave— No. No, sir. I understand. Yes, I understand. First of the year." Suddenly, the judge looked as sick as Coal felt. "I will meet with him, yes. As soon as I see him. I'll let him know. Yes sir, I will. I expect to hear from him soon. Yes. Thank you. Merry Christmas to you too."

For ten or fifteen seconds after it was obvious there was no longer anyone on the other end of the line, Judge Sinclair kept the phone to his ear. He finally sucked in a big breath, and the handset of the phone drifted down without apparent purpose to the base. It settled in like a petrel alighting in the rocks, and his hand remained there on it, as if it must be held in place or would take wing again and escape. He looked over at the piece of paper in his typewriter, and then at last up at Coal.

"How strange that the phone was silent when you answered it. I could hear it fine."

Coal made a facial shrug. No other defense could be better than his silence.

"So . . . That was Attorney General Hepner. Coal, he, uh . . . Coal, you are to be suspended until a hearing can be held. And Jim Lockwood is to be returned to jail."

Coal's face was still. His heart beat like it was working in molasses. "Why should Jim be in jail? We both agreed—"

"Because Mister Hepner's an ass," the judge cut him off.

Coal was silent for a moment. "Until when?"

A smirk came to the judge's face. "Until forever, I suppose. He'll always be an ass."

Coal really wanted to laugh at that. It actually was funny, and it was the first attempt at real humor he had ever heard Judge Sinclair make. He just couldn't find his supply of laughs, or even a polite chuckle.

"Until after the first of the year," the judge finally said.

"And Christmas?"

"They don't care. After all, *they'll* be home with *their* families."

"When does this happen?" asked Coal.

"I told him I would let you know as soon as I hear from you—whenever that might be."

Coal stared at the judge. The judge did not blink. Coal was trying hard to grasp what he meant by his words. If Coal had spoken the same words, it would have been with a very obvious double meaning. Was he to expect that kind of talk from *his honor?*

The judge walked back over to the typewriter and slumped down in front of it. He started typing on the warrant, his fingers ponderous on the keys. A feeling of hope rose in Coal's chest. But then the judge slouched forward, his head falling into the palms of his hands. He scrubbed at his hair and pushed it back on his head. Finally, he sat up straight again and huffed out a big breath.

"All right, let's face it. There's no use." With those words, he tore the half-finished warrant from the typewriter and wadded it up, throwing it like a hand grenade into a round trash can beside his desk. "Once again,

Phil Harringer—" He stopped himself mid-sentence, and his eyes darted over to Coal. Finally, he slapped the arm of his chair.

Judge Sinclair stood up and turned to look at Coal, Maura, and Ray. His gaze settled on Coal. "So I told that— I told Mister Hepner I would relay everything as soon as I saw you. Between now and whenever I *do* see you, I don't suppose I'd have any control over whatever happens in the case of Jim Lockwood." He stared into Coal's eyes, trying to drill his meaning home.

"Sorry, Judge," Coal said. "I want to understand your meaning, but I don't dare. I don't want to get either one of us in more boiling water than we already are."

Sinclair nodded and let out a sigh. "Understood. I'll carve it plainer. If Jim had gone, say, to visit his family for Christmas, then it would be hard to put him in jail before the first of the year. Wouldn't it?"

"Uhh . . . Sure, I guess it would."

"I understand if you are afraid this might put you in even more *boiling water,* as you put it, but I will back you to the hilt if it comes to that. After all, I gave you my blessing on releasing Jim. Plain enough?"

"Yes sir. So . . . Where does Jim go? He can't run forever."

The judge's face seemed to draw down in lines of weariness. "No, he can't. But he could sure enjoy possibly one last Christmas with the woman he loves. And wherever he spends that Christmas, I guess that would be completely up to the two of you—if you were to happen to see him, of course."

Coal stared into Judge Sinclair's eyes. He thought back to the two cigars the man had given him as a Christmas gift. He would never have guessed back then how he would come to feel about this man in so short a time. About now, he was thinking he would do just about anything the judge asked of him. For a man who had come across so stern and unbending at one time, Judge Wiley Sinclair had a heart made of rough diamonds.

"Just leave the badge on your desk whenever you get feeling that you and I have had a chance to connect," Sinclair went on, acting for all the world as if they weren't actually face to face at that very moment. "We can only make them believe for so long that we haven't had some kind of contact. In the meantime, I'll make all the arrangements with the state trooper, Stinger. They're going to have him take over for you until after New Year's."

Coal studied the judge's face for a few seconds, weighing his words. He started to speak once, stopped, then forced himself to go on, needing to speak but somehow not really wanting an answer. "What about this Stinger? Do you know him?"

The judge's eyes flickered. He didn't answer immediately, and Coal was afraid he knew what that meant. His heart started to pound harder.

"Yes, Coal. I do know him. Of course I do."

"And . . . ?"

The judge drew in a deep breath and sighed. He reached up and rubbed his jaw. "And I'll do everything in my power to see that you get that badge back as soon as humanly possible."

That was all Judge Sinclair needed to say. He could remain sounding neutral yet reveal to Coal about all that was necessary to know about state bull Willie Stinger.

His eyes settled into Coal's at last, and in his gaze Coal could read true sorrow. "I'm sorry, Coal. I truly am."

And Coal believed him.

CHAPTER TWENTY-SEVEN

Driving toward home, Coal passed the property of the family of one of his old rodeo teammates. The Bar H ranch had been in the Snowball family for generations, with old Billy Snowball being the current owner. Billy's third oldest son, Jeremy, had been probably the best calf roper on the rodeo team, and a good, squared away kid.

Suddenly, Coal slammed on the brakes, and the pickup skittered to a halt in the middle of the highway. Both Ray and Maura turned shocked eyes on him after recovering from nearly slamming into the dash, but he didn't favor them with a look. He simply threw the truck into reverse and screamed backward down the road until he was even with the Bar H gate again, then cranked the wheel and swung into the lane. He needed a telephone, and he needed it now, along with someone he could trust to keep his mouth shut. Billy Snowball was just that man.

In the yard, he stomped the parking brake down and left the pickup running. He didn't look over at Maura and Ray. "I'll be right back."

Jumping out, he went and rapped on the door. A tough-looking woman whose left eye stood slightly off-kilter to the outside and whose long hair was fashioned on top of her head in wrapped braids opened the door. She grinned with surprise when she recognized him.

"By jigs, it's Coal Savage! Come on in, Coal. Well, look at you, all growed up." Wow. Had it been *that* long?

Coal tried to meet her smile with enthusiasm, stepping in to let her shut the door. She came back around and grabbed both of his upper arms, looking him up and down. "Well, boy howdy, son. You look fine. Just fine!" She turned toward another room and hollered, "Hey, Pa, come on in here, would you? Come see what the buzzards didn't eat."

Soon, a wizened looking man with half-purple, half-brown leather for skin stepped around the corner. The dome of his head ran far back over the crest without a hair in sight. Only tufts of blackish silver remained over his ears. But he bragged a monumental silver walrus mustache that more than made up for it. There he stood in gray-blue polyester cowboy cut trousers and a snap-front white shirt with thin silver stripes, the buckle that held up his pants about as big as a saucer—a relic of his own rodeo days. Remembering the old Billy Snowball, Coal half expected him to turn and spit tobacco juice on the floor before he spoke.

After the happy greetings were over, Coal asked if he could use the telephone. He told the Snowballs the conversation he needed the phone for was top secret, and that anything they heard would make them accomplices to something they might not want to be part of.

Billy Snowball turned to his wife, Gertrude, and laid his hand to her shoulder. "Come on, old woman. I think we need to go check that hay again. I noticed the tarp's gettin' leaky." With that, they went out toward the back of the house, and in less than fifteen seconds Coal heard the door shut.

He ripped the phone off the base and dialed Jim Lockwood's number, his heart pounding.

Yello, came the greeting from the other end. Jim's country twang.

"Jim. Coal. Pack up some clothes and traveling stuff. Anything you'd take on a trip if you were leaving for a week." Jim started to say something, but Coal cut him off. "Jim! We don't have much time. Pack up, then get Betty in the car and drive. Get over to our place as fast as you can and get Mom to clear out a place in the barn where you can park the car. Then cover it with a tarp."

Damnit all, Coal. What're you tryin' to do? Scare the hell out of an old man?

"Jim, for hell's sake, just shut up and do what I say. Get packed up and get. Don't be at your house in half an hour. Now move."

With that, he dropped the phone back on the base. Even if Jim had any questions for him, he could have no idea where he had called from, so he couldn't call back. Coal had left him with no choice but to obey.

Coal went out the front door, avoiding looking over at Ray and Maura, then walked around back, finding Billy Snowball smoking a cigarette, and Gertrude cuddling an adolescent gray kitten. They both straightened up and drilled Coal with their eyes.

"It was sure great to see the two of you," Coal said. "But you didn't. Understand? You didn't see me at all. I was never here, and nobody borrowed your phone."

Not that anything would ever be able to be traced to the Snowballs, but Coal wanted to impress secrecy upon them at all costs.

Without skipping a beat, the old man took out his cigarette to spit that infamous stream of tobacco juice near the side of the house. "I don't even know who the hell you are. Get offa my property, stranger. But I hope you can come back sometime when you can talk about the old days." He gave Coal a wink.

All the way back to the KSRA radio station building, the only sound in the cab was the hum of the tires on the road. Apparently reminded of the silence by sight of KSRA, Maura reached out and flipped the radio on. As chance would have it, old Merle "Hag" Haggard was partway through a nineteen seventy-one country song called "Bigtime Annie's Square."

Merle was singing about some Oklahoma girlfriend of his named Annie who had moved out to California, and he went out to find her. He managed to do so, and was accepted by her, but everyone out in California called him "Bigtime Annie's Square." After listening to a few more rhymes about how he was, among other things, "Annie's leaning post she turned to now and then," and how "Annie called him feeble," Coal casually leaned forward and turned it back off, offering Maura no explanation. He had a feeling she needed none anyway.

He came up to the stop sign and made a full stop, feeling the vibes from Maura and Ray. When he glanced to the right, for traffic, he also stole a quick look at Maura, and there was a little smile on her lips. No doubt she was thinking back on the words of the song, probably where "Annie called him feeble." Women.

Still without speaking, he drifted his hand out and flipped the radio knob back on. Jim Reeves was singing "Silver Bells," his favorite secular Christmas song. Much more to his liking than a song about someone named Annie and her loser of a beau, even if it *was* being performed by the inimitable "Hag."

He turned right onto Courthouse Drive and started up the Bar, making the hard left into the courthouse driveway and rolling back to the parking lot. He stepped out to the comforting sound of the creek rushing along in the gully beyond the asphalt. Maura climbed out behind him.

Without speaking, Coal walked to the concrete steps and went down to ease open the door, with Maura and Ray following in complete silence.

Coal stepped just far enough inside the office for Ray to come in behind him, and Maura and shut the door. He scanned the room, smelling old, burned coffee, not even sure what he was looking for. Almost in a daze, he walked over to the desk and unpinned his gold badge, sliding the pin out of the material of his jacket and snapping it down on the hard, cold, once-blond surface of the desk, oft-scarred and stained by dozens of coffee cups, fingerprint ink, and substances unknown. His fingers rested on top of it for one thoughtful moment.

Walking over to the coffee maker, he started to reach for a cup. Then he realized the half-full pot was as cold as October spuds in the field. He scanned the room again. There was nothing here that he needed. Only his pride and his dignity, and he was taking those with him. That damn state bull, Willie Stinger, could have the rest.

On second thought, there *were* some particular things he might find handy later. He went around to the business side of his desk and opened the middle drawer, pulling out a little key on a wire ring. He walked to a tall, gray metal filing cabinet in the far corner and unlocked the top drawer…

When he had gleaned everything he needed from the filing cabinet and put it in a cast away paper bag, he looked over at Maura and gave her a wink he didn't feel. Then he looked at Ray. "You saw nothing, right?"

"What? I'm not even here."

"No, you're most definitely here, but you saw nothing."

"Have it your way then. I saw nothing. But why *am* I here?"

"Because they're only calling for my badge, not yours. Nobody said you couldn't still be deputy."

Ray stared at him. In his soft voice, he said, "I really only signed on to hang around with you."

Coal smiled. "Heart-warming. But there's a method to my madness, buddy. At least if you'd care to play along. It might not hurt to have somebody on the inside. I won't tell you what to do one way or the other, but it might come in handy if you keep that badge for a while. We can still hang around together."

Thoughtfully chewing the inside of his lower lip, Ray's eyes danced around the room. Maura was gazing at him expectantly, and on her face his eyes stopped moving. He gave a little nod before she looked away.

He sighed and looked back over at Coal. "Guess I'm a deputy then. I never filled out any tax paperwork or anything. Am I even on a payroll?"

"Well hell no," Coal replied with a funny glance. "I put you on as a volunteer. You think this county's made of money?"

Back at the house, a somber scene of worried concern greeted Coal and the others. It centered around the Lockwoods, who waited front and center to greet him.

It only took a few minutes to tell Jim and Betty everything that had transpired. Although there had been nothing that completely disproved Jim's guilt, Coal felt it looked promising. After all, even if the murder could somehow be blamed on Jim in the semi-aware state in which his physiological disorder might sometimes render him, it seemed quite a stretch to believe that same semi-aware murderer would conspire with other people to dispose of the body—especially the man's own family. The final decision, of course, would rest with a jury if Jim ended up being indicted for the murder, but Jim was a popular man in Lemhi County, while Bern Hargis was not. This fact alone had come to give Coal immense hope.

They sat around the living room and sipped scalding hot, tar-black coffee Coal made himself because he wanted it as strong and rich as possible. The aroma of not only the fresh brew itself, but of the newly ground beans, permeated every corner of the kitchen and living room and was complemented by the smell of Connie's cookies. She had felt the need of comforting Jim and Betty so deeply that she had made up two kinds: soft molasses, and frosted pumpkin. Mixed with the smell of the freshly cut Douglas fir tree and a cinnamon candle, the scents promised a night of Christmas magic.

With the inexplicable but driving desire not to let Maura disappear for the rest of the night, when the woman announced that she had to go home and feed her animals, Coal volunteered to go with her. He could see in Ray Christian's eyes that he was inclined to invite himself as well, but apparently he had experienced enough of Maura's aloofness for one day, so he announced that he was going to run into town and stop by the infamous Lantern Bar for a few minutes. By the thinly veiled look in Virgil's eyes, had it not been for the purpose of the visit to town, he might have asked to tag along with Ray.

The sun had gone down a while earlier, and the sky, the mountains, and seemingly the air itself rolled out around Coal and Maura in velvety soft shades of blue and dusky violet as they pulled into her yard. The horses, Homer, Sarah, Hilly, and Brusher, nickered with happiness as Coal and Maura slammed the truck doors and went to throw them flakes of hay, and the heelers ran out to see them as well, wriggling themselves into a frenzy.

Against the light metal siding of the house, the windows glared like off-set, malevolent eyeballs or mine entrances into the side of a lonely mountain. The utter darkness made Coal think of Maura's boys, Ty and Sky, and inside he cursed. He had had no time since his last visit here to follow up on the legal issues that were going on with them, so he had nothing of comfort to offer the woman. In fact, he had simply forgotten. He chose the intelligent path of complete silence on that raw, painful subject. He followed her into the house, where she flipped on the living room light, then went to turn her kitchen faucet on to allow the escape of a pencil's diameter-sized stream of water—just enough to keep the pipes from freezing. She turned and almost ran right into him.

Before Coal knew what was happening, Maura's strong hands had come up and closed on his biceps. She looked up at him. He looked down at her. The light was dim, but nothing could hide her beauty and her wonderfully expressive eyes. He had never felt a stronger urge to kiss her.

And then, wonder of wonders, the phone rang.

Maura's head jerked around. She stared at the phone through two more rings. Coal looked from it to her. Another ring, and she kept staring.

"There's no law about answering that," Coal said hopefully. He wanted her to ignore it.

It rang again. At last, her hands fell away, and she gave a little, hopeless sounding laugh.

She walked to the phone and picked it up. "Hello?" A moment to listen. "Oh! Hi, Jordan! Wow. This is a surprise." Her eyes roved the kitchen cabinets, the refrigerator, the stove—anywhere but to Coal. He was staring at her, but his pride made him stop and walk away. He pretended to study a Remington print on her wall up close and very personal. But his mind was running rampant. *Jordan?* What Jordan could she be talking to? Surely not Peterson, his deputy.

"Well . . . Wow. Okay, you sure caught me off-guard. Hey, I am really flattered, but . . . Could you give me a day or so to think about it? I'm sorry. I don't like being wishy-washy. Okay. Thank you. No, no—it's me, not you. I'll call you, okay? Are you sure? Okay. What's your number?" She picked up a pencil and jotted a number down on a pad of paper, and as she repeated it back to the caller, Coal listened while pretending not to. It was Jordan Peterson's number. His throat felt tight. He didn't know why. It was a feeling he didn't like.

"Okay, so I'll give you a call back in a day or two. I'm really flattered that you'd think to ask, but I'm just… Well, I just need a little time. We'll see. All right. Have a good night. Goodbye."

The phone came down very slowly from her ear, and she set it on the base and left her hand there, seeming to press it down as if it would jump back off the hook if she let go.

Coal was trying to make out individual hairs in the tails of Frederic Remington's horses. His jaws were starting to feel stiff from clenching his teeth, but until right then he hadn't noticed.

Dead, cold silence filled the house. Only the clock on the wall and the trickling water from the tap made any sound. Finally, Maura drew in a deep breath and sighed it out. Was she going to say anything? Should Coal? Both of them must be posing that same question to themselves. Both ignored it.

Then Maura took the easy road—the dark path of pretending something uncomfortable had never happened at all.

"Well, I think I'm done here. Want to head back?"

"Yeah, you bet," Coal replied, turning and giving her a smile. "Great painting," he added, jerking a thumb at the Remington, which showed a man resting near a water hole down in what must be a bison wallow. He spoke of the painting, but at the moment it was the very last thing he cared about.

Maura shrugged. “Yeah, Sky bought me that. I’m a Charlie Russell fan more than Remington, but I didn’t want to hurt his feelings, and it’s nice enough.”

Another time, Coal would have been happy to hear that, because he agreed about her estimation of Russell and Remington. Right now, he didn’t particularly care. All he could think of was Maura PlentyWounds and Deputy Jordan Peterson—together.

As Maura drove back out to the house, Coal tried to push the phone call far from his mind. Success in that endeavor came unexpectedly when he was jolted to remember he still needed to go back to Barracks Lane and make casts of the tracks left at the scene of the murder. But it was dark now, and cold. That was going to have to wait until tomorrow.

Friday, December 22

The day grew light—too soon, and not soon enough. Coal sat on the edge of his bed and listened to people stirring downstairs while he wiggled his toes and broke the icicles that seemed to be forming in them. Big, muscular Dobe raised his head up from the bed just enough to give Cole a curious, squinting gaze before settling back down. Only his head was in sight, with the rest of him deep under the covers. Coal would never need an electric blanket while Dobe was around. In contrast, Shadow lay over by the window, soaking in all the cool air she could from outside.

In spite of appearing completely content where they were, both dogs jumped up when Coal got dressed and followed him downstairs. While he headed for the bathroom, they went to see what Connie was cooking in the kitchen.

Coal lathered up in the shower and scrubbed his hair. The hot water ran down his head and face as he thought of Maura. And Jordan Peterson. And then he forced himself to think of his old friend Jim instead. Thinking of Maura and Jordan was a distraction he could ill afford right now.

Jim and Betty Lockwood did not like being treated like fugitives, not after a lifetime of respect and honor. But if they must be fugitives, they could not have found a better place than at the Savage ranch.

While they were in the kitchen drinking coffee, eating toast and eggs, and talking to Connie, Coal took the phone upstairs to his room, where he plugged it into a seldom-used jack. He dialed a long-familiar number and waited. A woman's voice he didn't recognize came on the line.

FBI forensics. How may I direct your call?

"Tony Nwanzée, please."

Oh, I'm sorry, sir. Mister Nwanzée isn't in today. Is there someone else you would like to talk to?

Coal did some off-the-cuff practicing on his new-found silent cursing skills. "No, not really. But could you have him call me?"

I can, sir, but he won't be back until after the holidays.

Silent cursing perfected. Coal was getting so fast and proficient at it that after he finished his whole repertoire he almost had to go through it again.

"Could I have his home phone number?"

Oh, I'm sorry, but I would lose my job if I gave out the private number of one of our employees. Would you like me to call him and pass your number on, Mister . . ."

"Coal Savage."

Silence. Long, brutal silence. Time enough to get in a few practice swings with some of his favorite words, had he thought about it. Then:

Coal? Coal, this is Mary! Mary Wright!

Embarrassed, Coal replied, "Mary! Wow! I'm sorry, I didn't recognize your voice."

Well, that doesn't surprise me! Take off like a wildfire and don't even call once in a while to see how we are. Of course you'd forget the sound of my voice!

For a few minutes, they exchanged pleasantries. Now that he knew who this was, secretary and stenographer Mary Wright, he was happy to hear her voice. It seemed like ages ago that he had worked there.

"Well, if you could call Tony and let him know I really need to talk to him, Mary, that would be wonderful. Can I leave a number?"

Oh, don't be silly! I'll just give you his number.

"Are you sure? I don't want you putting your job in jeopardy."

Stop it, Coal. You're just like family.

With a suddenly warm heart, Coal jotted down Tony's number, thanked Mary and wished her a merry Christmas, then softly lay the phone on the base. Drawing a deep breath, he dialed Tony's number. Now that his fingers were prodding into the holes in the dial, making those old familiar clicking sounds, they seemed familiar to him, although he and Tony had lived some fifty miles distant from each other and seldom did anything in their off-time together that would have required a personal phone call between them.

The phone rang. Then rang. Then rang some more. Ten rings. Each one squeezed Coal's heart harder. At last, he dropped his chin on his chest, then used up what hopefully was the last of his quota of curse words for today and wished he was able to stop himself from swearing. With disappointment, he called Mary Wright back at the FBI and asked her to leave that message for Tony after all—in case he called there first for any reason before Coal had a chance to try again.

Coal sat down on his bed and looked toward his door. Soon, he had to go back down and mingle with one of his lifelong heroes, and while he did that he was going to be sorting out a lot of feelings. Did Jim kill Bern Hargis, or did he not?

He was ashamed to admit it, but it had taken the serving of the search warrant at the Hargis residence and Ray Christian's dogged insistence about trusting old friends to bring Coal to the point he was now: He didn't know who had killed Hargis, and an awful lot of weight was going to lie in Jim's lap if Willie Stinger, the state bull, got hold of all the information and evidence gathered so far in the investigation, but down in his guts he somehow sensed that Jim really was innocent.

Yet it wouldn't matter much what Coal's guts might tell him, without hard proof. The wolves of justice were going to come howling down on Jim Lockwood in a big way, and soon.

The biggest thing standing between his friend and a possible prison term was one ex-lawman-turned-rogue-private investigator—two hundred forty-five pounds of fury about to unleash on the seemingly untouchable rancher Phil Harringer, and whoever else was involved in this murder.

One thing Coal knew without a doubt: Harringer might have killed Hargis all alone, but at least two other people had helped him dispose of the body.

Harringer would go down, but he would not go alone.

CHAPTER TWENTY-EIGHT

After Coal got a firm commitment from Jim that he would not leave the house, for any reason, he told Connie and the children goodbye and promised to be back as soon as he was able and spend whatever was left of the day with them. They were on Christmas break, and he had already missed way too much of it.

As for Virgil, he still didn't need to worry much about saying goodbye. Although his oldest son didn't care for sharing his innermost feelings, it was obvious even to Coal that he was far from the point of forgiving him for the faux-pas of giving away Burro. There were two more problems he could not afford to waste time thinking out: Virgil and Kathy.

None of that really mattered at the moment. What mattered was trying to prove Jim's innocence, even if he never did manage to prove who the real killer was.

The day was gray and glum. It hadn't quite reached the point of freezing again during the night, but the lack of blue skies made it seem colder and harsher than it really was. In spite of being around thirty-four degrees, there was still a look and feel of nighttime frost over the Savage world, but the air was absolutely still, imitating the inside of a refrigerated semi.

Walking out toward the pickup, snugged up in his blue and black buffalo plaid coat and brown Carhartts, and carrying his work backpack, a jug of water, and a paper bag full of Plaster of Paris with the top rolled over to keep it secure, Coal heard the front door shut, and he turned to see Ray Christian shrugging into his tan overcoat as he bounced jauntily down the steps.

"Where are you going?"

Ray stopped on the sidewalk and stared at him. "What do you mean? With you."

"Uh . . . You seem to forget, you are still bound to the law. I'm a private citizen. You probably shouldn't taint that badge by hanging around me." Maybe Coal should have grinned, but he wasn't feeling it. The fact was his words really were no joke.

Ray didn't skip a beat. "I wear a badge, and you don't. You're messing around with a criminal investigation. All the more reason for me to stick with you. I wouldn't want to have you breaking any laws."

After a few moments of what Coal intended to be an unbending, cold stare, he let one side of his mouth come up in a mini-smile. "All right, then get in. We're going over to the other side of the highway to make some plaster casts."

With that, he popped open the driver's door of the GMC, threw his backpack, the jug, and the paper bag into the middle of the seat and hopped in. The engine fired up with amazing ease after its long night's rest, but Coal had to feather the gas for several minutes to iron the wrinkles out of the idle.

He made a point of studying the countryside, not looking at Ray. When he finally looked over, Ray was unscrewing the lid off a heavy green thermos, and the bold smell of coffee erupted into the cab. Ray raised the thermos in the manner of a toast, then thrust it toward Coal.

"Stole this from your mom. First sip?"

"You must have stolen it from Betty. Unless Mom was making it for Betty and Jim, she only drinks Postum and Pero."

"Oh. Okay." Ray grinned sheepishly, then repeated, "First sip?"

Coal shook his head. "I'll have some later. Jim and Betty may as well be ticked at both of us." With that, he threw the truck in gear and wheeled it around in the yard, got to the road and checked for oncoming traffic. One seldom needed to bother on this road, but after spending four years in D.C., it was a deeply ingrained habit.

Out at the road to Hargis's dairy, he pulled off Barracks Lane and parked in the brittle yellow weeds, which were rimed with frost, and got out. The slamming of the door made a hollow barking noise in the still of the yet-to-be sun-lit morning, echoed half a second later by Ray's door.

Hearing the crunch of gravel breaking free of the frozen mud behind him as Ray followed along, Coal went back out to Barracks Lane and walked along it carrying the water and his paper bag which contained the makings of future plaster casts.

He strode with purpose to about where the first couple of dead cottonwoods towered to the right, and here he slowed down, scanning the mud and gravel road for sign of where the cowboy boots had started leaving their first tracks.

He had already come up to the third tree when he stopped, his eyes darting over the road, confused. As he slowly pivoted around, studying the roadway, Ray stood patiently.

Finally, his self-appointed watchdog could no longer hold his peace. "What's up, boss man?"

Without skipping a beat, Coal shook his head. "You're my babysitter, remember? I'm not the boss of anyone anymore. So. . . Do you see those tracks?"

Ray looked around as if suddenly realizing why they were there. "Haven't got to them yet, have we?"

Coal scanned farther along the road. "Well . . . I don't know, I guess . . ." He glanced toward the Hargis property, beyond the dead cottonwoods. "I was thinking the blood pool was between the second and third tree."

Ray looked around as if trying to get his bearings, but otherwise he made no indication that he had heard. Finally, with an irritated sigh, Coal turned back and walked to the Hargises' road, turned onto it and walked along the tree line until he got to the place where he thought he remembered the blood being. It was exactly where he recalled. Confused, he let his eyes trail along, finding the drag mark where the dead man's head had scraped the ground, leaving a thin skiff of blood. But . . . There were no tracks—anywhere. Cowboy boot or otherwise. And then he began to notice something else strange. The soil in small areas along the blood path was a different color. It was only slight, and it took some studying to really make it out, but it was definitely not the same as the surrounding area.

A warning bell began to go off in Coal's head. Without looking at Ray, because he was hoping not to see in the homicide detective's eyes the same doubt he felt in his heart, he went to the biggest pool of dried up blood, which appeared exactly as he had left it. Sure enough, right alongside the blood were two small areas where the soil looked slightly off-color. Somebody had sprinkled new dirt there to hide the tracks!

Without a word to Ray, he went over and jerked free a handful of yellow grass to use as a makeshift broom, then walked back to where he knew the tracks were hidden. The murderers must think they were dealing with some local hick. A little dirt wasn't enough to cover tracks he had already seen with his own eyes. Crouching down, he began carefully to whisk away the now obviously fresh dirt, which brushed to one side with ease, for it wasn't frozen in place like all the rest of the recently snowed-on dirt.

It was then that panic set in. The freshly sprinkled dirt was not simply placed on top of the tracks. Rather, it lay over the top of ground that Coal now saw had been carefully shaved with some kind of tool like a hoe or mattock. With his heart starting to pound feverishly, Coal made his way along the blood trail from one fresh spot of dirt to the next, brushing the dirt away carefully from each to reveal exactly what he suddenly knew would be the same along the entire path: The ground had been shaved of tracks. There was no doubt once the dirt was removed where each track had been, but it didn't matter. There was no longer a single track to make a cast of.

Coal's thoughts raced. These tracks, in his mind, had been what seemed a certain link to Phil Harringer, if Coal's suspicions held any weight. Now they were gone. Gone forever.

He turned to Ray, hoping his dismay didn't show in his face. Ray looked back at him, astute enough to realize what had happened.

"I'm not imagining things, right?"

Ray pursed his lips, then frowned. "No. Somebody came and obliterated the tracks."

Coal stared at him. He felt sick. "What about the pictures? I took some pictures, right?"

"No."

Coal was incredulous. "I didn't?"

"No." Ray met him gaze for gaze, then gave him a little smile and nudged his shoulder with his hand. "Come on, buddy! You gave me the camera, remember? *You* didn't take pictures—*I* did! I got photos of everything. I even put the lens cover right next to the best left and right tracks, to show the size."

A feeling of relief rushed through Coal. He clapped Ray on the shoulder. "You saved me! That'll be good enough, right? Even without the casts?"

Ray shrugged. "Well, it won't be as good as casts, but it'll be pretty good. Relax, buddy. We'll be okay."

"Relax? How? Somebody's been in here messing with evidence, and they did a damn thorough job of it. I don't know about you, but I think this cuts out the Hargises as any kind of suspects, at least in my mind. I don't think any of those people would be sharp enough to think of doing something like this."

With another shrug and a nod, Ray responded, "Yeah, you know, you've probably got something there. But I think your big rancher sure would be."

* * *

Coal drove back home feeling even more glum than the weather should have made him. The sun had come up over the Beaverheads while he and Ray were still scouring Barracks Lane and the Hargis property in hopes of finding at least one track that had been missed. But there was no luck, as far as the sun *or* the tracks. The heavy gray clouds relegated the risen sun to no more than a brighter spot in a cheerless sky, and the tracks all safely eluded their searchers. It was the fact that the sneaker tracks and the other two sets of tracks had been removed as well as the cowboy boot tracks that seemed more than passingly strange. Had it just been Harringer trying to keep himself out of the spotlight, why would he have cared if any other tracks were found and had casts made of them? On the contrary, it seemed that would be something in his favor as the investigation went along.

There was no speaking in the pickup as Coal drove back home and parked. No speaking all the way into the house.

Coal didn't even dare look at Jim or Betty and risk drawing their attention. He took the phone and returned again to his room. Dobe tried to follow him so he could reclaim his warm spot in the bed, but Coal shut him out. In his current state of mind, he wasn't in the mood even for the company of one of his most beloved buddies.

He had just plugged the phone back in and was about to pull it off the hook when it rang, startling a curse out of him. He then cursed the fact that his habit of cursing had gotten the better of him and then cursed his foul mouth, which seemed to be magnified over the last day or so.

On the fourth ring, he picked up the phone, more to stop the noise than because he cared who was on the other end of the line or what their problem was.

"Hello." A short salutation to match a short temper.

What's cooking, Coal?

Coal gave the wall a blank stare, the wheels of his mind processing. His silence went too long.

Jeez, bro, you forget me already?

Coal's heart seemed to jump. "Hey! Tony! Oh, man, is it ever good to hear your voice!"

Tony Nwanzée, a native Nigerian as dark as a Hershey bar, laughed with glee. His good humor rolled all the way across the continent and into Coal's heart. *You wouldn't have known that five seconds ago when you didn't even know my voice! So what you up to, brother? Wishin' you were back here in the big city?*

That forced a laugh out of Coal. "Ha! You'll never see the day. But I sure do need a hand from my old big city partner."

Really? Man, cut me a break! The only time you ever call is when you need something. An' here I thought you were calling just to wish your old partner a Merry Christmas!

Coal laughed again. Tony sure was good medicine. After obliging him with the desired Christmas wishes, he went into his latest backwoods Idaho problem. He told him he had some evidence that needed processing as fast as possible—a watch that needed to be fingerprinted by a real pro, particularly as it had spent a good amount of time under water, and some blood and soil samples that needed a work up. He would also need some photos of a head wound analyzed.

Last of all, he left his one-time partner with: "I'll send everything off to you in the mail today. As fast as you possibly can, give me a call back. But call me at the house. I'm on vacation until further notice." It was only a small white lie.

From the other end of the line came Tony's rollicking, fun-loving laugh. *Yeah, brother! Sounds like a real vacation, all right. You haven't changed much, have you? When you gonna stop working and have some real fun?*

Coal hung up the phone wondering the same thing.

* * *

Coal was lousy company. Jim and Betty, of all people, should have understood, but it didn't seem like they did. They sat watching *The Joker's Wild* and then *The New Price is Right*, and now and then Jim or Betty would look over at Coal and comment on something, but he had little to say. The fact was, it was all he could do even to stay in the room. Besides the fact that he couldn't stomach game shows, there was a driving urgency in him to be up and moving, to be doing *something* on the Hargis case. But what?

Deep in thought, he stared at the television screen, but none of the goings-on registered on him. The scenes playing out in his mind were all of the search of the Hargis place, the disgusting nature of the inside of the house, and the disturbing, suspicious manner displayed by Sherlene and Moby Hargis and Leroy Yarwood, in spite of the fact that he had nothing more to go on with the three of them than circumstantial evidence. One thing was for certain: In time, he was going to have to pull all three of them into his office for questioning, and . . . That was the thought that jarred him back to reality. He was no longer the sheriff! He had no right even to talk to them, other than simply as an interested citizen or, at best, an unlicensed private investigator.

He contemplated the man who would be standing in as sheriff, state bull Willie Stinger, a man he barely knew but who seemed to have very few supporters in the county, and few if any friends. What kind of an investigation was such a man going to run? From all Jim had told him, it sounded like they had spent a lot of time at odds, as it sounded like Stinger was the same way with just about everyone around. And, further, what kind of investigation *could* he run, since in all reality Coal had just about crippled him by absconding with all the evidence so far collected in the case?

He thought about the discovery of the body lying in Wimpey Creek, the blood that had still been on the belt knife Hargis was carrying, even after who knew how long under water. He thought—

Coal sat abruptly up in his chair. The pickup! The pickup! Why hadn't he thought of it before? He suddenly had a picture in his mind of the rickety old fifties Ford pickup he had seen going up Savage Lane the night of Jim's fight with Hargis. That old pickup had veered to the right, heading east up Lemhi Road. That was the way to Bohannon and Wimpey Creeks!

With his heart pounding, Coal jumped up, attempting to look nonchalant, and walked out of the room as if he needed to use the bathroom. He went on past that door, however, and into his mother's room. By her bedside, he found a pencil and a pad of paper, and he sat on the bed and tried using his trained powers of recollection and description to rebuild that old truck, on paper.

It was a fifties Ford. He remembered seeing that, because both of his were General Motors products, and in his mind he had been comparing the three. Dark in color. He remembered thinking maybe dark blue or green, although it could certainly have been brown. But the remarkable thing had been the driver's door. It must have been in a wreck at one time, because the door was mismatched. If he recalled correctly, in the darkness it had appeared to be yellow, or maybe even white. For that matter, it could have been light pink. Alternately, it could have been primer gray. Beyond that, it sounded as if it would break down right there in front of the house if the driver had tried to push it even one mile an hour faster.

Absently, Coal sketched the pickup and stared at it as he made notes all around it. He even put a driver in the front seat, a fact he didn't notice until his hands stopped moving. His subconscious must simply have wanted someone there, since the vehicle had been rolling when he saw it.

He jumped up, thinking he would head into town and find Bob Wilson so he could get the vehicle description to him and see if he might recall any such rig. Then he thought of that ever-so-irritating contraption, the telephone, and knew he had no good reason to leave his family alone during their Christmas vacation.

While he was thinking all this, that very contraption, which seemed to sense when his mind was on it, began to ring, up in his room.

Connie must have believed Coal was in the bathroom, because she sent Katie upstairs to get the phone, and soon she came back down, just as he was walking casually down the hall, for all the world as if he had been in the bathroom, not in his mother's room making notes and drawing sketches of murder vehicles when he should be relaxing and enjoying his family.

"Dad, that call was for you."

"Oh yeah?" He smiled at his beautiful girl. "Who was it?"

"He said Officer Stinger."

Coal's mood instantly darkened. Willie Stinger, the state policeman chosen to rule the county while he was on leave. "What did he say?"

She told him Stinger was up at the courthouse and urgently needed to have him call back at the earliest possible time. So Coal didn't.

Instead, he called Eric Hansen.

Yello.

Coal smiled. "Hello, Trax. It's Coal Savage."

Hello, Sheriff.

"Hello. And let me tell you, you can drop that title. I'm on leave right now. A private citizen."

A moment of silence. *Really. Well, I won't ask why. How does it feel?*

"I'd like to say relaxing. But . . . current circumstances? Probably the opposite."

Sorry. What can I do for you?

"Well, I think we're missing something at the Hargis place. Something big."

So? You're not wearing a badge. Not much you can do about it, right?

Coal had to chuckle. "Well, I'm going private eye. And the Hargises don't know I've been suspended."

Wow. Sounds illegal. Maybe dangerous.

"Yeah. You in?"

Hansen's turn to give a chuckle. *You bet.*

"Meet me out at the Hargis place?"

When?

"As soon as you can. Better yet, drive out to my house, and we'll go over together."

Hansen got directions to the Savage place, then hung up. Coal drank scalding coffee and ate a fat beef steak and swore that next year he'd be eating elk or deer meat. Beef never had been his thing.

Later, he and Hansen pulled up at the Hargis place. This time they didn't even bother going to the door. Hansen got his dogs out, and they went to the scene of the murder—or at least what Coal was guessing now was where it took place, where the biggest spot of blood stained the ground. Coal tried to stay out of Hansen's way as much as possible while he took the hounds around that area, then helped them through the fence out onto Barracks Lane. Coal followed along while the dogs tracked the path the man in cowboy boots had used. Finally, they veered off into the grass on the side of the road.

Coal wanted to ask Hansen if his hounds were onto something, but both Hansen and the dogs seemed so intent that he kept his questions to himself.

They went along in the grass, the hounds pulling more and more insistently against their collars. Finally, they came to the line of barbed wire and sniffed at it briefly, then tried to take a dive between wires. Hansen had to jerk them back, but the Walker kept fighting him.

"Clint!" Hansen's tone was sharp.

Hansen eased the wire up with some help from Coal and got the hounds through, then crossed over himself, leaving Coal on his own.

On the other side of the fence, the willows had begun to grow thick, and they intermingled with other trees, some of them thorny. Hansen swore a couple of times as the hounds dragged him a little too fast through branches too thickly interwoven or too prickly.

"Hey! Clint! Bogart! Stop it! Heel!"

Hansen barked the words at his dogs in much the same stentorian voice they would have used to tell him they had treed a cougar. They stopped and sidled around, but they certainly didn't like stopping.

Finally, Hansen stood up. "I think he turned around here and headed back to the road. It's thicker than a fur coat in here."

They met on the edge of Barracks Lane, not very far from where it forked and Phil Harringer's lane cut off to the left.

"Where'd he go when he turned around?" Coal asked.

Hansen shrugged. "Back on the road. From there, who knows? There's been way too much traffic on this road now to ever know for sure."

But Coal had a good guess. His intuition and suspicion drew his eyes along the road toward the Harringer place. The deeper he got into this case, the more he suspected the rancher of being connected to the killing. Somehow, he had to get onto his land.

CHAPTER TWENTY-NINE

When Coal returned to the house and let Eric Hansen and his dogs out to climb into their Jeep and head home, a silver mist was drifting out of the sky. This year didn't want to snow, but it didn't want to send out the sun either. It was depressing—a good mood for current circumstances.

Ray Christian came out and stood on the landing as Coal walked toward the house. He tugged a cigar out of his pocket and lit it, puffing until a cloud of blue smoke billowed out around his mouth.

"Where've you been?"

"Hansen and I went back over the trail at the Hargises'."

Ray stood there puffing his cigar. Coal had stopped at the bottom of the steps. Finally, he walked on up. Ray stood in front of the door and didn't seem inclined to move. "So what, buddy, you cutting me out?"

Coal stared at his friend for a moment. "Cutting you out?"

"Sure. I would have gone with you."

Coal grunted. "Sorry. I went on a whim. It wasn't any big deal. Nothing you could have done anyway, and it looked like you were having fun with the kids."

Ray answered with a grunt of his own. "Okay. But it would have been nice to be asked."

Coal frowned and again said, "Sorry." As he moved his hand toward the door handle, Ray finally stepped aside, saying nothing.

Coal went into the too-warm front room and frowned over at the blazing fire in the stove. Steam from what smelled like soup or stew added to the stifling sense about the place. Coal was anxious and restless. He wanted to be here with his children. And he should have been happy to spend some time with Jim and Betty. But inside him things were stirring. He didn't know why, or honestly even what. He just felt an urgent need to be doing something other than sitting here visiting.

Jim was watching *Jeopardy!* on the television. When Coal glanced over, he saw Betty looking at him, and she gave her husband an almost imperceptible nudge. The older man looked over at her, then followed her eyes toward Coal. He nodded, patted Betty on the shoulder, then got up and ambled over.

"Hey, son. You all right?"

Coal shrugged. "Not sure I even know what all right feels like anymore. You?"

"I'm fine. I'm out of jail. Sitting here with good company. It's warm. Nice aromas in the air. Yeah, son, I'm good. So what's the rest of your day lookin' like?"

"I guess I'd better get into town and start talking to people. Maybe start searching for a pickup I saw going up the road the night Hargis was killed."

Jim nodded knowingly. "Say. Do you want to go outside for a bit?"

With a frown, Coal glanced out the window. He weighed the dangers to Jim. "You know Willie Stinger called a while ago, and I'm supposed to call him back."

"That little prick can stuff it," said Jim. "Let him go."

That wrangled an actual laugh out of Coal. "No worries about that, Jim. I didn't plan to call him. The only reason I brought it up is I'm half afraid of him driving out here to find out why I didn't call. And if you were outside . . ."

"Oh. Yeah, I see what you mean."

"Yeah."

"Well, then, why don't you go ahead and call him back? See where he is. If he's miles away we can go outside and feel safe."

It wasn't a bad idea. Keep your friends close—and your enemies closer. So to speak. At least keep them on your radar. Coal went up to his room with the phone and made the call to the sheriff's office, which was where Stinger had been earlier. To his surprise and satisfaction, it picked up after three rings.

Courthouse. Stinger.

"Hello, Stinger. This is Sheriff Savage. My daughter said you called."

A pregnant pause. *Uh-huh. Yeah, I did. Quite a while ago.*

Coal ignored the sound of irritation. He already had plenty of his own irritation just at the grating sound of the voice on the other end. He swallowed, pretending nothing was wrong. "What did you need?"

Well, I've been trying to go through your files and notes on this Hargis murder case, trying to make any sense I can of things. I see some jumbled notes, and what looks like a partial report. But I can't find any solid notes I can read or any of the evidence that's listed in here. Not even an account of where it might be.

Here it was. Coal had to play all his cards. When he had commandeered all the evidence he had collected, he knew, of course, that this conversation was in his future. He just hadn't been sure when.

"I sent all the evidence off for processing."

If Willie Stinger's earlier pause had been merely *pregnant,* this one felt like an entire pregnancy. *So . . . when exactly did you plan to finish the report? And especially the part about the disposition of the evidence?*

Coal wanted to keep playing the soul of patience. But he had never been very good at it, and Willie Stinger, by voice alone, made him feel impatient.

"When— Listen, Stinger. I *planned* on finishing my report today. I *planned* on indicating the disposition of the evidence at the same time.

Unfortunately, what I planned and what actually happened don't seem to be the same thing. It wasn't exactly by my choice."

Meaning your suspension.

Stinger's voice had a ring to it like he meant the use of those words as a weapon. A knife he thrust in under Coal's ribs and then gave a hard twist.

"Yes, meaning that."

Well, you need to come down and finish the report anyway. I can't very well continue any kind of useful investigation without a full report. And by the way—where is Jim Lockwood? He's supposed to be back in his cell.

Coal heard a chuckle. It took him a moment to realize it was coming from him, a noise that surprised him because he thought he was far too angry for any such sound. "I don't know how they do things where you come from, Stinger, but I guess that investigation is going to sit and wait, because I'm not going anywhere. I've been relieved of my badge, and right now I'm relaxing at home with my family, and that's where I intend to stay. I'll be damned if I'm coming down there to write up any report just so you can follow up on *my* investigation." Of course Coal had no real intentions of staying home, but Willie Stinger sure didn't need to know that Coal the sheriff had been replaced by Coal the self-appointed private investigator, and that his driving need to exonerate Jim Lockwood hadn't lessened in the slightest.

"As far as Jim, I have no idea where he is, but it's not my job to round him up right now. Is it? I don't have a badge, and any arrest I made would be false arrest. I guess you're going to have to find him yourself."

With that, he hung up—both on the acting sheriff and on any chance the Lemhi County sheriff's department might ever have had of an amicable relationship with the Idaho State Police.

Coal took a few deep breaths, then slowly bent down and unplugged the phone. Collecting all the cord, he took another deep breath and went downstairs, plugging the phone back in and hanging it up, then walking over to where Jim Lockwood was once again sitting on the couch.

"We can take that walk now."

Outside, Ray Christian had vanished. Apparently, so had Virgil, because Coal hadn't seen him inside, and he couldn't imagine from the way he had been acting lately that he would allow himself to be very far from Ray.

On the porch, Jim pulled out a Marlboro and lit it, squinting at Coal through the first fresh cloud of smoke and smiling with closed lips. "Smoke?"

Coal shook his head. "Gave it up."

Jim nodded and shook out his match, flinging it out into the gravel. "Yeah. Me too. Just before bed last night."

Coal chuckled.

"Still keep all your tools out in the barn, Coal?" Jim asked.

Coal gave a shrug. "I suppose. I haven't had any call to look for them since I came home."

Jim jerked his head sideways. "Let's go see."

So out they went to the barn, where the tools were right where they had always been kept, and, true to Connie's nature, perfectly ordered. Jim scanned the long tool bench until locating a big yellow construction measuring tape, a hundred-footer. He picked it up, then walked outside, the cigarette pinched firmly between his lips.

Wordlessly, Coal followed him like he knew he was supposed to.

Jim stopped out in the middle of the yard. "Say, Coal, what is the life expectancy of a man supposed to be nowadays, do you know?"

Coal thought for a moment. He had read this somewhere not long ago. "Sixty-eight, I think. Why?"

Jim pulled out the cigarette and tapped it, making loose ash drift toward the ground like this winter's snow that wasn't to be. "All right. Here, take this tape out to sixty-eight, would you? Then set it on the ground."

Puzzled, but not enough to ask again why, Coal took the tape and walked out until he could see the number seventy on the tape. There, he locked the tape and laid it on the ground, with Jim still holding onto the zero end.

"Now walk back along that tape, buddy, until . . . Say, how old are you now, anyway?"

"Forty-two."

"Okay. Walk to forty-two and stop."

Coal obeyed. Jim looked at him when he stopped. "Got it? Forty-two?"

Coal nodded. "Forty-two. What's the game, Jim?"

"Well, Coal, it's just this: Look here at me. I'm at zero. And you set that tape at sixty-eight, right?"

Coal shrugged. Seventy was close enough. "Right."

"So I want you to look at where I am, Coal. Zero. This is where you started when you were born. Every inch of this tape is a year of your life. Forty-two years where you're standing. Now look back toward sixty-eight." Coal did, then looked at Jim. "Which one is longer?"

Coal answered merely by an uplift of one side of his mouth, and after a moment Jim went on. "If you live to a man's life expectancy, son, you've got . . . what, twenty-six years left?"

Coal was stunned. Jim made it sound so final. And twenty-six more years seemed so incredibly short.

Without thinking about it, Coal looked to the tape at Jim's feet again, then swiveled to see where the sixty-eight lay on the ground. He was standing at the beginning of the short end of his life. He had lived twice the years studies expected him to have remaining. Sober, Coal leaned down and retrieved the tape, slowly reeling it in as he walked back to Jim, where he stopped.

"Coal, by that number you just told me, I've got less than five years left to live. Now you can spend the whole rest of this day runnin' around the country wastin' your time tryin' to prove me innocent, or you can spend it here with me and Betty and your family, enjoying our company while we're still around. What's it gonna be?"

With his heart pounding, Coal stared Jim down. He had a big rock in his guts. Life was too short. Jim was right.

This "Jim Lockwood tape rule," as he intended to call it from here forward, didn't need to be analyzed much.

He spent the entire remainder of the day sitting in the house, laughing and visiting with his family, eating mashed potatoes with gravy and tender steak, and then, for dessert, cinnamon and sugar on pie crust. Connie and the kids kept Christmas music on the record player, and when Maura got off work and happened to come by after feeding her animals, Coal's day of rest and enjoyment was complete. He shocked Maura by asking her to dance with him to Nat King Cole singing "Silent Night," and he smiled each time he saw the looks on his family's faces as he came around in the tight circle he and the woman were making on the brown shag carpet.

He went to bed that night feeling not as if he had accomplished any great deeds, but like he had done everything that was important.

CHAPTER THIRTY

Saturday, December 23

In the morning, Connie was up first, as usual, and cooking pancakes, bacon, and eggs. Bill Withers was on the radio in the huge cherry wood console phonograph singing "Lean On Me," and the scent of breakfast, woodsmoke, and the warmth of a wood fire filled the house. Jim Lockwood sat in the La-Z-Boy in his Levi's, a crisp white tee shirt, and a pair of gray wool socks, his feet kicked up on the ottoman. As Coal saw him there, a thought struck him, and he made a mental note of it. With two house guests on top of a house that had already been pretty full of people, places to sit in the living room were really at a premium. It was Christmas season, and time to do something about that.

The sun wasn't up, but the cold steel blue of the sky promised a bright and beautiful day. Christmas was the day after tomorrow, and Coal guessed Jim would spend it as a wanted fugitive—but at least in the company of people who loved him.

When the phone rang, Coal had just sat down on the cowhide sofa and looked over at Jim. He didn't feel as relaxed as he tried to make himself look when he yawned, but he casually got up to go for the phone. Connie beat him to it, said a few words, then held the phone out to him without a word. He didn't bother to ask who it was. By her look, he already knew.

"Hello?"

Hi, Coal. Good morning.

Inwardly, Coal sighed, turning his back on Jim and Betty and lowering his voice. "Good morning, Kathy."

After the niceties, Kathy paused and drew in a deep breath. *So, Coal… Christmas is almost here, huh?*

"Yep. Almost." He couldn't help sounding distracted, and not just a little stressed. He felt a bit like he had back in high school talking on the phone to some girl: For the moment, he only wished his mother would go away.

Coal… Kathy stopped. Now Lynn Anderson was singing "Rose Garden" on the radio. *I beg your pardon. I never promised you a rose garden…*

Hey! You playing that just for me? Kathy teased.

For a moment, Coal didn't follow her. Then the song registered on him. He chuckled. "Ha! Sorry, took me a second. I didn't think you could hear what was playing over here."

I think Larry promised me a rose garden, the first time we heard this song together, Kathy said. Coal didn't reply. *Hey, you're sounding really distracted. Did I call at a bad time?*

Coal froze. Was there ever going to be a good time? "No, of course not."

But the woman knew. *Hey, Coal, I need to say something.*

"Yeah? Don't tell me: My dog puked on your floor."

Kathy forced a laugh. Coal instantly felt foolish. *That's funny. But no, nothing to do with the dog. Coal, I've been doing a lot of thinking, and I know I've been pretty selfish. I know you're under a lot of stress right now, from every side. I heard about what happened with your job, and I'm sorry. I'm sorry about Jim. I'm sorry about . . .* Coal waited. *Listen, Coal, I'm going to let you just have your Christmas with your family, okay? And… Well, I guess that's all. You know where I am. If you want to come see me, you're going to have to tell me, all right? Me and the girls, that is.*

Coal wanted to say something. He wanted to tell her she was wrong, and that he did have time for her. But he didn't, at least not right now. And both of them knew it. Before he could form any words, she said,

Hey, sweetie, I've gotta go, okay? I hope you're gonna be okay. Bye-bye. On the last word, Kathy's voice broke, and then the line went dead.

Coal could hear only two things: Lynn Anderson singing about how "there's got to be a little rain sometime," and the sodden pound of his suddenly cold heart.

* * *

Although it was Saturday, Christmas vacation, and, according to his own decision about the "Jim Lockwood Tape Rule," Coal should have stayed home with his family, he knew a different crowd of people would be frequenting the places in town than he would have found on a weekday. Besides, he had a little Christmas chore to do in town. He would try to get back home before the kids started waking up enough to really want to do anything, but he had to get into town and see what information he might be able to stir up. He had questions on his mind that people in the community might be able to answer, and the sooner he asked them the fresher people's recollections were going to be.

Coal took the phone back upstairs on a whim because he wanted someone to bounce ideas off of and didn't feel like being with Ray all day today. He would most likely have called Maura, but she had to work at McPherson's today.

He got the phone book out and dialed a number, and after four rings was getting ready to hang up. Then it rattled off the hook on the other end of the line, and a sultry voice he hadn't heard in a while came over the other end.

Hello?

"Hi, Annie. Hey, don't have a heart attack, but it's me, Coal."

Well, hi! Wow, what do I owe the pleasure of a phone call to?

Coal couldn't hold back a chuckle. "I don't know if it's such a pleasure, but . . . Hey, I was wondering if you might be interested in stopping in a few places around town with me today."

A pause on the line. Then: *Ohhh-kay. Why me, though? You and Maura have a falling out?* The question caught him completely off-guard, and it showed. He didn't dare tell her the real reason he couldn't call Maura.

"What's that supposed to mean?"

Oh, never mind. Sorry I said that.

"No, hang on a second. That didn't come out of nowhere. What's up?" He had been wondering since the night of Sissy's birthday party what the significance of the handshake between Maura and Annie was. Maybe now was the time he would finally learn.

Really, it's nothing, Coal. No, I'd be happy to go with you to town.

"But what?" he pushed.

Her uneasy laugh rang across the line. *But nothing.*

Coal drew in a deep breath. He wasn't always as direct as he might be, but being direct was something the Marines tried to instill in their recruits, and maybe this was one of those times that called for it. "Annie, I've been needing to ask you something."

Okay. By the sound of her voice, she was getting uncomfortable.

"So what was the handshake the other night all about?"

What?

"Come on. The handshake. Between you and Maura, out in the rain."

The pause this time went on way too long, but Coal decided not to interrupt the silence. At last, Annie said, *Coal, that really isn't something I'd like to talk about or even would feel good discussing. Okay? I really do want to go to town with you, all right? I do. But please don't ask anything about that again. It's private.*

Speaking of direct. Check mate. Coal took another deep breath. It was obvious Annie had made up her mind. He wasn't going to take a chance on upsetting her, and anyway, he knew all too well what it was like to have someone pressing for information it wasn't their right to know.

When he picked Annie up at her house, he could see she had hastily applied some eye makeup, but she looked like she hadn't slept all night. Halfway concerned, he started to ask if she was all right, but asking why a woman looked so tired was like asking her why she looked uglier than normal. Coal prided himself in believing that even he, the king of social blunders, wasn't quite that big of a fool.

Sleepy looking or not, Annie was still beautiful. In a way, sleepy eyes flattered her. Standing there in tight-fitting blue jeans with the ugly flare at the bottom, and a red and white plaid shirt interspersed with stripes that appeared to be made out of silver tinsel, Annie managed to look lovely as always. Some of the ugliest styles imaginable plagued the seventies, but just as with Maura, even ugly clothing couldn't make Annie Price less than attractive. She gave Coal a big smile and threw her arms around him. Before he could think about turning his face, she kissed him, right on the mouth. He wanted not to like it, but it stirred a strong, sensual memory in him, and there was no way not to like it. After all, he *was* a man.

"How have you been, Coal?"

"Good. Good. You?"

"Great."

As he let go of her, he dared step into territory that wasn't his business. "Say… You worked last night, didn't you?"

She giggled. "Okay. That obvious, huh?" She fluffed one side of her hair with her fingers. "Sorry I look like a troll." And there it was—the reason a smart man didn't mention a woman looking sleepy.

"No! You're funny. No, I didn't mean that. I just . . ."

"What?"

"Nothing."

"I look pretty tired, huh?"

"I guess. But you still look great." Trying to salvage something. "Why didn't you tell me you were trying to sleep?"

She laughed again. "Because then you would have changed your mind about coming to get me, right?"

"Probably."

"And I don't get enough chances to see you anymore as it is. So why would I have told you that? I'd rather go around town with you while I'm half asleep than not see you at all. If you'd rather, we can just sit on the couch for a while and have some hot chocolate or something."

"No! I mean, I'd love that, but I really have to get into town and start putting my feelers out on some questions I have. I've got to start figuring things out on this murder case."

The mention of the murder seemed to spark something in Annie, and her eyes widened. "Hey! That reminds me. I almost called you last night but then decided I should let you have your Friday night with your family."

"Thanks. But what's up?"

"Well, a man came into the hospital with a nasty infected wound in his side. He was with that woman from the fight at the grocery store—Hargis's wife, I think."

"What?"

"Yeah. She sat in the waiting room, but it was obvious they were together." When Coal asked for the man's description, it seemed plain she was talking about Leroy Yarwood. It sounded like he had a pretty bad puncture wound in his side, and they had had to fix him up heavily with antibiotics. This explained the painful looks Leroy had kept getting on his face when Coal was with him, and the way he kept clutching at his side.

"Did he say how he got the wound?"

"He said he fell on a sharp branch, but . . ."

"But?"

"But it didn't look like it. Both Dr. Bent and I thought the edges looked a lot cleaner, more like a knife wound."

Coal's heart was pounding. A knife wound. He remembered Bern Hargis's sheath knife having crusted blood on the blade. He thanked Annie profusely for her information. "But why didn't you call me?"

"Like I said, I didn't want to bother you. And . . ."

"And? What? Spit it out."

"So . . . I'm sorry, Coal, but I heard you had been suspended. Is that true?"

"It is."

"Oh. Wow. I'm sorry. Okay, so when I told Dr. Bent that he said it probably wasn't up to you to have anything to do with that man, and he told me not to call. He asked me to call the State Police officer instead, but I guess he was out on the road. We never reached him."

"Good. Do me a favor and keep that man out of anything you can. I'm going to work on getting him out of the office as soon as I can, and in the meantime, I don't need him muddying up this case. Forgive my language, but so far he sounds like a real prick."

Annie giggled, and Coal reinforced his apology.

They drove into town, and Coal's first stop was the Coffee Shop, where the curbs on both sides of the street were packed with vehicles.

Surprisingly for a place the size of Salmon, the Coffee Shop was considered nationally to be a five-star restaurant, and it showed. Inside, the place was packed almost as full as it could get. Coal and Annie took two stools at the counter, and after ordering a black coffee Coal swiveled around and spoke loud enough to gain the attention of everyone in the room who would listen.

"I guess you've all heard that I've been suspended as sheriff." There were immediate yells of support from a fairly large number of people. Coal thanked them, then went on. "Until I can get myself reinstated, after the holidays, I might as well let you all know I'm still working the Hargis murder case—as a private investigator. I have good reason to believe Jim Lockwood is innocent, and I'm going to need all the help I can get to prove it."

The rising din was cacophony, but from out of it Coal gathered two things, both from looking at the faces in the crowd and from the few comments he could actually make out and the tone of their voices. One, the people of Salmon apparently had such a lack of good judgment that they actually seemed to like him. And two, if the courts tried to prosecute Jim Lockwood for the murder of Bern Hargis, there was going to be hell to pay.

In law enforcement, there is no better card to hold than a favorable public opinion—both for Coal and for Jim.

Coal decided to go against so much of the etiquette of a law enforcement officer, justifying it by the fact that at least for now he wasn't wearing a badge, and he lined out as much of the case as he could. Prudently, he left out the part about Jim's condition, because Jim had to be able to hold up his head in town, and he would never have forgiven Coal for giving that away.

But he told about the muddy condition of Jim's vehicle, the muddy boots, the watch found at the site of the body dump, the description of the pickup he suspected as the one that was used to haul the body, and anything else he could think of that might get people's minds stirring.

In spite of his high hopes, nobody in the room could come up with anything helpful, but he wasn't going to let that disappoint him. People would stew on all he had said, and they would talk to their friends and acquaintances, and eventually, if there was anything to be gleaned from the citizens of this town, it was going to come out.

After the Coffee Shop, Coal and Annie moved on, and they made the rounds of every restaurant and bar in town, and even the library, the hotels, and the shops. Coal couldn't leave a stone unturned. He had certain rights at the moment, without the constraints he would have been under as a sworn keeper of the peace, that he had to exercise, and he couldn't wait. Once he had that badge back on, the parameters under which he would have to conduct the investigation would be much stricter.

Coal had saved Wally's purposely for the last, mostly because he had plans of buying Annie and himself lunch there. Holding the door for Annie, they walked in to greet the one-thirty residual crowd from lunch. The place was choked with a pall of cigarette smoke Coal almost felt like he had to duck under to see who was at the counter, and the strange mixture of the smoke, burgers, and fries made him instantly hungrier than he had been all day.

Young Karen Richardson, dressed in her white apron, with her chocolate-brown hair pulled back in a ponytail, gave them a huge smile from behind the counter. She was such a beautiful girl, and her smile so genuine and happy Coal couldn't help but want to give her a big hug. Wally and Beulah Richardson had passed on wonderful genetics, and they were doing a great job raising this one.

"Hi, Mr. Savage."

Coal smiled. "Now I thought we were better friends than that, Karen. It's Coal, remember?"

Blushing, the girl gave him a big grin. "Oh, sorry. Coal! So there are just the two of you?"

"Yep, just two. Do you know Annie?"

Karen gave a little shake of her head, so Coal introduced them, and they shook hands. She seated them in a booth, but Coal didn't settle himself in yet. He still had to make his spiel to the crowd of diners before they started clearing out.

A middle-aged man wearing the muddy, worn boots, tight jeans, and sweat-stained hat of a working cowboy seemed to be especially interested in the part about the mud on Jim's truck and boots. When Coal was finished, and requested the diners to ask around and see if they could help him answer any of his questions, the man cleared his throat.

"Hey, Sheriff." Nobody seemed to care that he had told them he was on suspension. He was still "Sheriff" to them. "That part about the muddy truck made me think of something."

Coal walked over to the man. "Do we know each other?"

"No, I don't believe so. Earl McKinney." The man held out his hand. "Good to meet you, Sheriff."

Coal shook his hand. "So tell me about the muddy truck."

"Well, it might not be anything to do with Jim's truck, but yesterday morning when I was in here for breakfast I heard old Garth Rumple grumbling about something that happened on his place. Something about a vehicle running down into the creek and knocking over one of his fence posts and then tearing up a bunch of bobwire. He said his cows got out and he had quite a time gettin' 'em back in there. He was pretty steamed, an' if he could have found out who done it, I think he woulda cleaned his clock."

"Where does Garth Rumple live?"

"Out on Pratt Creek," replied McKinney. "He has the Box R Ranch."

Coal thanked McKinney for his information, then went back over with Annie and ordered dinner. He knew the tidbit from McKinney was unlikely to pan out into anything, but it was better than whatever he had so far.

After dinner, Coal found Garth Rumple's phone number and dialed it from the pay phone at the front of the café. It didn't surprise him when the phone rang off the hook.

To salve his disappointment, Coal decided it was high time to accomplish one of the most important tasks that had brought him to town. It was another reason he was glad to have Annie there with him.

They drove over to Thrasher Furniture, farther down on Main, and when Coal walked in with Annie at his side the smell and the look of the place gave him a feeling of peace. Those feelings were few and far between.

He told Annie what he was planning, and then with her expert feminine help he picked out a new couch for his mother's living room. With a fast-expanding family and so many guests, it was sure high time. The piece they picked was a wonderful pale brown with inch-wide Christmas-green stripes and would seat three good-sized adults or four emaciated ones. The brown matched the La-Z-Boy already in the house, and the green would give the house a feel of Christmas and nature the whole year around.

As they were walking back to the pickup to wait for the staff at Thrasher's to bring out the couch and load it, Annie reached over and took Coal's hand. He turned to face her and looked down at her, which gave her the opportunity to take the other hand. She made his heart pound. Who was watching this display?

"So I know it's totally rude to ask, with it being so close to Christmas and everything . . ."

"What?"

"Well, I was wondering if you'd like to go see a show tonight. They're playing *The Getaway*. You like Steve McQueen, right?"

He laughed. "I guess so, but . . ."

Annie smiled. "Okay, okay. I knew it was rude."

"It wasn't rude at all. But we'll make it another time, okay?"

"All right. After Christmas, I guess?"

"Yeah."

Disappointment swam in Annie's eyes. He could see she wanted to drop his hands, but she didn't want to be obvious. She was still holding them when Maura PlentyWounds came walking down the sidewalk from the direction of King's.

The woman made a right turn on her heel and shoved into the door that happened to be in front of her—a real estate office.

CHAPTER THIRTY-ONE

Coal Savage, blissfully ignorant to the fact that Maura had seen him and Annie holding hands, drove Annie home and opened her door. She had been silent all the way back to her house after telling him it would be nice if he dropped her off so she could try to catch up on some sleep.

Coal was astute enough to know he had hurt the woman's feelings by not jumping at the chance to go see *The Getaway,* but also plenty smart enough to know how that date would have gone over at home. For once in his life, he made a right choice. But he was saddened by the cool goodbye Annie gave him at the door.

When he got home, a party was in full swing. Connie was making fudge with the girls, with Jim and Betty in the front room with Ray Christian and the boys watching some Western. Since the boys were sitting on the floor, it seemed like the perfect time to announce his mother's early Christmas gift.

Before Coal could even open his mouth or take off his coat, a car pulled up outside, announced by the deep-voiced barking of Dobe. Shadow went and joined her younger compatriot, and al-though she had a lot of years on him, her voice was no less deep and intimidating.

Coal looked up at the clock, his heart jumping. Two o'clock. Probably too early for Maura to be off work.

Greeting the others with half his attention, he turned and looked out the window, then swore.

"Coal!" Connie's hard voice barked from the kitchen, maybe more intimidating than the dogs.

Coal looked over at her but didn't apologize. "Willie Stinger's here."

"Oh, Jim," said Betty in a hushed voice. Connie swore, and Coal didn't even jump on the golden opportunity to berate her.

He looked over at Jim and Betty as the state policeman's car came to a stop near Coal's pickup and the door flung open. "You two just sit there and don't move. Don't come by the windows."

With that command, he grabbed his blue Wrangler jacket and stepped out onto the porch.

"You must be Stinger." He didn't feel like following any rules of decorum, and he certainly didn't think Stinger deserved a "Mister" or an "Officer" in front of his name.

"Yes, Officer Stinger. And you're Sheriff—er, uh . . . *Mister* Savage."

"Yes. *Mister* Savage. What brings you all the way out here?"

"Well, I got a phone call. Somebody suggested I might find Jim Lockwood out here."

Coal felt his jaw harden. It was a natural reaction. "They did, huh? Who was that?"

"I can't give out my sources."

"So I guess you brought a warrant."

The state bull stopped in his tracks, halfway from his car to the concrete steps. "Well, no. Do I need one?"

"You're joking, right?"

Willie Stinger stared up at Coal. Coal stared down. The thought crossed his mind that it was close enough for him to spit, and it couldn't possibly miss the officer's shirtfront. He almost smiled.

"No, I wasn't. Listen, *Mister* Savage, let's cut to the chase. You are already in enough trouble as it is, from the sound of things. And even more trouble if I can prove you absconded with all the evidence from this murder investigation. I suggest you cooperate."

"I'm guessing that being state bull gives you the grounds to be bull-*headed*," said Coal casually. He was tired, cranky, and he flat-out didn't like the looks or voice of Willie Stinger.

Stinger's angular face looked something like a wood splitting wedge, long and thin, and sharp at the chin. The tops of his eyes were flat—something like those of a rattlesnake. He was a man of medium build and stature, with a pencil mustache and thin, tight lips, but large sideburns—apparently, a man whose sense of style was dictated by current fashion. Altogether, he looked just about like his reputation.

"Can I come inside, Sheriff?"

"Wait," said Coal. "Now I'm *sheriff?"*

The cop scoffed. "Just let me in. I won't be a minute."

"We should be able to work together, Stinger," said Coal casually. "When this is all over, come see me, and maybe we'll sit down to a cup of coffee and find out if we have any common ground besides a badge. But for now, I'm spending Saturday with my family, it's almost Christmas, and I'm not in the mood for outside company."

"So I seriously need a warrant to look around?"

"If you can get one, come back. My mother's in the middle of making fudge. Maybe she'll even share a piece."

"I have a feeling we're not going to get along together." Stinger's voice was tight.

Coal nodded. "That's probably more than just a feeling." He raised his chin and used it casually to point out toward the road. "So long."

Rather than go back inside, Coal stayed standing on the porch. He didn't trust Stinger not to find some excuse to come up to the door and peek in. Stinger backed away without so much as a nod, then turned and got back in his car. Very sedately, he backed it around in the yard and drove back out onto Savage Lane. Once out there, he gunned it and was all the way to Highway 28 in ten seconds.

Coal's gaze followed the patrol car until it turned toward Salmon, then went back inside. Everyone was watching him.

"I guess Willie Stinger wanted to pay you a friendly visit, Jim."

Jim watched him quietly. Betty asked, "What did you tell him?"

"I told him he was uninvited to our party." Coal then said, "Now that he's gone, I don't suppose you're feeling spry enough to come help me bring in something big and heavy."

"I'm always spry enough, bud."

While Jim was getting his boots on, Coal looked over at Ray and Virgil. "Why don't you two come along?" Both of them got up, but neither seemed particularly excited about it, and Coal didn't take the time to try and figure out why.

Warning Connie to stay inside, Coal led his three coerced assistants out to the pickup, where they unloaded the heavy carton and brought it to the bottom of the stairs. Coal produced his Schrade, popped a blade open and started sawing on the cardboard, laying the beautiful couch out for all to see. Even Virgil voiced his approval, more so with his eyes.

Coal went back up to the house and told Connie to sequester herself to her room, and then they began the strenuous task of getting the couch inside. Once it was situated across from the old cowhide couch, to the *oohs* and *ahhs* of Katie, Cynthia, and the twins, and Sissy's big eyes, which were tantamount to praise, Coal called Connie out, and she marched down the hall, concerned about why she had been locked away.

When Connie saw the beautiful new piece of furniture, Coal got more than he had bargained for: a huge hug, and a mother's face wet with tears. "Thank you, honey," she whispered into his coat. "It's perfect."

* * *

The family gathered around the table for stew and rolls, with hot apple pie for dessert. When they were finished, Ray Christian got Coal's attention. Coal started to look away, but Ray's expression was so intent that his gaze was drawn back to him. Ray indicated the front door with a tilt of his head, so Coal got casually up, and the two of them put on jackets and went outside into the swiftly falling blue of evening light.

Ray fished a Saratoga out of a pack and looked a question at Coal. "Still not smoking?"

"Still not."

Ray nodded and lit his cigarette. Its orange tip cast a glow on his face in the dim light.

"What's on your mind?" asked Coal as the smoke curled past Ray's eyes, making him squint.

"Well . . . I don't know how to put it, but . . . Coal, have you decided you don't need me?"

"What do you mean?"

"Well, you've been out once with Trax Hansen, and now with somebody else, working this investigation. I'm not trying to push you, but if you don't want my help anymore, I'll back off. I just thought . . . Well, since you wanted to keep me on as your deputy, I figured we were going to be connected at the hip."

"I was tired of bothering you, Ray."

Ray nodded, trying to read behind Coal's eyes. "Who'd you take to town?"

"Her name's Annie Price. She was at the grocery store with me when the fight happened."

"Ohh . . . Yeah. Beautiful woman."

"Yeah. Her."

"If you were just on a date, I guess I can understand that."

"No date. Just . . . a change of scenery."

Ray drew deep on his Saratoga. "So what about Maura? I had the feeling you two were . . ."

"What?"

"Well, it seemed like you were an item."

"Not really. I don't think anybody is an item with Maura PlentyWounds." Sometimes Coal wished that weren't true for him. But one thing was certain: Things didn't seem the way they had before, and it felt like Maura was pulling into a shell.

"Wow. So if I were to ask her to a show or something—maybe a ride in the Caddy—that wouldn't be stepping on your toes?"

Coal was taken aback. "Are you serious?"

"Why not?"

"She seemed a little cold around you."

"Aww. Hard to get. I've seen that before."

Coal tried to laugh. He didn't know why he suddenly felt jealous, but he did. "I guess if you ask her on a date and she says yes, then I couldn't say a thing about it." Inside, he knew Maura would turn Ray down flat. He didn't know everything about her, but he was pretty sure he could tell when she didn't like somebody.

Coal remained politely with Ray until his friend finished his last drag on the cigarette, stooped down to snub it out on the concrete, and then put the butt in his pocket to discard in the house.

He turned toward the door, but Coal's touch on his shoulder stopped him. "Thanks for not throwing that butt."

Ray looked bewildered, then allowed himself a little smile. "Sure."

"So, you really serious about feeling left out of this case?"

Turning back, Ray shrugged. "Sure. I stayed to help you out."

"Well, I have to go back out—just for a little bit."

"When?"

"Right now."

"Your mom's not going to like that."

Coal contemplated that for a moment. He was guessing this was more than just intuition on Ray's part. Connie must have been talking to the others about how Coal was constantly leaving them alone. But he had a job to do. He was pretty much alone in a huge county, to do the job of many people. He had no choice. Did he? Certainly not now, not when his friend's freedom was at stake.

"I can't help that. With some things you have to strike while the iron is hot. One of my dad's favorite sayings."

Ray grinned. "Okay. Where we headed?"

"Back to Hargis's. I've got to interview Leroy Yarwood."

* * *

In the winter's dark, they pulled up in the yard at the Hargis dairy, the brights of the headlights sending a splash of golden-white over the weary old house. Coal thought about his sheriff's badge. He wished he had kept it, or at least pulled out an old, worn one he had found in a desk drawer a few weeks back. But these people already knew he was sheriff, or at least thought he was. Would they even notice a missing badge?

He looked over at Ray. "Hey. Mind pinning your badge where they can see it? Just a reminder for them."

Ray complied, attaching the badge to today's gaudy sweater, this time one with long sleeves, and they went together and knocked on the door.

Sherlene opened it. The bruises on her neck were starting to turn from dark red to more of a purple, and she still held her right hand cocked at a funny angle.

Coal studied both of those obvious injuries for a moment, long enough for her to know he noticed, but not so long as to seem prying.

"Hello, Mrs. Hargis. Hey, you're doing okay, right?"

"What's that, Sheriff?" He liked hearing that title. That meant she didn't know.

"Your arm," he said, indicating it with his thumb. "Looks like you could use a doctor."

"Oh, no. It's all right." Before he could say anything else about it, she asked, "Is there something I can do for you?"

"Well, yeah, there is. Do you think I could talk to Leroy?"

"Um, sure, I s'pose. But he's not feelin' too good."

"Oh yeah? Why not?" Coal was trying to act nonchalant. He knew good and well why not.

"Well, he uh . . . He fell on a sharp stick, and I guess it's gettin' infected. Doctor has him on antibiotics."

"I see. Well, is he sleeping?"

The woman's eyes told a story: She really wanted to lie. But a lie got over-ridden by the truth. "Um, no, not right now."

"All right. Call him out here, will you?"

Too late she realized her mistake. "Well, I think if he could sleep a few more hours he . . ."

"I thought you said he wasn't sleeping."

"Well, I meant . . ."

Coal had to take advantage of the situation. Sherlene Hargis thought he was still sheriff, and he had to use that belief to gently coerce her.

"Call him out here, ma'am. I won't take long."

The authoritative voice swayed the woman over. Lowering her eyes, she turned back into the room. "Hey, Leroy? Leroy, can you come here a minute?"

Coal could hear grumbling from back in the house, and in a minute or so Leroy appeared. He was tilted to one side, and his hand pressed against that side. His pain was no longer something he could try to hide.

"What's up?" Leroy's eyes were two things at once: pained, and surly.

"We need to talk. Ma'am, we'll just be a minute. Excuse us." With this basic order to go back in the house, Sherlene Hargis bowed out, and Leroy eased outside and let the torn screen door shut behind him. He stared at Ray for a moment, and in his eyes was a strange accusing sort of look. Then he turned back to Coal, but he said nothing.

"Leroy, the hospital called me. They said you came in with a hurt side."

"Am I under arrest?" Leroy blurted out.

The question took Coal by surprise. "Under arrest? Why would you be?"

Leroy's eyes shot back and forth between Coal and Ray again. "Well, no reason, I guess."

Coal nodded. "No, you aren't under arrest. We just need to talk about this side of yours."

"What about it?"

"How'd you hurt it?"

Leroy glared into Coal's eyes. There was no question he was trying to decide how much the hospital had shared. That, and maybe trying to remember the story himself.

"I fell on something."

"What was that?"

Leroy's gaze faltered before he seemed to recall his story. "A stick. A sharp stick."

"Can you show me where that was? Where the stick is?"

Another belligerent glare. "Well, no! Of course not."

"Why?"

"Well, it was up in the woods."

"When did this happen?"

"After I last saw you."

Bingo. Confirmation of Leroy's lie. He had been favoring his side already when Coal saw him last.

"I think I saw you holding your side the last time we talked and acting like it hurt."

Leroy stared, challenged as a liar and unsure how to react. He reacted in a way he must have spent years being trained to. "You can go to hell! I told you when it happened."

Coal raised placating hands. "Take it easy, Leroy. I just happened to notice that you seemed to be hurting the other day. What are you afraid of?"

Leroy tried to take a big breath, looking for calm. With the breath, he winced. "Sorry, man. This just hurts."

Coal's face went serious. "I'm sure it does. Leroy, let me tell you something. When we found Bern Hargis, he had a knife in a belt sheath, and it had fresh blood on it. It's at the lab right now. If we find out that your blood is what's on that knife, what am I going to think?"

Coal didn't bother telling Leroy that there was really no way to prove anything about that blood other than what type it was. It was a way of narrowing things down, but far from fatal proof.

"I don't know what you'd think! But it ain't my blood." Coal noticed that little droplets of sweat were starting to form on Leroy's chin. And it was still cold out.

"Leroy, I think it *is* your blood. Come on. Hargis got drunk, he was beating his wife, you tried to stop him, and he stabbed you. So you grabbed a crowbar or something and smashed in his head. It was an accident, right? You didn't really mean to kill him. You were just protecting yourself and Hargis's wife. Everyone has that right, don't they?"

Leroy's mouth seemed to clamp tighter with every word out of Coal's mouth. His gaze faltered. It went to Ray, where he found no harbor, then skipped around the yard a bit before being put blinkingly back on Coal. Even then, he could barely hold his gaze.

"I didn't hit him with no crowbar!" he blurted. "And I fell on a stick."

"We're going to know that for sure, Leroy. Real soon." Coal was bluffing. He doubted the tests would be done at forensics for some time still. "When we do, and you haven't talked, we're going to assume what that means. And so will a jury. Just tell us what happened, right now, and you'll probably walk away clean." He said nothing of how it looked to have tried to conceal the dead body. No need muddying the waters now. And watching Leroy, he saw a faint flicker of hope . . .

"You know what, Sheriff? You can go to hell."

Coal stared for a moment. Inside, he felt defeated. But he also felt anger. And the anger was all that showed on his face. He had felt so close.

"You killed Bern Hargis, Leroy. I'm going to hang you for it."

With that, Coal glanced over at Ray, then turned and walked away. But before he went far, he was going to play his last card. Reaching into his pocket, he pulled out a quarter, then turned. "Hey! One more thing. I found this quarter out here by your car the other day. I guess it must be yours." Saying that, he flung the quarter through the air. Leroy caught it deftly with his right hand.

Coal turned and continued on to the truck, Ray doing double time to keep up. They got in and slammed the doors, and Coal could feel Ray watching him all the way out to the road. As they turned left onto it, Ray said quietly, "You really so sure Leroy did it?"

Coal shrugged, letting one corner of his mouth almost smile, in spite of himself. He often found humor while coming down from heights of angry passion. "No, not at the moment."

Ray laughed. "Wow. Could have fooled me. It sounded good."

"I'm not sure he didn't, either. I just wanted to back him into a corner and play off fear a little. Maybe a little anger, too."

"Well, I think you got both those. Good play, actually. I'm impressed. But what was that quarter toss for?"

Coal glanced over. "You can't guess?" Then to Ray's bewildered shrug he replied, "If we ever find that murder weapon and the fingerprints from it match the angle of how it went into Hargis's head, we'll have a good idea if the killer is right- or left-handed. I figured we might as well get started on that tack as soon as we can, without having to do something obvious like making people sign their names on something."

Ray nodded quietly. Coal looked at him, and although his deputy said nothing in words, the expression on his face told Coal enough: About now, it looked like maybe Ray was starting to think Coal wasn't the pure amateur he had made himself out to be from the start.

Back inside the house, Ray walked along with Coal until they were close to the telephone. There, he touched his shoulder.

"Hey." Coal turned. "When I talked to you earlier, I was serious about calling Maura. You sure you're okay with it?"

Coal looked at Ray. How could he not be okay with it? He didn't own the woman. He shrugged, feeling sorry for the embarrassing situation Ray was soon going to find himself in. "Suit yourself."

"You got a number?"

Coal told Ray the five digit number from memory. Ray studied his face for a moment longer, trying to read the truth behind his eyes. Finally, he turned and picked up the phone.

Coal walked away. He didn't need to hear Ray make a fool of himself. He had been on Maura's cutting board himself.

The whole family settled onto the couches and the La-Z-Boy, and the teenagers pulled in chairs from the kitchen to watch *Audubon Wildlife Theater.* They had been watching for only half an hour when Ray got up and went down the hall. When he came back, he was wearing flare-legged black slacks and a dark blue shirt with white piping around every edge, and huge, ugly pocket flaps. He had a glaring white denim jacket in one hand.

Coal looked up at his friend. The question must have been written on his face.

"Heading into town," Ray said.

Coal nodded, a little surprised. "Oh. Should we wait up for you?"

"Uh . . . probably not."

Coal didn't know what else to say. He was determined to mind his own business. He guessed Ray was going out drinking. He wished he could send him with a list of investigative questions while he was at it.

Ray beckoned Coal, so he got up. They converged together by the front door, with Dobe clamoring to get out, and Shadow hanging back behind Coal. "You really don't mind about Maura, right?"

Coal stared at Ray. It took a moment for his friend's words to register. He thought back to Ray's earlier phone call, his thoughts rattling around in his head. "So . . . she actually said yes?"

"Yeah. Nice as can be. So I guess we're going to see *The Getaway.*"

Coal did his best to keep looking casual. "Sounds good. We'll leave the front door unlocked."

"Thanks, buddy," said Ray, clapping Coal on the arm. He turned then to the room, where some faces were already tipped up toward him. "Hey, everyone, I'm going out for the evening, so maybe I'll see you all later. Have a great night."

Virgil leaped up off his chair, whirling. "Hey, Ray! Can I go?"

Ray looked a little uncomfortable. It was plain he felt bad. "Hey, bud. Sorry, but not this time, all right? I'm going on a date."

Virgil's face flushed. It was hard for the boy to put himself out there as it was, and now to have his hopes dashed would be doubly rough on him, because everyone had seen him shot down. "Oh! Yeah, that's okay then." The boy plopped back onto his chair and pretended to be once more engrossed in the show.

A piece of the life seeped out of the room when Ray went out and got in his Cadillac. A little morsel of light had already gone out of Coal. Maura PlentyWounds was going to a movie with Ray Christian, something she and Coal had never done or even talked about.

He went back and sat in the La-Z-Boy and stared at the TV. It might as well have been a black screen. He couldn't see a thing.

The phone rang half an hour later, and Coal jumped. He didn't want to answer it. In fact, he had no intention of it. So Connie, with a disgusted look, went and picked it up. By now, it was commonly expected that every call was going to be for Coal.

Connie's voice brightened. "Oh, hello. It's nice to hear from you, Rick. How have you been? Oh good. Good. Yes, he's here. Just a moment." She held out the phone toward Coal as he was getting up. Putting her hand over the transmitter, she said, "Rick Cheatum."

Surprised, Coal took the phone. "Hello, Rick."

Hi, buddy. Hey, sorry to bother you so late.

"You're no bother. What's up?"

Well, I wanted to tell you how sorry I am about all that's going on.

"You heard, huh?"

Rick laughed. *Of course! Where do we live? It's Salmon, man! Say, I wanted to let you know that the other commissioners and I made a call in to the Attorney General's office, trying to make them change their minds—about the suspension."*

"Well, thanks, Rick. I'm guessing by the sound of your voice you had no luck."

No. Needless to say, they're all gone until after Christmas, and nobody's taking calls at home. I just wanted to try.

"Sure. Sure. Well, I appreciate the thought."

Sure, Coal. Anything to help a friend. Say, do you need anything? Even a quick visit? I could bring you something from town if you want. In fact, I've got a nice bottle of Dewar's White Label Scotch, if you're interested. Might lift your spirits.

Coal chuckled. "Thanks, Rick. I'd probably end up drinking the whole thing and then wanting to go into town and beat somebody up. Thanks anyway."

Rick's friendly laugh echoed through the phone line. *All right. Well, if you change your mind... Hang tough, bud. This'll all work out. You've got a lot of friends in this valley.*

* * *

Coal couldn't sleep much that night. Around midnight, he heard the front door open downstairs. And if he hadn't heard it, Shadow's low-throated growl would have clued him in. He waited half an hour until he heard the creak of the stairs and then someone walking down the hall making every attempt at being quiet. Finally, the door to Virgil's room clicked shut. Ray Christian had made it home.

Coal should have been able to sleep now, but all he could do was think of Jim Lockwood and Bern Hargis, Ray Christian and Maura PlentyWounds. He lay awake and stared at the ceiling until long toward dawn.

CHAPTER THIRTY-TWO

Sunday, December 24

Sunday would have been an ideal day for Christmas Eve. Being the time of year to celebrate the Savior's birth, what better way to spend the day than at church? But of course Jim and Betty Lockwood couldn't go, and that meant Coal couldn't either. He wasn't about to leave them here unattended with Willie Stinger lurking around. He could see him coming out to snoop around, illegal or not, and Jim would be helpless to go out and stop him from finding his car in the barn, since that would play right into Stinger's plan.

In the end, Ray Christian came to save the day once more. He volunteered to stay with the Lockwoods and make sure they got no uninvited visitors so Coal could accompany his family to church. If Ray had known about Connie's plans for the day, Coal wondered if he would have so easily agreed to stay home.

In another mile or two, Connie turned to Coal as casual as a worn-out pair of sneakers and said, "Say, Son, would you swing by and pick up Maura? I asked her to come with us."

After a glance over at his mother to make sure she was serious—which of course she was, because Connie didn't joke about things like this—Coal drew a deep breath. He glanced around the already-crowded Chrysler and in another quarter-mile found his tongue, without a direct reply to his mother.

"Looks like things are about to get even friendlier, kids. Why don't you all start figuring out who else is going to be on whose lap?"

With the current passenger configuration in the car, Coal was driving, with Katie in the middle of the front seat and Connie in the passenger seat with Sissy on her lap. In the back, Virgil sat right behind Coal with

Morgan on his lap, and then Wyatt in the middle and Cynthia next to him. Wyatt would be astute enough to know who was soon going to be sitting on Maura's lap in the back. And a glance at him in the mirror showed that maybe he didn't even mind.

But Connie threw Coal another curve. When they got to Maura's, Connie got out and re-seated herself in the back, still with Sissy on her lap, and that allowed Maura to be up front. Coal figured he had missed his guess of the actual seating arrangement by only a smidge, but Connie wasn't through just yet. In a voice as earnest as can be, she said, "Say, Katie, you said the middle has been making you a little car sick." Before Katie could reply, she continued: "Why don't you scoot out and let Maura sit in the middle. I think sitting by the door will be better on your stomach."

Coal almost grunted out loud. He had known Katie for her whole life, and never once had he heard her complain about motion sickness. And even if she had it, how would the side seat be any better than the middle? But of course he wasn't going to be the heel who brought this up, thus casting doubt on the sincerity of his mother's concern for the well-being of his family. Instead, he sat there quietly as Maura's sense of obligation to Connie made her slide in right next to Coal, and Wyatt scrambled to get up onto her lap.

Trying to be self-confident, Coal tried to make eye contact with Maura after she greeted everyone else, but she wouldn't look at him. He dropped his eyes to Wyatt, who had a big grin on his face as he looked out the windshield. On any other day, Coal might actually have envied him, but today Maura seemed so cold, at least toward him, that he was afraid his little shadow would get frostbite on his south end.

Although Maura wouldn't look at Coal, she was more than friendly with Wyatt and anyone else who wanted to talk to her. In church, she seemed mildly distracted as Connie once again worked her magic and managed to force Maura and Coal to sit together. In spite of Maura's cool demeanor toward him, Coal was pleased to listen to her melodic voice singing the chosen Christmas hymns. It made him think back to the first time he had heard her sing, as she strummed his guitar and sang John Denver.

On the way home, the Christmas songs continued a cappella, but of course they didn't last long before they were back to the house. Katie immediately put on an LP of the Mormon Tabernacle Choir singing Christmas hymns, while everyone else settled in around the living room except for Connie, Betty, and Cynthia, who started preparing dinner in the kitchen, and little Sissy, who of course had to be there to officiate.

Wyatt had become so attached to Maura that she was allowed a reprieve from helping with meal preparations so he could remain sitting on her lap. When Side A of the Mormon Tabernacle Choir album ended, and the needle came up off the record, Wyatt looked up at Maura.

"Hey! Will you sing some songs and play Daddy's guitar? Like before?"

Maura looked down at him. Coal felt for her. She was caught flatfooted. "Uh… I'm not sure anyone else would want to listen to me, Wyatt. Not when that beautiful music is on your record player."

"Yes they would!" Wyatt replied excitedly. Morgan echoed him on the instant, and the consummate eavesdropper, Connie, spoke her approval from the kitchen. Was there anything in this house that woman missed? If a stinkbug had been walking down the upstairs hall, he was pretty sure she would hear it.

Before Wyatt was done, his excitement had spilled over to everyone else, and Coal agreed happily with Wyatt's estimation of Maura's wonderful singing voice. For the first time that day that Coal knew of, Maura looked at him, and he gave her a sheepish shrug.

It would have been in Coal's best interest not to push Maura to sing, because she made it clear after only two songs that she wasn't going to go down alone. After that, she ended up relinquishing the guitar, and although everyone but Jim took part in the singing, Coal was the coerced guitar player for the rest of the impromptu concert.

Then, while the Christmas tree lights glowed soft and warm in the deep green branches and the fire simmered down, Coal put the twins to bed, and Connie did the same with Sissy. Coal said good night to Katie, and by the time he came out of her room, Virgil had vanished, to no surprise of Coal's. Also to no surprise, the seating arrangement had changed, and while Connie sat in the La-Z-Boy, and Jim and Betty on the new couch, Ray was alone at the right arm of the cowhide couch, with Maura in the middle, about four inches away from him. That left exactly one reasonable spot for Coal—the left side of the cowhide couch, nearly touching Maura.

Nonchalant, Coal walked over and squeezed down next to Maura, who happened to be holding his guitar. When the others tried to coax just one more song out of him, he didn't feel like he had a choice.

He sang, but by that point his thoughts were afire with Maura. She was sitting too close to him. He wondered if Connie had somehow arranged that again, although he wasn't certain how she would have gone about it, with Maura as a second unwilling party. However she had done it, he was pretty sure she had, and Maura sat so close that he couldn't help but smell her hair and whatever laundry detergent she washed her clothes with. He found himself wanting to ask her outside, to confront her about her date with Ray. With every part of himself he wanted to know if there might still be anything between them like what he had felt before.

But the Marine in Coal Savage was never going to let that happen. When Maura stepped out into the night, Coal followed her, but only in order to keep Ray from doing it, because he knew his friend well enough to believe he would.

Maura's steps on the way to Connie's Chrysler seemed faltering. Much slower than her normal pace. Her hands were thrust deep into the pockets of her dark green, quilted coat with the fur collar that fluffed up around her face, framing it perfectly.

She stopped and turned, looking back at the Christmas lights a-glow along the eaves of the house. Coal felt his heart pounding. It seemed like it had grown to nearly the size of his entire torso, as if he were the Grinch getting over a hatred for Christmas, and he could feel its throb in the pit of his stomach and in his throat. He could almost hear it echo in his ears. The multi-colored lights sparkled red, orange, green, and blue in Maura's eyes of magic.

He wanted to take Maura in his arms, and he hated himself.

She turned and looked at him, and the lights in her eyes seemed to flicker even brighter. She put out a hesitant-seeming hand, and it surprised him so that for a moment he could only stand and stare. Then he reached out and took it, and the smile on her lips grew a little brighter.

"I don't know why this matters to me, Coal, but . . ."

Her voice stalled. Coal stared. The keys to the Newport were frozen in his hand. Her hand was frozen in the other.

"What?" Coal finally pressed.

"Nothing happened." She shoved the words out between them like a big, awkward armchair.

He cocked his head. "What's that?"

"Nothing happened. With Ray."

For a moment, Coal didn't grasp her meaning. When he did, the question leaped into his mind why she felt he should need to know that. Then the obvious answer: She was reading his damn mind.

"I didn't think you'd tell him yes."

"I didn't think it really mattered, Coal. I saw you and Annie holding hands in town."

Coal was stunned. He didn't even know what she was talking about. "Holding hands? With *Annie?"*

"Oh, come on. You don't remember that?"

"No!" And his voice was adamant enough, even without his meaning it to be, that she must have believed him.

"Coal, are you and Annie . . ." She paused. He waited. His heart was pounding harder. He didn't want to hear her question, and he certainly didn't want to reply. He didn't have to.

Before Coal knew it, Maura was in his arms, and their lips formed together. Her hands roved around on his back as if looking for a better purchase, a better way to pull him in to her closer. But his embrace was so strong she could not have gotten them closer. Peanut butter and jelly in a sandwich could not have been meshed together better than Coal and Maura were right now.

Coal hadn't planned a kiss. He doubted Maura had either. They were two people who never seemed to plan anything in a relationship, and so it happened in nature's time and in her way. The kiss seemed eternal, yet it seemed but a flash. Then Coal and Maura were standing in the yard, holding each other, and the smell of the woman's hair, where Coal had buried his face, was like a California rose garden.

Coal could hear Maura's breath slowing down. She shuddered. She finally spoke. "I'm sorry, Coal. I didn't mean to do that."

He pulled back and looked into her eyes. "Are you really sorry?"

She tried to smile, looking down like a bashful school girl. He could tell she had to force herself to look back up. They weren't still in a tight embrace, but their arms remained gently encircling each other.

"We both have pretty complicated lives. You know?"

He nodded. And waited. It wasn't his place to pressure her on whatever she had to say.

"I know a lot of people need you, Coal."

His heart started to pound even harder than before. He hated to admit it, but he had waited for this kiss for so long, and now . . . Was she about to destroy its memory?

"A lot of people?"

"Oh, come on." This time she was able to force her eyes directly into his, and they didn't falter. "You know what I'm talking about. People. *People?*" She didn't want to have to go further, but she did. "All right. Kathy MacAtee. Annie. I don't even know who else."

Coal stared at her, hating this moment because he had no good way to respond. He wanted to respond to her with another kiss, yet he couldn't, because if he had never realized it before, he suddenly did: Maura was right. People needed him, and every one of them had something different to offer, and Coal Savage wasn't even smart enough to know what he wanted. Or needed.

"I don't know what's in the future for us, Maura," he finally said, drawing strength from her apparent stoicism. "But I don't want you to be sorry about this. I'm not sorry."

She shrugged, and somehow a giggle escaped her. "Well, that's *something.*"

"I'm serious. Hey." He drew her chin upward with a crooked finger. "Listen. That wasn't just you. I wanted it too. I'm sorry your life's so complicated. And I'm sorry mine is. I'm sorry if neither of us really knows what we want or need in this life. I'm sorry this jumped up and bit us like this. But maybe for two people like you and me that's how this kind of thing has to happen."

She nodded and smiled. She let out a short, fast sigh. "Yeah. Maybe. Hey, Coal?"

"What?"

"Let's don't let this change anything with us. Okay?"

"What would it change?"

She shrugged. "I just don't want anything to be uncomfortable. I want us to keep being friends. I want to be able to have fun with you the way we do. I want to be there for you, and I want you to be there if I need you, too."

"That won't change."

"Promise?"

"Promise."

"So . . . if you want to go to Kathy's, or you feel like you need to see Annie, I'm just going to be okay with it. We don't own each other. Okay?"

He stared at her. How did a man reply to this? Was there a right answer?

He could only echo her word, and hope it wasn't the wrong one: "Okay."

Coal drove her home, and but for the rushing sound of the tires on the pavement, the drive was quiet. Peaceful. There was nothing Coal needed to say, or at least nothing he dared to, and if Maura needed to talk she managed to hold it inside.

He pulled into her yard, and Dart and Chewy ran out to greet them, barking their fast-paced cow dog barks. The horses nickered from out in the dark.

Maura started to open her door, and Coal reached over and clutched her other arm. "Hey."

"Hey what?"

"Can you just stay put until I come around?"

"I can open my own door."

"It's not a question of whether you can or not. It's just not right."

She laughed. "Not right? How?"

"Well, I mean . . . I'd rather do it for you."

"Technically, I think that's only for married couples or somebody on a date."

He gave her a mock stern glare. "Would you just sit there?"

She heaved out a breath and relaxed back into her seat. Coal went around and opened her door, and took her elbow when she stepped out. "There. Now that wasn't so terrible, was it?"

She smiled a warm smile and shook her head. "Coal, do you want to come in for a bit?"

Coal had been aware of his pounding heart ever since he kissed this woman. Now it started beating harder again. "Will you ask me that again in a few days?"

Confused, she searched his eyes, then finally gave a little nod. "Sure. But not tonight?"

He stared down at her, searching his soul for words. Finally, he said softly, "I think I'm a little scared to tonight."

She smiled again, and the look in her eyes told him without a doubt that she knew what he meant. Suddenly, he said, "Wait. Can I come in just for a second and borrow your phone?"

She giggled, then shrugged. "Yeah, I guess if that's all I can do for you. Sure. I'll feed the horses."

He shook his head. "No, come in with me." He reached out and took her hand, leading her up onto her rickety porch, where she fumbled for her key and pressed it into the lock.

"I'm going to come out and tear your porch apart and make a new one before we crash through this piece of junk," said Coal. "Merry Christmas."

She laughed. "Now *that* is a deal."

Inside, she flipped on the light, throwing measly yellow highlights across a too-somber room. Coal walked to the phone and dialed his mother. When she was on the line, with Maura standing there watching him because he was holding her hand and wouldn't let her walk off, he said, "Hey, Ma, it's me."

Yes, Son! Is everything all right? He had no need to see her face to know the worry she was holding back.

"Sure. It's all good. Hey, I know it's short notice, but . . . Can Maura come spend the night?"

Watching Coal, Maura's eyes flew wide, and her hand clamped down harder on his. A pause on the other end of the line. A laugh. *Well, of course! She knows she's always welcome here. I guess I'd better change my sheets, huh?*

Coal returned her laugh. "I guess that's up to you. See you soon."

Coal? Connie stopped him short of hanging up. *I love you, Son.*

When he hung up, he looked at Maura. She was holding back a smile. "Well, I guess it's a sleepover."

"I guess so."

"I guess I don't have any say, right?"

"It doesn't really sound like it."

She shook her head. "You're something else, Coal Savage."

"Besides what?"

"Besides an egotistical smart aleck."

A laugh escaped him as he took her other hand, almost as if it was natural to do so. "What else am I?"

"Well, you know what? I haven't quite figured that part out. It might take me a lot of years, but I'll let you know."

CHAPTER THIRTY-THREE

Monday, December 25

Santa Claus must have come along in the night, because in the morning the twins came yelling to wake Coal up and tell him there were things in their stockings and under the tree. No accounting for how tired Coal was. He certainly hadn't stayed awake long enough to see the jolly old elf himself.

When the twins managed to drag Coal out of his room and down the stairs, while Dobe and Shadow were sensing the excitement about the house and running around in circles, he saw something he wanted for Christmas.

Of course he hadn't been snoopy or bold enough to follow Maura into her bedroom when she was packing to come over for the night, so he had no idea how she would be dressed this morning. In truth, it had never even crossed his mind. So the sight before him now stunned him, and for a moment he forgot all about the dogs and their antics, to say nothing of their probable need to go outside.

Maura's long yellow hair tumbled down past the sides of her face, lying like tangled gold threads and ribbons against the deep green satin of a chemise that was almost as long in the sleeves as it was at the bottom, where it ended about the middle of her thighs. With his mind racing backward, Coal couldn't remember ever seeing so much of Maura's legs before. In fact, he was fairly certain he had never seen *any* of her legs before, other than through a pair of jeans. The skin of her thighs was flawless, and Coal Savage speechless.

When he forced his eyes back up to meet hers, she was staring at him—as any fool should have guessed. The look in her eyes begged description. It was perhaps a look of questioning, of wondering. Her eyes seemed to ask him if she looked okay, if he was moved by her appearance in any way. The reality Coal was positive of was that no human being could look at his face and still believe he wasn't rendered weak in the knees.

Finally, she smiled, not a brazen smile, but a warm, soft, merry Christmas kind of smile, and Coal guessed she had read his feelings in his face. Her eyes, even still full of sleep from the hours they had spent sitting on the cowhide couch watching the fire, long after all the TV stations had gone to bed, were still beautiful, still full of a sleepy kind of mischief.

Connie came herding Virgil, Katie, Cynthia, and Sissy in, and one of her eyebrows arched up when she noticed Maura standing there in her "come hither" chemise. Had his mother not already witnessed this display? After all, Maura had spent the night in her room. Connie glanced at Coal, then used her right to remain silent and marched the children on past. Ray and the Lockwoods, perhaps wanting to relive a bit of the magic of Christmas by watching the twins, came in and found chairs from the kitchen, which they dragged in close, obviously planning on letting the younger set have the soft couches and the La-Z-Boy.

The usual Christmas excitement lit up the house, so much so that Coal left the dogs outside longer than normal to run off some energy. The twins unwrapped their Louis Marx Company Johnny West action figures, which by now were the customary high point of Christmas for them. For the older girls, it was mostly clothing, and Sissy had a Jane West figure that matched the cowboys, while Virgil got clothing, Western novels, and art supplies.

It was almost impossible to buy for Coal, and when he picked up his few gifts, he could easily guess each one. Two shirts, one soft gray, the other dull green plaid, and four boxes of ammunition. Otherwise, homemade jerky, a tie anyone should know he would probably never wear, and a can of boot polish—another item he didn't use near often enough. Oil would have been much more useful, but he kept the thought to himself.

Connie had even managed to wrap gifts for all of the adults, including Maura. Considering his last-minute invitation to her to spend the night, Coal had to wonder about that. Connie might have been planning to have Maura over later today, or maybe she herself had been planning on making the invitation. Either way, in Connie's eyes she had probably counted coup.

It didn't take long for the twins to disappear, along with Sissy, and the older children settled in to eating Christmas candy or oranges. The room now smelled of fresh oranges, besides the scent of Douglas fir and peppermint, and Christmas, at last, was complete.

Through all the day's festivities, Coal seemed to hold his breath, and he had a feeling that Connie, and maybe Maura, were doing the same. The ploy must have worked. They got through breakfast and dinner, and a huge overload of Christmas television programming, along with a couple of long walks up and down the road with the dogs, and the phone managed never to ring.

Coal couldn't help but wonder how Christmas morning had gone for Kathy MacAtee and the girls and for Annie Price, but his foolish male weakness ended at wondering. He held back the urge to call and check on them. That would have to wait until tomorrow.

About mid-afternoon, Maura sat down on the arm of the La-Z-Boy, while Coal was trying to wrap his numb mind around another TV show. She reached down and feathered a hand onto his shoulder.

"Hey."

He looked up. "Hey."

"What would you think about a ride?"

Coal thought of the pickups. He thought of the Chrysler. Didn't seem that inviting. But this *was* Maura, after all. Maybe a ride would be tolerable. He pointedly avoided looking over at Ray.

"Where to?"

"Up in the hills."

Coal's mind shifted gears. "Oh! You talking about a horse ride?"

"Of course."

"Sure. But we only have the two, you know."

She frowned playfully and cocked her head, just a little. "Yeah, that's what I thought."

"Oh. I see how it is."

She giggled. "That's how it is."

"I see you're a little more appropriately dressed for it than you were earlier." Coal looked her up and down, from her Lucchese boots and her dark blue jeans, to her plaid shirt, which was mostly white but intermixed with wide stripes of light brown, and thinner ones of bright green.

Maura raised an eyebrow. "You didn't like the outfit?"

Flat-footed. Yes. She had caught him. "I didn't say that, did I? But you have to admit it would have been interesting for a riding habit."

"I have lots of bad habits."

Coal laughed. "But that was a good habit."

And so the two of them went riding—Maura on Connie's younger, dark bay horse, Bolt, and Coal on Cody, who was still big and strong but had seen his better days.

* * *

Overall, it turned out to be the perfect Christmas Day, although Virgil still remained a little subdued. By this time, Coal was realizing he was going to need to take his oldest boy aside and talk to him about giving away Burro without his permission. But that kind of confrontation was not his forte. And on a beautiful albeit overcast day like this one had turned out to be, it just never felt like there was a place.

Late that evening Coal drove Maura home again. All the way to her house, he found his heart pounding like he truly didn't want it to. He let her out of the car—she stayed demurely seated until he reached her door—and then they stood there in the deep dark of the winter night, lit only by her pathetic porch light, and felt the first small pattering of hard snow pellets.

Coal could still taste Maura's lips from the night before. He had no right to want more, but he did. Instead, he held himself in check, gave her a long, warm hug, and then bid her goodbye.

He drove home with his thoughts on anything but the road.

When he went in the house, Connie caught him even before he could take off his coat.

"Well, it finally happened."

Coal's eyes snapped over to his mother, hiding a vague sense of alarm. "What's that?"

"The phone rang."

Coal stared at her, discerning. He could finally see the humor demonstrated by her eyes and the slightly upturned corners of her mouth. "I take it the world isn't ending."

"Not tonight."

"Who was it?"

"Eric Hansen. The tracker?"

"Yeah," Coal replied, unable to hide his impatience. "Yeah, I know who he is. What did he want?"

"You to call him. Oh—and he said for you to come eat some of my pumpkin pie."

Coal stared longer, this time until he realized she was trying to make him laugh. He relaxed. "He said that, huh?"

"Well, no. What he actually said was to tell you not to eat it all, and to save him a piece."

A laugh escaped Coal, and he turned and went to the phone. He had to look up Hansen's number, although he was beginning to suspect it wasn't going to be long before it was entrenched in his memory bank.

"What's up, Trax?"

Hello, Sheriff. Er . . . What do I call you now?

Coal chuckled dryly. "Sheriff. I'm going to get that badge back."

Nice. I like your confidence. Say, I've had some restless naps today. I can't stop thinking about that Hargis case.

Good, thought Coal. *I hope you don't ever stop thinking about it.*

"Yeah, what about it?"

Well . . . I'm not going in to work tomorrow. Maybe we can go back out there.

Coal felt heartened. "Sure, sure. I'd be happy to. You think of something?"

Just one of those nagging feelings. I want to give the dogs one more chance to look for tracks and your murder weapon—and me too.

They chose a time and hung up, and then Coal turned and looked at Jim, who sat on the cowhide couch with Betty, watching him. He just nodded. He wanted to give his old friend some real hope, but there was one thing that wouldn't stop nagging at his mind every time he thought of something new and hopeful.

No matter what started to look good, the memory kept returning of that damned watch found under Bern Hargis's dead body: a watch well-known throughout the Lemhi Valley, with absolutely no innocent reason to have been under Hargis.

Tuesday, December 26

Coal took the dogs with him the next morning to meet Eric Hansen at the Hargises'. He also took Ray Christian, for even though Ray was still officially a sworn deputy, he had seemed so hurt the last time that Coal couldn't find it in his heart to leave him home.

They were driving toward the highway, just after leaving the house, when Ray volunteered: "So nothing happened, Coal. Just so you know."

Coal looked at his friend. It was instantly obvious what he was talking about, because he had half expected it.

"I know. She told me."

They reached the highway and stopped to let a truck pass.

"Ahh . . . So she didn't kiss but told. I see."

Coal grinned. “Yeah. She told me nothing happened. About the same way you just did.”

“But I wanted it to,” Ray added.

Coal nodded. “Can’t say as I blame you, buddy.” He kept watching Ray, because Ray had something more to say.

His friend didn’t let him down. “So I have something you need to hear.”

“Figured you did.”

“I’m that obvious? Well all right. So you might have thought there was nothing between you and that woman, Coal, but I’d bet my Caddy you’re wrong. She has a thing for you that anybody can see a mile off. And I won’t step into it again. I’m sorry I ever did, in a way. But I guess I just had to know.”

And that was that. Coal couldn’t even think of words to reply, so he gave another nod and drove across the highway, despising his pounding heart.

At the Hargis dairy, Coal parked by Eric Hansen’s Jeep and left the dogs momentarily in the truck. Before he could ask Hansen’s permission to let them out, Dobe let out one of his teeth-numbing barks, which seemed to shake the whole truck, and even the yard. If nothing else, it rattled Coal’s vertebrae.

“You can let your dogs out to run around if you want,” Hansen volunteered when Coal was still twenty yards away from him. “I don’t really know what I’m lookin’ for anyway.”

With a thanks, Coal went back and opened the pickup door to release a couple of earth-bound rockets, Shadow running way too fast for her supposed advanced age although nothing short of a motorcycle could have put her in Dobe’s league for speed.

Coal and Ray walked over to Hansen. “What I’ve been thinkin’ about is this road,” said Hansen, indicating the new road, which really was only a half-beaten vehicle path.

“What about it?”

“Don’t ask me questions like that. I don’t know. It just keeps naggin’ at me.”

“I don’t have any authority here,” Coal reminded him, “but . . . Do you want to check it out?”

"You're only trespassing, right?" said Hansen. "Who's gonna say anything?"

Coal had to chuckle, glancing over at Ray, the only official lawman here. Ray gave a half-hearted shrug.

"Most people might not even know I'm suspended—including the Hargises, I'd bet."

"Better make hay while the sun shines."

Coal laughed, and Ray commented with, "Nice saying, but I wish the sun *would* come out."

"Well, first things first," said Hansen. "I'd like to look at that pool of blood again, and then follow the path where the body was dragged."

They started this process while Dobe and Shadow ran sniffing along the rough-broken new road. As they got close to the trees, Coal broke away from the others. He had been thinking a lot about these cottonwoods, and he realized he had never really given them a very close examination.

Almost immediately, perhaps because of the slant of the daylight, he saw something in the side of one of the roots that he had never seen before. A hole. A very clean-cut hole, as if made by a half-inch drill bit.

This didn't look like the work of any insect. Coal began to walk around the tree, and as he went he found several more of the holes, and all of them at fairly even intervals. With his curiosity in high gear, he walked to the next tree over, where he discovered the same thing. These roots also had six holes, in all, and all of them the same size, and far too perfect to have been made by anything in nature.

While Ray and Hansen were still searching for any of the cowboy boot tracks that might have been missed, Coal went over every tree in the row. Every single one of them had the same marks in the exposed parts of their roots. These were drill marks. He would have bet a new hat on it.

Taking several Q-Tips from his backpack, he twirled each of them around in a different hole, then placed them each in separate plastic bags and marked the bags with a number for each tree.

Finished, he went over to Hansen and Ray, and Ray looked up at him. "You looked pretty intent over there? You find something?"

"Yeah. Something really strange. Each one of those trees has about six holes drilled in the roots."

Ray stared at him. "That's bizarre. What would cause that?"

Coal shrugged. "Well, a drill, I'd guess. Go take a look."

Ray walked away, then came back over and confirmed Coal's prognosis. "I'm no tree guy, but I've worked with tools, and that's about as perfect as any hole I've ever seen made by about a half-inch bit."

"I thought so too."

"No offense, buddy, but my question is, why are you worried about that right now anyway?"

Coal smiled. "Oh, that dispute I told you about between Hargis and Harringer. Maybe Hargis really did kill the trees."

"With a drill?"

"Well, I was thinking he could have poured something into the holes after he drilled them."

"Oh. Sure, that makes sense."

All this while, even as preoccupied as he was, Coal couldn't help being impressed by Hansen's well-behaved hounds. He had left his German shepherd, Luke, home, but Clint and Bogart stayed right by him as he searched the ground, seeming overly interested, even almost fascinated, with whatever was too hidden here for Coal to see.

Meanwhile, his own numbskull dogs, after an initial greeting and butt-sniffing ceremony with Hansen's hounds, were off entertaining themselves in whatever way they could find.

Even as he thought about the dogs, he glanced around, trying to find them and make sure they weren't making too much mischief. Both animals were stopped at quite a distance off, in a wide clearing in the brush and shrubbery.

Dobe was sniffing intently at something on the ground, and Shadow had stopped maybe fifteen yards away, her head now up, her body in a position of high alert. She was obviously worried that Dobe had found something of interest to play with and she hadn't.

As Coal watched, Shadow ran to join Dobe, and the two of them picked something up off the ground and began tussling with it like a fresh bone.

He called to them, and whatever they had been fighting over fell to the ground as both snapped to attention and stared his way, ears sharply erect.

Suddenly, as if he thought he was the greatest retriever on earth, Dobe dipped his head and came up with his prize find, then started toward Coal. Shadow ran along beside him, bumping her shoulder against him as she tried to head him off so she could share in his treasure.

With a sudden intuition, Coal yelled at the dogs to stay, and on the second command, when they realized at the same time what he had said, both dogs stopped. He yelled sit, and both dogs dropped to their haunches.

By now, Hansen and Ray were watching the whole performance, and Hansen laughed. "That's pretty impressive, Sheriff."

Coal returned the laugh. "No, *your* dogs are impressive. Mine are a couple of clowns. Hey, I'm going to go see what they found. I'll be right back."

"I'm sure it's just a stick," cut in Ray. "No point messing around over there, is there?"

Coal looked at Ray but hardly heard his woods. He took off at a fast walk, until he got to the wall of bushes and thorny shrubs. It took him a few minutes, and more than a few thorn punctures, to get through the maze. Both dogs played their part well and stayed sitting. Coal was going to have to remember to reward them well later for not making too big a fool of their owner.

As he got into the clearing and reached the dogs, Coal slammed to a stop. He stared at the ground. With a sharp command to the dogs to *Stay,* Coal turned and looked back. "Hey! Get over here! We got something."

Then he turned back to the object on the ground, and a wave of chills swept over him. He was thankful, very thankful, for the lack of real moisture this December. The evidence before him was probably very pure.

There at the feet of his wonderful dogs lay a ball peen hammer.

There was blood and brain matter all over the peen end, clear up nearly to the wood. And bigger still, there were blood smears on the handle—in the shape of fingers.

CHAPTER THIRTY-FOUR

Eric Hansen stood looking at the hammer, then finally glanced over and met Coal's eyes. "Well. Glad you brought the dogs along. Even a dog that's just out to play can pay off sometimes."

Coal was a little embarrassed about his dogs playing while Hansen's were such well-behaved working dogs, but Hansen was right: At least this time they had come through.

"They carried it over here, right?" Hansen asked.

"Yeah."

"Any idea where they found it?"

"Yeah. I was looking right at Dobe when he first started sniffing at it."

Coal took Hansen over to the area where he had first seen Dobe stop. Ray followed along in silence.

Coal pointed to the spot where he thought Dobe had found the hammer, then stayed put. Hansen went across the last part of the clearing, then turned back toward Coal and carefully began to survey it, getting down and studying little signs from every possible angle.

It took him half an hour, but finally he came back over to Coal.

"What?"

"Well, I found where that hammer first hit, and it bounced and rolled a few times before stopping. It looks like it was thrown here, and as far as it traveled after hitting the ground, it was thrown pretty hard. I think. All guessing, of course."

"So then… no tracks around it. Is that what you're telling me?"

Hansen nodded soberly. "None that I can make out. Well, except for right over here." He took Coal back over, knelt down and waved his hand around a couple of inches above the ground, some seven or eight feet away from where Dobe had found the hammer. "Can you see that?"

Coal looked closer. "Not really."

"There's two round indentations. At least I think that's what I'm seeing. But I have no idea what to make of them."

It took Coal a bit of imagination, but finally the two spots began to emerge for him. "Yeah. I guess I can see something."

Hansen shrugged and stood up. "Anyway, like I said, I don't know what it might mean, if anything. But when we get a chance to study those finger marks on the hammer, it ought to tell you a few things. Can you get fingerprints off all your suspects?"

"Ha. Well, I *could* have. I don't have any authority now, though."

Hansen jerked his head toward Ray. "But he can, right?"

"Yeah. Yeah, I guess he should be able to get a warrant to have somebody printed."

Coal turned and looked toward Ray. He was standing with the dogs, petting them, acting like he didn't even care what Coal and Hansen had found. Apparently, Ray didn't know how deeply he was going to end up in this investigation. He should have known better than to throw his vacation in on something like this.

Coal left Hansen at the clearing and made his way back over to where Ray was waiting. He showed him what the dogs had found and told him the plan of action.

Then they turned back to Hansen. The reason for having the tracker stay back where the hammer was found was so he could guide them in a straight line that matched the landing path left by the hammer. After leaving the cleared area, they made their way back through the heavy brush and thorns. They had reached the rough new road before they found any area where someone might have hauled off and thrown the hammer. Here, dubiously, Coal turned and looked back at Hansen.

They stared at each other. Coal couldn't know what Hansen was thinking, but he himself was thinking there was no way someone could throw a hammer that far. There had to be some place closer they could have tossed it from.

Hansen tied a handkerchief high on a bush to mark where the hammer had lain, then made his way to Coal and Ray. He studied the terrain as he came, and when he finally reached Coal, he stopped, half out of breath.

"Why'd you choose to stop right here?" asked Hansen.

"It looked like the only place someone could have stood to wind up and throw that hammer."

"That's what I was thinking too."

"But no one could throw that far," said Coal.

Hansen shrugged. "Well, maybe I missed something. Maybe the killer waded through the brush for a ways before throwing it."

"Why would he do that?" asked Coal. "Why not just throw it as far as possible and be done with it? If it hadn't been for the dogs, we never would have found it."

Hansen gave a nod. "Yeah. Yeah, I know. You're thinking all the same things I am. It seems like anybody with half a brain could see they were just as well off throwing it into that jungle from just about anywhere."

A picture of Moby Hargis flashed through Coal's mind, and he spoke almost without thinking. "Maybe it was somebody *without* half a brain."

Immediately upon saying it, mixed feelings overcame him. He felt guilty for thinking such a thing, for after all, it wasn't Moby Hargis's fault how well-developed his brain might be. But at the same time, a warning bell started ringing. Was this that gut instinct cops and other people in dangerous occupations sometimes got? Should he start paying closer attention to Moby Hargis? And then, last of all—was Moby really as mentally handicapped as he made himself out to be?

Coal looked at Ray. "Hey, Ray, do me a favor. Grab my big measuring tape out of the pack, would you?"

Ray complied, and Coal recruited his help in going back toward the place where Dobe had located the hammer. It was only a one hundred-foot tape, so they had to measure in sections. When they had finished, Coal stared at the final number on the tape: seventy-five feet. They had gone almost four full lengths of the measuring tape from the closest place where it looked like someone might easily have launched the hammer.

An incredible three hundred and seventy-five feet!

The three of them met back together near the new-broken road, and Coal shared the measurement with the others. Hansen shook his head. "There's no way. No way somebody could throw that far."

Coal looked over at Ray, who shrugged. "I'd have to agree. How far can a human being throw without throwing out his own arm?"

"Well, I guess that's what I'm going to find out."

After a big thank you and a handshake, Coal parted ways with Hansen, then headed with Ray down to the public library. Ray didn't seem to have anything better to do. To Coal's dismay, they found the library closed. Apparently, they thought they had special privileges, and they were prolonging their Christmas vacation.

The Quality Motors car lot, however, was not closed. Far be it from the owner to take the chance of missing a sale—Christmas spirit be damned. Coal parked the truck and watched three men vomit from the sales building and other areas of the lot and start toward him. They must have been as bored as Ray was, for even when all three of them had to have recognized the fact that they would converge on Coal and Ray at about the same time, they still came on, undaunted. Any commission made they could fight out later.

"Hello, Sheriff," said one tall man in a slick-looking, flare-legged steel-gray suit. "Doug Conlin. What can I do for you?" Conlin caught Coal glancing over at the other two well-dressed hopeful salesmen and deigned to introduce them as Lance Garber and Robert Lawdon.

After obligatory handshakes all around, Coal told the salesmen he was interested in looking at the tires that were typical of the trucks on the lot. He hoped to find that the tracks located at the scene of the body dump and the tires on the trucks in the lot all shared a typical tread pattern.

The five of them walked around looking at tires. It didn't take long for Coal's suspicion to be affirmed. The treads at Crime Scene Number One—the dumping spot—and on Jim Lockwood's truck were pretty standard. He counted this as a good thing.

"Say, here's something crazy for you," volunteered Lance Garber all of a sudden. "Speaking of Bern Hargis."

Coal looked at him but didn't need to reply. A typical salesman, Garber was already set to say more. "This truck you're leaning on was bought and paid for by him."

Coal didn't know if he hadn't gotten enough sleep, or the out-of-the-blue revelation really did need to be processed as deeply as his mind wanted to gnaw at it. For several seconds, he stared at Lance Garber, then bounced his gaze off Conlin and Lawdon before settling it once more on Garber.

"That can't be right. You say Hargis *bought* this pickup?"

"That's right."

"Where would he come up with that kind of money?"

"Beats me." Garber shrugged, acting almost defensive. "But he paid it in cash. Ordered it custom from the factory, and it just came in this morning."

Coal stood back from the pickup. It was the brand-new 1973 model four-wheel-drive Styleside F-100, painted in Ford's "sea pine green" on the bottom, and the lighter "winter green" on top, with custom rims and big, bold tires. The seats had been custom-covered in leather.

Coal walked around the truck, trying to gather his thoughts. Hargis ordering this truck made no sense, considering the look of him and of his place, and his family. And it made far less sense that he was able to pay cash for it.

As he came back around the truck, his eyes locked on Garber's. "You're sure about this, right? One hundred percent?"

"Sure! Sure as we're standing here."

"What does a rig like this cost?"

"With all the extras, it cost him thirty-five hundred."

Coal repeated the number back, more to try and get the wheels of his mind spinning again than because he had any problem hearing.

"That's not all, either," Robert Lawdon cut in, as if afraid he wouldn't be remembered as a salesman if he didn't have something important to add to the conversation. "When Hargis was in here he was bragging it up about how he was having plans drawn up to build a huge new dairy barn, twice as big as his old one."

This was too much for Coal. "I don't believe that. Who's building it?"

"He didn't say."

Coal let all this strange new information float around in the currents of his mind. Finally, he just shook his head. Thirty-five hundred dollars for a new custom truck, and possibly a big new barn? There was suddenly a lot more to Bern Hargis than met the eye. He wished he could go up to the jail and look through reports of recent robberies in the vicinity. With Hargis being the man in question, the price of this pickup alone couldn't possibly have been earned legally—and that was even *if* he wasn't really going to pay for a new barn.

"Well, thanks for your help, boys," Coal said, and he and Ray turned to go.

Robert Lawdon's voice stopped them, and Coal and Ray turned to see him looking at Ray. After a moment, realizing Lawdon was speaking to him, Ray said, "What was that?"

"I said, did you find yourself any land?"

"I'm not sure what you mean."

"Land. I'm trying to buy a place, too. Saw you in the realtor's office a while back."

Ray made a strange face. "You must have me mistaken for someone else."

"Uh . . . Really? Wow," said Lawdon. "You're not trying to buy land?"

"Not that I know of!" said Ray with a laugh. "It's too cold in this country in the winter."

"Well, sorry then. I would have bet my paycheck it was you."

"I just have one of those faces, I guess," said Ray with a grin.

* * *

As soon as they got back to the house, Coal grabbed a pad of paper and a pen and called up the operator. He had them look up and then dial him in to the state library in Boise.

Two rings, and then a warm, husky voice: *Boise library. This is Jessica. How may I help you?*

Coal asked for the information desk and got it promptly. Another woman's voice came on the line, sounding older than the first, but no less pleasant.

Information desk. This is Ann.

"Hello, Ann, this is Coal Savage—sheriff of Lemhi County." For the moment, it was a lie, but a harmless one. "I wondered if you might look something up for me."

Of course I can, Sheriff. That's what we're here for.

"All right, could you tell me how far a person can throw a . . . Let's say a baseball. How far can someone throw a baseball?"

Ann gave a dry chuckle. *Hmm . . . I can't say I've ever heard that question before.*

"Too hard to find?" asked Coal, feeling a little disappointed.

Oh, Sheriff! Ann's voice feigned hurt. *Now you have challenged me. Hard to find, maybe—but not impossible. Do you want to hold, or should I call you back?*

"Well, why don't you call me back—since you offered." Coal gave her his number and disconnected, then went to the kitchen and helped himself to six ounces of cold steak and two frigid fried eggs, all to feed the hour-long workout he had done first thing that morning. He had hardly even bothered to greet Jim and Betty, who sat together on the cowhide couch watching TV, now joined by Ray and all of the children but Virgil. Connie was nowhere in sight—which meant she was out with Cody and Bolt. That also explained the absence of Dobe and Shadow.

Coal was wiping his mouth with a napkin when the phone rang, and he strode to it and jerked it off the hook. "Savages."

You sound so official, Sheriff. A light laugh. *This is Ann, calling you back from the library.*

"Hello, Ann. Did you find anything?" Coal tried to hold back his excitement.

I did. But you might not believe it. My boss says it seems far-fetched. Personally, I don't know distances, so to me it doesn't mean much.

Come on! thought Coal. He didn't have time for chitchat. "Okay, throw it at me."

He realized too late how much that sounded like a pun, and he wasn't surprised when Ann laughed and said, *Cute. Okay, Sheriff, well here it is. In the* Guinness Book of World Records, *it says that a man by the name of John Hatfield held the record since 1872, with four hundred feet seven and a half inches.* The enormity of that distance mandated a moment of silence by Coal. After giving him a moment to react, Ann continued: *But then on August first of 1957, a man named Glen Gorbous, from Canada, broke his record by throwing a baseball four hundred forty-five feet and ten inches. And I guess that's where the record stands, Sheriff. Is that anywhere near what you expected?*

Coal laughed. "Even three hundred feet seemed way out there to me, Ann. How can I thank you for your help?"

Just call me now and then, Sheriff—and give me something to do.

CHAPTER THIRTY-FIVE

Ray acted duly surprised when Coal told him about history's farthest throw of a baseball. The hammer toss didn't appear to have been nearly as far, but then it was nowhere near as aerodynamic as a ball, either. Three hundred seventy-five feet, with the new-found knowledge, seemed quite a throw, but no longer impossible.

"So what now?" asked Ray. "Go ask everyone at the Hargis place and Phil Harringer to throw a hammer as far as they can?"

Coal chuckled. "Yeah. Yeah, I know. It doesn't seem like there's a lot we can do with the information at the moment. So . . . what are your plans for the rest of the day?"

Ray laughed. "Plans? Hey, I'm here on vacation, remember? A *lazy* vacation. I don't have plan number one."

"Want to go riding horses, Ray?"

Both Ray and Coal jerked their eyes over to where Virgil stood at the opening to the hallway. Apparently, he had been doing a little eavesdropping.

"Uh . . ." Ray looked back at Coal. "What're you going to do?"

"Keep on working this case, I guess."

"Like what?"

"I haven't got that far."

"Come on, Ray!" cut in Virgil. "You'll love it!"

Ray had an almost put-out look in his eyes, but he hid it well. "Okay. All right, Virg. I'll go with you. You'll give me the easy horse, right? I'm just a city slicker."

Virgil laughed. "Sure. I can ride Cody."

Coal gazed at his son and stepped a little closer. "Hey, Virgil, you be careful, all right?"

The look in Virgil's eyes went from friendliness for Ray to a cool look of reserve when he put his eyes on his father. "I can handle him, Dad."

"I know you can, buddy. I'm sure of it. Just remember, Cody's getting a little tender in spots, and he can go off without much warning. He can't buck as hard as he used to, but he's still really strong. I just don't want to see you get hurt."

"Okay." Short and sweet. A common Virgil Savage kind of sentence. *Stop talking now, Dad* was what he really said.

Coal nodded and looked at Ray, then back at Virgil. "And keep the city slicker safe, too."

Ray grinned, but not before Coal saw a look in his eyes that disturbed him. Ray really didn't want to go riding with his boy. Considering how Virgil seemed to idolize Ray, that offended Coal in some strange way he didn't understand. Maybe it was because he would have loved to go riding with his boy—if this valley would ever let him and if Virgil were to ask.

It wasn't until after he watched Virgil and Ray ride off up Lemhi Road that it hit Coal: This *valley* wasn't making him do anything. Jim was his friend, and Jim needed him. But he had had plenty of time to go riding with his boy if he had really tried. For the rest of the day, that knowledge was hard to get off his mind.

* * *

Besides the guilt of not spending time with his family barging in regularly, Coal's mind was in a complete whirl thinking of all the things he needed to accomplish. He finally decided the complicated details of this case were something he needn't go through alone; Jim Lockwood was right here, and Jim had worked more cases than Coal might ever see in a lifetime. He was feeling so sure of Jim's innocence of the murder that he had no qualms asking for his help.

When Coal pulled Jim over to the kitchen and asked him for help, Jim let out a dry chuckle. His narrow eyes gazed into Coal's, and that patent almost-smile hovered on his lips.

"Ain't this crazy, Coal? Here I am your number one suspect in this murder, and you're askin' me to help. You know I could give you a bunch of bad advice and point you completely away from me as a suspect. I bet the authorities would frown on this one a little."

Coal laughed. "Yeah, I'm sure they would. So . . . you want to hear the case so far?"

* * *

Coal might not always have the best instincts. But in this case, his intuition paid off. Asking for Jim's help was the right thing to do. Within an hour, he had three pages of good notes, thanks to Jim's vast experience, and he began to compile a list of things he needed to do, along with a number given to each of them in order of their importance.

He started making phone calls right afterward. First, he attempted once more to call the rancher, Garth Rumple, who had complained about damage to his fences. Rumple wasn't there, and when he tried the jail, hoping to find Jordan Peterson there, state bull Willie Stinger picked it up, and Coal depressed the button to disconnect the call.

He called Flo, the dispatcher, and asked her to try Garth Rumple's number every half hour or so, and to see what she could do to raise Jordan and then have him call the house. He had a list of chores he needed to set his one-time deputy on.

Finally, he left Connie in charge of waiting for Jordan's call, and he drove into town to try and get things stirring. Until he could get hold of Jordan, he was just going to have to wade into the to-do list on his own.

He stopped first at the courthouse to talk to Barry Hoag, who was in charge of weed management in the county. When he told Hoag about the apparently dead cottonwood trees on Harringer's property, Hoag nodded. After a few specific questions, he said, "Well, from your description, I'd say you're right: They're probably dead. They shouldn't have their leaves turn black and just stay on like that. As for your swabs, I don't have any great news for you. Testing for some kind of herbicide would be real expensive and would take quite a while. And quite honestly, I don't even know how conclusive it would be.

"But even having said that, I think you're right that the drill holes are the key. I can't think of any other reason for drilling holes in tree roots—unless they were trying to make cottonwood syrup." He chuckled lightly, but his humorous delivery was a little off, and Coal wasn't in the mood for humor anyway. He tried to pretend he hadn't noticed.

"Well, anyway," Hoag went on, clearing his throat, "I think what you're lookin' at is a herbicide called . . ." Here, he paused. "You ready for this? It's a humdinger."

"Hit me."

With a tiny smile at the corners of his lips, Hoag pronounced the following word carefully: "2, 4, 5-Trichlorophenoxyacetic acid." Then he stared and waited for Coal's reaction.

Coal's eyes widened, and his chin dropped. "You're joking, right?"

Another laugh escaped Hoag's throat. "Okay, they also call it 2, 4, 5-T. Is that better?"

"At least I think I can remember that one."

"It's being used in Nam even today, far as I know. Mix it with another chemical with a big, difficult name I won't bother boring you with, and you have a little something called Agent Orange."

Agent Orange… Being at the military prison, Coal had had no experience with the infamous defoliant, but of course he had heard about it.

"I think it was back in seventy that the USDA halted the use of T on any food crop but rice, but you can still get it for killing trees and brush, or weeds along the road. I think it's getting a lot less common, though, so in this case of yours, if you can find a can of it on your suspect's property, you might be well on your way to proving who murdered those cottonwoods."

* * *

Next stop, the Salmon police department. Lady luck smiled on Coal, and he found Bob Wilson sitting inside at his desk filling out a report. Bob was already looking up, ever-vigilant, his pen stilled in his hand, as Coal came around the corner. A big grin spread across Bob's face, and he jumped up and clamped on his brown cowboy hat out of habit.

"Hey, Coal! How are you doing, buddy?"

"Good. Fair to middlin', anyway." Coal grinned back at his friend and shook his hand. "Hey, Bob, I have a favor to ask of you. I need your help trying to locate a pickup I saw the night before Hargis's murder, going up my road."

Coal handed Bob the drawing he had made of the truck, with his notes about the possible colors he thought the body and the off-color door could be.

"So you have some idea it might be around town?"

"No. Zero idea. I'm just desperate. I'm going to sneak back out and go all over Harringer's property and Hargis's, but I don't have a lot of high hope for finding it out there. So really, it could be anywhere."

Bob gave Coal the quick once-over, his face serious. "So . . . You're still suspended, aren't you? Did something change?"

"I'm a private eye," said Coal with a smile. "I don't know the first thing about it, so I'm going to start tuning in to *Mannix* a lot more religiously."

Bob laughed along with Coal. "Well, that will sure do it. One thing you'll have to learn to do is run into lots of beautiful women and start kissing them within five minutes of knowing them. Joe Mannix has that part down."

Coal left with Bob's promise not only to start spreading the word, but to come up with an official-looking poster about the pickup in question, which he would copy on the department's Xerox machine and post all around town as he worked his beat.

His next stop was nearby at the Coffee Shop, where he ordered a cup of strong black coffee, then used the pay phone to call Flo. The dispatcher's news was good. She had reached Garth Rumple, and he was waiting at home to talk to Coal.

Coal dialed Rumple, got his quick version of the damage that had been done to his fence and his creek bottom, then jotted down directions out to his ranch, where Rumple promised to meet him in twenty or thirty minutes.

Jay Castillo was waiting at the counter when Coal hung up, and he motioned him in. "You're running like crazy, Coal. You get anything to eat?"

"Coffee."

Jay laughed softly. "I said 'eat'."

"It's thick coffee."

"Okay, be serious."

"No, but I don't have time now. I've got to make a run out south of town."

Jay smiled. "I figured that much. But I got you half another thermos of that coffee, anyway. At least I can help you stay awake, if nothing else."

"Well, thanks, buddy." Coal nodded at his friend. A man could always count on Jay Castillo to be thinking ahead, trying to help a friend.

He flew out of town to the Box R ranch, way down on Pratt Creek. The day was overcast, as most days lately seemed to be, but it had gotten up a little over freezing now. Still, there was no sign of new moisture coming. With the thermos open, the smell of powerful coffee permeated every space of the pickup cab. It was amazing what the small comforts could do for a man's spirit.

When Coal pulled into the yard, a man wearing an Elmer Fudd hat with the earflaps down stepped out of a simple gray ranch-style home zipping up a brown Carhartt coat over a red and white plaid flannel shirt. His seventies sideburns were big enough to jut out beneath the earflaps, and twin creases came down either side of his mouth, making him look something like a ventriloquist puppet.

Coal started to get out of the truck as the man strode around to his side. Even as his foot touched the ground, the man said, "You Coal Savage? Prince's boy?"

"Yes, I am."

"Good t' meet you. Surprised we never met before."

"I didn't used to get back to the valley much."

Garth Rumple, who appeared to be in his mid-fifties, offered Coal a firm but cold and callused handshake. "Well, no sense you gettin' out, less you want to. If I can ride with you, I'll just take you on down to where the damaged fence is."

They drove down to a curve in the road, where in the obvious recent past a vehicle had slid off the pavement and down into the creek bottom. There a barbed wire fence crossed to divide Rumple's property from the neighbor's.

They got out and from the edge of the road surveyed the tire tracks and the broken barbed wire and brand-new juniper post Rumple had erected to replace the old one. It was obvious that whoever had done this had done what damage they did fairly quickly. Other than a little spinning, it didn't look as if it had taken much work to pull back out. Coal actually took that as a good sign. Had it appeared that the vehicle had been down in here longer, it would have led Coal to think it probably wasn't Jim Lockwood, who would surely have come out of his trance state had he spent much time out in the cold and mud. But then even that was a simple layman's diagnosis of a condition that most medical doctors probably didn't even have a grasp on.

Garth Rumple said, "I hope I didn't make this all seem worse than it is. The damage to the creek bottom wasn't really that much, as you can see. It was just that they broke my post and wire and then took off without telling me that really galled me. I don't hold slidin' off the road against anyone, but at least come admit what happened."

Coal nodded, only half hearing what Rumple was saying as he slid down the bank to where the bottom strand of wire was newly patched together. The strand up from it was bent, where the vehicle had obviously been pushing pretty hard against it as well, but it hadn't broken all the way through.

Rumple had stayed up on the road, so Coal asked him to get his backpack out of the truck and throw it down to him. He extracted the measuring tape and made a measurement of the height of both wires. The top wire of this three-strand fence didn't seem to have been touched at all, or at least no mark had been left.

He took measurements of the width of the tire tracks, then several photos of the tracks themselves, which were clearest back up on top, where the suspect vehicle had rolled gently back onto the road after freeing itself from the fence and creek bottom. He also took two different soil samples from the tire tracks and sealed them in plastic baggies, which he slid back into his backpack. The last thing he photographed was a set of boot prints, and he took measurements of them as well, from front to back and side to side.

"I doubt you'll ever find who did this, Sheriff. Er—I guess I gotta call you Coal, right? Somebody said you been . . ." Rumple paused.

"Yes, they suspended me. I'm doing this on my own for now."

"Well, I doubt you'll ever find who did it. So do you mind me askin' why it was so important to come all the way out here?"

"It's a long story, Garth. It's about a different case I'm working. Hopefully someday when it's all over we can sit down over a cup of coffee, and I'll tell you all about it."

Coal drove straight from Rumple's ranch to Jim and Betty's abandoned log home, where he got a hose and washed all the mud off the fenders of the truck. Fresh scratches on the left rear fender at approximately the same heights as the bottom and middle fence wires as good as proved it was Jim's truck that had slid into the creek bottom the night the damage was done. He photographed the scratches with a smile on his face.

Then, for good measure, he retrieved Jim's boots and went back to Rumple's to fit them to the tracks. In spite of any weather that had worn on them since the night of the murder, the boots were an almost perfect fit.

Coal gave a sigh of relief as he set Jim's boots back on the passenger floor of his truck. There was no positive proof that Jim hadn't been at Wimpey Creek the night of the murder as well as Rumple's place, but his wet boots and muddy truck now were only circumstantial evidence, as far as any court would be concerned.

* * *

When Coal got home, Virgil and Ray were just riding in on Cody and Bolt, and Coal parked and followed them out to the barn, where he filled Ray in on everything he had been doing.

"That's great, buddy. Great news. Sounds like you're doing a good job covering things," Ray said as he used a curry comb on Bolt the way Virgil had just shown him.

"You can't think of anything I'm missing?"

"Not at the moment. I'm sure curious to see how you're going to follow up on those drill holes in the cottonwoods, though. Just going to waltz onto Harringer's place and start snooping around?"

Coal laughed, then sighed. "Not sure on that one. I guess I'll have to do some thinking." He looked over at Virgil, who was quietly working on a tangled place in Cody's gray mane. Then he returned his eyes to Ray.

"Hey, Ray, I'll finish up here." He winked and jerked his head sideways at his son. "You go on back to the house and get warmed up."

After Ray had gone inside, Coal ran the comb down over Bolt's mottled bay hide, making a shiver run across the horse's side.

"Hey, Virg. Can we talk?"

Virgil was silent until Coal repeated his name.

"I guess so." The boy's voice was on the verge of being sullen.

"I've been meaning to talk to you about Burro. Son, I didn't know you were so attached to him. I didn't mean to hurt your feelings."

Virgil didn't look over at him. "Oh, that dumb old dog? I don't care. He didn't mean anything to me."

The words in Virgil's journal flashed through Coal's mind. They had long since been burned into it: *Today Dad gave my dog away to some of his friends and didn't even tell me. I guess Katie was right. He doesn't even care about us.* Words in a journal are more likely to speak the truth than words said out loud to one's father—especially when they were being shared by Virgil Savage. But how did Coal tell his son he had read those private thoughts?

Once more, he was at a dead-end. Without knowing his father had read his most personal thoughts, Virgil had once more done the classic shut-down. For Coal, there was nowhere else to go. Unless he could get his boy to open up, which had seldom happened before, they were going to keep on living with a wedge between them.

In silence, they finished currying the horses. And in silence, Coal wished he had Burro back from the MacAtees.

CHAPTER THIRTY-SIX

Coal felt scattered. And he felt lost. The lost feeling was over Virgil, but he was simply going to have to hope that worked itself out. Surely a fourteen-year-old boy would get over something like that, given a little time.

What was far more important at the moment was unraveling the murder case. And that was where Coal felt scattered. There were so many unanswered questions, things he felt might have a bearing on the entire mystery, but without exploring them there was no way to know for certain.

There was still a little daylight left, and a big question that had been rubbing a sore on Coal's brain. If Phil Harringer really was the murderer, or at least involved in the murder, this piece might play a part in bringing it out. He went in the house and invited Ray to come with him, then drove over to the Hargis place. This wasn't something he felt he needed Ray for, but having that deputy's badge in sight would at least keep serving as a reminder for the Hargis family.

Already able to smell the fetid odors from inside the home when he was five feet from the front door, Coal steeled himself. He had a feeling this kind of smell was something he would have to get used to if he was going to remain sheriff here. People who lived this way always seemed to be in the middle of something that required interception by the forces of the law.

Sherlene came to the door at Coal's knock, and its opening allowed a wave of soft yellow light and harsh brown stench. At least it smelled to Coal like it should be brown.

"Hello, Sheriff."

"Hello, Mrs. Hargis. Sorry to bother you again with evening coming on. I just had some questions for you."

"Okay." The woman's voice was hesitant.

"This won't be incriminating now that your husband is gone, I want you to understand. It's just that I might be able to make more sense of this case if you can answer some questions for me."

The woman nodded.

"All right. I guess it's just one big question first. I don't remember talking with you about this, but you were here when your husband and I talked. I'll ask it flat-out: Did your husband poison Phil Harringer's cottonwood trees?"

Sherlene pursed her lips, her eyes shifting back and forth between Coal's. She seemed to be struggling with her thoughts. Finally: "I don't think so. He talked about cutting down three of them so he could see the sunrises better. I don't think he would have killed them all. But if he did, he never talked to me about it."

"You're positive."

She paused, then gave a small nod, which turned to a very definite one. She didn't want him to miss it. "I'm positive."

"Positive enough to allow me to look around in your barns and sheds for the poison we think might have been used?"

She shrugged. "You said it doesn't matter, right? Because Bern's dead?"

"Right. It would just eliminate doubt for me." He kept it inside his own vest that he was working up a theory about the death of the trees. But there would have to be a lot more questions answered before the theory came to mean anything, if it ever did at all.

"Then go ahead and search."

"All right. Where are the boys, anyway?"

"In the barn, I think. Or somewhere out here, anyway. Not in the house."

Coal nodded and thanked her for her cooperation, and then he and Ray started out toward the milking barn. There were several outbuildings, but it was the closest and the largest.

Coal hesitated at the barn door, seeing light coming from inside it, and he and Ray discussed a plan. With the barn being lit, and with evening falling fast, they decided it best to start on sheds that might not have any interior lighting. With this plan of action, they started through the sheds. They had completely covered one of them, looking both for some kind of herbicide and for a drill and drill bit, when they heard voices outside.

Not wanting to surprise anyone unduly, they stepped outside, where Coal saw Leroy and Moby standing some distance away, but close enough to make out their words.

"I wish I had my gun," Leroy was saying. "I'd take care of him."

Coal's heart jumped. But he watched Leroy bend down and pick up a rock out of the yard, and drawing his right arm way back, he let fly with it. It was getting near dark, but there was enough light to see movement, which turned out to be two dogs, out sniffing around some bushes possibly three hundred fifty feet away, toward the highway. One was a big black and white mutt with long hair, and the other a possible yellow lab, but very light in color, even in the fading day.

Coal saw the rock strike the ground far short of the dogs and roll out of sight, and Leroy cursed. "You hit 'im, Mobe. Come on! They didn't even see my rock."

"Naw, I don't wanna hurt 'em, Leroy," Moby spoke in a whiny voice.

Leroy's tone became impatient. "Now come on, bud. They've been pestering the cows for too long, and it's gonna mess up how they give milk. Just hit one of 'em. Then they won't come back."

Reluctance showed all over Moby's body, and he shook his head. Regardless, he bent down and scooped up a rock that anyone could see was way too large to use for an effective throw. Coal was watching Moby, and the boy seemed more interested in looking for more rocks than in throwing the one he had. So far, they had no idea Coal and Ray were behind them.

"Come on, Moby! Throw the damn rock before they run off!"

Moby looked over at his friend, and Coal could imagine the hurt that must be in his face. He sucked in a deep breath, then hauled back and threw the rock. It flew, and flew, and flew . . .

And then something shocking happened. The dogs, in unison bolted to one side and took off like somebody had thrown hot water on them. A second later, a yelp sailed back to Coal's ears.

His eyes spun over to look at Ray. "Did he actually hit one of them?"

"No!" Ray replied. "I saw it hit the ground and roll."

Leroy and Moby whirled around without warning. They stared in angry surprise at Coal and Ray. Or at least Leroy looked angry. Moby seemed scared.

Coal's gaze flitted quickly to the side, where the dogs had made Barracks Lane and were going at a hard run out toward the highway. He looked back at Leroy and Moby Hargis.

"Sorry to surprise you." Coal could feel his heart pounding as the realization of what he had just seen sank fully in. "Moby, did you just hit that dog?"

"No sir," Moby said, his eyes widening. "Honest, I never tried to."

"Shut up, Mobe," Leroy growled. "Don't talk to them."

Coal started to edge toward Leroy and Moby, holding up his hands, palm out. "Hey, Moby, I'm not mad, and you're not in trouble. I just . . . That looked like a pretty long throw."

Ray piped up from the side. "I don't think it was all that far, man. It's just the late light making it look farther than it was."

Coal paused. Could that be right? It didn't seem *that* dark yet.

"It *was* a long throw," Leroy said, puffing out his chest. "Nobody can throw like my buddy can." He clapped Moby on the shoulder.

Five feet from the two of them, Coal stopped, and Ray stopped beside him. Coal felt breathless. "Can you show me that again, Moby?" he managed to ask.

"What?"

"How you can throw. Can you hit that same spot again?"

"Uh-huh."

"Of course he can!" Leroy chimed in. "If he wasn't so scared of hurting the damn dogs, he could have hit one. Go on, Mobe—show 'im!"

With a half-smile on his lips, Moby leaned over and picked up another rock. Avoiding Coal's eyes, he turned and threw that rock, and Coal studied its trajectory. The rock didn't go to the exact same spot as he thought the first one had. But it was close. Very close. And regardless of what Ray said, to Coal it still seemed an awfully long ways out.

But there was something every bit as important to Coal, and maybe more so: Moby had thrown that rock with his left hand.

CHAPTER THIRTY-SEVEN

Coal didn't say anything more to Ray about the throw or the fact that Moby was a lefty. He fell into one of those moods when he didn't want to talk at all. He only wanted to be lost in his own contemplation, and perhaps there some things would sort themselves out without expending any energy talking.

They continued their search of the Hargis barns and outbuildings, and by the time they finished the milking barn, it was well after dark. They had found nothing of consequence. Certainly no weed killer, at least nothing that wasn't long since expired. And the only half-inch drill bit anywhere on the property as far as they could tell was one they found in a tool box, lying loose in a jumble of screwdrivers, awls, and wrenches, where nobody could have located it easily even if they had been looking for it. And more importantly than that, it was crusted with rust. There was no way it could have drilled all of the holes in the cottonwood roots and still been so corroded and ugly.

Coal turned off the barn lights as Leroy had told him to do before he and Moby went to the house earlier. He and Ray walked back to the house and knocked, and fifteen seconds later Sherlene opened the inner door. She looked at the two of them questioningly.

"Ma'am, we didn't find any brush killer, and we didn't find a drill bit that might have been used."

She stared back at Coal. The wheels of her mind were turning behind her eyes, but he didn't wait for questions.

"I need to ask you about your financial situation now."

Sherlene only blinked.

"You said you have plenty of money. Right?"

She nodded. "Yes sir."

"Did you know your husband went into town and ordered a new pickup?"

"He told me he was going to."

That answer surprised Coal. He had assumed Hargis would be the kind to keep any knowledge about their finances strictly under wraps, even from his own wife.

"Is it true he was also getting ready to build a new barn?"

Sherlene shrugged. "Well, he talked about it. I think that was all."

"All right. Well, if he *did* decide to build a barn, do you know where he might have come up with the money? And the money for the pickup?"

She shook her head, a slow, deliberate movement. The look in her eyes told Coal she was half worried about saying too much. She wasn't smart enough to think ahead of him. Or at least that was the way Coal took her demeanor. Maybe he could use that to his benefit.

"Do you know Phil Harringer, ma'am?"

Again, she stared. Finally, she said, "Well, he's come over here."

"A lot?"

"Yes sir."

"Why?"

"First, it was telling us to keep our cows away from his."

"And then?"

"And then he started coming over to ask Bern if he could let his cows come over and go down to water from our side, because the banks are too steep over on his."

"What did Bern say to that?"

"He told him to get off the property."

Coal nodded. "Is there anything else?"

The woman's glance jumped back and forth between Coal and Ray. It lingered for a time on Ray, gazing at him as if she was waiting for him to speak. Then she looked back at Coal.

"Yes."

"What's that?"

"Well, they fought about the trees, and . . ."

"And what?"

"Then one night he came over and asked to talk to Bern alone, and when Bern came back in he was real quiet for a while. I finally asked him what was wrong, and he said Mr. Harringer had offered to buy our place from us."

Coal took a moment to digest this. Then: "What did Bern say to that?"

"I guess he told him he'd think about it, an' then later he said he was gonna sell."

This revelation took Coal aback. He stared at Sherlene and waited for more. Nothing was forthcoming but uncomfortable silence.

"So . . . what happened?"

Sherlene gave a huge shrug. "I'm not sure. Bern suddenly told me he changed his mind, and he called Mr. Harringer up and yelled at him over the phone that he wasn't selling."

"How did Harringer act about that?"

"Well, I heard him yelling real loud on the other end of the phone, and Bern told him he was going to have to get 'im a lawyer, and then he hung up."

"You couldn't tell what Harringer was saying?"

"No. It was just loud noise."

At last, Coal let out a sigh and looked over at Ray. He wanted to ask the woman another question. He wanted to shock her so bad that she would be caught flat-footed. It was no longer anything about Harringer. It was about Moby. He wanted to say, *Did Moby kill your husband?* But he didn't. For some reason, he held back. There were too many other things to think about, and that point-blank question was one he needed to save for just the right moment. The moment he most needed the terrible weapon of shock and surprise.

* * *

When Coal and Ray got back in the truck and started out of the yard, Coal took a deep breath. "Well? What do you think?"

Ray looked at him. "About what?"

"Oh, Judas. About tonight!"

"What about it?"

"Come on, Ray. Throw me a bone. You've got to have some strong opinions about how this case is going. What are you thinking?"

Ray sighed. "All right. Sorry. Okay, I have to admit I didn't know for sure where you were going with that line of questioning, but… Without trying to read your mind, I have a hunch that maybe Harringer gave Hargis some money down for the place, and then Hargis welched on the deal and wouldn't give him the money back."

Coal chuckled. "Okay, you sort of read my mind anyway. That could really point toward Harringer as the killer. At least I think so." He was saving the part about Moby being left-handed and being exceptionally good at throwing things for last. "So what about the trees? Did you get anything out of all that?"

"I'm not sure I follow."

"Okay. I had a weird suspicion about something, and I went after it. I don't think I know enough yet, and I'd like to get onto Harringer's place somehow and snoop around, but a weird thought popped into my head the other day about Harringer and those trees, and now that Mrs. Hargis told us what she did about Harringer wanting to buy the place, it has even more teeth than before."

Ray shrugged. "You lost me on this one, partner."

"No problem. It's a wild shot. But I'm thinking as much as Harringer likes throwing his weight around, my hunch makes at least some sense. What if Harringer went down there and drilled those holes himself and killed his own trees? Then called me up wanting to file a complaint. He seemed pretty sure his word was powerful enough to get Hargis in court over the trees, and as unpopular as Hargis was, once he was in court, Harringer would sure think it was a foregone conclusion that he'd be convicted. And I'm sure he looked into it enough to know killing that many well-established trees would likely be considered a felony."

A light came over Ray's face as they were nearing the Savage place. "Ohhh . . . So let me see if I'm starting to follow you. You're thinking Harringer offers money, and maybe even pays some out, then Hargis welches on the deal. Maybe Harringer was too cocksure to have Hargis sign anything, so he knows he can't get the money back, but he decides to kill his own trees and get Hargis sent up to the big house. Then Harringer can go in and offer money to the missus—or even go and get the place cheap when it ends up going for auction because the woman goes broke and can't keep it. How's that?"

Again, Coal chuckled. "Wow, Ray, you're pretty sharp, for a city boy."

"Why thanks, buddy." Ray grinned.

"But then there's something else." As he said that, Coal pulled into the yard and stopped, setting the brake and turning off the ignition.

"Something else? What?"

"Moby." Coal left the name hanging between them.

"Moby? What about him?"

"Come on, Ray. You're acting like that was hardly a toss the kid made with that rock. I'm going back out to measure it first thing tomorrow, and I'll bet it wasn't less than three hundred-fifty feet. *And* he threw with his left hand."

Ray stared at Coal. "Are you serious? Well, Coal, maybe you're right. Maybe my eyes just aren't as good as yours, and maybe that really was a super long throw. But that's a little beside the point."

"Why?"

"Are you telling me you think that dopey kid could actually have put a hammer in his own father's head? Jeez. Did you see how bad he felt about the thought of throwing a rock and hitting that dog? How could a kid like that be so worried about hitting a dog with a rock but be okay with slamming a hammer through his dad's skull? Come on. I don't buy it."

Coal studied his friend in silence. What Ray said would have made some kind of sense, to a lay person. But how could a homicide detective go his entire career without seeing enough cases of so-called "crimes of passion" to make him swear off judging someone's ability to kill when he had only seen that someone in fairly calm circumstances? He told Ray as much.

Ray shrugged. "Okay. Yeah, okay. You got me there. So . . . Where does that leave us?"

"Leave us? I guess we wait for the fingerprints on the hammer to come back."

Ray nodded but didn't speak. He took a breath and let out a long sigh. "And . . . what about your friend's watch, and the threats, and… What about all that?"

"I don't have the slightest clue yet, Ray. I'm not sure I ever want to know. I guess when it all comes down to it, if Jim's fingerprints are on that hammer, there won't be any more questions."

Inside, even voicing those words made Coal feel sick.

CHAPTER THIRTY-EIGHT

Wednesday, December 27

After a restless night, Coal rose early. It was still dark out, and too early to do what was most on his mind, so he ate ten ounces of cold steak, then went to the basement and threw weights around for a while. It felt good to make his muscles hurt and forget everything but the iron.

When he came back upstairs, he looked out the window at the silvery haze in the eastern sky and glanced at the clock on the wall. His mother would be out with the horses, he guessed, for he had heard her moving around on the floor above him when he was lifting, but now the house seemed quiet and cold with her absence.

He went upstairs and knocked lightly on the door of Virgil's room, where Ray was sleeping, then went in. Ray was stirring, and Coal spoke his name. The ex-detective sat up with a jolt, looking around. It was obvious he was trying to gather his wits.

"Time to get up, buddy. Or I'm going out alone."

Ray blinked, then blinked again. He rubbed his eyes and looked up at Coal. "What time is it?"

"Six-thirty."

Ray swore. "Where we going this early?"

"Nowhere yet. But I've got to get a shower, and then I'm going back out to the Hargises'. I've been tossing and turning all night long, and it hit me I'm missing a really big piece of this case."

Ray stared at him.

"I haven't interviewed anyone but Jim and Betty."

Again, Ray blinked. He wiped a hand down over his mouth.

"Why didn't you say something, Ray? Throw me a bone."

Ray sighed. "Sorry. I guess I'm getting rusty. And besides, I didn't really see much point in it."

"No *point* in it? You're kidding me, right?"

"Not really. It just kind of looks to me like your best suspect is Phil Harringer. Or . . ." His voice trailed off.

"Or Jim," Coal finished his sentence for him.

"Yeah."

"So all that stuff about not throwing my friend to the wolves so easily, that was just talk, huh? And even after all that talk about how far that hammer had to be thrown, and then seeing Moby throw way farther than either of us thought possible, *and* with his left hand, you still don't think he should be a suspect?"

"I don't know. Yeah, I guess. I still think he's too simple-minded to kill somebody, but . . . Whatever. Where are you going to interview them, anyway? At the house?"

"Don't have a lot of choice. I can't take them to the office."

With a nod, Ray started searching around for his clothes. He ran a hand around his head, making an even bigger mess of hair that already looked like it had been the battleground in a war of rats. "Okay. All right, I'll be ready."

After Coal's shower, he downed two big glasses of milk, dressed, and found Ray sitting in front of the TV with a cup of coffee. Out at the pickup, they found the sky had cleared off and turned to a brilliant blue, and there wasn't a breath of wind. Although it was probably below freezing, it didn't feel that cold. Hardly even jacket weather, for Coal. But of course Ray was wearing his heavy overcoat, with one of his customary sweaters beneath it. Coal still had enough sense of humor to grin at him, but he didn't say anything. He would have been just as bad off in Reno, he was sure, but sweating, not shivering.

They drove to the Hargises' as the sun was kissing the foothills and flirting with the tops of the taller trees along the Lemhi. Sherlene answered the door at their knock, her hair appearing to have lost a fight with a scythe. She and Ray made a great pair, although to Ray's credit at least he had found a brush. "Mornin', Sheriff."

"Morning, ma'am. Are the boys around?"

"Out milkin' still."

"Oh. All right. Say, I would like to sit down somewhere with you and the boys and talk a little about what happened."

"Umm. Why?"

"We just need to get some things cleared up. I need to wrap my mind around a few things."

Sherlene gave him a blank look while he figured she was trying to wrap *her* mind around a few things. "Okay. I guess that would be all right."

"Maybe we could do it out in the barn." It was a sad comment on the guts of the Hargis home that Coal preferred the stink of dairy cows and pigs to the fetid innards of that house.

"Sure. Should I get dressed?"

Coal scanned down to Sherlene's bare feet, realizing that she was still in a nightgown, which appeared to have been pink once, but now was some unspeakable mélange of earthy shades. "Yes, that would be best. But I'll go out and start with the boys."

When they went in the barn, Moby and Leroy were cleaning up, and they had shunted their train of cows back out to the pasture, their udders hanging wrinkly and slack. Coal watched the last old girl out the door and thought idly what a relief that must be for them as Leroy looked up from wiping his hands on a paper towel and caught him and Ray standing there. For a moment, Leroy stared, and they stared back, and no one spoke.

"You like to sneak up on fellas, huh?" Leroy seemed to be getting braver the more Coal knew him.

Coal decided to play nice. "Sorry about that. We didn't mean to startle you."

Leroy eyed him, his eyes baleful. At last, they softened, just a little. "That blood was from a deer."

Coal's thoughts shifted around, caught flat-footed. "Come again?"

"The blood. In my trunk? It's from a deer, not from geese."

"Really. Then why didn't you tell me that before?"

" 'Cause I know it's against the law."

"Deer hunting?"

"Not hunting," said Leroy. "I found it fresh dead on the road outside o' Leadore and threw it in the trunk to take home."

Coal nodded. "So roadkill."

"Yeah."

"It's just as much against the law now as it was then."

Leroy's face hardened. "Sure, but I asked a guy in town, and he said the statue of limits run out."

Coal held back a chuckle. "Statute. Statute of limitations. Well, I don't know if it did or not, but I'll tell you something that might surprise you: That isn't a law I really care about anyway. I'd rather see it go to some use than lie there and stink up the highway. But it sure would have been easier if you told me the truth in the first place."

"How should I know you ain't just like the rest o' them cops, writin' people tickets for every little thing?"

"I guess you wouldn't. But now you know."

Leroy only stared, so Coal went on. "We need to talk to the two of you. Separately."

Leroy's glance flew to Moby, who stood there with his hands hanging at his sides, staring at Coal's knees. "Mobe can't carry on no conversation with you. What's it for anyway?"

"Just to clear this thing up so we can all move on."

"Well, I can talk to you. You don't need Mobe."

Coal's mind raced. He couldn't lose the chance to talk to Moby Hargis altogether, so he would do well not to anger the young man's self-appointed bodyguard at this stage of the investigation.

"All right, let's wait on that. But how about we have him do one thing for me?"

"What?"

"I'd like to see him take a hammer and see how far he can throw it—like he threw that rock at the dog."

"Huh? What for?"

"Curiosity. I want to see if a hammer flies the same as a rock, and I need it to go a certain distance. I'm pretty sure only Moby can throw that far."

Moby almost smiled, although he still would not look up. Coal felt a surge of sympathy for him. How must it be to be so simple? Leroy patted his friend on the shoulder. "You got quite a arm, don't you, Mobe?" Suggesting that perhaps all in all Leroy wasn't much more advanced in the brain than his friend. He seemed to have no clue at all what this test was might do to Moby.

Coal turned to Ray. "Hey, would you take Moby with you to the house and see if you can make a phone call to Trax Hansen? I'd like him to be out here if you can find him."

While Ray marched off with Moby, Coal and Leroy went into the milking barn and found two stools. It was dark and dank in there, and the warm, earthy stink of new milk mingled with old, dirty cows engulfed the place. There was enough manure and straw around that Coal wondered how this place ever passed a health inspection. It wasn't like anywhere he could ever have imagined holding an interview, but as bad as it might be, it beat the house from every angle.

Although Coal hadn't been involved much in the intricacies of homicide investigation, he had had plenty of experience interviewing criminals. Besides firearms proficiency, this was one of his fortes. But although he took every approach he could think of, he wasn't able to get anything that seemed useful out of Leroy. Leroy had apparently done a lot of thinking about the eventuality of being questioned in-depth, and he must have drilled himself with the same answers over and over. The gist of what Coal got out of the interview was what he already knew or had been told: The blood in the trunk was from a deer—which would be ascertained when the blood tests came back, and which fit the fact that his car wouldn't have made it out of Wimpey Creek anyway—and he had gotten the wound in his side when he fell on a sharp stick. He had never seen a ball peen hammer on the property, according to him, and he knew absolutely nothing about Bern Hargis's financial dealings. In short, Leroy was a rock-solid interviewee, and Coal couldn't break him. Had he been on his own turf, in a real interview room, with time to kill, and a partner, the odds would be different. But he couldn't set foot near the sheriff's office, and he had nowhere else to go.

When they went outside, Moby, Sherlene, and Ray were standing there patiently. They were still waiting on Trax Hansen, who had said he would get there as soon as he could, so Coal took Sherlene inside the barn, fully expecting to fare far better in her interview than he had with Leroy.

To his surprise, Sherlene didn't help much either, and halfway through the interview Coal thought of something. Had he been clear-headed enough at the start of the investigation, and his mind not been clogged with thoughts of Jim Lockwood committing murder, he would have interviewed these people as early as possible, before they had a chance to sit and put together an ironclad story. That was something Ray should have jumped on, since homicide investigations had been his job. It seemed so strange to Coal that a big city detective had let something like that slide.

But it didn't matter now. The fact was Leroy had stuck to his story, and now Sherlene clung to hers as if to a life raft, and unless they allowed him to interview Moby, the one person he was sure he could get to crack, he had painted himself into a corner now, as far as anything useful he would gain from interviews with these people outside of an official setting.

He thought of Phil Harringer with a sick stomach. Was it going to be any better with him? The only chance he had there was if the rancher was so arrogant as to believe he wasn't even a suspect. That gave Coal a glimmer of hope, because nobody was more arrogant than Phil Harringer.

Trax Hansen wheeled his Jeep into the yard not long after Coal and Sherlene stepped out of the milking barn. Coal set up the hammer-throwing test as he and Hansen were guessing it must have happened. It came as little surprise when the hammer thrown powerfully and accurately by Moby Hargis went to almost the exact place they had asked him to throw it, then bounced away.

It was the results of the test once the hammer hit the ground that baffled Coal.

CHAPTER THIRTY-NINE

Coal stood at some distance and watched Trax Hansen carefully inspect the clearing where Moby had thrown the hammer. He moved with purpose in every step, and by his furrowed brow his mind was working furiously.

After twenty minutes, he walked with the hammer toward Coal, having to step over a few bushes to reach him and Ray. The others had stayed back in the place Moby had thrown from.

Hansen stared at Coal until Coal got nervous.

"What?"

Hansen shook his head, throwing a glance back toward where he had picked up the hammer. "Well, I feel a little stupid."

"Why?"

"Because. Hammers aren't round rocks."

After a moment waiting for Hansen to expound on his cryptic comment, and realizing that he was expected to bite the hook first, Coal replied, "Well, it's obvious you're no caveman."

The reply took Hansen by surprise, and he laughed. "Thanks, Coal. That's the nicest thing you've ever said to me."

"Don't mention it. Now what the hell are you talking about?"

"I should have thought of this before. With the shape of a hammer, it's going to be something more like a football than like a baseball. It isn't necessarily going to keep traveling in a straight path, even with momentum. Depending on how it hits, it could bounce anywhere."

"Okay . . . and?"

"Well, this thing bounced clear off to one side. And if he threw it ten more times, it might bounce ten different ways. I feel pretty ridiculous not thinking of that sooner."

What Hansen was saying struck Coal hard. "So the whole theory of the hammer being thrown from where Moby just threw it . . ."

"Doesn't mean a thing. And another thing. Look where this hammer hit the mud."

Hansen held up the hammer, and Coal studied it. It took about four seconds to realize what the tracker was trying to point out. A large section of the hammer head had flecks of mud on it.

He didn't voice his conclusion, but Hansen did it for him. Any hammer thrown from that distance into this same soil type, with more or less the same amount of moisture, was likely to sink down into the mud, and there had been no mud at all on the murder weapon.

Hansen and Coal realized the same two things separately and corroborated them out loud: The suspect hammer could have been thrown from any number of other places and still bounced to where Dobe had found it. And had it been thrown three hundred and fifty feet, it surely would have had mud on it, somewhere, for there had been no heavy rains since the night of the murder, and nothing else would have cleaned it off.

Moby's incredible throwing ability, while remarkable, only proved he had a special talent. As sure as Coal had been before, he was just as sure the opposite way now—so far there was nothing pointing to Moby over anyone else as the killer of his father. It was all going to come down to the identity of the fingerprints on the hammer handle—and that was on the off-chance that any of them ended up being clear enough to identify.

Before leaving, Coal tried once again, in a very gentle way, to get Leroy and Sherlene to let him talk to Moby alone, but neither would budge. They kept saying it would traumatize the boy—although of course that wasn't the wording they used, since using such a huge word would probably have traumatized the both of them.

In the end, Coal could only leave. If he was going to interview Moby, he would have to put him under arrest.

When they got back to the house, everyone was awake, and the house was in its usual controlled pandemonium. Connie had finally come to her senses and realized everyone might have already had enough of her sugar-loaded cookies for a while. So instead, she and the girls were making a cake. She was proving to be just about what every serious bodybuilder didn't need in his home.

"Daddy!" Morgan came running in and hugged Coal. Of course he had to inform his father of the obvious, even though Coal could see the cake-making under a full head of steam.

Connie motioned Coal to her, so he picked Morgan up and went into where the decadence was taking place. The other children greeted him happily, but the one that touched him the most was Sissy, who gave him a shy smile, nearly as rare as an honest politician. He tousled her hair and smiled back at her, melting at the happy look in her eyes.

"What's up, Mom?"

"You'd better call Jordan Peterson as soon as you can."

Coal felt instant alarm. "Why? Something happen? Is it about Todd?"

She shook her head. "No, I don't think so. He would have told me that. But he sounded pretty serious and made me promise to have you call him at the office as soon as you could."

Morgan wouldn't hear of having his father set him down so soon after their happy reunion, so Coal took him into the other room and dialed the office. Willey Stinger's voice came over the phone, and Coal disconnected. After a moment's thought, he called up Flo and heard her slightly raspy voice answer.

"Hey, beautiful."

Flo laughed. *I think you have the wrong number.*

"Nope. That sounds like the woman I'm looking for."

Well, you must want something really important, Coal. What can I do for you? I mean, after a greeting like that, I have to do something.

"Okay, you got me. Yeah, Flo, do you think you could try to get Jordan on the radio and have him landline you back? He wanted me to call him, but when I tried the office the state bull picked it up."

Oh, yes. Him. The tone of her voice changed completely.

"Why, Flo, I detect a hint of displeasure in your voice."

Ha! Is that what you would call it? Okay. Well, you're right. Displeasure at the very least. I hope I never have to speak with that man again.

"That bad, huh?"

That bad. Anyway. You've got it, Coal. I'll raise Jordan and have him call you. At the house?

"Yes. I'll stay here and wait for it."

It was half an hour before the phone rang, and Coal set down a fat sirloin steak and went over to pick it up, answering around a mouthful of beef.

Hey, Coal. I'm glad you're back, came Jordan's voice.

"What's up, buddy?"

Well, it's not good. I don't know how he found it out, but I guess it just proves this whole valley has loose lips. Stinger knows you're still working Jim's case, and he's madder than a slapped wolverine.

Coal chuckled at the colorful simile. "No surprise. Some people just have to talk. So what was he saying?"

He told me he wouldn't be surprised if I talked to you before he did and ordered me to tell you you'd better stop. But don't worry—I won't tell him we spoke.

"Ha! No, Jordan, by all means, let him know. I don't take orders from that windbag."

Really? You don't care if he knows?

"On the contrary. I'd like to rub it in his face. He'll soon find out he might be able to bluff some people, but some he can't."

All right, then. If you're sure.

"I'm sure."

Coal hung up, his mind already working feverishly. Stinger's warning about working Jim's case only served to dig spurs deeper into his ribs. He needed to think of something to do on the case now just to feel the pleasure of "going against direct orders". When he told Connie that, she frowned.

"Coal, you be careful, okay? Why do you always have to be this way? Even back when you were in grade school. So obstinate and contrary."

Coal grinned. "Not with the people I cared about."

She smiled and patted his cheek. "I just don't want to see you get in trouble, honey. Be careful."

Coal smiled back at her, enjoying the feeling of his mother watching out for his well-being, even after he had been grown up for more than two decades.

He went and sat in the soft easy chair for a while and chatted with Jim and Betty. Nobody said anything about it, but it didn't take very long to sense the restlessness building up in his old friend. Somehow, he had to bring this whole thing to a head. As far as he knew, Jim Lockwood had never had to hide from anything in his life. This feeling of being cooped up in the Savage home, unable to step out and breathe in some fresh air whenever he felt like it, must be wearing him down.

"I'm going to stir something up, Jim. Kick the hornet nest over."

Jim gave a lopsided grin. "Don't do anything dumb on my account, son. I'll be okay."

Coal eyed him closely. "Well, buddy, I don't believe you. You act like a cat in a cage."

"That obvious, huh?"

"Yeah. Listen. Stay in the house, would you? I'm going to go do something that's been gnawing on my mind for a while."

"What's that?"

"I can't tell you. You're a wanted felon, remember?"

Jim grunted. "How could I forget?"

Ray Christian came out of the bathroom and followed Coal outside when he put on his coat and stepped out on the porch, sucking in a deep breath of the cold, crisp air.

"What are we doing now?"

"Not we. Me."

"Wait. You aren't taking me?"

"Listen, Ray, I'm only willing to pull you into this thing so far. I have to go do something that might be a little shady. I'd rather you didn't know anything about it until later."

Ray stared him down. Coal didn't budge. "I don't like it, Coal. I'm just as much a part of this as you. I think I should be around in case you get in trouble."

"Nope. I'm doing this one alone."

A look somewhere between irritation and anger flashed across Ray's face. "Well, I guess I'll just go take a drive then. Don't get your tail in a crack you can't get it out of."

Coal drove away knowing Ray was put out. Right then, he didn't care. He truly was planning on doing something illegal, if it came down to it. He wasn't going to feel responsible for getting Ray brought up on charges too.

He drove the pickup across the highway onto Barracks Lane, continuing on past the Hargis and Harringer places.

Shortly, he came across a field hand mending a section of barbwire fence with a scattering of fat red Herefords in a field on the other side, ignoring him as they grazed at the dead yellow grasses. Coal drew a deep breath. This was what he had been hoping for. He stopped and got out, and the man, obviously one of Mexican descent, stopped and straightened up from his work. His eyes jumped to either side of Coal as his hands came all the way down to his sides, one of them clutching a pair of fencing pliers.

"Howdy. How are things?"

The man stared at him. He had a not-so-hidden look of trepidation in his dark eyes. He shrugged, glancing around. "No comprendo. No . . . En-*gleesh.*"

Coal sighed, trying to decide with his interrogation skills if the man was playing him. He guessed he wasn't. And beyond a few words like *amigo, adios, casa, cerveza,* and *burrito,* he didn't know enough Spanish to hint with a bucketful of gravel. If he were down in Mexico, he couldn't even have asked where the restrooms were.

"You don't understand English?"

"No, hombre."

With a shrug, Coal scanned the area around them. This man was alone. "Anybody else work with you?"

A pained look in his eyes, the man gave a little smile and a shrug. "Perdóname."

Coal just nodded and used his prize *adios,* then went back to the pickup and drove on. Once he was past Harringer's property and on federal ground, he parked the pickup, took his binoculars from behind the seat, along with a folded tarp, and mounted the first of the foothills that started the march up to the westernmost point of the Lemhi Range.

He was going to be forced into doing things the harder way. The Coal Savage way.

Coal's original idea was to find one of Harringer's ranch hands and offer him fifty dollars to sneak into his shops and look for the weed killer known affectionately as 2, 4, 5-T, which hopefully they would locate somewhere near a drill. It was no surprise that a man like Harringer was using Mexicans to do his work—and probably paying them a good fifty cents an hour to do it. Men like that didn't get rich by being generous.

The idea of enlisting the help of an inside man was not going to work. So Coal was going to have to do it himself. But he couldn't simply waltz onto Harringer's place and start digging. He didn't need to end up in jail for trespassing at this point.

He settled down in between sagebrush, his butt resting on the folded tarp, and raised his glasses. From where he was seated, he couldn't see the front of Harringer's house, but he had seen the rancher's pickup parked directly in front on his way by. He didn't know how he was going to stand sitting up here for long, but what else did he have to do today?

Another big question: Was it really so important if he located the weed killer on Harringer's place? Anyone could buy that stuff at the local hardware store, according to the county weed control man. Its presence by itself didn't prove anything substantial. But he had a hunch about Harringer and the Hargis killing, and he wasn't going to let go of it easy. If he was grasping at straws, then he would keep grasping.

As Coal sat there, he scanned the country around, and several minutes after sitting down he saw a heavy cloud of smoke come up from down in the trees. It appeared to be on the Hargis place, but he could see the top of their house from where he sat, and the smoke was coming up from closer, toward the foothills. At first, he thought maybe they were burning leaves or something, but after a few minutes it settled down to a gentle, continuous wisp. A campfire? What was in those trees that would make anyone go there to camp, especially in December?

It almost startled Coal when, only twenty-five minutes into his wait, he saw the pickup belonging to Phil Harringer pull into view from behind the house and head down to Barracks Lane. He stared at it through the glasses, his heart starting to pound. How could this be so easy? He had already asked around, and it had come as no surprise to learn that Harringer's wife had left him some years ago, and all their children were grown and gone. Harringer lived in that big house all alone, because it was unlikely anyone else could stand him long enough to make it a permanent home.

Knowing what he did of Harringer's personality, it was about as likely that he would let his field hands have access to his house as it was that Coal could fish for bass in the Sea of Tranquility. So if the rancher was driving away, that place now stood empty.

Coal picked up his tarp and glasses and took off down the muddy hill so fast he nearly went head over heels a couple of times, and once he slipped and went down, sliding several feet on his hip and the side of his leg and muddying up his Wranglers.

He threw the glasses and tarp into the front seat and leaped in, firing the truck up and fishtailing it out of its parking spot until he was slipping along the road some twenty-five miles an hour, right past the astonished field hand and on to the house.

He paused as he made the turn-off to Harringer's, glancing in his rearview mirror. If the Mexican field hand was paying any attention, he would see him turn in. But it was a chance he had to take. He sat there and looked along the road toward Highway 28, hoping Harringer would stay gone at least until he had a good chance to scour all of his outbuildings and his garage, if need be.

As he was about to turn in, he stopped. He looked toward the Hargis place, then back at Harringer's house. At last, he gave out a sigh. He was being too reckless. Setting himself up for real trouble. If nothing else, he at least had to park the truck somewhere besides right on Harringer's land. So he drove on, looking for a wide spot in the road.

As he feared, there was no wide spot. But there was the Hargises'.

Gritting his teeth and glancing back toward Harringer's, he made his decision and turned into the Hargis place, then made a sharp left and parked in the weeds. He could smell smoke, and a gentle wind was puttering along the new road Hargis had been cutting. He had no doubt it was the same smoke he had seen from the hill.

Glancing around, he shucked his Smith and Wesson from the holster and checked for six loads in the cylinder, pulled his backpack out from behind the seat, then crossed the fence and headed for trouble.

CHAPTER FORTY

Coal hated the feeling that ballooned in his guts as he crossed Barracks Lane and ventured onto the property of the enemy. He despised this feeling inside, the terribly pounding heart, the wretched moths that fluttered in his stomach, the ringing in his ears. It brought back memories that already were always far too close to the surface—memories from Korea and Nam.

He had to force himself to breathe deeply to keep his hands from shaking. He was on the property of a man he not only deplored, but a man who possibly had already committed murder, and if so would not likely balk at doing it again.

The most mild consequence he could imagine from being caught on this property was a trespassing charge—a stripe that would not look good on the record of a man trying to retain his seat as county sheriff when the next election rolled around. He could not afford to be caught here, and especially not inside Harringer's buildings. It was the kind of offense that could find him working in a hardware store or lumber yard the rest of his life.

But he had to take the risk. His gut instincts told him Harringer was his killer, in spite of any other evidence. Or maybe it was only that he wanted so bad for him to be.

There was nothing to hide his passage as he moved along Harringer's lane, so he chose to do it in the most nonchalant manner possible, like a man strolling along to visit a friend. Ironically, that in itself would be suspicious, for most people in this valley had to know Harringer was unlikely to have very many friends. And if he did, they would be haughty men such as himself, men who would never lower themselves to walking up to his house when they could drive.

Heart pounding faster than ever, Coal looked back at the highway, then at the front door of the house. He couldn't take unnecessary chances. What people in town claimed, and what could be the truth, might be two completely different things. What if Harringer had a maid? Or what if some relative were visiting? He had to know.

Taking a big breath, he walked to the front door and knocked, with the backpack hanging on one shoulder. He waited. Seconds ticked by, sounding as real as if he had a clock in his head. Of course that was simply his thunderous pulse. He waited. And waited. Started to turn away, then waited some more.

Finally, he knocked again. And nobody came.

Turning from the door at last, he looked along the lane back toward the highway and toward Hargises'. He could just see his pickup beyond the dead cottonwoods. A brown Cadillac flew east on 28. Then a blue Ford pickup. A pale green Plymouth went the other way, headed toward town. Coal gulped a breath of air and went down the steps. Here he was. It was time to do what he had come for.

The biggest shop sat directly behind the house. This building, while not as opulent as the house, was at least twice its size. The doorknob turned without effort, and the door eased open. Coal threw a glance behind him. He saw dots of black and red that were cattle, across the highway. But no other sign of life.

Leaving the door open, Coal looked around and found a light switch to the left of the door. He flipped it on, then gently closed the door, letting his eyes adjust to the light. In here was parked a beautiful new Lincoln Continental, sleek teal in color and as long as a river barge. There was a sixty-six Corvette convertible in Nassau blue with a white top. A cute car, but one that had never tickled Coal's fancy.

Other than these, there were three monstrous pieces of farm equipment, a disker and two others whose use he could only guess at. But he was pretty sure any of the three was worth more than his mom's house.

Along the far wall, lit by a couple of windows, stood a workbench, and to its left some kind of enclosed room, maybe twelve to fourteen feet square. Coal moved toward the bench, hating the pounding of his heart, thinking of the enemy beyond the walls of this building, knowing there would be no friendly chopper coming for him if he got in trouble in here. In fact, he had no means of communication at all with the outside world.

There was plenty of light from the banks of fluorescent lights overhead and the windows for Coal to see everything on the workbench. The array of tools was impressive, although he noticed with a little amusement that most of them appeared to be unused. Some men collected tools like Coal collected enemies. Harringer no doubt had a massive accumulation of both.

Coal stopped. He stared at a big bucket squatting in shadow on the floor under the bench. It was dark gray metal with a pour spout coming like a chimney from the top, and on the front of it was glued what appeared to be a very important white label. Moving closer, he set his backpack on the workbench and crouched down.

The words that greeted him were not what he expected. But they were close enough.

In huge black letters, it read: 2, 4-D. Beneath this attention-grabber, it read, more technically: 2, 4-Dichlorophenoxyacetic acid. It then went on with directions for use and cautionary statements. This was not the 2, 4, 5-Trichlorophenoxyacetic acid that the county weed guy had told him about. But its label made it plenty obvious that it was used for the same purpose.

It would have meant very little to see it here, for this was, after all, a ranch, and every ranch or farm must have something similar. It was the open-top wooden toolbox that sat beside it which seemed suddenly to explode Coal's innards like a big balloon. Inside the toolbox was a drill, a drill with a half-inch bit still attached.

With an almost trembling hand, Coal reached for the drill, a Skil, made of heavy gray metal and looking like some kind of fat, ugly space-age pistol. He hefted it and looked at the spade bit, and there, unmistakably, were flecks of wood. He brought the tip of the bit to his nose and sniffed. He couldn't be positive, but he smelled, or at least wanted to smell, the aged scent of cottonwood. It all seemed too easy, but there it was. Glancing around, he saw a portable gas generator not far off. Bingo. Everything a tree killer could want or need seemed to be right here.

His instincts had been correct. He knew it. It would be impossible to prove it, but he knew with everything inside him: Phil Harringer had killed his own trees. The implications seemed obvious. Coal had mulled over the idea for some time that the rancher intended on having Hargis cited for this felony, and then, when he was convicted and sent up to do time and couldn't pay off his fines, and consequently his property taxes, Harringer would waltz in and buy the Hargis place for pennies. The whole plan had gone awry, and Harringer had turned to plan-B. Murder. Either way, Hargis would not be able to pay his taxes. One way was just a little harsher than the other.

Coal suddenly heard the grind of gears and of gravel beneath tires. Barracks Lane was mud. The only gravel lane nearby was the lane coming up to Harringer's!

Coal didn't think his heart could run any faster without physical activity. And run, perhaps it didn't. But it did leap.

Throwing the drill back in the toolbox, he scanned the room, looking for places to hide. There was a walk-out door in the far corner, going out to the back of the property. It was just beyond the small enclosed room that he assumed had been built so it could be heated if someone wanted to do work in the winter time without heating up this entire building.

Coal walked, swift but silent, to the front wall, reaching it about five feet from one of several windows. He heard the vehicle coming on, ever closer. But it didn't go on to the driveway of the house. Unless his ears deceived him, it was pulling along the front of this shop!

He looked around again, starting to feel like a trapped animal. His job as sheriff of Lemhi County seemed to flash like mud spatters before his eyes. He eased along the wall to the window, then steeling himself, poked an eye just past the window frame. Phil Harringer's pickup was stopped not ten feet away! He could see the sparkling brown back fender. The door slammed. Harringer was out!

Coal rushed the door and turned the lock. He heard footsteps in the gravel outside, and then the rattle of the doorknob as he fast-stepped across the concrete floor, headed for the back. He heard Harringer's voice, cursing.

Keys rattled as Coal ran into the sharp edge of a piece of huge yellow machinery. He heard the door opening. The back door was still ten feet away. He whirled around. His time had come. There was no getting out of this. He could make a dash for the back door, but he could never make it without being seen and recognized.

The sound of another vehicle's tires in the gravel outside registered on his panicked senses, and the door ceased opening. He scooted over behind the little enclosed room and stepped to the side of it that was farthest from the front door. Flattening himself against the wall, he waited, detesting his racing heart. And why was it so hard to catch his breath? He hadn't even exerted himself.

He heard a voice speaking faintly in Spanish. A voice he was pretty sure was Harringer's replied, also in Spanish. He looked toward the back door. If he made a run for it now, he might make it. Harringer was preoccupied. But he could also be caught midway between this hiding spot and that door, and the unfortunate thing about being Coal's size was that, even from the back, it would be hard not to recognize him, especially with his telltale white hat.

He drew another big breath and stared at the door. It was time. He had to try.

He started away from the wall just as he heard Harringer's voice get louder, and the door swung open. With one step, Coal threw himself back against the side of the little room. He flattened up against it like a suction cup.

Footsteps sounded hollow inside the building, and then a second set. Voices spoke, all in Spanish. He was sure the one was Harringer's, and the other he was fairly certain was the man he had tried to speak to. He heard them walk to the tool bench.

It was only then that he remembered his backpack. He had left it sitting in plain sight on top of the bench!

Harringer's voice rose in apparent anger. He spoke sharp words, and the other man replied with meek ones. The rancher spoke again, and the only word Coal caught and understood was the last one: *Pronto.* Then footsteps sounded again, going farther away, and half a minute later he heard an engine fire up. A vehicle wheeled around in the gravel, and he heard it fade away toward Barracks Lane.

Silence. Silence cold and dead and frightening.

Had Harringer gone too? He had never heard the door shut. But no! He heard the rattling of tools. He was almost amazed that he could hear anything over the terrible pounding of his heart in his ears. What about his backpack?

Footsteps approached the little room. Coal pressed back harder, as if he could disappear into the drywall. *Go in the room!* he thought. *Go in the room!*

Instead, the footsteps continued on past where Coal knew the door was into the room. Two more seconds, and their owner would round the corner where Coal was hiding.

Without warning, the footsteps ceased. For a moment, dead silence filled the vast space of the shop. It was thunderously shattered by the sound of Phil Harringer's voice.

"What the hell are you doing in here?"

CHAPTER FORTY-ONE

It was all Coal could do to keep himself from stepping out from the wall, ready to face a confrontation. He wasn't afraid in any way of Phil Harringer. But he certainly feared being left without a job and a way to feed his family.

In spite of the urge to move, he held still, not even realizing he hadn't let out his breath for a while until he felt faint.

"Come on, you rascal. Let's go."

The words seemed strange, and the voice was off—not gentle, really, but softer than the voice of the Phil Harringer Coal had met. Puzzled for a moment, Coal heard a cat start to meow as someone grabbed it, cutting the sound short. He heard the footsteps again, this time headed toward the front door.

Coal's gut instincts moved him. With the softest feet he could manage, he rushed the nearest piece of farm equipment. Just as he reached the far side of it, which was only five feet beyond the back door, he heard Harringer mumble something, and then the front door slammed. Soon, the rancher's footsteps came his way again, on a collision course for the back of the shop.

Coal knew his legs and feet were visible underneath the machinery if Harringer looked that way. But in Korea he had learned the value of absolute stillness, and now he put it to use. He took shallow breaths and kept his eyes on the floor. He didn't need the energy of his glance drawing Harringer's attention.

Harringer reached the back door and threw it open, causing a rectangle of brightness to fall across the dusty concrete floor behind Coal. The footsteps went outside and receded, but with the door still wide open it was obvious he intended to come back this way. Coal looked around the room. He listened for a moment for the sound of footsteps returning.

There was a dirty canvas tarp over something at the back side of the shop. Fifteen feet away. Coal eyed the doorway. An empty yard greeted him, and the foothills beyond. No sound. Turning, he scrambled for the tarp. Reaching it, he threw it up to reveal a black and white Honda CB750. He was thankful for canvas, as a plastic sheet would have sounded like thunder inside the walls of that shop. Dropping to his knees, Coal started to whip the tarp over his head just as he heard gravel crunching at the back door. He didn't even have time to straighten the tarp. Harringer was back inside.

Again, Coal drew shallow, almost meek breaths. He heard Harringer grumbling something under his breath before he slammed the back door. The next words were audible: "Well, where in the hell . . . Huh." A long moment of terrible silence followed.

Finally, Harringer started moving again, and this time he was headed right for Coal. By the sound, he had walked right past the front of the machine where Coal had been hidden only half a minute earlier.

Harringer walked so close to the tarp Coal swore he felt air movement at the bottom. Harringer stopped. Coal allowed himself to draw in a long, deep breath. If this tarp was about to be torn off the Honda, he was going to need all the air he could get for the fight that was sure to follow.

"Okay," he heard Harringer mumble. "About time."

Then he turned and marched to the front door, and Coal heard the sound of some soft object striking the floor. The door screeched open, then slammed shut. Dead silence descended on the musty shop.

In another moment, Coal heard Harringer's pickup fire up, and then gravel crunched as it pulled away. Still, he waited. He was too pessimistic to believe Harringer was really gone. But what if he was going for reinforcements? What if this was Coal's only chance?

Again, instinct drove him out from under the tarp. He ran to the closest window and peered out. Drive-able space must go all the way around the house, because he was just in time to see the pickup appear from around the front of the house, once again headed down toward Barracks Lane. Harringer was behind the wheel, his eyes dead ahead. Whatever he had been looking for, he must have found it.

When Harringer made it to the lane and turned toward the highway, Coal whirled back to the workbench. His backpack was gone! In a panic, he moved along the bench. Nothing! Gone! In a frenzy, he tried to think of everything in the pack. Was there anything that could identify him as its owner? He swore, feeling sweat break out on his face.

Turning, he started for the door. He had almost reached it when something caught his eye, and he looked down. His pack lay on the floor near the door, among a heap of life jackets and a couple of oars. Harringer must have thought it was his own pack! It was the sound of it falling Coal had heard before Harringer opened the door.

Sucking in a breath, Coal swept up the pack, took one last look around the room, then opened the door and headed toward Barracks Lane at a trot. It might look suspicious if he was seen, but he had to get off this property as fast as he could.

* * *

Coal set his backpack behind the seat, pushed the seat back, and crawling inside, he leaned his head back against the window. He found his heart still pounding. He didn't like thinking about how close he had come to facing certain trespassing charges. Maybe even burglary, depending upon how well the prosecutor and Phil Harringer got along.

He drew a breath and let it sigh out. After a moment, remembering, he stepped out of the pickup again and sniffed the breeze. What about that smoke back in the trees? His guts told him he needed to look into it further. And what better time than now, when he at least felt like he could get away with a lot more than he could in an elected position such as sheriff.

He took a couple of steps along Hargis's rough new road. His nose told him nothing. The wind had even picked up, and yet there was no longer any smell of woodsmoke. As he glanced back toward the pickup, he heard the crackle of the radio. A voice he was sure was that of Flo Hawkins was calling for him. He started to turn back, then looked along Hargis's road again. Flo's voice came on once more, a little more urgent. He wasn't even the acting sheriff right now. What could she possibly be saying that would be important to him?

Finally, he walked back to the pickup and climbed in, pushing Hargis's road and the woodsmoke out of his mind. He picked up the radio mic and started to key it, then sat there for a moment pondering. He had a bad feeling about saying anything to Flo over the air. He was, after all, not even supposed to be on the radio, since it was an official channel, and he was anything but official. Besides, anything he said Willie Stinger could hear.

Finally, he decided he would just drive home and telephone Flo. He fired up the truck and headed out to Barracks Lane. Exploring the mysterious woodsmoke would have to wait.

He was still some hundred feet from the highway when he realized that a car he had been watching come toward him at a fast clip from the other side of the highway, Savage Lane, had a light bar on it, with a single red dome centered on top. What he could see of the car was baby blue in color—the State police!

Trying not to be conspicuous, Coal eased off the gas, allowing the police car, a new Dodge Coronet, to come to a stop at the highway, then turn toward town. As it turned so Coal had a good view of its white driver's side door bearing the legend STATE POLICE over the top of a gold-colored image of the state of Idaho, he saw through the window glare someone seated in the back.

His heart leaped, and he gunned the truck the rest of the way to the highway and almost got himself t-boned trying to tear across after only a cursory glance both ways. He had missed a low-riding Pontiac, and he cursed the car's extinguished headlights just as the driver was likely cursing him.

The last time Coal had driven this fast along Savage Lane, he was going the opposite direction, right after having a rifle shot taken at him. He slid into the yard, and before he even got out of the cab the front door flew open, and Connie ran out, with Betty Lockwood on her heel.

"Coal!" Connie ran down the steps. Betty was ringing her hands as she followed her down, and he met them in the middle of the yard.

"Coal, that damn state cop came and took Jim."

Coal stared at his mother. Her cursing didn't even register on him. He turned his eyes on Betty. He had never seen more anguish on her face.

Turning, he strode to Jim's wife and took her in his arms. "I'm so sorry, Betty. I'm so sorry. I'll get him out. I promise. What happened?" He pulled away and held her shoulders as he looked down at her.

"Someone had to have seen Jim and called the police," Connie's voice cut in. "How would he have known to come here?"

"All right. All right, let's all calm down. This isn't over. I need to make some phone calls. Let's go in. Jim will be all right."

With his arm around Betty, he walked her back up the steps, Connie coming right behind.

When they got inside, before Coal could grab the phone, Connie clutched his arm, making him turn back to her. "That's not all, Coal."

Her tone of voice clutched something deep inside him, and he felt his insides go still. "What, Mom?"

"That officer said he's going to the judge right after he puts Jim in a cell to get an arrest warrant for you too. For—"

"For harboring a fugitive. I know."

Connie stopped and gave a brisk nod. Her eyes filled with tears. Coal suddenly let out a laugh and pulled his mother to him. "It'll be all right, Ma. Easy does it." But it didn't matter. This one had gotten to her. This tough woman Coal had seldom seen shed tears was crying now, and the kids stared the two of them down. Maybe until now this had only been worrisome. Now, seeing Connie Savage reduced to tears, he saw real terror come over their faces.

After calling the jail, with no answer, he called Flo to make sure she knew he had gotten the message about Jim, and asked her to try and reach

Jordan Peterson and have him call the house. He jerked out the phone book and looked up Judge Sinclair's number, then dialed it. The judge's secretary answered.

"Wilma! I need to talk to the judge. Is he in?"

He's in court. But Coal?

"Yes?"

Hey, I'll be in huge trouble if anyone finds out I talked to you, but . . .

"What is it, Wilma?"

Well, I think Judge Sinclair is going to sign an arrest warrant for you.

Coal felt a kick to the guts. He stood silent for several seconds.

Coal?

"Yeah, Wilma. I'm here."

What are you going to do?

"Not get arrested, I guess."

Please don't tell them I said anything.

"I'd never burn you for trying to help me. This is our secret. Thanks, Wilma."

There was no calling the judge now. And suddenly he couldn't remember why he had wanted to talk to Jordan either. Coal turned to see Connie standing close by, her hands clasped together in front of her.

"You eavesdropping, Ma?"

She smiled, and again tears filmed her eyes. He guessed she was unable to speak, because she didn't.

"I have to go, all right? I'll call you as soon as I can."

"Where are you going?"

"I can't say. If they come asking you about me, I don't want you having to lie."

"Coal . . . What's going to happen?"

"I wish I could tell you, Ma. I really do."

As he drove down the highway in the GMC, he was unworried about his speed. The only officer who could have been on the road to pick him up for speeding was Stinger, and he would be in town by now booking Jim into jail. Coal had taken only the time needed at home to throw some clothes into a duffel bag, pick up his Winchester and a box of .357 magnum rounds.

He reached his destination and pulled off the highway, checking ahead and in his rearview mirror to make sure no other car was in sight. He pulled all the way around the back of the house, then took out a huge tarp he carried behind the seat and shook it out over the pickup, tying it in place.

He already knew no one was home, because there was no vehicle in the yard, but he stepped up onto a rickety wooden porch at the back of the house and knocked. No answer. When he tried the door, it was locked, so he went around front, making sure once again that no cars were coming. As he went to rattle the doorknob, it turned, and the door popped open. He slid inside and shut it behind him, turning the dead bolt knob. He was now alone.

And now he would wait.

CHAPTER FORTY-TWO

As far as Coal could find, other than some Chicken of the Sea, there wasn't a scrap of protein in the house. And at twenty ounces of protein to the can, over the two meals he helped himself to, Coal cleaned out four cans of the six available before daylight started to fade.

Frosty evening engulfed the valley of the Lemhi, and across the highway deer crept out of hiding in copses of trees to venture into the pastureland. The tops of the Beaverheads shone in brilliant white tinged with orange-gold, while the lower flanks, like the valley, lay clothed in purple and blue.

A car pulled up alongside the house and cut its lights. Coal was up, standing in the shadows. Should he peek out and make himself known? Or did he lurk here in silence and scare the hell out of the home's resident when he was found here?

Footsteps on the front stairs. Stamping feet on the porch. Maybe it was too late for such decisions now.

Coal swore. He wished he had acted sooner. He didn't know how this person was going to react to the shock of his appearing out of nowhere, but he knew how he would have felt in their place.

The doorknob rattled. Then it rattled again. This person must be remembering the door had not been locked. A pause of seconds. Then keys jingled. Coal cursed himself again. He should have left some kind of sign.

The door opened, and the keys were extracted from the key hole. Then she was inside. The door shut. What did one do to remedy what was coming? Nothing seemed a good fix. So he did the only thing he could. He spoke her name softly.

Annie Price whirled. Her next reaction was to spin back to the door and grab the knob. He said her name more forcefully, and she jerked back around and with as much feeling as Coal could imagine spoke a little word that started with the letter s. It was a simple, almost meaningless word, but the way Annie enunciated it made it seem to stand out in letters four feet tall.

"Annie, I'm really sorry." Coal stepped closer as she put her hand to her chest and took a deep breath.

"Coal! Damn it! What are you doing? Why are you here? You scared the hell out of me."

Some things cannot be helped. For Coal, letting out a laugh was one of those. "What?" Annie's voice was a mixture of anger and relief. "What's so funny?"

"I'm sorry. I really am. And you're going through my whole list of curse words. I'm afraid of which one comes next." Another step took him to within arm's reach of her. She stared up at him. Even in the dim light, he caught the glitter of tears in her eyes. "Hey. Annie."

Without warning, she struck his chest with the side of her fist. It shocked him more than it hurt. But then she fell against him, and she was crying. He redoubled his efforts to curse himself.

"Hey. Hey now. Annie. Annie." It was all he could say. He stood holding her and felt like the biggest fool in the valley. It was only now starting to sink in what a terrible shock finding an unknown man in her house must have been to her.

At last, she sobbed to quiet and scrubbed the tears out of her eyes, stepping back from him. No more niceties. "Why are you here, Coal?"

"I didn't have any place else to go."

A moment passed. "Your mom kicked you out?"

The question struck Coal with more humor than it should have, and again he couldn't hold back a laugh. Annie flared up at the sound. "This isn't funny! Do you know how bad you scared me?"

It took Coal too long to stop laughing, long enough for Annie to turn and throw the light switch on, turning back again to jet her purse onto the couch. She ripped her coat off and threw it on top of the purse. "Are you finished?"

"Hey, Annie, listen. I think the judge issued a warrant for my arrest."

"He *what?"*

"Yeah. I know."

"Why?"

"Harboring a fugitive. I was letting Jim stay at my house." Coal had to believe that if Judge Sinclair really had issued a warrant, it was only for the sake of trying to make it look like all was above board. After all, he had as much as suggested that Coal let Jim stay with him over the holidays. But be that as it may, a warrant was a warrant, no matter how it had come about.

"What are you going to do now?"

"I don't know."

"Do you . . . Why me, Coal? Why did you come here? Why not Maura's place?"

Nothing like direct questions. But Coal wasn't too interested in producing a direct answer. The truth was he was afraid too many people would think to look for him at Maura's first. Otherwise, that was where he would have gone. But he couldn't admit that to Annie.

"I just . . . I thought of you, Annie. Isn't that enough?"

She smiled up at him, taking a big breath and letting it gust out of her. "Yes. Yes, it's okay. Of course it is. I just wish you could have warned me."

He smiled, embarrassed. "I know. By the time I could think of any way to do it it was too late."

She looked around the room, seeing that he had closed all the blinds. She glanced over at the kitchen. "Did you find anything to eat?"

"Tuna fish."

"That's all?"

He chuckled. "Weight lifter diet. Old habits. I'm sorry I just about cleaned out your tuna supply. I'll buy you five times what I ate to replace it."

"No you won't do anything like that. I'm happy you felt comfortable enough to eat."

Annie started to walk into the kitchen, then suddenly let out another sigh and walked to the living room sofa, throwing herself down onto it. "You wanna sit for a while? I'm spent."

Coal walked over and sat near her, with a carefully calculated eight inches between them. She looked at down at his leg and the space between them. "I guess you don't want my cooties on you."

Embarrassed, he let out a little laugh. "Well, I didn't want to sit on top of you."

"Well, I wish—" Whatever she had started to say, she stopped.

"You wish . . . ?"

"Nothing. Nothing. Wow, it was sure some day at work."

"Yeah?"

"Yeah." She went on and told him about all the things she had had to deal with during her twelve-hour shift. As bad as they sounded, they didn't sound as stressful as his time spent in Phil Harringer's shop, but he didn't bring that up. No point in tipping his hand, to friend or foe.

"You want a drink?" asked Annie.

"What do you have?"

"Wild Turkey. Like before."

"Never much variety around here."

She laughed. "Well, I told you . . . Besides, you hardly drink."

"I know. Know what? I think I will. Wild Turkey, here we come. But next time I'm in town I'm bringing you some Jim Beam—just in case."

They sat side by side on the sofa and sipped alcohol. Annie got up and turned on the TV, and for half an hour they numbed their minds and said nothing.

It was growing warm in the little trailer house. Annie had turned up the heat before pouring the drinks, and of course there was always heat of another kind whenever Coal was alone with this woman. The show ended. Commercials came and went. Another show started. Coal couldn't have said what it was.

"Would you rather have some music?"

Coal shrugged. "Sure. Either way."

Annie got up and walked over to a beautiful mammoth of a Zenith stereo console and reached down to pick up an LP from beside it. She turned as if by accident so he wasn't able to see what she pulled out of the sleeve, then set the record down carefully on her turntable and set it to play. After the initial crackle of the diamond needle biting into the outer grooves, Glen Campbell's voice came on singing "By the Time I Get to Phoenix."

"Nice."

"You like it?"

"Like it! Glen's one of the best things that ever happened to music."

She sat back down. Somehow she forgot the eight inches he had so carefully measured out between them. Coal acted like he didn't notice.

Leaned against the couch back, they listened without talking to "Homeward Bound" and "Tomorrow Never Comes." Apparently, those words were all Annie could stand.

"Oh, for heaven's sake," she burst out. Reaching down, she took Coal's arm and raised it with a little help from him, then slid down under it and let if drape over her shoulders. Not looking up at him, she sank back into his warmth. "That feels better."

Coal's heart was pounding. He knew he shouldn't be here. Maybe he should have gone to Andy Holmes's place, or Ken's. Probably about anywhere but here or Maura's—or Kathy's. Come to think of it, there were a lot of foolish places in Lemhi Valley for him to go.

Annie finished her two fingers of Wild Turkey, sipping at the empty glass as if something more would magically appear in it. At last, she lowered it and looked at Coal's still half-full glass. "Refill?"

"Still finishing what I have."

"Do you want to do some heavy petting or something?"

Coal stared down at Annie, and then they both burst out laughing. Apparently because he only laughed and didn't actually reply, Annie struggled up off the couch.

"I'm going to make us something to eat. Tuna Twist?"

Coal thought about the negative health benefits of the throw-together-from-a-box tuna fish meal and laughed again. "Sure. Might as well finish off the last of it."

She got up and started cooking, and Coal watched her move about the kitchen. Maybe it was wrong, but it felt good being here with her. It also felt a little deadly. He cringed when he thought of Maura and wondered how she would react. He frowned when he wondered why he would think it was any of her business.

Annie turned off the stove and covered the saucepan, moving it to another burner. When she came back with another two fingers' Wild Turkey in her glass, she didn't sit down by Coal. Instead, with an absolute poker face, she straddled him, her knees sinking down into the soft blue fabric of the couch on either side of his legs. She looked into his eyes with a direct stare that said nothing of her thoughts.

He smiled, but inside he was squirming.

For a long twenty seconds, she gazed at him, then raised her glass to her lips and sipped, trying not to let him out of her eyes. She raised a fingertip to her moist lips and dragged it along them. Then, embedded in his eyes again, she raised the same finger to slip it along his lower lip. He reacted by kissing her finger and instantly thought better of it, but too late.

She smiled. "You *are* alive."

"Yeah. A little too much."

"Why don't you finish your drink?"

He looked down at it, sitting clutched in his fist on the cushion. He returned his eyes to meet her direct gaze. "I don't know. Maybe because I've done that before."

"So?"

"So I do stupid things when I finish drinks."

She wouldn't remove her eyes from his. Super Glue couldn't have held them there any more effectively. "Stupid things? Like making love to me?"

She had to say it. She couldn't have said any number of other things. It had to be that. He should never have come here. But then, maybe it was time. Time for him to put things right between him and Annie. He didn't believe he would ever have an opportunity this clear and obvious again.

"It's not stupid, Annie. But right now it's impossible."

She tried to give him a little smile, covering a look of hurt in her eyes. "Can I ask why?"

"Of course you can. I'm just not ready. One of my best friends is sitting in jail right now, for murder. It seems like I'm the only one who can get him out. And…" He guessed it was time. Coal didn't like telling the story of Laura, but Annie had to know.

CHAPTER FORTY-THREE

Initially perhaps too embarrassed to move, Annie stayed astraddle of Coal as he recounted the events leading up to Laura's death, and what had followed after it with the children. As he spoke, she slowly sank down and down, until all the weight of her hips and torso rested on his legs. As he had expected, this story had taken a lot out of her, as it had him. She was shocked to silence at the horror of it, and, in the end, paralyzed.

As he was finishing the story, he knew it was enough, for now. It was enough, and he knew he would be safe here now with this woman. She would make no more advances on him, at least not tonight. And he was glad, as there was one other reason for his reluctance that he hadn't dared tell her. Something he would keep inside, and no one else would ever know: If he made love to Annie, the time would come, somehow, that Maura would learn of it, either because he would have to tell her, or by some other means. It was inevitable.

And although he and Maura had agreed that they had no hold on each other, there was something deep in the heart of him that still could not imagine having that conversation with her. He had had enough difficult confrontations in his life, and too many of them because of something rash he had done. He didn't know why he felt like he owed anything to Maura PlentyWounds, but still, he did.

But in spite of every other reason, he couldn't hold Annie Price the way she wanted, or Maura, for that matter. Or Kathy MacAtee. Not until he knew in his own heart what was right. And until he could put Laura fully from his ravaged mind.

Annie tried to make light conversation while they ate their Tuna Twist and watched *Dragnet* on the television. But of course, inevitably, the atmosphere in the room had changed, and the glum aura of the television show didn't help.

When he was finished eating and had lost interest in Joe Friday's dry voice, Coal called Connie. He didn't bother leaving the room for the conversation. One thing Annie had proved was that he could trust her.

"Hi, Ma, it's me."

Connie's voice broke when she tried to reply.

"It's okay, Mom. I'm all right."

Son, where are you?

"Someplace safe. Someplace you don't know about, and when they ask if you know—which they will—you'll be able to look them in the eye and tell them truthfully that you don't know."

A little laugh. *You think you're pretty smart, don't you? So . . . You're safe?*

"I'm safe."

You promise?

"Mom! Yes, I'm safe. Safe as in a church."

Okay. Well, you need to call Rick Cheatum. He called looking for you again.

Before hanging up, Coal told Connie he loved her. He didn't tell her that often enough. And he asked her to give each of his children, as well as Cynthia, Sissy, and Betty Lockwood, a hug for him.

You want me to give everyone *a hug?*

"Of course."

His mother paused for a few seconds. *Then I will. Son?*

"Yeah?"

Maura's here too. She lowered her voice, as a feeling of longing seeped into Coal's heart. *She's worried about you too.*

"Tell her I'm all right."

Coal?

"Yeah, Ma."

She didn't say it, but I think Maura is hurt that if you had to hide you didn't go to her.

"That's the first place you would have suspected. And a lot of other people too." He said no more. Annie was too near.

The woman was pretending to watch TV when Coal hung up. But he could tell she had been tuned in to his every word. The base of the phone sat on top of the phone book, and Coal pulled it out and looked up Rick Cheatum's home phone number. As always, Rick seemed happy to hear his voice. They spoke for a while, and to Rick's credit he never asked where Coal was, although he admitted that Connie said he had gone into hiding.

Rick suggested talking to Elmer Keith, because Keith was known far and wide, and he had many connections.

I can call him for you if you want me to.

"That's okay, buddy. Thanks. I'll call him."

Without even setting the phone down, Coal flipped through the White Pages until he got to Elmer Keith's name. Even as a man of renown, the old codger refused to have an unlisted number. Coal figured it was his way of daring someone to come to his house with any idea of harming him or his wife Lorraine. Keith had enough firearms and ammunition in his house to supply an army, and more than enough skill to use them. There were plenty of them he had developed himself, or had a big hand in.

Yello. Coal laughed when he heard Keith's gruff voice on the other end of the line.

"Hello, Elmer. It's Coal Savage."

Well damn, son! Don't you know you're interrupting Dragnet*?*

"I can call you back later."

Keith gave a dry chuckle. *The wife's into it. Me, I'd just as soon be out throwing lead into something as listen to Joe Friday. What's up? Last time you called we was gonna go up on a hill and shoot a rifle.*

"Nothing fun like that, I'm afraid. Elmer, I'm in trouble. I need your help, but this time a different kind of help."

Spit it out and let me see what I can do.

"You heard they suspended me from the sheriff job."

Yeah, those sons o'— He must have looked over at his wife because he didn't finish his sentence. *I heard.*

"And now the state bull had an arrest warrant signed for me."

A what? What the hell for?

"Harboring a felon, I assume. Jim Lockwood was staying at our place."

Good for you! How is the old coot?

"Not so good, right now. Stinger came over and arrested him today when I was out."

Curse words erupted on the other end of the line until Coal heard Lorraine Keith shush her husband. *That boy never broke a law in his life,* Keith said. *All right, that tears it. What do you need me to do?*

"Well, I know this is a long shot, but you don't happen to know the governor, do you?"

Know him! Hell yes, I know him! You want me to call him?

Coal hesitated. This seemed almost too good to be true. But then just because Keith was willing to make a phone call didn't mean anything would come of it. Governor Cecil Andrus was a tough man. He seemed fair, and Coal took him as a man who cared about his constituents, but he didn't seem like the type to be coerced into doing something he didn't want to.

"That's what I was sort of hoping for."

It's as good as done. You got a number I can call you at?

Again, Coal hesitated. Even his mother didn't have this number. But it wasn't likely that anyone would go to Elmer Keith asking questions about his whereabouts—and even less likely that Keith would give a sign of knowing anything. Coal read off the number printed on the phone, and they hung up.

After a few minutes listening to the silence of the now long-dead stereo, Annie looked over at Coal. "Know something?"

"What's that?"

"Since you were here last, I decided to be a better host."

"Yeah?"

"Yeah. I'll show you."

She got up and went to a cupboard, then opened it and stepped out of the way so Coal could see. There were several bottles of wine that he could see, three or four of them dark in color, and at least one white.

He laughed. "I thought you said you only had Wild Turkey!"

"Well, that's because I thought we could use something stronger."

"You're going to turn into an alcoholic."

She gave him a wry face. "No, I won't. I haven't even opened any of them yet. They're a lot milder than the Wild Turkey, so . . . Would you like a glass?"

He had disappointed this woman enough for one night. "Sure."

"Which one?"

Coal laughed. "Which one? I'm no connoisseur. Just pick one of the dark ones."

She opened a bottle of Chateau Palmer, straight from the winelands of Bordeaux, France. At least that was the claim on the bottle. Bringing two glasses, she sat down near Coal and handed him his glass. He sipped it with pleasant surprise.

"Can I ask you something?"

Coal looked at her. "Sure."

"Would you at least hold me for a while?"

He didn't even know if doing that much was a good idea. But the point became moot, because he was just putting his arm around her when the phone rang. She answered it, then handed it to him.

"Hello?"

Yeah, Coal—Elmer. Not good news.

Coal's heart fell and he grimaced. "No go, huh?"

Not that *bad. I just couldn't reach him. But I'll keep trying. You going to be at this number for a while?*

"What's a while?"

Hell, I don't know. A day, at least.

Coal looked up at Annie. "Am I going to be here for at least a day?"

This managed to get a giggle out of her, and she nodded and made a playful kissy face, then giggled again.

"My boss says yes."

All right, good. I'm going to keep calling Andrus, and as soon as I find out anything I'll call back. Don't go far from the phone.

Coal hung up feeling only slightly disappointed. He knew Elmer Keith could be pretty persuasive. He could even be as sweet as honey, if he wanted to be—not that sweetness would necessarily work with Cecil Andrus. But even though he knew nothing yet, at least there was hope. Big hope. And as the wine began to warm him, that hope got stronger.

And so did his yearning to taste Annie Price's lips once more.

CHAPTER FORTY-FOUR

That night, Coal slept on the sofa. The wine and Wild Turkey worked on his head, and more than once in the night he had to fight the urge to go to Annie's room and crawl into bed next to her. Perhaps worse, sometime around three in the morning, she came to him, wearing a flannel nightgown that reached to her knees but did very little to hide her womanliness from sight or smell.

By the dim glow of a stove light in the kitchen some fifteen feet away, she sat on the edge of the couch and took his hand. Her backside was pressed up against his hip. When the heat of the moment finally began to fade, and Coal felt himself slipping back into unconsciousness, Annie's hand came out, caressing the loose hair off his forehead, her gentle fingers touching his whiskered cheeks. That was how Coal fell back to sleep. He could never guess how.

Thursday, December 28

The next day, Coal woke up to a cold, quiet house. It was just light outside, and the steel-gray sky promised in time to turn blue, but he could see at a glance that it wasn't going to be a warm day. Still no sign of moisture. Would this winter end up being as dry and cold as Coal's love life?

There was no sign of Annie, so she must have decided to let him sleep and headed in to Steele Memorial and another long day of work. That thought gave him a lonely feeling and left him a little disappointed, apparently because he was a fool. But he would have liked at least to say goodbye.

He took a chance and made a call to Jordan Peterson at home. After six rings, the phone rattled off the hook, and a very tired voice came over the line.

"Hey, Jordan. It's me, Coal."

Jordan seemed to go from zero to sixty. *Coal! Where are you?*

"Someplace safe."

Coal, no you aren't. The judge signed an arrest warrant for you, and now Stinger's cooking something up. I don't know what it is, but he was saying some things yesterday. I think he knows something.

Coal hated the feeling that crept into his guts. He didn't like feeling unsure of himself, of his safety. Could Stinger really have an idea where he was holed up? How? No, there was no way. He forced himself to calm.

"Jordan, I don't see how he could know anything. I came here and covered the truck, and I'm pretty sure nobody saw me."

Long silence. *All right. I hope you're right. But maybe you should change locations—just in case.*

Coal thought suddenly of Eric Hansen. If anyone would be willing to thwart the law around those parts, he had a feeling it might be Hansen. He wondered where the tracker lived, and if he was home right then.

"I'll be careful."

Jordan said nothing.

"So what's Mr. Stinger been up to? I assume his investigation is pretty much stalled, right?"

This time Jordan gave a little laugh, and it sounded like he was struggling to sit up on his bed. *Yeah, man, I'll give you that. He's madder than a busted gambler. I think he's pretty sure Jim did the killing, so instead of even trying to find out the facts, he's spending all his time trying to locate you. That's one thing you've accomplished, Coal, whether you wanted to or not: You've made Willie Stinger hate you more than anybody. And I don't think he's going to rest till you're in jail with Jim. Everybody in town is saying you made a top-notch fool of him, and I don't think he's going to forget it. He's a pretty scary guy, Coal. I'm not even sure he's quite all there in the head.*

Coal tossed Jordan's words around for a moment. He decided that although he might have to rely on Willie Stinger in dangerous situations from time to time, having made him hate him was actually an important accomplishment. If Stinger had liked him, he would have felt bad. He told this much to Jordan, and Jordan gave a little chuckle, then was silent.

After a few more seconds, just when Coal was going to say goodbye, Jordan cleared his throat. *Hey, listen, Coal—I need to tell you something, so you don't hear secondhand.*

"Shoot."

All right. Well, I've noticed it doesn't really seem like there's anything big between you and Maura, right? Jordan's voice was the most timid Coal had ever heard it.

His heart began to beat a more sodden rhythm. Why did thoughts of Maura make him react this way?

"No, not that I know of. Why? You want to ask her out?" He didn't let on that he knew Jordan had already asked Maura out over the phone the night he was at her house.

Well, I already did. And the second time she said yes.

Coal was stunned to silence.

Hello?

"Yeah, I'm here."

You heard me, right?

"Sure. So it sounds like you're going to take Maura on a date." Coal hated how the words tasted like acid on his tongue.

Yeah. Tomorrow night, I guess. I hope that's okay.

Coal forced a light laugh. "Of course it's okay. It's not like Maura and I are married."

He could almost hear the tension rush out of Jordan's voice, but it was obvious that he still wasn't completely convinced. *All right. Just wanted to make sure.*

"Maura's got a right to choose what she does in her free time, Jordan. I promise." He hated saying the words, but they were true.

After hanging up, Coal went and sat down on the couch, facing the picture window. He had the blinds open just enough that he could see out but it would be almost impossible for anyone to see in. Misty looking streams of sunlight were exploding out of the southeast, lighting up the crest of the Beaverheads, and the black and red cattle across the highway were starting to come to life. Two last deer trotted along the other side of the fence, looked once toward the highway, then vanished into a screen of willows.

Coal jumped when he heard Annie's bedroom door crack open.

He was too far over on the couch to see her leave her room and start down the hall, assumedly heading for the bathroom. But she passed it up and came on to the edge of the kitchen. All of a sudden, there she stood, her hair in beautiful disarray, her well-formed shoulders bare, as well as her legs from mid-thigh down. A bright orange typical seventies towel covered just enough of the rest of her to instantly stir to life a man who hadn't been with a woman in more than half a year.

"Good morning—Sheriff." She gave a little giggle and ran the extended fingers of her right hand through hair that had apparently seen a long night of tossing and turning.

"Morning." He stopped himself short of finishing the greeting with the word "beautiful."

"Hey, I'm going to take a quick shower, and then I'll come make us some breakfast. How does that sound?

Coal had to admit he was hungry. Two kinds of hunger, in fact, were doing battle with each other. "Yeah, sure. Or maybe I'll make us something while you're in there."

"Really?"

"Sure. Might as well get some use out of me while I'm here—especially since I invited myself."

She let out another giggle. "Wow. I never knew a man to get up and make breakfast for a woman."

After she had gone back down the hall, leaving her image lingering in Coal's mind, he got up, turned on the radio, and put on his boots. In the back of his mind, he found himself wondering about Annie's comment. How many men *had* she known, anyway? And really, what did he know about this woman, other than the fact that she was gorgeous, she had a wonderful smile, and eyes that looked right through him. And she was some six years his elder, hard as it was to believe.

In the fridge, he found much to his relief that Annie had brought home a dozen eggs and some thick-sliced bacon. He dug a box of Bisquick out of a cupboard and mixed up biscuits, not so much because he enjoyed Bisquick's biscuits or because they were good for his weight lifting regime, but because they were simple, and fast.

He fried the bacon to the Carpenters singing "Ticket to Ride" until it was still five minutes away from firm enough to snap in half, then poured most of the grease out and fried himself six eggs, and two for Annie.

The shower had shut off several minutes ago, but there was still no sign of the woman, so when the biscuits were done he turned off the oven, put the eggs and bacon on two separate plates, and slid them inside, leaving the door cracked.

He had no more than done so when the bathroom door creaked open, and he listened for Annie's feet pitter-pattering down the hall. They did indeed pitter-patter, but toward him, not away.

And then there stood Annie once more, looking much the same as earlier, only now with wet, but still disheveled hair and water droplets on her shoulders, upper chest, and cheeks. Coal couldn't help the way his heart started to beat.

Her greenish brown eyes, now behind a pair of black-framed glasses, gazed him down, unmoving. Her lips were slightly parted, and her normally dark blond hair looked almost brown. It framed the pink of her skin perfectly. He couldn't move. He stared, she stared, and he listened to the petrifying pound of his heart in his ears, and to the notes of Waylon Jennings singing about how "Ladies Love Outlaws" on KSRA.

Was it common courtesy to tell an incredible looking woman fresh out of the shower, clad only in a towel, with shapely legs and shoulders exposed, that she looked amazing? Or was it an invitation to disaster? It was only a two-choice question, with a fifty percent chance of getting it right. Coal didn't even need to draw on any past experience to pick his answer. He had only to look into Annie's eyes.

"As soon as you get dressed, I'm keeping breakfast warm in the oven."

Her eyes flickered. His red-blooded American heart missed a beat. And time stood still. Annie had made her nonverbal play, Coal had parried skillfully, and part of him hated himself for that.

The eyes fell away, and Coal didn't know much about women, but he knew the look of defeat. He wanted to rush to her and take her in his arms. Instead, he stood his ground.

"Okay, that sounds great. I'll be right out."

And then she turned, and her feet whispered down the hall. Coal averted his eyes to the front window until her bedroom door was closed—and safe.

Maybe it really was time for him to think of a safer place to stay. He was sure Hansen's would be a safe bet. Or Ken's, Jay's, or Andy's. Maybe even Rick Cheatum would take him in, or Elmer Keith himself. Anywhere might be a better choice than here.

Annie returned in a few minutes wearing a pale green paisley shirt with its long tails untucked over flare-legged blue jeans. Her feet were bare. She sat down without a word as Coal took the plates out of the oven and set them on the table.

Breakfast was a quiet affair. The table was small enough that no one even had to ask for anything to be passed. It was all within arm's reach. Coal studied his food as if secret messages were imbedded in it. He felt Annie look up at him now and then, but like that wise old cutthroat that haunts the deep green pool below the falls, he let that wet fly sit there just below the surface and swam on by. Maybe some younger fish would take that fly, but Coal would not. He had been hooked before, and hard.

Only once or twice did he meet the woman's eyes, and then it was she who looked quickly away. The second time, he frowned. He wanted to break the silence. He could almost hear the woman screaming questions out at him—anguished questions that he knew were haunting her.

But exactly what those questions were, that was a guess even an experienced man would not take a chance on.

"This is good, Coal."

Someone might as well have fired a rifle in the bathroom down the hall, the way Annie's voice made Coal jump.

"Oh, thanks. It's not much."

She shrugged. "Well, it kind of is after cooking your own meals for . . . well, a long time. And . . ." Her voice trailed off, and like a fool he looked up into her eyes.

"And?"

She let out a little laugh. "And, like I said earlier, I've never had a man make me breakfast, not unless I was paying him."

That comment made Coal hurt, and he didn't even know why. What had Annie's past really been like? He wanted to ask. Then he thought maybe he would take a wiser road, go out in back and shoot himself in the foot with his .357 instead.

"I was glad to do it. You didn't have to let me stay here."

"I know. But I'm glad you came."

"Hey, Annie." He stared into her eyes, which somehow the glasses almost seemed to make more intriguing and beautiful than before, and prepared to be really stupid.

"What?"

"I'm sorry."

Silence. Deadly silence. The kind that makes you start to sweat, even if the day is cool.

"Sorry?"

"Yeah. Hey, I really shouldn't have come here."

"Why?" A look of concern had overtaken her face.

"I know now how it must have looked. Like . . . Well, I'm really sorry."

"You don't have anything to be sorry for."

"But I am."

"Why? Because I'm a desperate woman and I can't keep from throwing myself willfully at you? Because I have no pride?"

He smiled, a sad smile. Now she had laid it all on the line. There was no way out but to face this. But before he could speak, she went on.

"Coal, can I ask you something?"

"Of course."

"Just for a minute, can you pretend there never was another woman? Your Laura didn't exist, and we're both here, single, together in this house. If things were that way, would there even be a chance for us then?"

He started to reply, but she jerked her hand up, palm forward. "And I want you to know I'm not just talking about sleeping together. I'm talking about . . . Could you ever see you and me being *together?*"

He stared at her as his feverish mind whirled.

"I'm sorry for putting you on the spot. I just . . . I don't know how I should act when I'm with you. But . . . I really like you. A lot. And sometimes I feel like you have the same feelings for me, but then I'm not sure. I have to know if I'm just dreaming."

Coal pursed his lips. For the moment, he was holding back words, while he tried to form his reply properly.

"You don't have to answer me, I guess." He had waited too long.

"No, Annie, I'm going to answer you. I want to."

She tried to hold his gaze.

"Annie, I don't know that I've ever been more physically attracted to any woman."

This brought a flicker of hope to her eyes.

"I love your sense of humor. Your laugh. I love how you smell, how you look. How you feel. Yes, I could see a chance for us. Okay? This is all me. It has nothing to do with you."

He could have said more, but the gist of his thoughts was out there between them, somewhat like a soft white dove holding an olive branch, hovering in front of her—an offering of peace and promise. Now it was her move.

Her answer was tears flooding her eyes and running down both cheeks. She jumped out of her chair, and he expected her to disappear down the hall. Instead, she came to him, and he scrambled up to meet her and crushed her to his chest.

She was crying, and he didn't know what to do. He was saved by the ringing of the phone.

Wiping her eyes in one quick motion of her thumbs, she stepped over and picked up the phone. "Hello? Yes. He's here." She held the phone out to Coal, with one glance into his eyes that then fell to his midriff and there remained.

"Yeah?" Coal said into the phone.

Coal. Elmer. Okay. Good news. I got Andrus on the phone, and we had a long chat. Listen, he wants you to give him a call. Just so he can make sure he has all the details straight. You got somethin' to write with?

Annie must have heard Keith's gruff side of the conversation, or at least bits of it, because she whirled and snatched up a note pad and pencil from an organizer that hung on the end of her cupboard and turned back to hand them to Coal.

"Yeah, Elmer, go ahead."

All right. Now this is his home number, understand. He's still off for the holidays. So he only requested that no one else be given this number.

Coal jotted down the Boise phone number as Keith read it out, then read it back to him.

He's expecting you to call right away, son. Says he's not going to be at that number in a while. Good enough?

"I don't know how to repay you, Elmer."

Then don't hurt your head thinkin' about it. I'm just happy to help a friend. Besides, I never could stand that state cop anyhoo. I'm happy to do anything that helps get some egg on his mug.

Coal reached out and depressed the disconnect button on the phone. While he was holding it and peering at the governor's number, the phone rang and made him swear. He looked an apology at Annie, who just smiled, when normally she would probably have let out a giggle and made some wisecrack.

"You expecting a call?"

Annie shook her head. Coal swore again, looking his distaste at the phone in his hand while he waited for whoever was calling to give up. They could call back later.

Third ring. "What if they're trying to call you in to work?"

"Huh. Good luck with that. I'm planning to hang out with you today. You really think I'm going to miss an opportunity like this?" She smiled. Her teeth were brilliant white against the pink of her lips.

Fifth ring. Sixth. Seventh. *Damn it! Give up,* thought Coal.

Eighth ring. "All right. Would you just answer it? Tell them you'll call back in a minute."

So Annie took the phone and answered it. Her eyes moved around as her mind was registering whatever was coming across the other end of the line. Her voice was at a higher pitch when she handed the phone across to Coal. "I think you'd better take this. He said it's urgent."

Coal grabbed the phone. "Hello."

Sheriff! The voice on the other end was in an obvious state of panic. *This is Vic, from the jail.*

"Hello, Vic. What's up?" Coal tried to keep his own rising alarm out of his voice.

Hey, Jordan told me to call you. They know where you are. They're on their way to arrest you. Now!

"What the— How?"

I don't know, Sheriff. But they're coming. Jordan and that Stinger guy and a deputy from Challis. They're on their way there right now.

Coal thanked the night jailer and dropped the phone on the base. His eyes shot to Annie, but he didn't dare take any time to explain. "Maybe you'd better get out of here."

"Why?"

"Annie! Just— You need to go."

"This is my house. They're coming after you, aren't they?"

He only nodded as he fumbled the phone off the hook again and started dialing the governor's number. There were three nines in it, and he cursed every one as the dial spun all the way back around like Methuselah taking a walk.

Annie stepped closer and clutched Coal's arm, looking out the front window. The phone started ringing.

"They can't come in here unless I let them, Coal."

Distracted, he looked at her as the phone rang the third time. Her words registered on him. "I don't know what that man's capable of, Ann—" The phone picking up cut him short.

Hello, this is Carol.

"Hello, ma'am. Sorry to be short, but this is Sheriff Savage from Salmon. The governor is expecting my call."

A pause. Just to aggravate an already aggravated fugitive. *Um, yes. Can you hold?*

"No!" He practically shouted into the transmitter. "I can't hold. I'm sorry. Please get him. It's an emergency."

His voice must have upset Carol, whom Coal assumed to be Andrus's wife, because her pause was pregnant.

"Please hurry, ma'am. I'm really sorry for sounding short."

Well, he's on the other line right now with a judge, okay? So you're going to have to wait, Sheriff. I'm sorry.

Coal was looking out the front window when three police cars, the blue and white Dodge of the state bull, a black and white out of Challis, and the Ford Jordan Peterson had been assigned to, converged on the front yard.

CHAPTER FORTY-FIVE

"I've got to go out the back door!" Coal said to Annie, turning that way and handing her the phone.

"What am I going to tell the governor?" Annie's eyes were wide with terror.

"Uh, tell him whatever. I can't get you involved in this any more than what you are."

Annie turned to look out the window. "Coal, they're coming to the door! What do I do?"

"Tell them they can't come in. I'm not here. Buy me some time."

But all of a sudden, he knew it wasn't going to work. Unless he left on foot, he wasn't going anywhere. In this kind of cold, it would take far too long to get the pickup warmed up enough to drive away. By then they would be all over him.

He looked at Annie again. "Tell them I'm not here!"

Pounding started on the door. "Open up! Police!"

"Coal!"

He grabbed Annie by the shoulders. She was still holding the phone. "Take a deep breath. Just don't let them in. They don't have any right in here."

"But what if—"

The insistent pounding, now louder, cut her off. "Open this damn door or we're breaking it down! This is the Idaho State Police!"

Coal grabbed the phone out of Annie's hand and put it to his ear. "Carol! Carol, are you the line?" he hissed.

No answer. "Carol, they're going to break into the house. I've got to talk to the governor now!" Silence.

"All right, we're coming in! Get away from the door!"

A hard bang on the door followed that command. The second one exploded the door inward, and Willie Stinger and a heavy-set younger Challis Deputy Coal didn't know came flying inside, the deputy brandishing a shotgun. Jordan Peterson, eyes scared, followed them inside.

Revolver in both hands and aimed at Coal's chest, Stinger yelled, "Get on the floor! Now!"

Coal hesitated too long, looking at the phone in his hand.

"Drop that damn phone or I'll blow your head off!"

Stinger's face was bright red, his eyes swollen. He wasn't joking. He was going to shoot Coal, here and now. Coal fell to his knees, letting the phone fall close to him. "All right, I'm down! There's a woman here. Don't start shooting."

He couldn't believe what was happening. It was like he had stepped into a nightmare state, or into some Communist country.

"I said get on your face!" Stinger was livid.

With his gun in only his right hand, he stepped in and grabbed Coal by an arm, shoving him toward the floor. "Cover him, Johnson. If he moves, you shoot him in the head, and I'm not kidding!"

Jordan stepped closer. He towered over Stinger in every way. "Hey! Hey, take it easy."

It was like the words only partly registered on Stinger. He turned and stared up at Jordan. "You shut the hell up and do your job. Get me your handcuffs."

With all the guns being pointed, and Annie in the room in a panic, Coal knew he had to obey this man. When Stinger shoved at his back, he went down on his face, and he felt a crushing pain as Stinger dropped a knee into the middle of his back.

"Hands behind your back!"

Above the ringing in his head, Coal could hear someone yelling on the phone, a man's voice. He made out the shouted words, *What in the hell is going on there?*

"Governor Andrus! This is Coal Savage! I'm being arrested!"

What? Who's there with you? Who has you?

"A state officer, Willie Stinger!"

"SHUT UP!" Coal felt the hard sting of what had to be Stinger's revolver, striking him across the right side of his head. He slammed the handcuffs on Coal's wrists, and he could not have done it less gently.

"Hey, take it easy on him!" Jordan said again. "Man, this isn't right! Johnson, we've gotta stop this."

The Challis deputy didn't reply. As most men might be, he was in shock at the way Stinger was acting, far above and beyond the actions of a responsible lawman.

Sheriff? Sheriff! Coal could hear the governor's angry voice yelling through the receiver of the phone. *I demand you put that officer on the phone—now!*

His face crushed against the carpet, and thankful Annie kept her place so clean, Coal mumbled, "Annie, pick up the phone. Tell him what's happening."

Stinger grabbed the back of Coal's neck and shoved his face against the floor. It felt to Coal like he was bearing down with all his weight. "Listen, bastard, I said shut up! You're in a heap of trouble already."

Annie snatched the phone off the floor before Stinger could stop her. "Sir?" she shouted into the transmitter. "Sir?"

"You drop that phone!" Stinger screamed. "Get her out of here!" he yelled at the other two. But neither of them moved.

"Yes, he's right here. Okay, I'll try." Coal heard Annie's pleading voice and guessed she was talking to Jordan or Deputy Johnson. "It's the governor, and he wants to talk to *him.*"

Coal couldn't even focus anymore. He could see a fuzzy rug and feel the hard pressure of Stinger's hand and the fury and fear in his own mind.

There was a moment of silence, and then he heard Jordan's voice. "Hello? Hi! Yes sir. Yes sir, he's right here. I'll try, sir. You'd better take this." His tone of voice had changed from one of deference to one of anger and disdain.

"Who the hell is it?"

"He says he's Governor Andrus and if you want any chance of keeping your job to answer the phone."

There was a long moment of silence, and finally the pressure of Stinger's hand went off Coal's neck, but it seemed like the knee dug harder into his back.

"Hello. Who is this?"

Coal heard angry yelling coming through the handset. This went on for some time, and even though there were several pauses on the other end and Stinger tried to insert a word or two, he was cut off each time.

Finally, the yelling on the line stopped. Coal felt a huge relief as the pressure came off his back and Stinger stood up. When he spoke, it was in a very subdued voice. With his hands in cuffs, Coal didn't even try to roll over. He just listened to the beaten sound of Willie Stinger's voice.

"But, sir, let me explain." He stopped for a moment while angry vibrations came once again from the other end. "But, sir, this man has been harboring a wanted fugitive—a murderer. He has hidden evidence in a murder investigation. He has done everything he can to keep me from being able to continue any kind of real investigation. He— Yes sir. Yes sir, I understand. Yes sir. But— I understand, but he— Yes sir. Yes. Yes. Thank you."

After a moment of silence, Coal heard the phone settle softly back on the base.

Complete silence filled the trailer house. A mosquito burping after a good draught of blood would have sounded thunderous. Finally, Coal saw Stinger's shadow as he turned and walked to the front door. He went down the steps, and in half a minute they heard his car door close, with just enough force to latch it. The vehicle turned around and purred out of the yard, and gravel ground under its tires as it pulled onto the highway, headed toward Salmon.

Still, no one spoke. Coal turned his head patiently to see someone crouch down, and he knew it was Jordan Peterson when he felt the handcuffs being unlocked from his wrists. Jordan's voice sounded like a bomb blast when he spoke at last, even though he wasn't speaking loudly at all. Every sound is relative.

"Give me your hand, Coal."

Coal didn't roll over and obey. He simply pushed to his knees, looking around him at Annie, Jordan, and Deputy Johnson. With a deep breath, he rose the rest of the way to his feet. The moment his eyes met Annie's, she ran to him sobbing and fell into his arms.

Neither of the deputies spoke. Coal would have bet both of them would rather be anywhere but here.

He finally turned his head when Annie settled down to sniffles and was just holding him. Big Jordan looked up.

"Well, that was entertaining," said Coal.

A laugh burst from Jordan. Finally, he said, "Is that what you call it?" The whiteness was just dissipating from his cheeks.

Coal shrugged. "Something like that."

Deputy Johnson turned his head to look past the broken door toward the yard, where Stinger's car had left a visible hole. "That man is a real peach."

With a chuckle, Coal massaged his red wrists. "I'll say. Johnson?"

The man nodded, and Coal put out his hand.

"Good to meet you."

"Yeah, you too. Sorry about all this mess. Sheriff Matthews said I had to go along with that guy and we'd straighten it all out later."

"Sure. Good thing he didn't shoot me."

Jordan nodded, a look of relief on his face. "Yeah." Everyone seemed to know that had been a real possibility.

* * *

When the two officers had gone, Coal made a phone call down to the hardware store and asked them to send someone out immediately to fix Annie's door. It wasn't more than thirty degrees outside, and she had done nothing to deserve freezing because of a madman like Willie Stinger.

Next, he made a call to Elmer Keith, told him briefly what happened, and asked him to call Rick Cheatum. Last of all, he dialed up Judge Sinclair's office, and Wilma's voice filled with relief when she realized who was speaking.

Within half a minute, Judge Sinclair's voice came over the phone. *Sheriff?*

"Yes."

Is everything all right?

"Yes sir. It is now." He wanted to ask why the judge had signed a warrant for his arrest. But perhaps that was not his place.

I got a phone call just now from Governor Andrus.

Coal hesitated. "Yes sir?"

You need to come down to my office, Sheriff. I'd like to have a word with you.

"Yes sir. I guess that's been a long time coming."

CHAPTER FORTY-SIX

Life had changed for Coal Savage by the time he walked smiling out of Judge Sinclair's office, past Wilma's Frank's desk, and back downstairs to his office in the jail. *His* office.

They were reinstating Coal forthwith.

His first order of business was to release Jim Lockwood once more on his own recognizance.

Within two hours, Coal was back in the courtroom, this time with his family, Maura, Annie, the Lockwoods, Rick Cheatum, and Jordan Peterson. The glaring absence of Deputy Todd Mitchell was felt deeply by Coal.

Judge Wiley Sinclair, dressed in his black robes, with a white shirt collar and tie just protruding from the top of it, came out of the back and called Coal up to the front of the room, while the others waited and observed from the hard wooden benches.

Coal wore a blue polyester suit and string tie, the latter making him look more like an 1880's Hollywood sheriff than one from 1972. His ever-present black boots almost glowed under their new polish.

Judge Sinclair looked at Coal and almost smiled. "Coal Savage, will you raise your right hand?"

The hand came up.

Giving Coal the directive to repeat the words of the oath after him, Sinclair read each section of words carefully. Coal repeated them.

"I do solemnly swear that I will support the Constitution of the United States and the constitution and laws of the State of Idaho. That I will faithfully discharge all of the duties of the office of sheriff of Lemhi County, according to the best of my abilities. So help me God."

Coal looked into Sinclair's eyes as he finished the last line. "So help me God."

At last, things in Lemhi County felt complete. The missing piece of the puzzle had been put in place.

The judge pulled out a paper, which contained the oath Coal had just taken, and he signed his name on the bottom. The judge then removed another piece of paper from the folder and handed it to Coal.

"This is your certificate of appointment. After the next elections, assuming you run again and are successful, we will replace it with a certificate of election. That should look good on your office wall."

Coal smiled. The others in the room clapped. Formal, Salmon, Idaho was not.

With the gold badge once more on his chest, Coal thanked everyone for coming, gave out hugs to any who wanted them, and returned at last to the sheriff's office—*his* office.

Dynamics in Lemhi County had changed quite a bit since waking up in Annie Price's trailer house that morning. Coal was once again the official sheriff, his hearing waived. Any legalities that might be forthcoming over the wrongful death of Roger Miley would only be in the case of some family member coming out of the woodwork to file a civil suit. The judge, going by Cecil Andrus's orders, had exonerated him of any legal wrongdoing in the case.

Perhaps more satisfyingly, Officer Willie Stinger had been temporarily relieved of duty, until such time as an investigation could be completed on his behavior and actions that morning. With Jim free until the end of the investigation, the situation as it stood could not have made Coal much happier.

Now to kick his investigation into high gear.

Having put Annie out of his mind for the time being, the one thing that still bothered Coal was the absence of Ray Christian. He had asked Connie to make sure he was invited to the swearing in, but Connie told him Ray had vanished that morning. The Cadillac wasn't in the yard, and no one had heard a single word from Ray.

After going through his mail and making sure there was nothing pressing on the schedule, Coal got in the truck and drove every street in town, searching for the blue Cadillac Eldorado. When he failed to find it, he flagged down the baby blue police car driven by Bob Wilson and asked him to keep an eye out for it, then call Flo in dispatch and have her get him on the air if he found it.

It wasn't like Ray to vanish like that. He wondered if something he had done had offended him, and then he shrugged it off. He wasn't going to start worrying now whether he was offending someone or not. He had little tolerance for overly sensitive people.

* * *

It wasn't until late that evening, a couple of hours after Coal had gone home to his family, that the Cadillac pulled into the yard. Connie pointed it out to Coal, and he got up and shrugged into his coat, since it was below freezing out and he thought this greeting might be prolonged.

Stepping out on the porch with both the dogs, Coal blew into his hands and rubbed them together, watching as Ray climbed out of the Cadillac and came his way, steam coming out of his mouth.

Dobe ran off the porch to greet Ray partway, still a little formal, but nothing like Shadow, who lingered against Coal's leg as if protecting him—or herself.

When Ray was close, Coal walked down to the sidewalk. "Hi."

"Hi, Coal."

"What'd you do, go out to see the sights?"

Ray chuckled. "Yeah. Up over the pass. Beautiful day."

"Mom missed you."

"Sorry. I should have told her I was going. But nobody was up yet, and since I had no idea where you were I didn't see much point in sitting around the house all day."

"Are things okay with us?" Coal asked. The question was blunt, but he didn't really care.

"Okay? Sure. Aren't they?"

"Just wanted to be sure. You still planning on staying around to finish up this case?"

"Actually, I'm glad you brought that up. You know, there probably really isn't much left I can help you with, is there?"

Coal shrugged. "You tell me."

"Well, the investigation part is all done, as far as all the evidence gathering and so on. And you told me you were trained in interview and interrogation, right? So what would you still need me for?"

Coal stood silent. "So… You're telling me you might be heading home."

Ray answered Coal, shrug for shrug. "Ah, I don't know. I've been kind of enjoying the company up here. I'm not sure I have all that much back there to make me want to leave. Would it be okay with you if I stayed a little longer?"

"Of course. I'm not in any hurry to see you go."

Ray smiled. "Thanks, buddy. I feel the same."

Friday, December 29

The next morning, the last day of the week, Coal was sitting in his office deciding what to do for the day when the phone rang. He kicked his feet down off the desk and picked it up. It was Annie Price.

Hey, Coal. Good morning.

"Good morning to you. What's new?"

I don't know. So . . . are you okay?

"Of course. Why wouldn't I be?"

Okay. Are we *okay?*

Now he understood what she was asking. "I think so. I'm sorry for putting you through all that yesterday, Annie. I should be asking about you, not the other way around."

I'm all right. I can't stay scared forever, huh? I'm just glad that creep got his.

"Yeah, me too."

Hey, Coal, there's another reason I called. You remember that guy that came in here and looked like he might have been stabbed? And he said he got poked by a sharp branch?

"Sure. Leroy Yarwood."

Yes, him. Well, he's back in here again.

"Why?"

Well, I'll call it a dog bite. But it's a lot more than just that.

"What does that mean?"

I think you should come down and see for yourself.

It looked like he wasn't going to have to do much planning for his day. As usual, it would plan itself. "How long do you think he'll be in there?"

It's going to be a while. You'll see.

* * *

Coal arrived at Steele Memorial just ten minutes later, with Ray beside him. The sky had clouded over, it was pushing the bottom side of thirty degrees, and trying to snow. They got out of the truck just in time for a particularly energetic flurry to whirl by on an otherwise completely windless day.

"I always thought Idaho would be a lot snowier," Ray remarked. "This isn't much wetter than Vegas."

Coal laughed. "Or Phoenix either, for that matter. Believe me, it's not a typical winter." He wondered offhandedly if it rained or snowed more in Reno, since Ray hadn't mentioned his hometown, choosing instead to bring up Vegas.

They slipped through the glass door to find warmth in the main hallway of the hospital, but it couldn't make up for the antiseptic and rotten flesh stink of the place.

Mandy the receptionist smiled at Coal. "Hi, Coal. Can I help you?"

"Sure, Mandy. Nice to see you. Hey, we're looking for the dog bite guy."

"Oh, yes." She made a distasteful face. "That guy is a mess. He's down in room three." She pointed the way with the eraser end of a yellow number two.

Coal and Ray strolled down the hall to room three. Annie was inside with Doctor Bent, and Leroy Yarwood was laid out on a table. Coal had seen plenty of blood in his time, but he wasn't prepared for so much of it just from a so-called dog bite. There were bloody towels in a heap on the floor behind Annie, and the sheets were almost more red than white, to say nothing of Leroy's left leg and forearm.

Coal stared for a moment until Annie looked over, her gaze followed by Doctor Bent's. "Hi, Coal. What brings you down here?"

Coal stared a moment longer until he realized he wasn't supposed to let on that she had called him. "Oh, I was just driving by and thought I'd say hi. What do you have here? Looks like a mess." A big understatement.

Leroy tried to raise his head and focus his eyes on Coal. His head swayed around in a sloppy circle, his eyelids fluttered, and he lay his head back again.

"Dog bite," said Doctor Bent, pausing his needle after just making a stitch through an ugly pink gash on the man's leg. "I guess one would call it that on the records, anyway. Or *bites.* Personally, I think 'attack' fits better. I'm guessing sixty stitches before I'm done here. At least."

"What did he say about it? It sure couldn't have been the old dog they have on their place."

When the doctor, concentrating on getting the next stitch just so, failed to answer him, Annie said, "He didn't say very much, just that a dog attacked him on his place. Oh—and his friend killed it."

"His friend? Huh." That could only mean Moby. Coal was surprised. Moby had seemed so set against even throwing a rock at a stray dog. It was remarkable how someone could change when a friend was in danger.

"How long until he'll be able to talk?"

Doctor Bent shrugged. "I'll be done in . . . I don't know, it might be an hour. He'll be out of the anesthesia in a couple."

"Mind if I look closer, Doc?"

"No, go ahead. Just be sure not to touch anything."

That went without saying. Whether for the patient's sake or his own, Coal had no intention of laying a finger on anything that had anything to do with Leroy Yarwood.

Walking close, he studied Leroy's arm and leg. Both of them had suffered severe damage, not just in the way of puncture marks, but in savage tearing.

"You think it was really a dog?"

Doctor Bent nodded briskly. "Oh yes. No doubt of it. This is typical of fighting breeds of dogs, which will latch on and then shake their heads back and forth and tear. It's very fearsome."

He was right there. Coal clucked his tongue. He didn't ask, but he wondered if Leroy would have full use of his arm after he healed.

Coal and Ray left the doctor and Annie to their nasty chore and went to sit in the waiting room. They weren't there five minutes before Sherlene Hargis and Moby came in from outside. On sight of Coal, they paused in the hallway. Moby looked at his mother, and Sherlene glanced back toward the door, then again at Coal.

Calculating which way to go.

CHAPTER FORTY-SEVEN

Finally, Sherlene settled something in her mind and came on down the hall. Moby was imitating an obese bag of Velcro, clinging to his mother like a life preserver.

Coal stood up as the two of them came close. He took off his hat. "Ma'am." She nodded. Moby looked away. "Do you want to tell me your version of what happened?" He didn't admit he hadn't spoken with Leroy yet.

The woman's eyes darted toward the door, and she licked her lips. "Well… Did Leroy tell you everything?"

Coal nodded but didn't exactly lie. "And now I need to confirm it with you. He's pretty doped up, so he might not have gotten everything straight." It wasn't even a white lie. He might not have.

Sherlene let out a sigh, her eyes flickering toward Ray and bouncing away from him as if lingering there would burn her retinas like the sun.

"Well, there was a dog, and…" Again, her eyes flickered toward Ray. "Okay, Moby was walking behind Leroy when a big dog came out and attacked him. You saw him, right?" This was a stalling tactic, observed a hundred times in Coal's last profession.

"Sure. He's pretty bad."

"Yes. So Moby, well, he grabbed a rock. Didn't you, Mobe?" She looked at her boy. Any more stressed and Coal guessed she would be shaking. Moby only nodded. "Well, Moby grabbed a rock," she said again. "And he ran and hit the dog on the top of the head."

"And?"

"And . . . I guess it died?"

Coal managed to keep a straight face. "You guess? Is it dead, or isn't it?"

"Well, I s'pose. Yes."

"Listen, Mrs. Hargis. Moby's not in any kind of trouble. I saw the shape Leroy's in, and Moby should get a medal for heroism. He certainly won't get in trouble for killing a vicious dog."

Sherlene almost smiled, looking over at Moby and patting his arm. "There, see? You ain't in trouble, Mobe."

"Where's the dog now?"

Sherlene's eyes shot over to Ray again. Her breaths seemed to be coming too fast. "It's still there, I think. At least when we left it was."

"And 'there' is . . . Where?"

"By our house."

"Where by your house?"

"Well, on that road."

"That road? I'm not sure what that means."

"That road? The one Bern was cuttin' out, over by them cottonwood trees."

Coal nodded. "Any objection if I go over there and have a look?"

Sherlene seemed unable to make solid eye contact. She wiped her hands on the fronts of her pant legs, seeming unaware of doing it. Drawing a deep breath, she said, "Well, you need a search warrant, right?"

The suggestion was a little startling. *A search warrant!* Who had Sherlene been talking to?

"Why would I need that?"

The woman fixed her eyes on Coal's face, her jaw tight. Somehow, she had gathered strength, and she was making her stand. Somebody had gotten to her. Coal knew that as much as he knew his own shoe size.

"On account of I just think that's the law." Her eyes fluttered, but she forced them to stay on Coal's face. Only a very close look revealed that she was actually staring at the tip of his nose, not his eyes.

"All right. I'll get a warrant and go out there."

"All right," she echoed. Then she turned toward the exit, and after half a second's pause, Moby turned with her.

"Ma'am?"

Sherlene stopped and turned. "Yes sir?"

"Didn't you come to see Leroy?"

"Uh, well . . . I remembered we have to get ready to milk the cows."

"Milk the cows? Well, it's almost ten o'clock, ma'am. You're not done milking yet?"

Her face reddened. Her eyes seemed to pinch up around the outer corners. "Yes, of course. But I'm saying we need to get ready for this evening."

And move some evidence around, thought Coal. What was going on out at that place? He thought about Judge Sinclair, calculating how fast he could get a warrant and follow the Hargises out to their property before they could disturb anything he suddenly felt it must be pretty important to see.

"Okay, well take care." He had caught himself just shy of saying, *We'll see you out there in a little bit.* It would be foolish to give them a warning, so they could speed out there and start tampering with something that might be evidence—or at least interesting, if nothing more.

Sherlene nodded, wordless, and she and her son turned and made for the exit with ever-increasing speed.

Not ten seconds later, Doctor Bent stepped out of the examination room, drying his hands off on a towel. He looked at Coal, then happened to glance down the hall.

"Oh, Mrs. Hargis!"

Already some thirty feet away, the woman turned. When the doctor registered on her, she stepped back down the hall, Moby holding tight to her side.

"Leroy's waking up, but he sure doesn't seem to want to talk much."

"Is he better?"

"Well, he's stitched up."

"Is he released?" Coal cut in.

"He will be when he gets his senses back. It shouldn't be but another half hour or so and we'll have him on his way," he said to Sherlene.

Sherlene stared at Doctor Bent, but Coal had the feeling she was much more aware of *him* than the doctor. "Well, we . . ." She stopped.

The doctor peered at her for a few seconds until it was obvious she had finished. "You *are* taking him home, aren't you?"

Frozen, Sherlene seemed to stare through Doctor Bent. All of a sudden, it was like someone had poked a pin in her, and her entire being seemed to deflate. She sighed. "Um. Yes sir."

Several minutes later, Annie cracked the door open and looked out. She saw Coal there and smiled to acknowledge him, but because Sherlene Hargis was there she spoke to her. "Leroy's waking up now if you'd like to see him."

Coal jumped up, and Ray came out of his seat a little more slowly. "I think we'd all like to see him," Coal said. "After you, ma'am."

Sherlene and Moby moved into the room as if they were walking into a gas chamber, looking about, waiting for a trap to spring. Coal and Ray went in behind them, and the door shut, leaving Annie and the doctor in the hall.

Blinking, Leroy looked up at Coal. Even barely waking up, the ever-present look of mistrust was there.

"Hi, Leroy. We'll let you visit with your friends in a minute, but I have to ask you some questions first."

Leroy blinked again. "Okay. Whatever." Even in two words it was evident how slurred his speech was.

"I need to know about this dog. Who owns him?"

Leroy scrubbed at his eyes, trying to convince them to stay open. "Well, he—"

A sudden knock on the door interrupted his words. Mandy the receptionist peeked in, with Annie hovering over her shoulder. Coal didn't speak, only looked a question at the two of them.

"Coal, I'm sorry to bother you, but it's really important. A Doctor Zane, from the University of Utah, is on the phone, and when I told him you were here he said he needed to talk to you. It's about your deputy."

Coal's heart leaped. Todd! A momentary feeling akin to excitement fled from him like a frightened sparrow. He wasn't sure he liked the tone of Mandy's words.

Todd . . .

CHAPTER FORTY-EIGHT

Turning to look at Ray with a feeling of dread in his chest, Coal said, "Will you stay here with them? I'll be right back."

He left the room. The walk down the hall seemed eternal. What was he going to tell Jan Mitchell? How would she break the news to her boys? What was he going to do about finding a new deputy that was as good at his job as Todd? The way the message had been delivered, he knew it could not be good. He was trying to steel his emotions. He took a deep breath as he reached Mandy's desk. A beige phone, fat and ugly like a bloated rattlesnake, waited on the desk for him, off the hook. He looked at Mandy, and she motioned for him to pick it up.

"Hello?"

Yes, is this Sheriff Savage?

"It is."

Sheriff, my name is Doctor Zane. I've been treating a Todd Mitchell—apparently your deputy?

Go ahead and tell me, Doctor, Coal was thinking. *Get it over with.*

"Yes, Todd's my deputy." He couldn't bring himself to voice the words, *How is he?*

Well, I think I have some promising news for you.

Coal pressed the phone harder against his ear and stared, unseeing, at the wall behind where Mandy had once more taken a seat. "Pardon? What was that again?"

I said I think I have some promising news. Mr. Mitchell started moving around about an hour ago.

Coal had a hard time making the doctor's words register on his brain. What he was hearing didn't seem a thing like what he had expected to hear.

"Wait. What do you mean by moving around?"

Well, not like a person with the severe case of brain damage we were afraid of. More like someone fighting to come out of a coma.

"I . . . Doctor, are you sure about this?"

I've been doing this for twenty-seven years, Sheriff, and yes, I'm pretty sure. It's not as if he's conscious, but it's still a bright spot, compared to where we've been for all these days since he came here. Whoever the doctor up there is—Doctor Bent, I believe? The job he did drilling the hole in Mr. Mitchell's skull to relieve the pressure, I'm pretty sure that saved this young man's life.

Coal headed back down the hall feeling more hopeful than he had since finding Todd Mitchell unconscious and bloody on the floor in the Batterton hallway. He still didn't dare hope Todd would soon be back being his deputy, but maybe at least his family could talk to him again, and that would be something.

Coal went back in the room with Leroy and the others. Leroy's eyes were open, and he was looking at Ray when the door opened. He dragged his eyes over to Coal.

"All right. About this dog."

Even as Coal spoke, Sherlene reached over and touched Moby's arm, and they stood up together. The movement drew Coal's attention for only half a second before he looked back at Leroy.

"I don't want to talk about it."

Coal stared. "What?"

Leroy stared back. No reply.

"This dog pretty much shredded you, Leroy. Just tell me what you know about it and I'll go see if I can find an owner to at least pay for the doctor bills."

As if bored, Leroy waved him off. "Just go on."

Sherlene and Moby walking to the door made Coal turn.

All Sherlene said was, "Excuse me, Sheriff," and she reached for the doorknob.

Assuming Sherlene and Moby must be going to sit in the hall, Coal stepped aside to let her out, then turned his gaze back to Leroy.

"You know today isn't the last of it, right, Leroy? They're still going to have to have you come back in to check on your wounds, and you're going to have to pay for some antibiotics to keep it from getting infected. This isn't going to be cheap."

"Whatever."

"Whatever? What's gotten into you? Just tell me what you know about the dog and I'll get out of your hair. I'm not going to come back and help you later if you can't tell me whatever you know now."

Leroy's eyes fairly sizzled as he looked up into Coal's. "Then don't. I don't need you. Get."

"Where's the dog's body?"

Leroy's eyes faltered. "Why?"

"I want to at least go get it and have it checked for rabies. I don't need some rabid redneck running around my county."

"Well . . . It's gone."

"Gone where?"

"Just . . . gone."

Coal had dealt with stubborn people before. In this case, he couldn't understand Leroy's attitude, since his cooperation could only help him financially. But Coal had better things to do than to push his help on the unwilling.

Then again . . . What if there were more to this dog attack than met the eye? The more stubborn Leroy became, the more curious Coal was getting. In fact, his curiosity now was downright intense.

He looked over at Ray. "Come on, we might as well hit the road."

Ray was up as if spring-loaded, and he walked to the door as Coal opened it.

As they headed down the hall, Annie erupted from a room, nearly colliding with Coal.

"Whoa! Sorry."

"You can run into me any time, Coal—you know that." Annie laughed.

"Where are Mrs. Hargis and her son?"

"They left. I was out at my car when they went out, and they got in their car and headed out of town. I watched them because I was surprised they were leaving without Leroy."

Without a word in response, Coal whirled toward the exit.

"Hey! You're just going to leave without a goodbye?"

Coal looked back. “I’ll talk to you later, okay? I’ve got a gut feeling I need to go after a search warrant. No time to explain.”

He started on, and Ray bumped his arm. “Search warrant for what?”

Coal didn’t reply. Ray had heard him tell Annie there was no time to explain, and he meant it.

As he was passing the receptionist’s desk, he tottered to a stop and turned to Mandy. “Hey, Mandy? Can I borrow your phone?”

“Of course.” She picked up the phone and pushed it across the counter to him. “Do you know the number?” The phone book was already in reach of her fingers.

Looking over at the book, then back at Mandy, he shook his head and grinned, and as if by magic the book appeared next to the phone. He had a feeling the number he was looking for would soon be a permanent occupant of his memory bank, but it wasn’t yet. He found Judge Sinclair’s number and dialed it, once again cursing all the long-dialing nines. Wilma Frank answered.

“Hi, Wilma. Coal Savage. Is the judge in?”

Well, hello, Coal. Yes, he’s in, and you’re not going to believe this, but I think he’s even free.

Coal laughed. “Great! Can you see if he’ll talk to me?”

I’m sure he will, she said, and not four seconds later the judge’s voice came over the phone.

“Hello, Judge. I have kind of a situation.”

What is it?

“Well, we just had a serious dog attack out on the Hargis property, and they’re acting way too suspicious about it. They don’t even want me to have it checked for rabies. And then Mrs. Hargis and her boy left the hospital in a hurry and didn’t even take the victim with them that they came in for.”

So you’re looking for a search warrant to go pick up the dog’s body? Over the phone, I assume?

Coal felt a little sheepish. “If it’s possible.”

Well, I don’t do it very often. It’s a little irregular. But it sounds like the circumstances are at least somewhat emergent. You say the attack was serious?

"More than fifty stitches' worth, I think. And I'm guessing on the low side."

Then yes, Coal. I owe you one anyway for having to sign that arrest warrant on you. Just do me one favor and keep us both out of hot water, all right?

"I'll do my best, sir."

In the warmest voice Coal thought Sinclair could muster, he said, *I know you will.* It still surprised Coal a little, but right then he felt pretty good about that hard-nosed judge.

Coal and Ray flew out toward Hargis's place, calling Jordan Peterson on the radio on the way to let him know what was up and asking him to try and get hold of Trax Hansen and see if he could come out as well. They couldn't wait for the tracker, however. They had to secure the scene before any potential evidence was disturbed. The whole trip out, Ray was uncharacteristically quiet. Coal guessed he had offended him by not answering his question about the warrant.

Before ending the radio communication, Jordan said, *Hey! Another thing, Coal: I got a call from some guy at the FBI headquarters in D.C. He said he used to be your partner?*

Tony! "Yeah. Tony Nwanzée. What did he say?"

He says your evidence is on its way back. He just mailed it out—overnight. And he wants you to call him whenever you get a chance.

"Thanks, Deputy!" Coal wanted jokingly to tell Jordan he'd like to kiss him, but he didn't want every crackpot in the county with a radio to think he was just as much a crackpot as they were.

Out of the corner of his eye, Coal saw Ray holding the door handle, and the man had stiffened up in his seat. He looked down at the seventy-five miles an hour on his speedometer and cringed as a car flew past heading toward Salmon.

Casting an apologetic look at his passenger, he said, "Sorry. I didn't even know it would go that fast."

Ray glanced over, trying to grin. "Yeah, neither did I."

Coal slowed back down almost to the speed limit, wondering how the pickup was holding up under the hood. As they passed the 28 Club, he eased down on the brake in time to make the corner onto Barracks Lane on two tires and half of the other two. Ray clutched his door handle tighter, and a swear word escaped his lips, making Coal laugh as they fishtailed along the washboard road for the first forty feet.

As they pulled off the main road onto the Hargis property, Coal saw Leroy's car sitting just off the new road, and Sherlene and Moby just beyond it. Moby was bent over, dragging something, but he jerked upright when his mother looked over and realized who the visitor was, then thumped him in the ribs.

Coal threw open his door and leaped out, followed by Ray. As he marched toward Sherlene and Moby, Coal studied the woman's nervous mannerisms. He couldn't see her face clearly from the distance, but she seemed to have a serious problem trying to decide what to do with her hands. As usual, Moby clung close to her as if afraid by moving away he would expose himself to real life.

"All right, Mrs. Hargis," said Coal as they neared the woman and her son. "You'd better leave the dog where it is."

"You can't be on my property without a warrant, Sheriff."

Coal was surprised at her sudden pluck. "Well, ma'am, I don't have a warrant on paper, but I do have a warrant. We can go over to the house and call the judge if you'd like, so he can tell you himself. But in the meantime, leave that animal right where it is."

Sherlene's shoulders sagged. Her face seemed to sag as well. She looked at Moby. "Okay."

"You want to go make the call?"

"No, sir."

Nodding, Coal walked close. The dog lying on the ground with a ragged, bloody hole in the top of its head was a brute. At a glance, Coal would have guessed him to weigh in excess of one hundred fifty pounds, and judging by his stocky build, black and russet coloring, and snub nose, he must be part Rottweiler. The other half was less certain, but a gamble on some kind of mastiff would have been safe.

Judging by the hole in the crown of the dog's head, in which he was pretty sure he could make out a tip of the responsible stone, the animal had died fast and had had no idea what was coming. A pool of blood had soaked into the ground six feet away. Coal made a mental note about trying to dissuade Moby Hargis from ever thinking he might want to chuck a rock at him.

"That's a big dog, Moby."

The boy couldn't quite meet his eyes, but he nodded.

"I know you probably feel bad about having to kill him, don't you?"

Another nod.

"But you might have saved Leroy's life. You did what any good friend would do. Did you see where this dog came from?"

Moby froze. Finally, he looked over at his mother. No one else spoke, and Coal held his tongue for several seconds. When he spoke again, it was to Sherlene. He was taking a gamble, but it was a safe one, considering his reasons for being here and the fact that Judge Sinclair had so easily approved this warrant.

"Ma'am, I'm going to need you to walk off a ways with Ray."

The first look that was more than worry or stress leaped into Sherlene's face. It was the look of real fear. "No! I have to be with Moby."

"No. You don't. The judge said I can talk to Moby alone," he lied. "I'll have to arrest you if you don't comply. Now you don't want that, do you?"

She stared him down. Her expression slowly metamorphosed from one of fear to the closest thing he had seen in her of hatred. But to her credit, she said nothing more. Robotically, she turned and walked to Ray, and the two of them went some distance back up the road behind Coal.

Coal looked back at the blob of young man in front of him, whose rose-colored tee shirt was two sizes too small and allowed three inches of belly and his dirty navel to be exposed to the frigid day above filthy blue jeans.

"I'm here to help you, Moby." Coal's voice was as soft as any he had ever used to interview or interrogate someone. "You'll be fine. I want to be your friend, all right? There's nothing to be worried about."

A lot of those words he had heard at the Bureau being spoken by other agents, and more often than not they were as full of deceit as the suspects they were talking to. In this case, however, Coal meant them. If he had ever felt sorry for someone, he felt sorry for this big, helpless oaf of a boy.

"You believe me, right?"

The boy managed to drag his eyes up off the ground long enough to touch on Coal's chin. It was as close as he could come to meeting his gaze. It took him over twenty seconds to thaw out his neck muscles, but at last the boy gave a little nod.

"Okay. Now Leroy's hurt pretty bad, and if it wasn't for you he might be dead. So we need to know where that dog came from—so we can find the owner."

Moby's eyes leaped over to his mother. She was so far away now. He looked back at Coal. Fear was written all over his face.

"Where'd the dog come from, Moby? You want to help Leroy, don't you?"

Moby gave it his best effort to look up at Coal. Finally, he motioned along Bern Hargis's would-be road with a wave of his hand. Before Coal could speak, he detected a sudden, faint waft of woodsmoke on the still air. With zero wind, he couldn't tell where it came from.

"It came from that way?"

Moby broke his silence: "Uh-huh."

"Have you ever gone back there before?"

Frightened round eyes popped up to stare at Coal, for the first time making actual eye contact. "Papa said never go in there!"

CHAPTER FORTY-NINE

Coal and Ray started along the newly broken road. A light, hard snow began to patter down on them, making little drumming noises on Coal's hat. The clouds hung low and ominous, and there wasn't even a breath of wind to stir the tops of the willows.

As they went along, the path seemed to grow unnaturally dark. Coal paused. An image of that big, ugly dog charging down this corridor with blood in its eye leaped into his mind. Ray came up beside him.

Something oppressive bore down on Coal, more than just the overcast sky. Trees blocked them in like aggressive foreign soldiers, some of them planted here by human hands, as they were big pines, and this was not pine territory. These big, overgrown pines and a number of ponderous cottonwoods prodded up out of the heavy screen of willows and wild rose. The trunks, although mostly straight and proud, seemed somehow to lean inward, closing in on the lonely and mysterious pathway that now was barely wide enough for two motorcycles to pass side by side—or one larger vehicle whose owner didn't care about scratching the paint.

Coal had once wounded a huge black bear, way up in the dark black woods of the Selway, and the feeling that had come over him while pursuing it was much like the feeling that overcame him now. His pounding heart irritated him, sounding like a distant, sloppy whip crack in his ears. His breaths came more quickly.

When he smelled the strongest waft of woodsmoke yet, just as he had long ago detected a scent of bear odor, he reached down and unsnapped his holster and drew his Smith and Wesson. From the corner of his eye, he saw Ray looking at him, but he didn't draw his gun.

The hissing of Ray's voice stopped Coal. Gun partly up, he turned. Ray had a cautionary hand up in the air, and he pointed toward the ground ahead.

"What is that?"

Coal looked. He saw nothing. "What's what?"

Keeping his hand in the air for a second, Ray edged ahead. Six feet in front of Coal, he crouched down. Turning his head both ways to peer among the trees, he motioned Coal forward. Within two steps, Coal froze, and a chill went over him. There about four inches above the ground, partly hidden in tangled willow branches crushed by tires, ran a wire.

Coal's mind whirled back to Korea, and his heart sped up even more. He moved sideways, following the wire, to find what appeared to be a package of some kind of explosives suspended behind a bird's nest in the crotch of a willow. The bird's nest appeared to have been stuck there by someone, not built in place.

It was time to call for help. But help was too far away.

Coal jolted to the sudden crack of a rifle behind them. He whirled and dropped to a knee, then realized the shot had come from a ways off, maybe even all the way back to the Hargis house.

"What the hell do you suppose that was about?" asked Ray, who by his face had obviously been startled as bad as Coal.

Coal shrugged. He spoke to Ray in a whisper. "You don't have to keep going, Ray. This isn't your problem."

For a moment, Ray only stared at him. Finally, he whispered, "I made it my problem the day you asked for help. I'm not backing out on you now, not when this thing looks like it's at its worst. But… Don't you think we should go call for more help?"

It took a moment for Coal to ponder that. He knew his warrant probably really didn't cover what he was about to do, but these seemed like exigent circumstances. After all, he was investigating a dog bite case, and Moby had said the dog came from this direction. What if he left to get help, and somebody had a chance to tamper with evidence of some kind? Besides, he had to admit that he had been curious about this road ever since the first time he saw it. Now his curiosity, because of the woodsmoke, the dog, and the explosive booby trap, had ramped through the roof.

Back in the trees ahead of them, the sudden sound of someone kick-starting a motorcycle made Coal jump. "Let's go!"

"Whoa!" Ray's voice stopped him.

Coal jerked his head that way, irritated.

"Buddy, I don't want to lose you now. If there's one wire, who says there aren't more? Let's go in easy."

Coal stared at Ray. Several seconds went by as he digested his friend's words. At last, he nodded. "You're right. Thanks." Ray only shrugged as the sound came back to them of the motorcycle revving up. But then the sound died, just before a second attempt was made at kick-starting. When the sound ended again, it came no more.

The woods seemed to close in even more as Coal moved ahead, Ray right behind him. There were more pines, more willows, more trees of several kinds. Yet even so, the closed-in feeling seemed to be more inside Coal's head.

And then he saw the first glimpse of the cabin through the trees. A gentle puff of smoke burped out of a tin chimney and filtered off into the trees.

Coal and Ray looked at each other, Coal with his gun poised. After several seconds, Ray shrugged. He spoke in a low voice: "It's probably empty now, right? You heard the bike."

Coal nodded. "That little word 'probably' has gotten people killed. And anyway, he obviously wasn't able to get that bike running, so he might still be here. Otherwise, I might guess you were right. So you going to waltz in there unarmed?"

"I'm not unarmed. I've got you." Coal chuckled. "Listen. I think you should go get a warrant if you're going in there."

"I have one."

"That's just to come and get the dead dog—and you did."

"Yeah, on the surface. But wouldn't this be considered exigent circumstances?"

"That's a huge stretch. Maybe if we chased some guy from the dog to the cabin and he ran in. But we didn't."

"Yeah, but this is Salmon, Idaho, not Reno. I say we go in."

Ray stared at him. He looked frustrated. Finally, he shrugged. "All right, I guess you know your judge better than I do."

"What's the big deal? It's just a dog bite, right?"

Again, Ray stared. It was getting to be a habit. He sighed. "All right. Sure. Just a dog bite."

Turning, his revolver still poised, Coal continued on.

The cabin sat in a clearing in the trees perhaps some forty feet across. It had been there for a while, but the chinking appeared to have recently been redone, and a coat of varnish applied to the grayed logs. The shakes on the roof were grown over with moss, but off to the side a pallet covered with a tarp made Coal wonder if there weren't new shakes or shingles there waiting to be put on. The ground around the place had been newly cleared. Someone had taken a recent interest in its upkeep.

Coal whispered to Ray. "You want to go around back?"

"Sure." Ray seemed calm. He walked around back. Coal watched him until he was gone from sight and frowned. Ray had decided to draw his pistol, but it hung down at his side as if he didn't know it was even there. With the failure of that motorcycle to start, whoever was staying here could be anywhere now.

Once he knew Ray had to be wherever he planned to watch from, Coal moved to the cabin, approaching from the front left corner. A porch ran the full length of the front of the structure, and he stepped up on it and moved to a window. He eased the side of his face around the frame and peeked in. It didn't take long to mark the place off as empty of life.

He called out to Ray to watch the back and made one last study of his surroundings, and then, stepping to the door, he looked all around it, searching for anything that could be the trigger to some kind of booby trap. Nothing was visible. He used the tail of his coat to cover the knob and turned it. The door was unlocked. Maybe whoever was staying here realized as remote as this cabin was, and as hidden from anyone's view, it made no sense to lock it because whoever wanted to gain entry probably would not hesitate to break his way in. Might as well save a good door frame.

The seasoned, drawknife-cut logs of the cabin had a backwoods lodge smell that any veteran outdoorsman would recognize and appreciate. The inside was no different. The warm, comforting smell of cottonwood smoke scented the room, and in the far left corner the orange-yellow flicker of the low-lying flames winked out from an aging cobblestone fireplace with a rude screen in front of it that was attached to what appeared to be a frame welded together out of angle iron—and a poor welding job at that.

The smoky smell mingled with the musty remains of hundreds of bygone fires that might have smoked in here for decades, smoke-curing the old, stained logs. Bacon and barbecue scent embellished these smells of a backcountry hunting lodge, and any other time and place Coal might have closed his eyes and breathed deeply of these welcoming odors. But in this room there were other smells, and sights as well, smells and sights that Coal would do well not to close his eyes over.

The overriding smells of burned gunpowder and Hoppe's Number 9 solvent mixed with gun grease only accentuated the appearance of an array of weapons—handguns, shotguns, and rifles—that decorated the tops of a rickety handmade table, shelves, and the one single countertop in beautiful disarray that only a gun buff would appreciate. Coal appreciated it even as he felt the gut-kick of its potential significance deep inside.

Aside from the guns and a stack of recently cut firewood that wreaked of resin, a few magazines cluttered the place, some sitting open on chairs, on the floor, and on one rude coffee table. A box of saltine crackers and half a block of uncovered cheese lay next to the *Life Magazine* which sat, cover closed, near another that lay open with eye glasses holding the reader's place. It was an issue of *Life* he remembered coming out back around June, not because he was a huge reader of the magazine, but because it had Raquel Welch on the cover, and a red-blooded man didn't soon forget the details surrounding seeing Miss Welch showing herself off in living color.

After another glance about, and a quick scan of the walls to make sure he wasn't missing any potential trip wires or the like, he went to a back door, which was in much worse repair than the front, felt around it for wires, and then opened it and looked out. Ray was waiting for him.

"Come on. There's nobody here."

Ray came up on the small wooden stoop just outside the door and stepped inside, taking a glance around as he holstered his pistol behind his waistband. He swore softly as he surveyed the room and its arsenal. "Good place for a guard dog," he said, still soft-voiced.

"I'd say. There's more to this guard dog story than we know."

Ray nodded. “Still, there’s no law against owning a bunch of guns and ammo. Right?”

“No. Only against letting your dog run loose and shred people on their own property. What do you see out back?”

“Not much. An outhouse. And looks like maybe some food in a metal drum. Canned stuff.”

“No bike?”

“Not that I saw, but I wasn’t really looking.”

Coal stepped out and off the porch, and seeing something on the ground, possibly a business card, he bent to pick it up.

The shotgun blast was incredibly loud in the closed-in woods.

CHAPTER FIFTY

From his bent-over position, Coal pitched forward and hit the dirt on his belly and elbows. Rolling to his left, he shucked the Smith and Wesson, then immediately rolled three more times to his left, and once back to his right.

He was hoping to draw more fire and get whoever had done the shooting to miss again so he could pinpoint them, but no more sound was forthcoming except a faint rustling in the woods. At a guess, it sounded to be some ways off, but he wasn’t going to stick his head up to make sure.

Glancing around, he couldn’t see Ray. But he noticed as he was searching that there was a substantial woodpile in front of him, some five feet high and perhaps fifteen feet across. Two large ponderosa pines served as its book ends. Gut instinct told him that wood was the reason he hadn’t been fired on again after hitting the ground. The same instinct told him to move, and fast. The gunman could be working his way around to a new vantage point.

Coal holstered the revolver, rose to his hands and knees, and scrambled right up next to the wood pile, which smelled very fresh-cut. With his back against it, he looked around, his .357 in hand once more. He spotted Ray at the corner of the cabin, scanning the woods with his gun drawn, and hanging at arm's length at his left side.

Ray suddenly raised his pistol and aimed it into the woods, paused, then slowly let it down to the side of his left leg. "Coal," he hissed. "I think he might be gone. He cut and ran."

Coal nodded. His heart was racing, and perhaps it was only his imagination, but on himself he thought he smelled the same raw fear he had felt the several times he had found himself under fire in Korea. Being shot at never got easier.

Getting to his feet, but staying bent double, he ran a zigzag line for the corner of the cabin and made it. Ray clapped him on the arm. "Damn it, Coal. That was too close. I told you we should have called for help."

Anything Coal said would have been in anger, so silence was his response.

Coal had seen a pair of binoculars among the paraphernalia in the cabin, so he scrambled back inside and picked them up. Through the back window, he surveyed the surroundings for a while. Then stepping back outside to his place of cover at the corner of the cabin, he began to scan the foreboding woods more carefully. These were quality optics, made by Zeiss, and the detail through them was superb. Among the things he saw was the flick of a squirrel's tail, on the far side of a big cottonwood, and parts of a beat-up red motorcycle, parked right where it must have been abandoned when it stopped running.

"See anything?" asked Ray, who stood at Coal's back.

Coal told him.

"You want me to go look at it?"

"Hell no. You want to get shot?"

"Come on, buddy. That guy's long gone by now."

"You're willing to take that chance?"

"How good of a shot are you?"

Coal grunted. "How good do you want me to be?"

"Good enough to cover my butt."

"That good."

"With a rifle?"

"Sure."

"Then let's go in and get you a rifle or a shotgun, and you can cover me with that. I'll go look at your bike."

Coal turned and looked at Ray. "You're nuts."

"No, I just trust you."

Finally, Coal shrugged. "All right. I'll keep an eye out here if you want to go pick out a good gun. Just remember, this is your bacon. But don't you dare get shot on me."

Ray grinned and headed around to the front of the house. When he returned, he had a Remington pump shotgun. He handed three green shells to Coal. "I already loaded it, but just in case you empty it . . ."

Coal chuckled. "I assume it's holding five shells already. If I empty it and that guy's not dead yet, you probably will be."

"Thanks."

"Don't mention it."

Ray moved off, peering about the woods. This time, Coal noticed he was wielding his pistol in his right hand.

He reached the bike and looked it over, then came back. "Well, not much to tell you except it's a road bike, but not registered."

"You get a VIN?"

"No."

"You want to?" Coal offered him a little notebook with a blue cover.

Ray laughed. "You're pretty easy about putting me back in the line of fire."

"It was your idea, buster."

Again, that laugh. "You win."

Ray returned to the bike and wrote down a VIN, then came back to Coal and handed him the notebook. "I told you that guy lit out."

Coal nodded. "You told me. Say, I've been watching you with that pistol first in one hand, then the other. Can you really hit anything left-handed?"

Ray laughed easily. "Sure can! I was blessed from birth to be ambidextrous. When I was little, I used to eat all my food with either hand, and I always changed hands back and forth to write until my third grade teacher forced me to use my right hand."

"Well, it only makes sense, silly. They don't call it your 'right' hand for nothing."

Coal went back to the cabin, looked around one more time, then scanned the woods outside from the front window. He couldn't deny hating the idea of going back up that dark, lonely road. By now, the hidden gunman could easily be lying in wait there for them.

When they headed out, Ray marched right up the road until Coal stopped him with a hiss. Ray turned with a question in his eyes, and Coal motioned him back. "Come on, man. You know better. We're taking to the woods—on the far side of the road."

"You're pretty paranoid."

Coal stared at him for a few seconds, trying not to be angry. "You think so? Try having a load of buckshot split your hair and see how paranoid you get."

Ray only nodded. They moved off some twenty feet into the woods, then paralleled the road, constantly scanning the woods on the far side. Other than another red squirrel, this one announcing its presence in an irritating, chattering voice, there was no sound and no movement.

With more than one thorn in the legs of his pants and in his coat sleeves from rose bushes, Coal finally made it back to within rock-throwing distance of where he had parked the pickup. He swore. There *was* no pickup!

Ray looked over at him. Neither man spoke, although in his head Coal was speaking plenty. He had seen no reason to take the keys out of his ignition, assuming he would be back shortly. Now, too late, he saw a fairly decent reason.

Still without a word, Coal walked to the Hargises', and Ray followed and knew better than to talk. Coal pounded on the door of the house with the heel of his hand.

Sherlene came to it and opened it a crack, but Coal shoved it the rest of the way open, pushing her off balance. "Who took my truck?"

The woman stared at him. Finally, she found the sense to utter the single word: "What?"

"My truck. It's gone."

The woman's face blanched. "I'm sorry. We've been inside."

"You're telling me you didn't hear or see anything?"

Cautiously, she shook her head. He stared sharpened darts at her for a second, then finally took a deep breath and sighed. It was a big house. It was possible if she had been inside the whole time that she really wouldn't have witnessed anything.

"All right. Well, I need to use your phone." The request made him cringe. He had half-contemplated walking back to his house to make this call.

They threaded their way through the filthy, germ-ridden disarray of the house to the now familiar phone, and Coal called the jail. No answer. He next called Flo and asked her to try and reach Jordan. Before she could hang up, he thought further and yelled into the transmitter. "Flo! Wait!"

Jeez, Coal! You about split my ear drum.

"Oh, sorry. Hey, do me another favor and tell Jordan when you get him that my GMC has been stolen and to be on the lookout for it. I'm out here at Hargis's dairy if he wants to come pick me up. And Flo?"

Yes, hon.

"Can you also put an APB out with the PD and the State? I don't know the license number, but it's a '72 green GMC with a white top."

I know, Coal. Everybody knows your truck by now. Hey—I'm sure sorry this happened.

"Thanks, Flo."

Jordan Peterson pulled up in the Ford LTD some twenty minutes later. He had been on his way down toward North Fork, where some hapless would-be photographer was stuck in the mud on the side of the road. As far as he knew, they were still stuck there. Coal felt bad for them, since it was his stolen truck that had caused their call for help to be preempted.

Remembering the VIN for the motorcycle, Coal called Flo back to have her check on it. She came back with a bike that had been sold most recently to a buyer in Wabaunsee County, Kansas, by the name of Gilaud B. Withers.

"It's a red Honda?" Coal asked.

Umm . . . No, it says a blue Honda.

Coal swore. Over the air. Then he apologized. Off the air.

"You're a mess, pard," said Ray from the back seat.

"Yeah. I guess. Hey, Jordan, turn the car around."

Jordan looked over at him. "Where we going, boss?"

"Back."

"To the Hargises'?"

"Yeah."

"You don't want more help?"

"You have the shotgun in the trunk, right?"

"Yeah," said Jordan as he pulled off onto a ranch road. "So?"

"So you're a duck hunter, aren't you?"

"Sometimes."

"Good. That makes you 'more help'. You can cover me."

Jordan got the car turned around and headed back toward the Hargises'. He had gone only a quarter of a mile before he said almost under his breath, "I never said I was a *good* duck hunter."

CHAPTER FIFTY-ONE

Back at the Hargises', Coal had Jordan drive as far up the bad road as they dared, then told him to stop and made sure to take out the key and put it in his pocket.

It was right then that a Jeep pulled in behind them, and Trax Hansen got out and stood looking toward them. Coal paused, glancing over at Ray. At last, he drew a deep breath and walked back, meeting Hansen halfway.

"This has turned deadly," he announced in a low voice. "I don't want you going in."

Hansen's expression never wavered. "Deadly how?"

"Well, somebody took a shot at me with a shotgun. I'd be dead if I hadn't been reaching down for a business card." Saying that made him think of the business card. He had meant to pick it up, but something about a load of buckshot cutting loose over a man's head can make him decide he has different priorities.

Hansen only stared. Apparently nothing about Coal's expression said he was fooling around. "Okay. That's fairly deadly, I guess. Will you let me take my rifle?"

"You're joking."

"No rifle?"

Coal chuckled. "No, I mean . . . You still want to come along?"

"Sure. Hunting bears and cats is getting a little boring."

"Well, bring the rifle then. I'd love to have some more backup. But for the record, I'm not asking you to come."

"For the record, I don't really care."

Without breaking his serious face, Hansen went back to his Jeep and pulled out an old 8 mm German Mauser, a rifle that looked like it had fallen from a two hundred-foot Sequoia and hit every branch on the way down. Its stock was stained a deep brown, almost black, from decades of sweat and weather.

"You don't squander money on frills, do you?"

"Just on my undies." Hansen almost smiled.

With pistols drawn, Jordan carrying the shotgun from the trunk, and Trax Hansen with his Mauser relic, they went back up the road, carefully stepped over the trip wire that Coal had marked with a rock in the middle of the road, and in a few minutes came in sight of the cabin. The fire had died down enough that smoke no longer puffed out the chimney.

Watching all around them, they went in. As they reached the back of the cabin, Coal was half expecting to find the motorcycle gone, except he was pretty sure that whoever had tried to start it was also the culprit who stole his pickup.

The bike was there, and Ray held out his hand.

"What?"

"Give me your notebook and cover me. I'll go see if I can find any better markings."

"No, *you* cover *me*," said Coal. He couldn't help the impatience in his voice.

"Hey!" He heard Ray's plaintive voice but kept walking out to the bike.

His eyes were still good enough to read VIN's, and he peered closely at this one as he checked off the digits in his notebook. They were one off.

With a grunt, he wrote down the number, this time replacing the code for blue with the actual code for red, and returned to Ray and Jordan. He guessed Ray was miffed at him, since he wouldn't meet his eyes.

"You need some glasses, Ray." He made the remark half in fun, but Ray didn't laugh.

"What?"

"That was a c, not an e."

"Oh."

"Yeah, oh."

Saying this, he looked down at the ground. He could see one white corner of paper revealed under the side of the sole of Ray's boot.

"Excuse me." Coal started to bend down. He had to look up when Ray didn't move.

"Oh. Sorry." Then he moved.

Coal picked up the business card and flipped it over. It bore Harvey Cupper's name from Lemhi Valley Realty. Without comment, he put it in his pocket.

They returned to the LTD, and Coal got on the radio and called the correct VIN in to Flo. She came back with the information of one William T. Barker, living on Shoup Ave., one street north of Main, in Salmon.

They were only a mile on their way when Coal glimpsed something off in the trees on the driver's side of the car and yelled out for Jordan to stop and back up, which he did, after some gnarly screeching of tires.

"What does that look like?" He pointed.

"Your truck!"

"Sure does to me. Find some place to pull over." Saying this, Coal jumped out and got on an unnamed road that came off Twenty-eight and snaked amid the thick trees. He didn't need to look back to know Ray was with him. Hansen had stopped his Jeep on the road behind them, but he hadn't heard his door shut, so he must be waiting with Jordan.

They neared the truck, and Coal studied it and the area around it for some time through the Zeiss binoculars commandeered from the cabin.

There was no movement, and no sign of anyone around. Throwing a cautionary glance toward Ray, Coal drew his revolver and walked on in, keeping his eye on the underbrush.

The keys were in the ignition. The truck was unharmed. He holstered the pistol and started to get in, then stopped as Ray headed around to the other side. "Wait!"

Reaching into his back pocket, he pulled out a pair of latex gloves and held them up to Ray. Ray nodded understanding. "You're starting to get the hang of this crap."

"Yeah. And I can read VIN's too." He immediately regretted the jab.

When he had donned the gloves and backed around, and they were driving back out to the highway, he apologized. Ray only laughed. "Oh, come on, man! I deserved a lot more than that. I guess I'm losing my eyesight."

"Happens to the best of us." Coal knew his own eyes weren't what they used to be.

After a hearty thanks, they parted ways with both Hansen and Jordan and drove into town, stopping at the address on Shoup Avenue where William T. Barker had been living the last time he registered the motorcycle. Before going in, Coal dusted all along the door, the steering wheel, and the gear shift for fingerprints, pulled the revealed prints with squares of strapping tape, and stuck them carefully on blank recipe cards. He put the cards back in his backpack and stuffed it once more behind the seat.

His knock on the door was answered by a man in a dirty ball cap and striped gray coveralls, with large teeth that didn't seem inclined to get acquainted with any dental hygienists and the eyes of someone too well acquainted with a jug of moonshine.

"Hi. I help you?"

"Maybe. Are you William Barker?"

"Yes sir." Suspicion sparkled in Barker's eyes.

"Did you used to have a red Honda motorcycle?"

Barker's mouth clamped shut. He shared a reasonable amount of his suspicion back and forth between Coal and Ray, then drawled out the word, "Yeah. Why?"

"You sold it?"

"Yeah. Hey, I haven't seen that bike in more'n a month, and I ain't got no claim on it. Is somethin' goin' on?"

"Who did you sell it to?"

"Just some guy. Big guy. Steve something. Maybe Riggins? I only remember his first name for sure because I got a brother named that, and this guy didn't look like no Steve. More like a Juan or Jose. And he sure didn't look like a Riggins neither."

"So you're saying he looked Mexican?"

"Yeah. At least I think. Kinda talked like one too. Not real bad. He spoke pretty good English, but you know, he had that kind of accent."

"You said he was big?"

"Yeah. Well, not meanin' tall, right? Five eight—maybe? A little shorter than me. But big like through here." He indicated his chest. "And especially across the back. Reminded me of a gorilla."

Coal nodded. "Anything else?"

"I never saw his eyes. He had some pretty funky big black glasses he never took off." Barker thought of something and laughed, putting Coal in mind of a donkey. "And he had a crazy big head o' hair—and a beard. Real bushy—like his hair."

"So black hair?"

"Sure."

"Anything else? What did he drive here in?"

"Nothin', man. At least I never saw no car out here. He just walked up, paid me cash for the bike, then rode it out of here."

"Did you notice anything else remarkable about him?"

"Remarkable? Well, I gotta say he wasn't real friendly. Never even saw him crack a smile. Listen, did somethin' happen with that bike? It's not my deal now, right? I mean, I sold it all legal."

"No, this isn't anything to do with you, Mr. Barker. Thanks for your help."

"You know, man—whatever I can do t' help the law."

Sure, thought Coal as he was walking off. He was an old "judger by the cover of a book," and William Barker looked like trouble with a capital T. But it wasn't likely that his trouble had anything to do with the current case.

* * *

They went back to the sheriff's office, where Coal went upstairs and sent the new fingerprints off to Tony Nwanzée at the Bureau by facsimile, then called him to make sure he would be watching for them. He put the cards in a heavy envelope then, and they drove to the post office and sent them by insured overnight mail to follow up the faxed versions, which Coal didn't trust to be all that readable. He and modern contraptions like facsimile machines had never quite become friends or respecters of each other.

They were going back to the truck when Ray said, "Hey, don't suppose you could drop me off back at the house, could you?"

"Really?"

"Really what? Do you need me?"

"I guess not."

"Okay. Well, I told Virg I'd go riding with him again."

Coal smiled, hiding the painful knowledge that Virgil didn't care to go riding with *him.* "Sure, no problem. Maybe I can grab a bite to eat too."

They were clear out almost to the 28 Club when Flo called to tell Coal he needed to see Joshua Olschewski at his saddle shop. Olschewski had found something Coal was going to want to know about. Beneath his dark sunglasses, Coal only blinked. "I didn't want to eat anyway."

CHAPTER FIFTY-TWO

After saying a quick hello to the family, which included hugs from both twins and even one from Connie, Coal left Ray at the house and drove back to town, exasperated that life couldn't let him relax long enough even to grab a bite to eat with his family.

He pulled off Main Street onto Church and stopped in front of Olschewski's saddle shop. The door bells welcomed him, but not so luxuriously as the smell of leather and leather dye.

"Hi, Josh."

"Hey, boss! How are you?"

"Fine, I think. Man, I don't know how you come in here every day and work. I'd be sitting around sniffing the leather all day. You know, with that smell your job must be pretty close to heaven."

Olschewski made an expression halfway between pursing his lips and a frown. "You'd think so. But I haven't been able to smell that in years."

"Why?"

"I don't know. Your nose just blocks it out after a while, I guess."

"Sad."

"Yep."

"So what did you need to see me about?"

"Well, I was out to Gil Warden's place—out past the cemetery, in the bushes—goin' to take measurements of a horse's back, partly because Gil's real particular and partly because that horse is so sway-backed there's no way he'd order an expensive saddle for it without letting me look at it first. But while I was out there I saw this old pickup parked out past his fence."

"Yeah?"

"Yeah, and I remembered that poster of yours on the door, describing a truck you were lookin' for."

Coal felt himself getting excited. "Okay."

"I looked at it real close, and if isn't the pickup you saw, it's a pretty close copy. I asked Gil about it, and he says it just showed up there a while back, and nobody's ever come to get it. It isn't on his property, so he just left it."

Thanking the saddle maker, Coal started out the door armed only with Olschewski's oral directions and his .357 magnum. He had almost made it to his truck when he remembered the business card retrieved from the cabin. He walked down to Main, then cut across the street to Lemhi Valley Realty. There was a receptionist, but no Harvey Cupper. He asked her to have Cupper call Flo as soon as he came in, left her the number, then went back to the GMC and headed out of town toward the cemetery.

Not far out of town, he passed Cemetery Street, then left the highway on the next road, Demick Lane, and drove nearly to the end of it, to a squat white house with a high-boarded round corral next to it, which according to Joshua Olschewski Gil Warden used for his horse training. Another fence, much shorter, adjoined the round corral, running out some hundred yards or so until it made a corner and headed west. In some thick brush just past it squatted an ugly Ford pickup, once-dark green but now severely oxidized, with a cream-colored door taken from some other truck of the same make. A small dent just behind the door was probably the only sign left from whatever had caused the other door to need replacing.

It had been so long since Coal saw the pickup going up his lane in the dark that he could of course never make a positive identification, but this rig fit everything he could remember of that one. Not surprisingly, the tires had the same tread, as he remembered it—or at least what was left of the tread. He had seen movies featuring monks who were not so bald as these tires.

It was also no surprise that when he started looking for a VIN there was none. The one inside the driver's door had been destroyed, as well as the one on the chassis, once he got underneath to look for it. That left no intact identifying mark by which he would be able to prove who its last owner was. But this was Salmon, Idaho. Small town USA. Somebody in town would know who this pickup belonged to. Of that he had no doubt.

There was no key in the ignition. Coal had hoped for a lucky stroke like that, but it would have shocked him if it had worked out that way. He went knocking on Gil Warden's door, failed to raise him, but found him out with a buckskin colt in a barn, where he was rubbing it down all over its body with a noisy piece of cellophane. The colt trembled at the legs, and its ears flipped back and forth and all around, while its eyes rolled in its head. But so far it was staying put.

"Almost got him, looks like."

Gil Warden, a young man in Wranglers and brown Acme boots, wearing an ugly green plaid shirt with pearl snaps, jerked his head up. "Damn. Scared me."

"Sorry."

"Oh, hey. You're Coal Savage."

"Yes."

"You come to see that pickup?"

"Yes, and I already did. You don't know anything about it, right? It just showed up there?"

"Yeah."

"Remember a day?"

"No. Just sometime before Christmas. Shortly before."

A perfect fit.

"I don't suppose I could use your phone."

"Um, sure."

"Or better yet, you don't know how to hotwire a car, do you?"

Warden laughed. "It seems like it might be kind of incriminating if I said I did."

Coal grinned. "I'll look the other way."

"Well, I wish I could help you, but no dice. Hey, if you could just go let yourself in through the front door, there's a phone on the far wall of the front room, right by the doorway."

"Thanks." Small town Idaho.

Coal went to the house and called Ken Parks at his shop. He was hoping he could explain something over the phone that would help him get the truck started, but mechanics and Coal were bitter enemies—or at least that was what Larry MacAtee used to tell him. He didn't know a solenoid from a cylinder.

In the end, Ken drove out to meet him, saying he needed a break from the shop anyway.

They walked out to the pickup, and Ken threw up the hood. He looked around for a moment, then took a long flat head screwdriver out of his pocket and looked at Coal. "See this?"

"What about it?"

"It's a key."

"What?"

"You heard me. A key."

"What's the punch line?"

"Listen. For future reference, if you had a real key, and it just wouldn't start for you, you'd just turn the key on and then touch a screwdriver across these two screws. It should fire up. You're bypassing a bad starter solenoid."

"Great. I was just thinking about that."

Ken looked up at him. After a moment, he decided he must be joking, and he grinned. "Anyway, you don't have a key, so it's neither here nor there, but if you did have, just touch that screwdriver there, and watch for sparks. I wouldn't do it too much, but it's a way to get you rolling if your starter goes out."

"Great. I'll tuck that away. But what about now?"

"Are you going to sue me for damages?"

"What damages?"

"The damage I'm about to do."

Coal laughed. "Go for it. I don't plan on adopting this thing."

"Okay, your call." Ken went to the cab and got in, with Coal tagging along. Ken held up the screwdriver. "Remember when I said this was a key?"

Coal nodded. Without another pause, Ken turned and jammed the straight-bladed screwdriver into the ignition, depressed the clutch and worked the gas for a second. Then he turned the screwdriver as if it were the real key.

The pickup fired up.

Ken gave Coal a smug look—a normal expression of his.

"If you ever find the key, you probably won't be able to use it."

"I'm pretty sure it's long gone."

"So what are you planning to do now? You just gonna leave your truck here and take this to town?"

Coal stared at his mechanical savior blankly. Finally, Ken laughed again. "I thought so. Too bad you didn't have me grab Andy and bring him out. Well, I guess if we can go now—and if you'll buy me lunch—I can drive it in to the jail for you and then you can bring me back out here to get my rig."

"You're a prince, Ken. I owe you."

"That's what I said. Lunch."

* * *

After shuttling the pickup to the courthouse, then going back out to get Ken's rig and afterwards feeding him at the Coffee Shop, Coal returned to the courthouse to look over the recovered pickup, determined that if there was evidence of any kind he was going to find it.

The entire time he was doing his search, all he could think of was how bad he still wanted Phil Harringer to be involved with the murder of Bern Hargis. He had to admit he didn't miss having a man of Hargis's fine qualities to deal with in his county, but putting Harringer in prison for the crime would be icing on the cake.

He had just found in the bed of the pickup what appeared to be a tiny drop of blood and had collected it when it hit him: He had never called Tony Nwanzée back about the evidence he was returning to him!

Taking a deep breath, he checked his watch. There was still time before Tony had to go home, and if he did Coal could call him there. He had to force himself to stick with the pickup and get all the evidence from it that he could collect before running off to the next task. He was starting to think the job of sheriff in a small county was more like five or ten jobs all rolled into one.

It took him a good hour to finish collecting what he could find from the truck, which included a few hairs, three spots of blood, and some dried mud from far up under the wheel wells. He measured and photographed the tires, carefully dusted for fingerprints in the cab and wasn't surprised to find absolutely none there. Whoever had removed the VINS would also have scrubbed the cab as clean as possible, and they had apparently done the same with the tailgate, for there wasn't even one minor whorl or a ridge there to indicate any human being had ever touched it with bare hands.

At last, he went in and washed his hands, and then he looked over at the phone and took a deep breath. It was time to place a call to the FBI.

And time to hang—or exonerate—Jim Lockwood.

CHAPTER FIFTY-THREE

The phone at FBI headquarters in D. C. seemed to ring off the hook. It wasn't hard for Coal to see where that saying had come from. He was starting to wonder what had happened back there, if they had dumped their budget and had to fire all their receptionists, when the phone rattled off the hook, then went dead.

For a few seconds, Coal listened to the dial tone, trying to believe he wasn't really hearing it.

He slammed the phone down on the base so hard it made the bell ring, and the reverberation went on for several seconds. Then taking a deep breath he dialed the number once more.

This time, on only the second ring, it picked up. There was a pause, and Coal was about to swear, when he heard, *Nwanzée's office. Burnett here.*

"Ross! Hey, this is Coal Savage, out in Idaho."

Hey, Coal! Man, that's a voice I never thought I'd hear again! What's happening?

"Well, I really need to talk to Tony. Bad."

Dang, buddy—he's out. He had to go out to the airport to pick up some big drug smuggler. Can I help you with anything?

This time Coal swore, but only in his head. "Umm . . . No, probably not. Do you know when he'll get back?"

Anybody's guess, but I'd say at least an hour.

"Ross, you've got to leave him a message to call me, okay? It's not life or death, but it's close."

I'll do it. I hope everything's okay.

Coal was hoping the same. No sooner had he hung up than the phone rang. With a false sense of hope, he picked it up. "Hello?"

Is this the sheriff's office? asked a man's voice.

"Oh! Yeah, sorry. This is Savage."

Coal, Harvey Cupper here. Lemhi Valley Realty? Nancy said you wanted me to call.

"Yes! Hey, Harvey, I found a business card of yours out in the strangest place, behind an old cabin at the back of the Hargis property. I'm sure it's a long shot, but—"

Hey, is this about the two guys who were looking for a vacation place way off the road?

Irritated by the interruption only for a second, Coal paused. "You tell me. What was that about?"

Well, two guys came in. It's been some time ago, way back before Christmas. Strangers in the valley. Said they had heard stories about rafting the river and thought this would be the place for them to retire.

"Do you remember what they looked like?"

They'd be hard to forget. Mexicans, for sure. One looked more like it than the other. Real big hair and beard. Heavy guy. Looked like a pro wrestler. And he wore some big, fat, black sunglasses that he never took off, even when we were in the office and the light was pretty dim.

This sounded like the man who called himself Steve Riggins. Coal repeated the name.

Like I said, Coal, it's been a while, but you know, that does sort of sound familiar. Whatever it was, I didn't believe it was real. He was for sure Mexican. I'd stake my life on it.

"What about the other guy?"

He didn't get involved in the talking. Always hung back. Also a dark-haired guy, but in a way he seemed maybe only half Mexican. He had a beard too, but a lot better trimmed. And shorter hair. Could have been a businessman, by his looks. Honestly, he could have been an actor. Pretty good looking fellow.

"I've got to ask you, Harvey—why did you think of these two guys after all this time?"

Well, because of what you said. They were asking about pieces of property off the highway—secluded. And a few days later the big guy—Steve—he came back in asking specifically about the Hargis place.

After Coal hung up with Harvey Tupper, he sat down at his desk and looked out at the gloomy day. Hard pellets of snow were bouncing in the parking lot. Not heavy, but enough to make believe winter might really come after all.

What was he dealing with now? Two men, not one. Two men, and surely they were living in the cabin behind Hargis's. But they must have worked out some other deal, since Harvey Cupper hadn't heard any more from them. They must have—

Coal felt like a fool. Of course! The new road Hargis was cutting. He didn't just *feel* the fool—he *was* a fool. This was all playing in together. Hargis's new pickup, paid for with cash. The new dairy barn he had planned to build—and if he spoke with any builders about those plans, that would be easy to nail down, since there were only a handful of builders in the whole valley. The new road. The new coat of varnish on the cabin, a cabin on the property of a man Coal could never imagine bothering to take care of an unused building, when he didn't even take care of his own house.

Coal's head started to pound with the fury of his thoughts. What if… What if Phil Harringer, so bent on buying the Hargis property, had found out that Hargis was selling it out from under him? What if he had already put money down on it, and Hargis wouldn't give it back, and Harringer, enraged, went over and . . .

Coal stopped. His entire body was tense, as if ready to explode. Suddenly, all the wind seemed to go out of him, and he settled back down into his chair, rubbing his sandpaper jaw. He pulled in a huge breath and let it seep out of his pursed lips. Then he did it again.

He had to get hold of himself. He knew one thing in this whole case: He despised rancher Phil Harringer, not only for what he had done to K. T. Batterton, but for the sheer fact that he was an all-out ass. But he was letting his hatred for Harringer cloud his vision. There was no reason why Harringer still couldn't be his main suspect. But it was by no means a sure thing. The scenario that had popped into Coal's head was plausible, yes. But even if it were true, there wasn't enough evidence so far to convict a man, no matter how much he despised him. He still had to talk to Tony Nwanzée. Until he did, he was counting chickens when he didn't even own any eggs. As much as he almost prayed the murderer would be Phil Harringer, he didn't even have enough to bring him in and talk to him yet—unless Harringer agreed to talk of his own accord.

Jordan Peterson pulled into the parking lot for his shift while Coal was sitting there, and he came downstairs still buckling on his gun belt.

"Hi, Coal."

"Hey, buddy. Say, not to saddle you with office time, but did you have any plans right off?"

"No, not really."

"Then could I get you to wait here for a while? I need to run up to the clerk's office for a bit, and I'm waiting for a phone call."

"Sure, that's fine. Say, Coal?"

Caught already partway to the door, Coal turned back. "Yeah?"

"I see you're in kind of a rush, but . . . I feel a little silly without one of us bringing this up eventually."

"What's that?"

"About Maura."

Coal froze. This was a subject he had been avoiding, a subject he had no intention of ever asking about. It wasn't his business. But the real reason was he simply didn't want to know what kind of date night Jordan and Maura PlentyWounds had had.

"What about her?" The coward's way of pretending he had no idea what his deputy meant.

"Well, we went to a movie together."

"Oh, yeah! How'd that go?" He really did want to know, but he really didn't. The air in the room seemed suddenly too thick to breathe.

"Great. It went great. We might do it again next week."

Coal's heart fell. But his poker face didn't. "That's great, Jordan. Good for you. She's a super lady."

Turning before Jordan could read his face, Coal went to the door, threw it open, and bolted up the stairs, going into the courthouse and into the county clerk's office.

When he returned from his information-seeking quest, Coal knew two things: As he had intuited, the two strangers to the valley had been in asking about tax records for the Hargis dairy. Both of them, according to the clerk, she would remember forever. But it wasn't only the two strangers who had been looking. Harringer had come as well, quite a while before the other two. Perhaps it wasn't Christ-like to wish a man a killer, but Coal did, with Harringer. At the very least, perhaps all three of them, Harringer and the two strangers, were tied up in the murder together. That didn't really fit with any other facts, but if there was one thing Coal had learned in life, it was that quite often murder made little sense of any kind.

Jordan stood up from the desk as Coal was opening the door. The sudden motion made Coal's heart leap. "Anything?"

"No, sorry. Your mom called, but that was all."

Coal's feeling of disappointment gave him a touch of guilt. He should have been happy to hear from his mother. But he felt so close to exonerating Jim from the murder charge that had been hanging over his head that he couldn't wait to call him and Betty with the news—or better yet, bring it to them in person. Any other call right now was only an unwanted distraction.

He sat down and picked up an issue of *Newsweek* from September that he had brought with him from Virginia. He had kept meaning to read it, but something always seemed to come up. The cover photo was a shot of Israeli soldiers moving a coffin containing one of the dead Olympians from the early September Palestinian kidnapping and murder in Munich, Germany, that rocked the world. It read, *Israel buries its dead.*

Jordan picked up his keys and put on his coat, stepping to the door as he did up his buttons with what seemed like more care than the job needed. He paused and looked back at Coal for several seconds, then said something, but Coal was so engrossed in the magazine he didn't realize it until his deputy was gone. The fact was whatever Jordan had said Coal really wasn't in the mood to hear.

The clanging of the telephone bell made him jerk in his seat. He practically knocked it off the base trying to scramble up and answer it.

"Salmon sheriff."

Hey! Coal, my man! Tony!

"Man, Tony, am I glad to hear your voice! What do you have for me?"

You want all of it?

Coal almost laughed. "Well, no, why don't you leave out all the important stuff? Of course I want all of it!"

Tony laughed with glee. He sounded so close he might have been next door. *All right, brother. You can try to jot some of this down if you want, but the report should be there early tomorrow, all nice and typed up for you.*

"Man, you're a prince!"

Don't I know it! All right, here goes. And you owe me a bottle of Chablis for this, buddy!

Tony started from the top of his list and read carefully down it. Much of it Coal had already figured out or guessed at, but this professional report represented the work of the best the country had to offer in the way of evidence analysis. It was a perk no other Idaho sheriff could have hoped to be blessed with.

He first covered soil types. The soil taken from Wimpey Creek didn't appear to be a match to the soil taken from Jim's undercarriage. The most significant difference was that the soil taken from Jim's pickup had a lot of what appeared to be cow manure mixed in it, while the samples from Wimpey Creek didn't. Coal was satisfied with that.

Tony had told his people to put a rush on working over the hammer, even though it had come in later than everything else. He wanted to get all the evidence back to Coal at the same time. The bloody finger grip marks on the hammer, the report indicated, were indeed from a left hand, someone with thicker-than-normal fingers. Coal almost chuckled about the last part, because he didn't have one suspect on his list who didn't have thick fingers, including Hargis's own wife.

Tony came out of the blue, however, with a revelation that there was a good, readable set of prints on the hammer that wasn't on the handle. Rather, it was on the head. There was a thumb print on one side, and the prints of an index and middle finger on the other, as if someone had carried the hammer away gingerly, and didn't want to leave any prints on the handle where they were sure to be searched for.

The blood on the hammer was a scientific mess. There were actually traces of three different blood types on the handle, and a fourth on the head—presumably Hargis's. And one of the three on the handle, according to the expert employed by the FBI, appeared to be from a dog! Coal would have to obtain blood samples from all the witnesses if they wanted to match the blood type to anyone.

"You're seriously telling me there are four different blood types on that thing?" Coal cut in.

Serious, bro. Serious as a heart attack.

"And a dog?"

Yep, no foolin'! Oh—I almost forgot. This is an important one. Judging by the photos you sent of that poor guy's skull, our expert said it wouldn't be impossible, but it would be a lot harder to make a blow like that for somebody who wasn't naturally left-handed.

Coal had somewhat absently been jotting notes down. Now he wrote *LEFT HANDED* in fat black letters, then underlined it three times.

Tony sighed. Well, t*hat's about it, brother. I'd better get, unless you can think of anything else.*

Coal stopped him from hanging up. "Not so fast, old pard."

What?

"You're not going to leave until you tell me more about those fingerprints on the head of the hammer."

Say what?

"Damnit, you heard me!"

Tony started laughing. It was a rollicking belly laugh, not just a chuckle. He was having a good time with Coal.

Okay, okay. Man, I wouldn't have hung up anyway. I just wanted to see if you even noticed.

"Of course I did. Did you get a match on those prints?"

Maybe I did and maybe I didn't. You still going to send me that bottle of Chablis?

"I'll send you a whole winery. Stop messing around."

Tony's voice went serious. *All right, bud. This is gonna be a weird one. You ready?*

"Shoot."

Well, two of the prints were pretty smudged, but our computers nailed this guy on the middle fingerprint. One hundred percent positive ID. The guy's out of Las Vegas, Nevada. A Mexican. Nothing big on him, just that he used to be a cop, but he got in trouble down there and basically had to resign or be fired. I talked to the Vegas PD, and they said he has some mob connections, mostly through his brother, who you've probably heard of: Angel Medina?

"Wow. Really? Yeah, I've heard of him. I think you and I have talked about him before."

Yeah, well, that's the guy. So the brother apparently got in trouble for tampering with evidence that could have put Angel away for a while. That's why they dumped him. They couldn't get him on anything else, but they also thought he might have been taking some of the drugs they confiscated and selling them.

"What's his name? The brother."

Hector. Hector Reynaldo Medina.

"You have any photos of him?"

Way ahead of you, brother. Vegas PD overnighted one off to you yesterday. Maybe you'll get your evidence back and the photo all at the same time.

"So let me make sure I've got this right: Hector isn't wanted for anything. Just his brother."

Not even his brother right now. He split Vegas before they could bring charges up on him for anything, and Hector had apparently made a big enough mess of the evidence that they probably wouldn't have got a conviction anyway.

"All right, Tony. I really do owe you a bottle—or a case."

I'm just messing with you, bro. If you want to, you knock yourself out, but I won't be expecting it.

Coal hung up with his old friend and partner knowing if he did *anything* in the next week it was going to be sending Tony Nwanzée at least one bottle of sweet Chablis.

He was lying in bed late that night before he remembered something. One of the most important reasons he had been so excited to hear from Tony, before he got sidetracked with all the information about the Medina brothers.

Jim Lockwood's watch.

CHAPTER FIFTY-FOUR

Saturday, December 30

Coal slept little that night. He finally fell into fitful sleep sometime after three o'clock, and he woke with a start and rolled over to stare at the clock until his eyes came into focus. Five o'clock!

Struggling out of the tangled covers, he pulled on his pants, almost tripping over Dobe and Shadow as he tried to get out of his room. He fumbled down the stairs into a dark world where apparently even Connie was still sleeping.

Going to the telephone, he sat for a moment in a daze. It would be seven o'clock in D. C. Tony would already be up getting ready for work, wouldn't he?

He made a decision at the same time that it hit him he had transcribed his old partner's home telephone into the lined pages inside the Ma Bell phone book where important numbers were kept. He opened the book and cursed until his eyes finally focused on Tony's number. What was supposed to be so great about one's "golden years," again? Sore muscles, bad eyes and ears, hairs growing in places where hair wasn't meant to grow, unless one was a dog. *Golden years.* The only thing Coal could imagine would be "golden" about aging was the color of one's pee he was no longer able to hold when he didn't want it coming out, or able to make come out when he wanted it to. *Golden.* Like hell.

Feeling only a little guilty, he dialed Tony's home number. But why should he feel guilty? Tony was the one who had forgotten!

A groggy voice answered.

"Tony?"

Uh . . . Yeah, I think so. Who's this?

"Coal!"

What the crap, man? You miss me already?

"Not really, but you didn't address all my evidence."

Huh?

"My evidence! You didn't tell me anything about that watch I sent!"

A long moment of silence. Even though it was after seven o'clock back there, Tony sounded even more groggy than Coal. *Oh, shoot!* The awakening. *Yeah, you're right. Uh . . . Let me think. Let me think. Okay, so if I remember right, there were several prints on that watch, but the ones that really struck me matched the prints you sent from the dead guy.*

"Wait. Now say that again?"

Your dead guy, man! The victim! His prints were all over that watch.

"Are you sure?"

Aw, come on, buddy. We got the best in the business back here. Of course I'm sure. Two other sets of prints on there, but none that matched any of our records. Oh—and the prints were on both sides of the band, outside and inside.

"Thanks, Tony! You're a prince."

Yeah, man, you better *butter me up! Oh, and you forgot something.*

"What's that?"

You're so sorry for bothering me at home so early in the morning—right?

Coal laughed. "Oh, come on. You're getting ready for work anyway."

Brother, you need a shrink. Man, it's Saturday!

* * *

Coal didn't want to steal his mother's thunder, but being with horses gave him a feeling of peace and contentment, and a chance to sort through his thoughts. So before Connie could get up, he went back upstairs, trailed by both dogs, and got dressed, then went out to feed Cody and Bolt.

A low-slung, smutty gray sky was spitting the same hard bits of snow as the day before, and thank heaven for zero wind and heavy coats, because it couldn't be much over twenty-five degrees. The gravel crackled as he walked out to the corrals. He missed the feel and sound of powder snow squeaking beneath his boots.

As Coal smelled the horses, a smell not quite as agreeable as the same smell in warmer times of year, it made him think of the smell of Herefords from when his father was still around and operating the ranch. He missed that. He missed all those things about working with animals, and with the land, the things he had grown up with.

Peace filled Coal's heart as he watched the horses munching on deep green alfalfa hay and a bait of grain, steam rising from their nostrils as the sounds of their chewing played like music in his ears. The dogs ran around the yard, ignoring the cold.

It was during this time of peace when Coal thought again of Jim's watch. Three sets of fingerprints. Whose could they be? And did it matter? What mattered was that one set belonged to Bern Hargis. He sorted through the possible meanings of this. Of course, as a cynic he might say Hargis and Jim were fighting, and somehow Hargis's fingers touched the watch during the fight, before Jim drove the hammer through his skull. Yes, there was always that chance. But he preferred another possibility: Somehow, Hargis had come by Jim's watch without Jim's knowledge of it.

Going back inside, Coal wiped his boots off at the door and smiled back at Connie, who was frying bacon in the kitchen. He went over to her and put his arms around her from behind.

"Ma, you sure cook a lot of bacon. You know, if butter's supposed to be so bad for you, then why isn't bacon?"

She laughed. "Well of course it is! But I love the smell."

Coal gave her a squeeze and then let go. "I do too. And I still say you're going to find out someday that bacon was all right to eat after all. If you keep putting all your faith in so-called health experts, you're going to die young."

Again, she laughed. "Yes, well, it's a little too late for that, now isn't it?"

Coal went and pulled off his coat, sitting in front of the television with Dobe and Shadow at his feet for a while as he sipped on a cup of his mother's Pero because he was too lazy to make coffee. It sure felt lonely here now that Jim and Betty were gone, but he was happy they were back in their own home, without fear of Willie Stinger coming after them.

He sank back in his chair and closed his eyes, thinking of the Lockwoods, the Hargises and Leroy Yarwood. He thought about Maura and Annie and Kathy MacAtee, and he thought about Virgil and their standoff over his giving away Burro. There were so many things he could be dealing with that a friend and father with a simpler vocation would have time for on a dreary Saturday in the middle of Christmas vacation. But he couldn't rest until this murder case was laid to rest.

Incredibly, Coal dozed off, and the next thing of which he was aware was Connie shaking his shoulder. "Hey, Son."

He blinked up at her. He hadn't felt so tired in days. He had been shoved down a rabbit hole by a jack hammer, and it seemed it would be days before he felt sober again.

"You okay?"

"Yeah, Mom." He struggled up to a straighter position. "What time is it?"

"Just five-forty. I didn't want to wake you, but I know you like your bacon fresh. And the eggs are going to get cold too."

"No, that's okay." He struggled out of the chair, which seemed to grow mobile arms that reached up to pull him back down.

Going to the table, he ate the food she had made him, some sixty grams of protein and plenty of fat, with a dry biscuit from the day before. It hit him as he ate that before anything else that day he had to go back and visit Sherlene Hargis. Maybe she had an answer to a question that had plagued him from the morning they pulled her husband's body out of Wimpey Creek.

Downing a glass of milk that topped his protein for that meal at over seventy grams, he stood up. He had eaten as slowly as he could, but the clock said it was just shy of six.

"I fed the horses, Mom."

"I know." She smiled. "I saw you out there, or I would already have been out. Hey. You okay?"

He had to laugh this time. "Mom, you just asked me that."

"Oh. I did?"

"You did."

"Did you answer me?"

"I don't remember."

"Oh. Then are you okay?"

He laughed, then shrugged. "I got up to call Tony Nwanzée, my old partner at the Bureau. He told me three sets of fingerprints were taken from Jim's watch."

Searching his eyes, she asked, "So what does that mean? Is it bad or good?"

"Well, think about it. If Jim was dumping Hargis's body in the creek and his watch broke and fell in the water, why would it have Hargis's prints on it?"

Her face brightened. "Then…"

"Yeah. Unless something really bizarre happened that made Hargis get his prints on both sides of Jim's watchband when he was killing him, I'd say this is great news for Jim. Now I've got to drive over to the dairy and see if Sherlene can tell me how her husband might have left his prints on someone else's watch. This is too important to do over the phone."

The fact that the Hargises ran a dairy gave Coal the only reason he needed to drive over so early in the morning. They had to be up early. Wasn't every dairy owner?

But Sherlene wasn't. Coal knocked, then knocked some more. The last several knocks weren't with his knuckles, which were starting to feel bruised, but with the toe of his boot. He had started to turn away toward the barn when he heard the door crack open.

Sherlene Hargis peered at him through the screen door. "Is something wrong?"

"Sorry, ma'am. I thought you'd be up."

She only stared at him.

"Ma'am, I'll let you go back to sleep, but I need you to answer some quick questions for me. Or maybe only one."

"Okay." He actually felt for the woman, who looked like he had felt earlier. He was starting to think he might have to catch her if she passed out.

"Ma'am, I have a watch that belongs to Jim Lockwood. It has your husband's fingerprints on it." Then, on a whim and a gamble, he took a shot in the dark and lied. "It also has yours. It's an expensive looking watch with elk tooth inlays. Oh—and the band is broken loose. Do you know anything about that?"

No dogfood-stealing skunk in the beam of a spotlight ever looked guiltier than Sherlene. She stared at him, her fear palpable even through the dimness of the door screen.

"Ma'am." Coal felt even sorrier for her than he had thinking about how sleepy she looked. "You aren't in trouble. I'm just trying to figure out why both of your fingerprints would be on another man's watch." Coal was going on the assumption that the third set of fingerprints on the watch were those of Jim himself.

"You promise I won't be in trouble?"

"You're not in trouble. Just answer me."

Her eyes flitted away. They didn't come back to his face as she spoke. "Well, at the store… You know, when Bern and the sheriff had that fight? After you all left, I saw that watch. It was just lying there on the floor with all them cans of food. I'm sorry. I honestly didn't know whose it was. I didn't mean to take it."

Coal's mind raced. He felt goose bumps racing up and down his body, and he was sure the small hairs actually stood up on the back of his neck. He was almost afraid to speak. "So . . . you found it on the floor of the store?"

"Yes sir."

"Ma'am . . . Why didn't you turn it over to the store?"

"Well, I would've, but Bern saw it an' grabbed it outta my hand. I thought it must belong to one o' you, but Bern told me he'd beat me if I told anybody he had it. He said it was finders keepers. I'm sorry. I really didn't mean to keep it."

Coal's heart seemed frozen. The goose bumps he had felt now covered him from head to foot, big nests of them. Even his breathing had seemed to cease. He fought back a sudden, strange rush of tears. How could this answer have been so easy, and right in front of him all along, for only the price of asking? Jim Lockwood had not killed Bern Hargis. Jim was only a victim of circumstance, a man with a very unfortunate seizure condition who had made a huge mistake, in his anger, of telling someone else he was going to kill them, and then having them wind up murdered shortly after. He was as innocent in this killing as Coal's twins.

Coal almost felt an urge to give Sherlene Hargis a bear hug. Instead, he simply thanked her through the window screen. And floated back to the pickup.

Jim Lockwood was an innocent man. And a free one.

As Coal drove out to the highway, he contemplated turning right and driving to Jim's to share the news with him. Then he remembered that he should get the watch today, with all the other evidence.

It would be like a kid longing for Christmas, but Coal was going to force himself to wait until he had that watch in his hand to go visit the Lockwoods. He could hardly stand waiting to see the looks on their faces.

* * *

Later that day, when Coal returned from the most satisfying job he had taken on in some time, that of handing Jim his newly repaired watch and telling him his worries were over, he drove right past Savage Lane back to the jail, where he had left Tony Nwanzée's package of returned evidence sitting on his desk next to the unopened envelope from a Lieutenant Zach Durfey, from the Las Vegas PD. He had barely paid any attention to the other items in Tony's package, since he had already gotten the run-down on them from Tony, and the watch was what he had truly cared about anyway. That watch, which in its way had held Jim a prisoner, now had set him free. Coal was floating a foot above the ground.

Now to find out more about this mystery former police officer, Hector Medina, and perhaps more about his brother Angel as well.

He took a letter opener out of his drawer, slid it under the flap, and pulled out the photo. Then he stopped. He stared. As had been the case too many times of late, his heart seemed to stop. Only this time it was not with the feeling of elation the revelation about Jim's watch had given him.

The photo was not a police booking shot, as he had expected, but a professional studio photo of a handsome young man with black hair and sideburns, wearing a conservative tan business suit and a yellow tie with diagonal navy blue stripes.

Coal could not see him as a man named Hector Reynaldo Medina.

He knew him as Ray Christian.

CHAPTER FIFTY-FIVE

Coal stared at the photo until it began to blur. It was the well-composed, confident face of the man who had become his friend, the man who had been beside him through so much in the past thirteen days.

He didn't swear. There were times when even that would not release the pressure in one's head. He set the picture down carefully on top of his desk and took in a deep breath, then got up and went to the bathroom. He didn't want to see his face in the mirror, but he couldn't help looking. As he turned on the water in the sink and let it get good and cold, he stared at his whiskered cheeks, now looking dark and dirty with the thickness of his beard. He stared at his dark, unkempt hair, which had started getting a little long on his ears, and at his blue-gray eyes, which were starting to look back at him with no less of a haunted look than he saw in Annie Price's. Those eyes had suffered irreparable damage. They had seen too much.

He leaned down and started splashing cold water on his face, over and over. He filled his cupped hands and then ran them back over his hair as the water spilled out and dripped everywhere. The sandpaper of his whiskers scratched his hands. Vaguely, he was aware that it felt kind of good.

He looked up at the mirror again and blinked as water ran into his eyes. He picked up a towel that had probably been used too many times by too many people and dabbed the water off his hair and face. He blinked again, attempting to clear his vision. Apparently, it had been clouded for some time.

Returning to his desk, he slumped into the chair, and Ray's suave face stared back at him, confident and good-looking in every way.

He picked up the business card that had come with the package, a card with a little gold badge printed in the upper left hand corner, next to which were the big bold blue letters LVPD, and Lieutenant Zach Durfey's name and office phone number in its center.

With no reason to expect that Durfey would be in, because for one thing it was Saturday, and for the other, Coal's luck never worked that way, he dialed the number, his finger moving slowly, automatically. He couldn't hear the clicking of the dial as after each digit it retreated back to its starting point. He saw it move, but heard no sound.

Las Vegas Police. This is Captain Wagner.

Coal had to force himself to come back to where he was. He was barely conscious of the voice and the words that came with it. "Hello, Captain. This is Sheriff Savage, from up in Idaho. I just received a photograph from one of your detectives. A Lieutenant Durfey? He wouldn't happen to be in today, would he?"

You're in luck, Sheriff. He's right here walking one of our rookies through a DWI booking. Can you hold?

"Uhh..." Coal tried to think of a way not to sound demanding. Captain Wagner saved him.

Never mind. Long distance call. Sorry, Sheriff. I'm a budget guy too. Hold on.

Another voice came on the line, manly, but at the same time gentle, with an obscure tone of caring too often missing from the voice of a man who spent too many years wearing a badge.

This is Lieutenant Durfey. Coal Savage?

"Yeah."

How can I help you, sir? Did you get the photo I sent?

"I did. I did." Coal paused. Durfey waited for several seconds.

Everything okay?

Coal shook himself free of his thoughts. "Yeah. Well, I've got an issue up here. I hope you can help me."

Sure. Fire.

Coal chuckled quietly. *Fire.* Maybe a strange thing for a cop to say. "So this Hector Medina character that used to be with your force. He's going by the name of Ray Christian now, and he's up here in Salmon."

So I gathered. Rey Christian, huh? Makes sense. Our guy didn't go by Hector. He always used Rey, with an e. You know, for Reynaldo? So he might be a suspect in a murder, you're thinking?

Coal paused, staring hard at Ray's photo. Murder? This was *Ray* they were talking about!

Sheriff?

"Sorry. I'm here. So . . . Well, that's the bad thing. I never had any reason to think he was involved until I got the fingerprints back from the evidence techs. The fact is, this guy's been helping me do the investigation." He was embarrassed even to admit this now.

Durfey swore. *Oh, man. I'm sorry, Sheriff. Wow. That's a rough one. What can I do to help?*

"Well, there's somebody up here that's been hiding out in a secluded cabin, and the other day he took a shot at me with a shotgun."

Holy crap! Thank heavens for bad shooting, huh?

"Yeah. Actually, I was saved by bending over to pick up a business card he had dropped. But anyway, I don't know much about this guy except for a description from at least four people that always seems to be pretty consistent."

And you think I can help?

"I just have a funny idea you might."

Okay, let me see. Throw it at me.

"So he's supposed to be a big guy. Not tall, just wide, like a pro wrestler. Maybe five-eight? Talks with what I'm gathering is sort of a Spanish sounding accent, more than Mexican, but the people who have seen him think he's Mexican. Wears dark glasses apparently indoors as well as out, and has a bushy head of black hair and a big beard. He's been telling people his name is Steve Riggins."

Well, Sheriff, that name doesn't mean anything to me. But that description... I hope I'm wrong, but if you've got Rey Medina up there with you, I'm thinking it's a real good chance that the other guy you're talking about is his brother, Angel. It's Jacinto Angelo Medina. And Sheriff, if that's the other guy, you might have some real problems on your hands.

Tell me something I don't know, thought Coal. He drew in a deep breath. "What kind of problems, exactly?"

Well, Angel is deep inside the Mafia down here. He's been up on several murder raps, but we were never able to sink him for anything. We thought we had him for interstate drug trafficking, but we're pretty sure Rey stole some evidence and kind of 'un-filed' some reports, and—

Well, anyway, the short of it is Angel got away again, but we were about to do a raid on his place when he up and split, maybe about a month ago, about two weeks after Rey abandoned his fancy apartment downtown and vanished.

That guy you're describing sounds just like Angel, and if it is, don't try to take him without two or three good men. Like I said, we couldn't prove anything, but we're pretty sure he's been the trigger man in two gunfights down here, one of them where a cop got killed. And we had a witness who was willing to finger him for two execution-style murders—until this guy disappeared without a trace—the witness, that is.

When Coal hung up, his thoughts turned to home. Rey Medina, formerly known as Ray Christian, had been living under Coal's own roof for almost two weeks. He had come to feel like part of the family.

The most devastating thing about this for Coal right at that moment was he didn't know if he could ever trust his own judgment about people again.

He thought of the hammer, and he thought of the Mafia man named Angel Medina, who was supposed to be a killer. But the fingerprints on the head of the hammer weren't Angel's. They were Ray's.

Coal stared at the phone. His hand was shaking. He wanted to dial his mother and have her take the kids and go somewhere. Then again, he was afraid Ray would sense something wrong and leave. But could he with a clear conscience leave his family there with a possible murderer?

He blinked his eyes and rubbed them with his forefinger and thumb. Whatever he did, he was going to need some help. Where did he turn?

He looked over at the clock. It was eleven-thirty. Jordan was probably still sleeping. What about Bob Wilson? And Chief Dan George? And what about Todd Mitchell? He sure wished his deputy was here with him now. He thought about Paul Matthews, the sheriff over in Custer County. But that was too far. He might be able to wait on Angel Medina. But how was he to wait on his brother?

Coal got up mechanically and picked up his holster, putting it back on his belt. His eyes swept the office, and he didn't even know what for. He looked at the shotgun rack.

Then he stepped to the door and went out, listening to the pelting of little snow pellets on his hat as he made his way to the GMC, as if in a trance.

Coal didn't know how he got back to his house. By driving his pickup, obviously, but he didn't remember a mile of the drive. He only knew that he came to himself making the turn onto Savage Lane. He reached down and wiggled the .357 in its holster.

And Coal, who had stopped some time ago being a praying man, said a prayer.

He hesitated and scanned the yard before driving in. When he had driven away earlier, Ray Christian's Cadillac was here. Now it was gone. He sat there in the truck, unsure how to feel but sensing the tension flood out of him.

Until someone stopped behind him in the road and honked, he sat staring at the house. The car horn shook him to his senses, and he waved an apology at the driver, then turned into the yard and parked in the driveway. His mother's Chrysler Newport was there.

Filling his lungs with ice-cold air, he slammed the pickup door and went up the concrete steps, looking through the front window with some trepidation. Until he got close, he could see only the light of the TV playing through the sky's glare on the glass. But up close he made out the twins and the girls all lazing around on couches and chairs, as relaxed as they could be.

He stepped inside and was greeted by Dobe and Shadow, both of whom he ignored. "Hey, kids. Where's Grandma?"

"She took Cody to the vet," Katie Leigh replied, pulling her eyes away from *The Rifleman* on the TV screen just long enough to acknowledge him.

"Cody? Why? What's wrong with him?"

"I think he got a nail in his foot."

Coal frowned. "Great. How long has she been gone?"

Without taking her eyes off Chuck Connors's face, Katie shrugged.

Coal sighed. He felt his heart starting to slow back down. Without realizing he had even drawn it, he slid his revolver back in the holster.

"Is Ray around?" This time no one replied. "Katie!"

His daughter turned to him, obviously disgusted at missing even one more moment of the show. "What?"

"Where's Ray?"

"I think he went to town."

"By himself?"

"No. He took Virgil. They're going to look at some guns."

CHAPTER FIFTY-SIX

Putting on the calmest face he could muster, Coal went over and unplugged the phone from the wall, then bounded up the stairs two at a time and plugged it back into the jack in his room.

He called the vet and got the receptionist, who found Connie sitting in the lobby and put her on.

Hello?

"Mom, it's Coal! Do you know when Ray and Virgil left?"

I'm not sure. Why?

"It's hard to explain. Now don't panic, but . . ." He went on to give her the shortest possible version of everything he had just learned about Ray.

Connie swore, a sound Coal didn't often have the pleasure of reveling in. But even his mother cursing couldn't lift his spirits right now.

"Do you know where they went?"

I'm not sure except that I know Ray got a star in his windshield, and I told him to take it to Andy Holmes's shop to get it fixed.

"That's all? Katie said they were going to look at some guns."

Oh, yes. Ray did say that. Please be careful, honey.

"I'm not going to let you lose a grandson, Mom. Just say some prayers, will you?"

Hey, Coal? Her voice stopped him just shy of hanging up.

"Yeah?"

Do you remember that boy from junior high that you were friends with? Mikey Parravano or something like that?

Coal thought back, while wondering why it mattered. Mikey Parravano was a scrawny kid back in junior high, not very good-looking, pretty poverty-stricken, and often the brunt of jokes and bullying. He had always liked Coal, but the day Coal came to his rescue against three particularly cruel bullies who had caught him out behind the IGA grocery and were working him over made Mikey Parravano a loyal fan and follower of Coal's forever. In fact, sometimes Coal couldn't get rid of Mikey if he wanted to.

"Yeah, sure I remember him. Why?"

Well, I thought you told me one time that he was somehow in with the Mafia down there in Las Vegas too. Do you think he'd know anything more about these Medina brothers?

"Mom! That's a great idea!"

He hardly told her goodbye before hanging up and dialing the LVPD back again. This time he had to settle for talking to Captain Wagner. He told him about Michael Parravano. "Do you know him?"

Not personally, but I know of *him. Yes, he's supposed to be a Mafia guy, but a pretty small fish. We've never gone after him because it seems like the Feds would rather ignore him and keep him on the back burner.*

"Do you have any way to locate him?"

Sure. I think he has an office in the Flamingo.

The captain managed to look up a number for the Flamingo, and Coal hung up and dialed it. It took a lot of patience, but finally he got Mikey Parravano on the phone. After a few words of happy greeting, Coal threw his old friend the curve ball.

"Mikey, I'm calling because I need a huge favor if you can help me."

Sure, Coal! Are you kidding? Anything. You name it.

"Okay. Well, there's a couple guys from down there. The Medina brothers? One used to be a cop, but he got in trouble and got ousted. And his brother's supposed to be a pretty tough cookie. Angel? Do you know them?"

Parravano's voice got quieter. *Hey, Coal. Man. Can I call you back?*

Coal had a gut feeling his old friend suddenly had cold feet. He wasn't going to call him back at all.

"Mikey, I really need some help on this, buddy. I've got to know why these guys are up here."

I know, man. I know! Parravano's words were hissed. *Just— Seriously, man, I gotta call you back. Give me your number. Hurry.*

Taking a leap of faith, Coal gave his old friend the house number, and after Coal's promise to wait for the call, the line went dead.

One of the longest half hours of Coal's life passed while he sat there on his bed listening to the dogs fawn around outside his door, wanting to be inside getting attention from him, and the drone of the TV downstairs, with the occasional outburst of laughter or shouting from one of the kids.

Without warning, a severe, sharp pain hit Coal in the guts. He looked down at the phone, horrified. He exercised his vocabulary of curse words. It had been twenty-five minutes. Mikey Parravano might be calling back any time. Again, he cursed, calculating how long a trip to the bathroom might take.

In the end, there was no choice. Nature won't wait on fools, and sometimes she gives no second warnings.

Jerking the phone plug out of the wall, Coal ran downstairs and plugged it back into the living room jack, then dashed down the hall to the bathroom leaving behind a final command for someone to answer the phone if it rang.

As fate would always have it, he had no sooner than sat down when he heard the phone ring. Something shot out of him at that precise moment, and it wasn't all curse words. "Get the phone!" he yelled.

It was five minutes before he felt safe to leave the bathroom, and he gave his hands a quick bath in rubbing alcohol rather than waste time on soap and water and ran back to the living room. The kids were watching television as if nothing had happened.

"Hey! Did someone get the phone?"

Katie looked over. "Um . . . Yeah, Dad. It was some guy from Las Vegas, and he said he couldn't hold on because it's long distance."

"What? Did he say anything else?"

"Yeah, Dad! Easy, okay? He said he'd call back again in a few minutes."

Relieved, Coal started to reach for the phone plug again.

Just as he touched it, the ring of the phone jarred him, and he swore and immediately regretted it but realized the kids were all so engrossed in Lucas McCain and an impending gunfight that they probably hadn't heard him anyway. He snatched the phone off the base and answered.

Coal? Mikey.

A huge surge of relief went through him. "Yeah, Mikey! Thanks for calling back, man."

I'll never forget what you did for me, Coal, Parravano said. *I'd do anything I could for you. But you gotta promise me you'll never tell anybody where you got this from. I'm begging you. My life won't be worth a Tonka truck if anybody ever finds out I talked to a cop.*

"You know this is safe with me, Mikey. I can't thank you enough."

Yeah, yeah. Sorry, buddy, but I've gotta talk fast. I'm in a phone booth in a seedy part of town.

Coal couldn't remember hearing a more nervous voice than Parravano's was right now.

Parravano went on to tell him how Rey and Angel Medina had been chosen by the Mafia bosses because of their legal troubles and the scrutiny they were already under in Las Vegas anyway to find some very secluded place where Mafia members who were wanted or who might be sought out and subpoenaed as witnesses could hide until they got word that the heat was blown over. One of the Mafia who had been on a rafting trip down the Salmon River suggested the area, and the two brothers took off in Ray's Cadillac to secure a place worthy of hiding important fugitives.

"Anything else?"

What else do you need? That's why they're up there, bud. That's all I know.

Coal thanked his old friend, promised him once more that his name would never come from his lips in law enforcement circles, and hung up.

Oddly, the first thing that came to his mind now was Phil Harringer. Whatever stake Harringer had had in this whole mystery, Coal didn't believe any longer that it was any more serious than killing his own trees in hopes of getting Hargis in enough legal trouble that he might be able to buy his land cheap.

The irony that Harringer, whom he had every reason to hate, was innocent in the Bern Hargis mystery, and Ray Christian, whom he had come to think of almost like a brother, was likely the hammer man who had put Hargis in his grave, was staggering.

His next thought was of Virgil. And that made him think back to his recent scare involving Katie and Hague Freeman. He would never have thought that being the sheriff of Lemhi County was so fraught with peril for him and his family.

Virgil . . . Just like the day Hague took Katie, they had never even had a real chance to make up.

CHAPTER FIFTY-SEVEN

Coal went and grabbed his father's Winchester out of his mom's closet, remembering how not that long ago it had saved his life, and Katie's. He sniffed at it and smelled the scent of new oil. Would it soon smell once more like burned powder, and death?

He carried it back out and looked at the kids. They were engrossed in their show. He started to tell them goodbye, because no one ever knew the time that was promised him. But it felt like saying goodbye was already admitting defeat.

Let his innocent ones watch their show. Let them revel in the happy ending Lucas and Mark McCain and old Sheriff Micah would surely bring to the screen. Who was he to spoil that?

Scrubbing each of the dogs a couple of times behind the ears, he left them both standing disappointed at the door and went back outside, destination: Andy Holmes's auto repair shop.

Coal passed a few cars on the way into town, and a number of logging trucks and dump trucks possibly hauling material from the mines. 1970's Salmon was a bustling place, and no one ever seemed to stop working, even on a Saturday.

Because of the traffic going both ways, he was forced to go the speed limit, and it took over ten minutes to get into town. When he pulled up at Andy's shop and looked in the garage door window, he saw the Cadillac, and Andy was working away on the windshield.

He stepped inside, making Andy turn around. "Oh, hey, Coal! What's going on?"

"Hey, Andy. How long ago did that guy leave the Caddy?"

"I don't know. Half an hour, maybe."

"Was Virgil with him?"

"Yep. Man, that's a good-looking kid."

"Thanks. Did they say where they were going?"

"No, but when they left here they went through Ken's instead of going back out the back."

Coal said a quick goodbye and went into Ken's. His friend was on his back on a creeper, doing something underneath a jacked up '66 Oldsmobile Toronado, a car Coal had always admired since watching Joe Mannix drive one around doing his detective job on television.

"Hey, Ken?"

"Hey. That Coal?" came the voice from under the Olds.

"Yeah. Did my boy come in here with Ray Christian?"

"Uh-huh." Ken started to slide out from under the car.

"Don't come out on my account. I've gotta go anyway. But did you see which they walked when they left?"

"They didn't walk." Ignoring Coal's request, Ken slid out from under the Olds and sat up, wiping his hands on a rag. "He asked me if I had a car he could take around town for an hour or so while Andy was working on his, so I let him use that ugly old Voyager with the bad fender. I figure if he steals it I'm not out much."

"Did he say anything else about where he was going?"

"Not really. I didn't ask."

"Well, do me a favor and call dispatch if they come back, will you? Tell her to please call me."

Ken said he would, and with that thought Coal walked back through Andy's shop and requested the same courtesy of him.

He went out and got back in the pickup, driving slowly around town as he searched every nook for the purple and white Mercury Voyager station wagon Ken Parks was talking about. His heart seemed to beat faster and faster the more he drove without seeing the Voyager.

On a whim, he went into Wally's and the Coffee Shop, and neither of them had seen Ray and Virgil. The Arctic Circle employees told the same story.

Frustrated, Coal got on the pay phone at the Coffee Shop and dialed the house. After six rings, Katie picked up the phone. "Katie! You've got to answer quicker."

Sorry. The simple apology, with no argument, made Coal feel bad.

"Hey, honey, that's okay. I'm just on edge. Have you seen Virgil and Ray yet?"

Her answer surprised him. *Yeah. They came back a while ago.*

"What are they doing?"

They're out in the yard. They— Dad? It looks like Ray's yelling at Virgil or something.

"What? What do you mean yelling?"

After a pregnant pause, Katie said, *Dad, Ray looks really mad.*

"Katie! What are they doing? Maybe you should go out there and listen. What's going on?"

They're coming back in. Dad, please come home. Something's wrong. I've never seen Ray look like this.

Coal heard Ray's angry voice, and then the line went dead.

The trip back home was grueling. Coal drove as hard and fast as the pickup and the traffic would allow. A couple of times he even resorted to putting his red rotating light up on the dash, but it hardly seemed to make a difference.

It felt like half an hour before he was flying past the 28 Club, and then squealing his tires as he made the corner onto Savage Lane. He punched the gas again to straighten out of a fishtail just before he would have jumped off the edge of the road.

Gravel flew as he came into the yard and skidded to a halt, looking around for the station wagon. It was nowhere to be seen.

He threw open his door and jumped out, taking his Smith and Wesson out of the holster as he started for the front door of the house.

Katie punched open the door before he could get up the stairs.

"Daddy!"

He got to her before she could come off the porch, and she fell into his arms. "Katie, what happened? What's wrong? Where are Ray and Virgil?"

"They're gone." The words came out almost in a sob.

"Gone? Do you know where?" He fumbled his revolver back in his holster.

"No. They came in the first time, and Ray was teasing us and having fun, and he asked where you were."

"He did? Did he say why?"

"No, but I told him you got a phone call from some man in Las Vegas and then had to leave."

Coal froze. It seemed like every part of his body froze too. He tried to bring calm into his voice, and more importantly his face.

Taking his girl by the shoulders, he said, "Okay, honey, so . . . This might sound strange, but did you notice anything weird about Ray when you told him about the phone call?"

"Yeah. He got really serious and stopped joking around with us. Virgil was getting a sandwich, and Ray started to go outside, so Virgil followed him out. That was when Ray started yelling at him—right after you called."

"What was he yelling at him for?"

"I don't know. They were outside and we couldn't hear."

"Then what? Then they left in the car?"

"No, just Ray."

Coal's heart felt like it jumped out of his chest. "Wait. Now say that again. You just told me they were both gone."

"They are."

Coal wanted to scream, but he managed to calm himself. "So they *did* leave in the car?"

"No, Dad, you're not listening to me."

"I *am* listening," Coal countered, trying his best to hold back his frustration. "You told me they both left."

With hurt in her eyes, Katie stared up at him. After a few seconds, she said, "Dad, why are you acting like this? You're scaring me." Apparently he had failed in his attempt to hide his frustration.

"I'm sorry, Katie. I just need to know what's going on. You said they left again, but now you told me Virgil didn't go."

"He *did* go, but not with Ray. Ray wouldn't let him go with him. Virgil just took off and walked up the road. I think he's pretty mad."

A rush of relief made Coal feel almost weak in the knees. "Okay. Okay. So where did Ray go?"

"He didn't tell us. He came back in really quiet after he yelled at Virgil, and he packed his stuff and left with his suitcase. He didn't even say goodbye to anybody. He was in some station wagon."

Coal took a calming breath. His boy wasn't with Ray. That was good. He was only walking off some steam. Something out of place caught his eye, over by the stove. He looked to see Ray's city slicker cowboy boots lying there.

"Why are Ray's boots still here?"

"He must have forgot they were there. He got 'em all muddy when he was on the side of the road looking at where the rock hit his window."

On a whim, Coal went over and picked up the right boot. It was obvious the boots had been muddy, and they were still wet, but the worst of the mud had been knocked off them. He flipped the boot over. There in plain sight on the outside of the heel was the very obvious nick Eric Hansen had shown him in the tracks that fled the murder scene toward Harringer's place. The evidence against Ray Christian was mounting like an avalanche—fast, and insurmountable.

Coal saw the danger going through the roof, so he said a proper goodbye to the kids, including Cynthia and Sissy. The little girl was still leery of hugs, but she let him squeeze her shoulder and gave him a shy smile.

Coal looked at Katie Leigh and took her by the shoulders. "Honey, if Ray comes back here, you can't let him in, okay? No matter what. If he tries to break in, sneak out the back and run."

"Daddy, what's happening?" Haunted memories were spilling out of Katie's eyes and painted all over her face. The look made him almost wish they had never come back to the Lemhi.

"It's too much to explain now, but Ray isn't the guy we thought he was, okay? I'll try to tell you all about it later."

He hugged his girl again, and this time they held each other for a long time, long enough for the emotions to well up inside him. With one last kiss on the forehead, he went out and got in his truck.

Traffic had slowed down considerably on the highway, so there were times when Coal was able to drive seventy miles an hour. He raced with the sure knowledge that the Cadillac would be gone, and that he had no way of knowing which way it would have traveled, either up over the pass toward Montana, down 93 toward Challis, or, if he had somehow slipped past Coal, even south on 28 toward Idaho Falls. For that matter, he might even have gone downriver toward the end of the road, but of course that would get him nowhere.

He slid up almost to the door of Andy's shop and jumped out. His heart leaped when he looked in the window, for there was the Cadillac!

Bursting through the door, he looked around. Andy came out of his office with an invoice book and a pen in hand. His eyes darted about as if something had just happened, or was about to.

"Jeez, Coal! What's up? You tore in here like the place was on fire."

"I'm looking for Ray—the guy with the Caddy."

"He hasn't been back."

Stunned, Coal stared at his friend. "Really?"

"Really."

"Is the windshield done?"

"Uh-huh. Probably twenty minutes ago."

"Andy, I've got to ask you to do something for me. Something kind of illegal. Well, actually *very* illegal."

"If the sheriff is ordering it, is it still illegal?"

Coal wanted to laugh, but he couldn't. "I need you to do something to the Cadillac. Not anything real obvious, but something that'll keep it from going very far if he gets back here and I'm not here."

"What's that gonna be?"

"I don't know! Think of something. Go ask Ken. I'm sure he can come up with a hundred ways to screw up somebody's vehicle. I'm counting on you, bud. Just make it so he can still leave. I don't want something going down in here."

He slammed the door and jumped back in the truck. From here, he had no idea where to go, so once more he began slowly to cruise the town. He only knew he couldn't get far from Andy's shop.

* * *

Rey Medina flew as far up Bern Hargis's battered new road as he dared in the Mercury station wagon before leaping out and going into a jog. When he neared the trip wire, he slowed down until he had found it and stepped over it, then ran on toward the cabin.

Still fifty yards out, he drew his pistol and fired two shots into the ground, then went forward at a walk, catching his breath. He saw movement at the cabin window, and the front door opened.

A heavy-set man in a black leather jacket, Levi's, and harness boots stepped out onto the porch. His bush of hair was everywhere, but the lower part of his face was freshly shaven. "What the hell, man?"

"Get your stuff, Angel! We gotta get out of here. Now!"

"What's goin' on, Rey?" The heavy man's voice was gruff, almost mean.

"They're gonna be coming for us. The sheriff's been talking to people in Vegas."

The big man swore. "All right." He turned and scanned the room, which looked like a gun store had been in an explosion. "All right. What ride did you bring here?"

"Some car I borrowed."

"A good one?"

"No!"

"Then go back and get them Hargises' car and bring it back here."

"Well, I'd say the one I have is better than theirs."

"I don't give a crap, man! Somebody might've seen you come here in it. We gotta change out."

"Okay. You want me to drive all the way in here? What about the explosives?"

"Just pull the wire off the tree on the side away from the bomb, man! Go!"

Rey knew better than to question Angel Medina any more. He whirled around and headed back up the road, undoing the trip wire and running it over to wrap it around the tree with the box of explosives.

Then he ran the rest of the way up the road and jumped into the Voyager. He raced it way too fast in reverse until he was able to spin it around where the Hargises' main road continued on into their yard.

Leaping out, he scanned the yard. A panicked feeling struck him. Leroy's car was here, but the Hargis car was gone! He wasn't about to take Leroy's piece of bald-tired junk. They'd be lucky to make it into town on those tires.

As if his wishes had called it up, he heard a motor approaching, and he turned to see the Hargis family chariot pull off Barracks Lane and come toward him.

He ran out to it and put up his hand, making it rock to a stop in the mud. He hurried around to the driver's side as Sherlene was rolling down her window. Moby was in back, and Leroy Yarwood was in the passenger seat, all of them staring at him.

"Hey! We have to take the car, all right? We'll leave it in town at the body shop."

"Why?" Sherlene dared ask.

Rey took a step back, his face reddening. "Just get out!"

Sherlene and Leroy flung their doors open and piled out, but as Moby opened his door, a thought hit Rey. "No, Moby, you stay back there. I'm gonna have you help us load up some stuff at the cabin."

With that, he leaped into the driver's seat, cringing at the stink inside, and flew up the road, giving the old car the kind of ride it hadn't seen in years as the tree branches scraped down both sides of it, screeching on the rusted metal, and the tires bumped over rocks, roots, and dips. They rattled into the yard, and Rey got out and slammed the door, yelling at Moby to follow him.

When Rey and Moby came into the cabin together, Angel looked over. For once, he wasn't wearing his sunglasses, and his eyes had a strange, ugly, pale look to them, not just inside, but all the way around. It was obvious that they seldom saw sunlight. "What the hell'd you bring the kid for?"

"To help us load, man! We gotta move!"

Angel didn't apologize for growling. He just turned to where he had piled some of the guns and swept a bunch of them up, taking them out to pour into the trunk Rey had opened. It only took a few trips, with the work of all of them, before the cabin was swept clean of anything that couldn't be sacrificed.

Angel went out to the car, headed for the passenger side. As he went, he racked a shell into the chamber of a Colt .45 auto. "You're drivin', bro!"

Rey looked at Moby. "Get in!"

"No! He ain't comin'!" Angel growled.

"I say we take him."

"Well, I say we don't! And if you don't shut up I'll put a bullet in his head right now!"

"Knock it off, man! Come on. Use your head. We can use him as a hostage if we have to."

Now with his almost ever-present sunglasses once more covering his eyes, Angel stared at Rey for a few seconds. Finally, he caved. "All right, whatever. Then let's go!"

Rey was able to spin the car around in the yard, and in less than two minutes they were barreling toward Salmon and Rey's beloved Cadillac Eldorado.

* * *

Coal had stopped Bob Wilson in his patrol car and asked him to help look for the Voyager. Now he was making another slow circle of town when something hit him like lightning.

Ray wouldn't be here in town! He would be out getting his brother and clearing out of the cabin. Coal let out a string of curse words and wheeled the truck around in the middle of the street, narrowly avoiding being struck by an oncoming pickup headed toward the Bar.

He went out of town way too fast, with only one thought in mind now: What if the Medinas simply abandoned the Cadillac? What if they were already racing for all they were worth down Highway 28 toward Idaho Falls?

If Ray knew he was going up on a murder rap, what was a car going to mean to him?

Coal mashed the gas pedal all the way to the floor. It was a long way to the Hargises'.

CHAPTER FIFTY-EIGHT

Some seven miles out, Coal glimpsed a car passing him on its way toward town. He had been concentrating more on driving like a GMC out of hell than watching any cars he passed, but thinking back it looked like the last one might have been the dark blue early 1950's Olds 98 Bern Hargis had owned.

He sped on his way and yawed off the highway onto Barracks Lane, careening off the road and into the Hargis drive, then slamming on the brakes again to make the left turn that would take him to the secluded cabin.

Out of his peripheral vision, movement registered on him, and he looked over to see dark shapes running at him from the direction of the Hargis home. He knew he had been going too fast when the truck started a sideways slide before he could bring it to a halt. Leroy Yarwood, then several seconds later Sherlene Hargis ran in front of his hood. The woman appeared to be in hysterics, while Leroy was yelling some garbled words he could make no sense of.

Coal jumped out of the pickup, keeping the door between them. "Calm down! I can't understand either one of you!"

Through her tears and sobs, Sherlene managed to cry, "They took Moby! They took my Moby boy!"

As the words registered on him, Coal stepped around the truck door, glancing back and forth between them. "What do you mean they took him?"

"They took him!" Leroy growled. "Them two Mexicans! They took him."

"Was one of them my deputy?"

"He ain't your deputy! Are you dumb?"

"I was!" growled Coal. "Where'd they go?" Suddenly, the old car flying past him toward Salmon flashed back into his mind. He turned and got back in the truck.

"Get my Moby!" yelled Sherlene between sobs.

Coal slammed the pickup into reverse and flew backwards, spun around and got back onto Barracks Lane. He had to purposely pull out only two hundred feet in front of an oncoming car to beat the next line of traffic, but the GMC didn't disappoint him, and he went through the gears fast. Soon he was going over seventy miles an hour once more.

But it was still a long road to Salmon.

* * *

Andy Holmes walked so fast he almost broke into a run going back down the sidewalk from the hardware store, darting through Ken's shop instead of going all the way around to his own outer door. "It's just me, Ken!" he said as he rushed by the pair of boots sticking out from under a car.

He heard Ken call back, "Good luck!"

The hacksaw in Andy's hand was brand-new. Even the tag was still hanging from it. He hurried to the Cadillac and popped the hood. For a second, he stared at the fan belt. Then he turned and scanned all around outside. He might only have minutes. Maybe seconds!

Reaching down, he grabbed the fan belt and started carefully to saw at its underside. Once he had gone what he hoped was a safe distance through it, he moved to a new place, then finally one last one, trying to space the cuts evenly all the way around the belt.

The screeching of tires registered on him, and he whirled around. He could see a dark older vehicle outside, and men were piling out either side of it. As he turned back, knowing he had but seconds, the handle of the hacksaw hit the alternator, and it broke free of his hand and fell. He could see the blur of it going down among all the parts of the car, but the outer door was opening. There was no time even to grab for the saw.

Andy reached up and took the hood in both hands, slamming it down just as he heard a voice behind him. "Hey! Man, what are you doin' in there?"

Andy turned, very slowly. He saw Ray Christian coming through the door, but the man who had spoken, a burly man with a bush of hair and black glasses, was staring at him challengingly from several feet away.

"Oh, hi. I just thought I'd check your fluids."

"What for?" The man's voice was a growl. "You ain't even no mechanic."

"Sorry. Just trying to be helpful and killing a little time before I close up for the day. Plus I wanted to admire your engine," he added, to fill the awkward silence.

The man kept staring at Andy until Ray clapped him on the shoulder. "Hey, bro, come on. Let him alone. We gotta go."

The big man ordered Andy to raise the garage door, then turned to Ray. "Go fire it up!"

Andy froze. What if he had sawed too far through the belt? What if it broke right here? What if they opened the hood to see what happened and found the hacksaw, still hung up inside? Andy casually looked toward the door going into Ken's shop. Did he have enough time to make the door if hell broke loose?

Trying to look casual, Andy walked to the door chain and raised the door. The Cadillac fired up on the first try, and Ray revved it a little to make sure it didn't die. After ten seconds or so, he leaned out. "It's great, man! Get out of the way!"

The big man stepped aside so Ray could drive out. He pulled up alongside the dark blue Olds they had come in and left running. The big man marched to it and leaned inside to shut it off and pull out the key, then went to the back and flung the trunk open.

Ray Christian stopped just beyond the garage door, but Andy hadn't reached it yet to close it, and he heard their exchange as Ray jumped up out of the Caddy. "Come on! We don't have time to get that stuff, man! You saw the sheriff go past us! He's gotta be on his way by now!"

The big man stared at Ray. Finally, he threw all his feeling into a string of curse words as he pulled two pistols and a rifle out of the trunk and slammed the lid. "All right then, let's go!" He went to the Caddy and opened the passenger side door, setting the guns inside.

Ray ran over to the Olds and threw the back door open. "Come on! Get out!"

"Leave him here, you idiot!" growled the bigger man. "We got no time for your stupid crap!"

Ray looked at the man, then yelled angrily into the Olds. "I said get out!"

A man Andy Holmes instantly recognized as the mentally handicapped son of murdered dairy man Bern Hargis stumbled out of the back seat of the Olds, and Ray grabbed him by the shoulder of his shirt and shoved him toward the Cadillac. "Go! We don't have all day!"

The man, more like a boy, scrambled for the Cadillac with big, frightened eyes and climbed in, to the tune of the vehement curse words that were streaming out of the heavy-set man's mouth as he sat down and slammed the passenger side door.

Ray squealed the tires as he slammed his foot down on the gas, and Andy watched them go. It felt like his heart was in his throat. In his mind, he was saying, *Go. Go!*

But they only made it barely into the street before there was a loud clanging noise, and the car skidded to a halt two car lengths away, facing north on Main.

Nearly panicked, Andy looked at his door. A vision of all his tools flashed before his eyes, but there wasn't a tool in the place that would be an effective weapon against the guns in the big man's possession, and he had no idea what Ray was carrying.

As the two men opened their doors and came out of the Caddy, Andy recognized an object lying on the sidewalk where it ramped out into the street. It was the brand-new True Value hacksaw!

CHAPTER FIFTY-NINE

Coal flew way too fast past the first of the Salmon businesses. Ahead, a vehicle sitting partway out in his lane of traffic registered on his vision. It was Ray Christian's blue Cadillac!

He saw two men striding from it back toward the sidewalk, and one of them was motioning wildly with his hands. Coal was still coming on too fast, trying to decide on his next move. The faces of the men came to him: the driver was Ray!

They both whipped their heads toward him at the same time, and Ray yelled something at the other man, obviously his brother, Angel. Both of them ran back to the Cadillac and got in, and the car raced north.

Coal slammed on his brakes as he closed on the parking lot of Ken's and Andy's businesses. He recognized Andy Holmes standing there just as Ken boiled out his front door. As the truck came to a stop, he jumped partway out, forgetting to put it in neutral and killing the engine.

He yelled at the other two, "One of you get over here! I need a driver! Now!"

Both of his friends stood like statues, but Andy recovered first and ran to the driver's side of the truck as Coal got back in and slid all the way over. "Go! Go!"

Andy, his face pale, fired up the truck. He killed it once trying to roll away, started it once more, and grinded the gears hard getting to the Salmon bridge. They veered to the right after the bridge, and Coal had the sudden, sickening thought of déja vu. It hadn't been so long ago when he made that same corner chasing Bud and Linda Miley's Riviera out of town.

"How fast will this thing go?" asked Andy over the roar of the engine.

Coal frowned and stared straight ahead. "Not as fast as that Cadillac. Just keep it to the floor."

On through the nasty gray day they raced, with snow pretending to fall, but now a little softer snow than before. Neither man spoke. All Coal could think of was how deadly this Angel Medina was purported to be, and now it was both him and his brother. And they had a hostage. Coal's only backup was a man who had never been proven in battle.

Then again, his backup was only going to really matter if Andy had managed to sabotage the Caddy enough to break them down. If he hadn't, there was no way they were going to catch that Cadillac before it went over the pass.

Almost as an afterthought, he got on the radio and called Flo, telling her to send any help she could his way and to call and get the Montana state police on the ready, in case they didn't catch up to the Cadillac.

They had just sped past the Carmen post office when Coal glanced up at the road ahead and swore. He had just looked down at his rifle and was trying to decide if he dared hand the .357 over to Andy in case of a confrontation. As he looked up, the Cadillac registered on him. It was pulled over to the roadside! A dark-colored vehicle was stopped in the road, and it looked like its driver had just stepped out.

Without warning, the new driver pitched sideways, and Coal saw something he wanted to pretend he didn't: the spray of red coming away from the man's head before he went down.

Andy instinctively slowed the pickup down as he got close, and three men came from the direction of the Cadillac and got into the other car just as Coal recognized the bronze Charger owned by Drew Runnigan, one of the principle characters in the beating death of Roger Miley.

Again, he swore. If that was really Runnigan's car, there was no way they could keep up in this pickup.

"Hit the gas!" Coal yelled. "Get on him now!"

Andy responded, and the truck engine roared. Another car had just flown past them, and it passed the Charger as well, getting in front of them right as a logging truck came in sight from the other direction.

"Get on him, Andy! Come on! Come on!" Coal was pounding on the dash with his fist, leaning way forward on the seat as if it would help them close on the killers.

As they passed the Caddy, Coal saw the form of the man lying on the road. It might have been Runnigan, or it might not have. Whoever it was, there was no sign of movement, and a lot of blood.

"Get up to him!" Coal roared again as he started to roll down his window.

"What are you doing?"

"Just drive!" Coal pushed down the door handle, locking it securely. He managed to get partway out of the window and aim his revolver. "Faster!" he yelled, but now the ice-cold wind was carrying his voice away and burning his eyes.

A man leaned out of the passenger side of the car ahead, and Coal saw an orange flash. The whine of a bullet passed Coal's ear. He responded by shooting at the back window of the Charger. Doing so scared him, because he knew Moby was back there. But he had to try and take out the driver and get that car off the road before someone else got killed.

To Coal's amazement, Andy got almost right up on the Charger, mostly because it was being held back by the car in front of them. Coal fired again at the back window. The shot only glanced off the severe fastback curve of the glass. He fired again, and again. Nothing was going in!

Turning, he dropped the pistol on the seat and picked up his dad's Winchester. Leaning out again, he yelled at Andy once more to keep the gas all the way down. This time when he aimed, it was for a much lower target—and much smaller. A tire.

On his seventh shot, he saw a poof of dust, and the Charger went into a swerve, then started fishtailing. It finally spun around in the highway, narrowly missing the last of the southbound cars as it came to rest at a right angle to the road.

"Stop!" Coal yelled. "Stop! Quarter us in!"

It almost surprised him when Andy knew what he meant, bringing the truck squealing to a halt at an angle. Unfortunately, now Coal's door was in line with the Medinas.

Coal blessed Andy's soul as he rolled out his side of the truck, clearing a path for Coal. He was crab-scrambling backward on the seat, and he just cleared the steering wheel as the first shot came winging from

Angel Medina. He expected to find himself in mid-air, and to hit the asphalt hard. To his surprise, strong arms closed around his torso, and then Andy was dragging him the rest of the way out of the truck.

He didn't even have time to thank his friend for saving him as the next bullet slammed into the side of the pickup. Without thinking or planning, he went up over the hood and snapped off a shot at Angel Medina. To his great surprise, he heard a cry.

Running to the truck bed, he looked over again, and Angel was holding his thigh with one hand as he jerked at another man and pulled him out of the back seat in front of him. Moby!

Angel's left hand let go of his wounded leg, and his arm went around Moby's throat. His right hand came up holding a pistol aimed at the side of Moby's head.

Ray's voice registered on Coal. "Hey! Hey! Angel, come on!"

"Shut up!" Angel screamed. "Just shut the hell up! Hey, cop man! You wanna come on, then come on! *Come on!"*

Ray was yelling again. "Angel! Angel, stop, man! It's over!"

His brother wasn't listening. "Turn around and get, copper! I'll blow this fool's head off now!"

Ray, peering up over the roof of the Charger, looked out at Coal. "Coal! Listen. He'll do it, man. Listen to him. Come on. Don't get this kid killed! Just turn it around and go. I'm begging you!"

Coal gritted his teeth. What right did Ray Christian—Rey Medina—have to beg anything of him? He was a fraud and a murderer. He was scum of the earth.

"Drop the gun!" Coal yelled at Medina. "There are going to be cops all over this place in a few minutes. There's no way out of here."

"I'll kill him!" Angel Medina screamed again. And all of a sudden, Coal knew he would. No matter what else Angel did today, he was going to open Moby Hargis's head like a rotten pumpkin.

Coal leveled his rifle toward Angel. There was a little of his head showing, part of one leg, and his gun hand. Of course his left arm showed as well, but it made no target, being wrapped around Moby's neck.

Ray must have seen the look in Coal's eyes. "No, Coal! No, man, don't do it!"

The Winchester cracked, sounding hollow in the still, icy morning, with the gentle flakes of snow sifting down.

Angel Medina started screaming wildly as Coal jacked the lever again. Angel's pistol had flown from his hand, and there was blood everywhere. Moby, in shock, staggered away from his captor, the right side of his face sprinkled with blood. He stumbled out of Coal's line of attention to disappear in a blur at the back of the car.

Angel dropped to his knees. He was groping blindly for his gun with his left hand—because his right one was shattered—but he couldn't seem to take his eyes away from Coal. Coal had only to squeeze off one more round to finish the fight, and end the life of one bad Mexican.

"No, Coal! Come on, man, don't make me shoot you!"

Coal had been staring so hard at Angel, kneeling pathetic on the ground, that he had temporarily put Ray out of his mind. Now Ray stood there with a rifle pointed at him across the roof of the car. Moby was slumped onto the asphalt behind the trunk, staring straight ahead as if he were dead.

"He's trying to pick up that pistol, Ray!" Coal yelled. "You'd better get him to stop. Now! I'm going to put a bullet in his chest." He knew he was calling a bluff. Yes, he would kill Angel, but then Ray's rifle would take his life too. "Make him stop, Ray!"

To Coal's shock, Ray lowered his rifle and worked his way around to the front of the Charger, where Angel had finally looked down and seen his gun. He started to reach out for it with his left hand. Ray grabbed him by the collar and jerked him backward, still holding the rifle in his left hand.

With Angel kicking and swearing, Ray dragging him bodily around to the other side of the Charger and out of sight. Finally, Ray yelled out. "Coal! I did it. He's got no gun now! Have some mercy, man. After everything I did for you."

"Everything you did for me!" Coal yelled. "You pig. Everything you did for me was a sham! I guess at least I know why you fought so hard for me not to think Jim was the murderer. You knew who it was the whole time!'

Silence.

"Give it up, Ray. Come out of there with your hands in the air, and bring Angel with you. Every cop in Salmon is on his way right now, and they're waiting for you over the state line too. There's no way out."

"There's a way out if I kill you!" Ray yelled back. "Give us your truck, man. Let us go! I've been your friend!"

Coal heard those words with disgust. His friend! Ray had more gall than almost any man Coal knew.

"Ray, I'm going to start throwing rounds under that car in half a minute, so that's all the time you have to decide. Have you ever seen what a ricochet will do to someone? Even if you move, I'm still going to nail your brother."

Ray's head popped over the roof of the Charger. He had the rifle leveled almost immediately at Coal, just like an old veteran. Coal found his target as well. He could have fired, almost on the instant. They both seemed to line up their sights at the same time.

Neither man fired. A Mexican stand-off in more than one sense of the word.

Without any obvious explanation, Ray slowly slunk down behind the Charger again.

Coal took a deep breath, finding new courage. "Five seconds, Ray!" He lowered the barrel of the rifle to aim at the underside of the Charger. Three seconds later, the barrel of Ray's rifle came up, vertically, and then leveled out and came to rest on the Charger's roof. Ray's hand spun it to face toward the front of the car.

"My brother's gonna bleed to death, Coal. Don't shoot. I'm coming out."

CHAPTER SIXTY

"You're going to have to bring Angel, too, Ray. I won't trust you."

"Come on, man," pleaded Ray as he stepped to the front of the car. "He's got one in the leg, besides his hand. Have some mercy. We were friends."

Coal let out a harsh laugh. "Friends, hell. You've played me this whole time, Ray. Get him out here or we'll just sit and wait for the others to show up."

Ray stared at Coal. Finally, his shoulders sagged. He went back behind the Charger and crouched down. He came up supporting his brother, and he limped him back around to the front of the car.

"Good. Now both of you turn in a slow circle, with your shirts untucked and raised up."

Both men followed the commands. If they had any weapon on them, it wasn't visible. Keeping the Winchester trained on them, Coal spoke to the side. "Andy, would you go over and get the kid up and help him over here?"

Andy did as he was asked, helping Moby up off the ground. The boy stared at the road, his eyes vacant.

He stood beside the pickup, and Andy dug for a first aid kit behind Coal's seat, as Angel and Ray started toward them.

Moby suddenly started blubbering. "You gonna shoot me? You gonna shoot my hand too? Please don't shoot at me!"

Coal looked over at the boy. He was staring down at Angel's bloody hand.

"Daddy did it! Daddy did it!" he cried out, all the while with his eyes glued on Angel's shattered hand. Coal frowned at him. The others all glanced around at each other, but no one spoke.

"Daddy was gonna kill Mama." Tears started streaming down Moby's cheeks. "He was gonna kill Mama." His eyes blurred by tears, he fell on his knees. All he could look at was Angel's bloody hand.

"Shut up!" Ray barked without warning. "Stop talking, kid! They know everything already!"

"No! No! Daddy did it! Daddy did it, not me!"

Ray looked a plea over at Coal. "Hey, man. Can I talk to him? I'll get him calmed down."

Coal stared at his former deputy, wondering how well he really knew the Hargises. What was he going to do to calm down a mentally challenged kid who was obviously out of his head in shock?

"Daddy did it." This time Moby's voice was quieter, and his chin quivered. He kept staring at Medina's hand, which he was holding with the other hand, while blood oozed between his fingers and dripped on the ground.

"Your daddy did what?" asked Coal.

"He tried to kill Mama. And Leroy. And he killed my dog. Daddy did it."

"I know, son," said Coal gently. "I know he did. I'm sorry."

"Please don't shoot my hand." Moby looked up into Coal's eyes for the first time. "Please don't."

"He's not going to shoot you, Moby," said Ray. His pleading eyes looked over at Coal. "Come on, man, let me talk to him for a minute." He took a step toward Moby.

Suddenly, Coal's guts warned him of a new danger. He made his voice sterner. "Moby, do you have a gun on you?"

Moby's eyes widened, and he came to his feet and took a step backward. "Don't shoot me. Please don't shoot me!"

Coal's rifle came up a little, and he stared at the boy, then glanced over at Ray.

Ray sighed. He was beaten and exhausted, and all his suave demeanor washed away.

"Give him the gun, Moby. Come on. You couldn't use it anyway. He's not going to shoot you."

"Go get in the truck and get my pistol," Coal ordered Andy. "Now."

Andy went and grabbed the Smith and Wesson and came back out. "Keep it on them."

Coal raised his rifle a little. "Moby, where's the gun?"

Moby's hands came up to the sides. "Please don't shoot me! I promise, Daddy did it!"

"Stop saying that!" Ray growled. "Stop it. Moby, he's not going to shoot you. Just stop talking!"

Moby started weeping like a child. Coal side-stepped to Andy and traded him weapons, then went holding the revolver to circle around behind Moby. He fished a .380 automatic out from the small of his back and frowned at it, then looked up at Ray.

"I guess now I know why you wanted to talk to him."

Ray actually looked sad, and he shook his head. "That wasn't why. I've had plenty of chances to kill you if I wanted to."

"You didn't have the same reasons before."

"Daddy was gonna kill Mama," Moby mumbled through his tears. "He made me stop him."

"Moby! Shut up!" Coal looked into the angriest face he had yet to see Ray make.

"No, you let him talk. Who made you stop him, Moby?"

Moby slumped down again, this time on his butt, bringing up his arms to fold them around his chest. It was as if he were giving himself a hug.

"I stopped him."

"What did you do to stop him, Moby?" Coal's voice was even softer than he had intended. A chill had suddenly begun to come over him as what Moby was saying began to register.

"I stopped him."

"How?"

"I got his hammer. He was comin' at me to hurt me, an' tellin' me Mama was no good, an' I was dumb, an' he looked real mad, an' . . ."

Coal felt his skin rise in goose bumps. "Okay, Moby. Then what happened?"

"Then I got his hammer . . . out of his truck. An' he started laughin' at me. An' he told me he was gonna teach me a lesson. A real good lesson. Like he did to Mama . . . an' Leroy . . . an' t' my dog."

Coal couldn't take his eyes off the pathetic figure of the emotionally broken boy, sitting on the ground embracing himself to try and find some kind of comfort, staring at the ground as he bared his soul.

"Moby, you don't have to keep talking," Ray said. His voice was as soft as Coal's. Coal looked up at him, and their eyes met. A great sadness had covered Ray's face that he couldn't try to hide. Coal didn't bother to reply to him. It was obvious there would be no stopping Moby from talking with Leroy and his mother out of the picture. A dam had broken in him, and he had to empty all that was left.

"Daddy did it. He made me hit him. I told him I would hit him, an' he laughed an' told me he would cut me in little pieces with his saw, and Mama too. Kill them. Just like he killed my dog. He made me hit him."

"You hit your daddy, Moby? Did you hit him in the head with a hammer?"

"Please don't shoot me," Moby mumbled. "I won't do it no more."

"Moby. Tell me. Did your daddy make you hit him in the head with the hammer?"

"Uh-huh. Real hard. An' then he fell. An' blood came out. It went all over. Just like my dog. An' I pulled him away and tried to cover him up, an' then I ran."

"Why didn't you tell somebody, Moby?"

Moby's glance went to Ray and fell away. "Ray's my friend. Ray told me not to tell, because some men would take me away, and maybe put Mama an' Leroy in a cage. An' me in a different cage. An' I could never see them no more."

"Come on, Coal," said Ray in his soft voice. "Leave the poor kid alone. What's the point of doing this?"

"What's the point?" He looked up at Ray. "What's the point? I had you down as the killer, Ray. That's the point. Why were your fingerprints on the damn hammer?" He knew his voice had lost any of the force he wanted it to have.

Ray shrugged. "I was trying to hide it. I fell and lost it in the dark, or that damn thing would have been buried forever. Man, come on. Look at the kid. What would you do? His dad was an ass. He deserved what he got. You want to see an innocent kid in prison? You know what'll happen to him in there? It's not going to be pretty. And now you're always going to know he went there because of you."

Coal stared at his one-time partner, his one-time friend. His heart softened as he saw all the truth behind Ray's eyes.

"Moby's not going to prison."

* * *

It was a solemn ride back to Salmon. The ambulance had come, and Jordan Peterson and Bob Wilson. Jordan rode back with the ambulance, so Coal let Andy take the pickup and Moby Hargis back to town, with the plan being that Coal would then be able to keep Ray Christian handcuffed in the back seat of the Ford.

But that wasn't how Coal played it. After everyone else pulled away, Coal told Ray to turn around, and he took off his handcuffs.

With confusion in his face, Ray turned back around and tried to read Coal's face. "Why'd you do that, man?"

"Hell if I know. Professional courtesy, I guess. Go get in the car. Front seat."

Everyone else was gone. No one was left to see Coal making a fool of himself once more.

Rolling toward town, Coal and Ray spoke in subdued tones. Ray told Coal many things he already knew, about the plan to hide important people in the Hargises' cabin, and, if things went smoothly, to build other ones back there as well. It was a good place to hide people. Until Bern Hargis started getting dollar signs in his eyes.

That was when Ray began to talk about things Coal could have only surmised. A deal had indeed been decided between Phil Harringer and Hargis, but the Medinas had come along at the perfect time and spoiled the rancher's plans. The Mob had paid out big money to buy the rights for keeping their people behind the dairy, to eventually put in a new road, with a high fence, and to buy Hargis's silence.

But drinking men sometimes find it hard keeping silent. That was going to be the big glitch in the plan, and it didn't take long after Hargis's purchase of the new pickup for Ray and Angel to begin to see it. They had made a huge mistake in judgment.

Before they could decide what to do, Hargis had gone off the deep end, and Moby, in a sad, unexpected way, had become their savior. Ray had sworn to himself that he wouldn't let Moby take the fall and go to prison. But then Jim Lockwood's watch ended up in the mix.

And Coal Savage went on a rampage of justice. There was no going back.

When Ray was settled at the jail, Coal stood looking at him through the bars. He felt like he should say something, but he didn't know what to say. He had felt deeply for the man he had thought was Ray Christian. He couldn't find the right words for Hector Reynaldo Medina.

He went down to Steele Memorial and visited with Jordan. The deputy was sitting at the foot of the bed where Angel Medina was handcuffed, and he understood that here was where he would spend his next many hours, trading off from time to time with the city police, who had been kind enough to offer their services.

They spoke of Drew Runnigan, dead at the scene of his car-jacking, and how fate plays a crazy hand in life, and how Roger Miley was avenged at last, in a way no one could possibly have seen coming.

Coal was walking past the front desk when Annie came from the other hallway and stopped him. She gave him a little smile and took his hands.

"You've had some rough days, Coal. Are you ready for a rest?"

"More than ready. I could sleep for two days."

"I was hoping you might want to come pop open a bottle of good wine."

"Sorry, but I'm headed for bed. After I go see my family."

She smiled again, ruefully. "That's okay. I knew you'd say that, but I had to try. So I'll just give you the good news here instead of over wine."

He smiled at her, wishing he could be the friend she wanted. "What's the good news?"

"The doctor from the University of Utah called again."

Coal perked up and searched her eyes, not daring to speak.

"And since you aren't going to ask, I'll just tell you," said Annie with a sparkle to her eyes. "It sounds like you have a deputy who is sitting up and drinking broth. And he really wants to see his family, if they can find a way to go down there."

Coal had to clench his jaws to keep his eyes from welling up with tears. “Todd? You’re not kidding me, are you?”

“You know me better than that.”

Coal stepped forward and hugged her, probably way too tight.

When he got back into his truck again and headed east out of town, he couldn’t help the little smile that was plastered to his face.

It looked like his two days of sleep would probably never happen. Tomorrow, when church let out, he was heading out on a road trip with Jan Mitchell and her boys. To Salt Lake City, Utah.

After that, when he got back home, he was going to take his boy Virgil on a road trip to Montana or somewhere, and they were going to have a good long talk about powerful guns, beautiful art, important books . . . and great dogs.

THE END

Look next for ***BOOK 4: LIKE A MAN WITHOUT A COUNTRY***

Note to my readers: If you have enjoyed this book, please considering giving it a good review, on Amazon, GoodReads, and elsewhere. This will help the book sales gain momentum, which will of course allow me to continue putting out more books in this series. It is extremely appreciated, more than you could ever know. Thank you so much!

Author's note

I just want to make a few quick comments here, since my "Author's notes" have become tradition, and I can't possibly leave one out.

First off, a big thank you to my friend Warren Webber, for portraying Jim Lockwood on the cover. Not only is he on the cover, but Warren is the very guy I modeled Jim's character after from the beginning of this series, so as a cover model it would have been impossible ever to replace him.

Thank you to all others who have been support in researching these books and who have purchased them and spent their valuable time reading them. It has been a fun ride, and I hope to have many more *Savage Law* books before this car finally rolls to a stop.

For those who might be feeling this one went a little heavy on the romantic subplots, I do apologize, but many of my female readers have expressed a liking for this side of my books, and since studies show that most fiction readers are women . . . Furthermore, I like the romantic interludes myself, so they probably won't disappear any time soon—as in, before the series ends. I hope my readers won't really mind.

My final note is to let you know, for your own curiosity's sake, that I have carefully researched out each day's weather, the music, and what was playing on the television at any particular time. While I of course can't know the exact programming available in Salmon, Idaho, every one of the shows I mention in these books were the actual shows playing on that date at that time—in *someone's TV Guide*. The music of course I can't do the same with, but any song mentioned in this series was actually out and being played at that time.

And if it's snowing, cloudy, sunny, or whatever weather is mentioned in the book, that is most likely what it was actually doing. So yes, although it might seem odd, that 1972 December really was every bit as dry as it is in the book—in spite of all the memories of your childhood that tell you there was five feet of snow on the ground every winter.

I know this is fiction, and I'm allowed to do whatever I want, but having these authentic touches within the pages makes it more real to me, and I hope it does that for you, my readers, as well.

About the Author

Kirby Frank Jonas was born in 1965 in Bozeman, Montana. His earliest memories are of living seven miles outside of town in a wide crack in the mountains known as Bear Canyon. At that time it was a remote and lonely place, a place where a boy with an imagination could grow and nurture his mind, body, and soul.

From Montana, the Jonas family moved almost as far across the country as they could go, to Broad Run, Virginia, a place that, although not as deep in the timbered mountains as Bear Canyon, was every bit as remote—Roland Farm. Once again, young Jonas spent his time mostly alone, or with his older brother, if he was not in school. Jonas learned to hike with his mother, fish with his father, and to dodge an unruly horse.

Jonas moved to Shelley, Idaho, in 1971, and from that time forth, with the exception of a couple of short sojourns elsewhere, he became an Idahoan. Jonas attended all twelve years of school in Shelley, graduating in 1983. In the sixth grade, he penned his first novel, *The Tumbleweed,* and in high school he wrote his second, *The Vigilante.*

Jonas has lived in six cities in France, in Mesa, Arizona, and explored the United States extensively. He has fought fires for the Bureau of Land Management in five western states and carried a gun in three different jobs.

In 1987, Jonas met his wife-to-be, Debbie Chatterton, and in 1989 took her to the altar. Over some rough and rocky roads they have traveled, and across some raging rivers that have at times threatened to draw them under, but they survived, and with four beautiful children to show for it: Cheyenne, Jacob, Clay, and Matthew. Middle son Clay has now taken up the writing of fiction himself, and is writing a series of fantasy-science fiction novels, so the legacy will live on.

Jonas has been employed as a security guard and Wells Fargo armed guard in Phoenix, Arizona, a wildland firefighter, Pocatello, Idaho, police officer, and municipal firefighter. After a full career, he retired from the Pocatello Fire Department in 2017 and is currently employed once more in armed security, guarding federal facilities and dreaming up more books for his fans.

Books by Kirby Jonas

Season of the Vigilante, Book One: The Bloody Season
Season of the Vigilante, Book Two: Season's End
The Dansing Star
Legend of the Tumbleweed
Lady Winchester
The Devil's Blood
The Secret of Two Hawks
Knight of the Ribbons
Drygulch to Destiny
Samuel's Angel
The Night of My Hanging (And Other Short Stories)
Russet

Savage Law **series**
Law of the Lemhi, part 1
Law of the Lemhi, part 2
River of Death
Lockdown for Lockwood
Like a Man Without a Country (forthcoming)
Thunderbird (forthcoming)

The Badlands **series**
Yaqui Gold (co-author Clint Walker)
Canyon of the Haunted Shadows (Kindle only)

Legends West **series**
Disciples of the Wind (co-author Jamie Jonas)
Reapers of the Wind (co-author Jamie Jonas)

Lehi's Dream **series**
Nephi Was My Friend
The Faith of a Man
A Land Called Bountiful
Shores of Promise (forthcoming)

Gray Eagle series (e-book format only—forthcoming in print)
The Fledgling
Flight of the Fledgling
Wings on the Wind
Death of an Eagle (e-book and large format softbound)

Books on audio

The Dansing Star, narrated by James Drury, *"The Virginian"*
Death of an Eagle, narrated by James Drury
Legend of the Tumbleweed, narrated by James Drury
Lady Winchester, narrated by James Drury
Yaqui Gold, narrated by Gene Engene
The Secret of Two Hawks, narrated by Kevin Foley
Knight of the Ribbons, narrated by Rusty Nelson
Drygulch to Destiny, narrated by Kirby Jonas

Available through the author at www.kirbyjonas.com

Email the author at: kirby@kirbyjonas.com or write to:

Howling Wolf Publishing
1611 City Creek Road
Pocatello ID 83204